Language Shaping

Jane Baldwin

Contents

Dedication

To my supportive husband

and two sons

Prologue

It had been a long day already, and Margo was exhausted. Now, Migel sat across from her, trying to make the connection. "Do you believe in karma?" Margo had just asked. She had timed the question artfully following the coffee spill incident that miraculously did not stain the pair of pants of the woman who had just earlier prevented an older man from knocking over his tea. It seemed such a natural segue—exactly how Margo liked her questions to appear. It's not that Margo had to stage drink catastrophes at every interview, but she certainly used opportunities to create situations that either demonstrated how the interviewee handled a situation or allowed Margo to directly ask questions that would otherwise seem odd at a job interview.

Migel was visibly startled for a moment, but then he recounted what his grandfather always said: everything that you say and do tells smart people something about you. Don't live in anticipation or fear, but be aware and sometimes be intentional. Migel began, "The concept of karma, as I understand it, implies that there is an external force that levels circumstances and events." He paused and then continued, "I believe that people have more control than that. People make choices from the opportunities that they have. I think that it is best to think critically and to be self-aware as much as possible. This fosters better interactions and opens the door to new possibilities." Migel exhaled. That was what he believed, he realized, as he spoke.

He had just never put it into words. Exceptions crept into his mind, so he quickly spoke again as if the pause had been intentional. "Not everyone can make their own situations, of course, because not everyone lives in fair, non-war zone territories or can control the events in their lives. Some people lack easy access to clean water, so it's very difficult for them to change their circumstances. Many people exist with hardships that are practically insurmountable. Others live in fear. I've known people who were brainwashed early to certain perspectives, perceptions, and explanations, and it is hard for them to see around these views. I think that in the best of circumstances, though, humans certainly can control how they internalize events and how they think about them. Although, of course, not everyone develops an awareness of what they can control. I can acknowledge that I am privileged enough to know that karma is not the only explanation that I can imagine." Migel sat back, satisfied with his answer.

Amazingly well done, thought Margo, "That's a thoughtful response," is what she said. *We can hire him now and move on*, she thought, but they went on to chat for the next 20 minutes. Migel was easy to talk with. He didn't appear to have any obsessive habits, he didn't relate fiercely with any particular group, and most importantly he was open to new ideas. Margo had learned what she wanted to know; Migel would adapt. Margo offered him the job.

Chapter 1: Margo Duc

Margo had created her own interview process. She had begun by thinking of qualities and skills that she needed her team to have, and then she worked backward, analyzing how a person might have developed each particular quality or skill. She was aware of the fact that society gets steered towards group thought at multiple life turns from fashion to peers, politics, pop culture, social media, values, and even schools. At best, many people dwell on what is theoretically possible or their version of the ideal. The result: it's harder and harder to find people who respond practically on a regular basis. If practicality is what you want to uncover in an interview, well… You can't exactly say, "Please tell me about a time when you demonstrated pragmatism when your ontology was threatened." So, Margo had carefully selected people and vetted them heavily before she interviewed them.

Margo identified shared characteristics and special skills that she expected her team would require in order to have a successful mission. She had tried to ascertain which types of experiences would encourage the development of such qualities. She needed a team of seven people with this determined set of skills who were physically and mentally fit for the challenge. They had to be intelligent but also very logical, adaptable, self-aware, and reflexively capable of critical analysis and redirection. They could not be misanthropic or cynical, but they couldn't have romantic visions of the world either.

Next, Margo explored how such people could be located. How would they self-select? With a little help from Samir's database access, she was able to further shift through her group of names and gain access to their contact information. She sent a selected group a brief job description, including pay, and an offer to interview. She could not offer traditional healthcare benefits.

Experience is the most valuable predictor of anything. People are the sum of their experiences, and everything counts. Having jobs, an education, relationships, a family life, daily activities, sports, and chores matter, and so does immigration, travel, sickness, and even death. Experiences develop character, particularly indicative of depth and desire. Margo didn't exactly exclude brilliant academics, but she was very cautious, to the point where she didn't interview anyone with a perfect GPA. People typically perform extraordinarily well in academics by putting a lot of time into their studies, and if they did that, well then, by definition, they had fewer real-world experiences. So, where some teams were composed exclusively of experts in various fields, Margo's team would not be. 'Breadth over depth,' she had decided. Smart and curious people will always make connections, whereas deeply focused people literally cannot. This was her explanation for the kind of people she was looking for, and she had explained it to Samir, justified it, and then gone on to explain her barcode idea.

"A barcode?" Samir had inquired, his tone incredulous as his eyebrows shot up.

"Yes," Margo had replied. "I have been mentally barcoding people for years."

"Explain."

"Binary Code is a series of ones and zeros, right? Each bit has a single value that is either a one or a zero, so I have a list of questions. One is 'yes' (on), and zero is 'no' (off), and if you ask the same questions in the same order to multiple people, then you have a 'barcode' for each person of ones and zeros, and they can be compared. See?" but she didn't wait for an answer and continued, "Among other things, I'm looking for certain patterns of similarities among interviewees. I'm certain it will work. It's like this:

Do you speak another language fluently?

Yes = 1 no = 0

Have you lived in another country for multiple simultaneous months?

Yes = 1 no = 0

Can you speak a tonal language?

Yes = 1 no = 0

Can you quickly think of trips you would like to take?

Yes = 1 no = 0

Do you have food allergies?

Yes = 1 no = 0

Have you traveled for 15 days or more to a region where you don't speak the language?

Did you take some classes in college just because they sounded interesting?

I have all kinds of questions—You get the idea. I call it 'barcoding' because I get a set of ones and zeros that represent the person's answers to simple factual questions. I also group eight questions of a theme in a byte. I map out individual answers and consider the byte answers. I'm looking for those patterns or those juxtapositions that I know fit well together."

"Sounds good," something that Samir always said when he was trying to end a conversation in a pleasant way. He did seem mildly amused at her nerdiness. "Just get the team together."

"I am," Margo said, and she left his office.

For some, exploring the unknown is more interesting than scary, she thought. *We've seen this throughout history. Some people wander and poke the unknown while others always remain close to home. Most exist somewhere in between. Even without large bank accounts, people who love to travel will explore. They debunk their own areas during day trips, they go camping, they take car rides, they eat in ethnic restaurants, and they read. Some talk to strangers, as this, too, forms a kind of travel experience to the unknown.* Margo knew that she needed to find people who were hungry for travel, more curious than fearful of the unknown and people who didn't mind when their beliefs were challenged. Beyond that, the team she was planning to build needed to have knowledge of human behavior, multiple cultures, linguistics, biology, cognitive science, history, and computer science. They needed to be able to demand evidence before blindly agreeing, but at the same time, also be open to surprises. The group needed to have a diverse skillset.

Humans generally choose whenever possible to be around people like them, people who reinforce the values and opinions that they already have, not challenge them. Many people want to be around others who speak a certain language or celebrate certain holidays, this is clear by looking at immigrant, ethnic, and religious communities. Some people want to live in certain zip codes, assuming that they will share much with people of similar social class or ambitions. Some people are attracted to others who attend a certain club or cultural activity or watch a certain sport. Others look closer at people who wear a specific brand of clothing, attend certain schools or social events, and work or volunteer for certain charities, political groups, or non-profits. People, in general, like others who are like themselves. Margo considered the kinds of choices that her team would make but also realized that at a certain stage in life, finances, educational goals and friends dictate a lot.

Americans like a choice. It is part of the collective culture. A quick glance at the laundry detergent aisle of any large store verifies this. And there are also hundreds of other options available online from small companies to companies that claim to sell natural products. Americans value options and the ability to individualize the choices that they make. Part of the culture is to demonstrate personal preference. In the last century, at an increasing rate, car stickers, license plates, t-shirts and online activity all show that many Americans also like to tell others about what they choose to do. Therefore, groups that people join, generally with an online presence, are particularly telling of the interests and inclinations that people have because those people have the option to choose freely from a myriad of choices with few limitations and often no initial buy-in. The decision can also be somewhat private. There are professional groups to join, hobby groups like knitting, interest groups like remote control car racing, and groups that actually plan to meet physically to hike, ski, visit a museum, a bar, or introduce people looking for partners of various kinds. The click of a button or an email can subscribe a person to an online affiliation group with often little other information. Compare that to joining a physical club that requires letters of recommendation from other members, a waiting list, and initiation fees, buying season tickets to a sports venue and joining an online group is quicker, cheaper and easier. Despite the ridiculous cost difference, online groups and physical clubs serve essentially the same purpose: to offer people an opportunity to meet others like them. Having thought deeply about all of this, Margo sought to identify potential hires by scanning the internet for unusual groups related to travel initially and then to linguistics and culture. Margo looked for people in their twenties who self-selected to affiliate with others who liked language, even if they had not necessarily studied linguistics, although at least one needed to have done so.

Months earlier, Margo and Samir had identified "gen z" as an ideal group to draw team members from. The group's cohesion, they had decided, would be dependent in part on the ages of the people in the group that Margo selected. They had concluded that Margo would interview only people born after 1996. Following Karl Mannheim's 1928 essay, "Das Problem Der Generationen," many others have considered how one's generation informs the preferences for communication and the work and spending habits of any given generation. Samir and Margo had explored their options. The Millennial generation was born between 1981 and 1996. This made them largely between the ages of five and twenty when the September 11th terrorist attacks occurred in the United States, and they all remember it at some level. Many countries have terrorist attacks, but to have had one on United States soil both shocked and formed opinions in the minds of the unexpecting Americans who lived through it. It also formed a generation's opinion about the nature of a government and international relations. Additionally, Millennials were raised during the era of the wars in Iraq and Afghanistan, and they seem to have developed certain expectations and intense political polarization as a result. They are a specific generation that gets along best with themselves, and a generation once removed, the Baby Boomers (born 1946-1964). Margo had said that they could put Generation Z candidates (born 1997-2012) and Generation X candidates (born 1965-1980) together, or she could put Millennials with Baby Boomers, but she wasn't going to do different mixes. In the end, they decided that the team should come from only one generation, and it would be Gen Z. This generation was diverse, optimistic, flexible, young enough, open enough, and typically still laden with college debt. They were perfect. So, Margo immediately began to explore online groups for potential Gen Z candidates within their publicized member list.

A group called "The International Association for the Study of Child First Language Acquisition" seemed good initially, but that society attracted mainly academics and medical practitioners. The same was true for "The Linguistic Society of America" and "The European Language Resource Association." Margo was trying to avoid people with demanding careers and highly focused interests. 'How to find devoted but less invested individuals?' she wondered. Then, one day, she logged into Facebook and scanned the endless number of affinity groups there and somewhat accidentally located the Facebook group for "The National Museum of Languages." Thousands, but not hundreds of thousands, of people chose to join this group, presumably because they were interested in language at a level beyond the average person. They could be students of linguistics, but they could also be just curious people. After opening its doors in 1997, the National Museum of Languages closed them permanently in 2008, opting to exist solely as a digital entity, an interactive website. The Facebook page hosted stories, comments, photos, links, and, at the top in the center, a list of subscribers at the click of a button. Margo pursued the subscribers. She looked at the pictures and self-descriptors of the followers. She picked one hundred appropriately aged people of interest, and she had a list of potential candidates.

Databases hold all these days. Where people live and have lived, their age, their religion, how many taxes they pay, and previous names they have used are a drop in the bucket of stored big data. Private databases hold information on purchasing habits, websites visited, physical locations visited, time spent on websites, and products or places reviewed. Navigation tools learn more from their users than users learn from the maps. Government databases have other useful information, such as voter registration, vehicle registration, taxes paid and taxes owed, data from criminal investigations, and data from the hundreds of billions of phone calls that people have made using major telephone carriers. There is data concerning who people call, what degrees people earn, where they work, and how much money people owe, and there is additional information in the very loose category entitled "information concerning matters related to possible threats to national security." Couple all that data with files from mass surveillance as well as cloud-stored personal video camera content and the ability to cross-reference any and all lists, and someone can create a solid background file on all but the highly reclusive. Margo was able to produce a long list of people she'd like to interview from the list of possible candidates simply by having Samir go through these databases. Her long list had people who had majored in psychology, history, English, biology, marketing, engineering, cognitive neuroscience, math, art history, anthropology, and one person with a geology/ environmental science/ sustainability kind of degree.

Samir had also scanned the list for potential deal-breakers such as people living with partners, and new homeowners. He weeded out anyone advancing rapidly in their careers, anyone without a college loan, and anyone with a net yearly income over eighty thousand dollars. Samir also tossed out people with Subscribe & Save prescriptions or pet product deliveries (people don't like to leave their pets behind), as well as anyone who owned property.

Margo then solicited the people who had made it through the initial screening. She had an enticing job offer for each of them – paid international travel and expenses to participate in a research opportunity concerning culture and language. A small stipend would be paid to each member, and (as the short-term project was sponsored by and service to the US Department of Education) current student debt absolution. The vast majority accepted the invitation to interview- who wouldn't? Debt absolution was a serious incentive; it was hard to believe that it got thrown in at all. For an anticipated eight-week project, albeit one with long hours, seven days a week, guaranteed jet lag, and somewhat unspecified but not 'dangerous' work, it was an incredible offer.

Some interesting facts about Americans: 92% of all student loans are federal loans (totaling nearly 2 trillion dollars of the federal debt), the average loan per student is over thirty-five thousand dollars, and over fifty percent of students at both public and private institutions of higher education have student loans. It wasn't hard to find people in debt to the US government, enthusiastic and willing to unleash themselves. Margo had quickly put together a schedule to interview those who responded to her offer. She talked with people who had previous immersive experiences in foreign cultures, a strong interest in language, easy-going personalities, and a lack of food allergies. Margo felt bad about this part, but it was too risky not to consider it. She was not sure what people ate in some of these countries, and avoiding trouble was a safety precaution. For that matter, she also had to screen out vegetarians as well. Vegetarianism, as a choice, resulted from affluence, and the group would be headed to a few not-very-affluent-countries. The group needed to be willing and able to eat all the food that was offered. In poor countries, with much less animal meat protein available than in the US, it was an honor to be served a meat dish, and she didn't want anyone refusing that on principle. Margo also looked for side skills that might come in handy (the ability to fix computers, for example, the ability to talk to anyone about whatever came up) and, of course, the fewer personal tethers people had, the better. Mentioning the word fiancé or significant other was an instant deal-breaker. Despite all of these restraints however, her interview process ended with seven shortlisted candidates.

One unanticipated occurrence: the interviews had also ruled out anyone who came across as potentially irritating in close quarters.

Margo had not initially thought of this, and then she met a guy who constantly ran one finger up the side of a finger on his other hand, down into where it joined his palm, and then back up the next finger. He did this over and over. She realized if he needed to self-soothe at an interview, he'd never make it through the trip without falling apart. Another person started every single response by saying, 'So to clarify, you are asking…' it grated on her nerves. Margo's English skills were fine, so this person was either buying time to think or just being difficult. Margo decided that when people spoke and repeatedly clarified or rephrased, it was a form of aggression as if the goal were to catch the speaker in contradiction. Anyone who seemed dodgy or overly suspicious was also eliminated, as were people who asked too many questions that seemed unnecessary (people like that often find themselves dissatisfied with the answers that they get). Anyone can become unpleasant after many weeks, but like a good summer camp cabin, this group should have enough group activity and self-guidance (as opposed to counselor guidance) to keep themselves in check.

During the interview process, Margo tried to uncover what people "do" with their time and how they react to the unpredictable. What people do explains a lot about them, and some people, quite frankly, do very little. But of the people "who do," their reasons vary tremendously. Take foreign travel: there are lots of reasons why people travel. Some are internally unhappy and looking for satisfaction that they can't find elsewhere. Some people just want to tell others where they have been. They are checking off boxes—been to Paris, to London, to Singapore, check, check, check. Some travelers tend to be trepidatious and stick to the known and group-affiliated kinds of travel. None of these types of people would work on Margo's team, but of course, neither would a person who hits adulthood and has never traveled to the city that is a few hours away. Traveling forces people to release control. When one travels, it's hard to know exactly what will happen, what the hotel pillows will be like, how long the wait will be, or what kind of food will be available. People who voluntarily travel (and like it) can roll with the punches and adapt. Margo needed that kind of travelers—the kind of people who had a desire for different perspectives but who were flexible enough to adapt to hearing surprising views. These kinds of people engage in little travel experiences. They ask people about where they are from. These people make connections all the time between what they learn and what they already know. Margo had to hone her ability to sort out these types of travelers from the others. These types of travelers were the most suitable for her group. They are generally reflective, willing to be surprised, and comfortable with the unknown.

As a final requirement, Margo wanted team members who could speak at least one other language well and understand basic concepts of the language-culture connection. They needed to be grounded and pragmatic; she could not emphasize that enough. It was unknown what the group would discover exactly, and the group had to be able to be believers—if necessary—while not being instant believers who overlooked incongruencies. People who speak more than one language understand their own culture and others better than people who only speak one language. That was a reasonable quality to interview for, but pragmatism (even with access to spending habits from the databases) was hard to verify in a limited timeframe. It is not easy to advertise a job with the line "the ideal candidate should have a substantial international travel experience that required them at least once to extract themselves from unpleasant situations. People who grew up in a war-torn nation or knew poverty but were able to escape without lingering trauma are desirable." That's what she really meant, but she could not advertise it as it is. So, Margo looked for opportunities to see people in situations where she could study their reactions, and she asked people to explain themselves. She watched them when they spoke. Sometimes, she asked simple, factual questions that could be answered with a one or a zero. She asked permission to record all interviews on her phone, explaining that she had multiple interviews in a single day and wanted to be sure to keep everyone separate, but really, she replayed the recordings to study tone and hesitation.

Some people lead soft lives. They quit when things become too difficult, and they don't have the flexibility that struggles, inconvenience, and long unfulfilled desires provide. On the other hand, too much struggle, too many dreams unfulfilled, and too much familiarity with death often produces a coldness, a detached hardness in people that makes them apathetic. Somebody with apathy or a general lack of enthusiasm could be a problem on the team. The group needed to get along and more or less like each other and be sensitive and appealing to those that they met. Margo needed people with a certain appreciation for what they had but who were still capable of dreaming about better circumstances. She knew well it was a tricky combination. She needed young, innovative, smart people who were resilient. Having a wide range of knowledge over a lot of knowledge in one area would be most helpful. She needed creative thinkers. If a person has thoughts and ideas, then connections can be made that spark new thoughts; the exact details could be looked up and put to someone else. The goal for this group was to witness first-hand and to explain.

Chapter 2: Migel Ngubá

Palenque de San Basilio is a village founded by runaway slaves, *cimarrones,* from Cartagena in the 17th century. Cartagena, the capital of Colombia, was established in 1533 and quickly became an important hub for the transatlantic slave trade. Once ships docked, their cargo—including enslaved people—was sold in markets and sent throughout the Western Hemisphere. As historians have pointed out, Cartagena is uniquely located on the Caribbean Sea in a way that quickly earned it prominence among trade ships in the 17th and 18th centuries. Subsequently, the city grew and developed in response to the needs of these ships. Industries in boat repair and farmed products such as coffee became important, as did the professions of notaries, foremen, and tradesmen.

The Malinke people are a large ethnic and linguistic group in West Africa, who come from the lands that are now Mali, Gambia, and Guinea. Benkos Biohó, born in the late 16th century to a royal Malinke family, was destined to be king., However, he was captured by a notorious Portuguese slave trader and sold twice. The second time was to a man in Cartagena in 1596. For three years, Biohó was forced to row the Magdalena River, but in 1599, he successfully escaped with a few other rowers and found refuge in the foothills of the *Montes de María*, the mountains on the northern coast of Colombia. The runaways refuged other escaped slaves and formed a small army to protect themselves. The army became formidable and unbeatable, and the Spanish lost every battle against them. Biohó ran the intelligence and strategic planning, and the village grew as more slaves were brought in and protected. In 1605, the governor of Cartagena granted autonomy to the people in Palenque but more officially secured it a few years later in writing in exchange for Biohó's promise that he would stop aiding and abetting further runaway slaves. Biohó was also commanded to tell the people that they could not call him king. This lasted until 1619, when Biohó was captured by the Spanish while walking in Cartagena. He was hanged and quartered in 1621.

Palenque's army remained so effective in freeing enslaved people that in 1691, a royal decree from Spain granted freedom to all the Africans living in the village. Accordingly, Palenque became the first African settlement in the Americas and remains the only surviving walled city established by escaped slaves. A statue of Benkos Biohó now dominates the village square of Palenque de San Basilio. In one hand, the statue clutches a broken shackle, while the other, still bound in an iron cuff, reaches upward toward the sky. Biohó's face is frozen in an expression of agony, his mouth open as if caught between a cry and a scream all at once. People remember their history, ever distrustful of the Spanish for breaking their first written agreement, the people of Palenque kept to themselves behind the walls for generations, teaching their African culture and traditions to their young. They spoke then and still do now the creole language known as Palenquero, and even in the 21st century, inhabitants have been heard saying, 'We are African first, Colombian second.'

San Basilio de Palenque is not a prosperous town in the twenty-first century. There is still no hospital, although there are 'medicine people' who practice ancient healing methods. In 2023, a medical study confirmed that a group of plants used by these medicine people in San Basilio de Palenque to treat inflammation-related diseases was so effective that they suspect that the dried and powdered plant components might be effective against cancer cells. None the less, few modern trained physicians come to this area. There is no wastewater treatment facility. There are no institutions of higher education. There are few paved roads. It is not easy to dream of a modern life while living in San Basilio de Palenque, but Migel Alvarez's parents did.

Miami, Florida, and New York City, NY, have the most significant Colombian communities in the United States, but when Migel's parents felt that they had to leave Palenque to offer their unborn children the opportunities of the modern world. Migel's parents were afraid of both large cities, and chose central Florida instead and started a family. Longing for the mountains, they moved north to Massachusetts when Migel was three. The reality of this was more complicated than the map had explained, as the Spanish-speaking communities in Massachusetts are further from the mountainous western side of the state than the Alvarez family initially realized. Rolling hills and a short drive to the ocean, though were an improvement over flatland and a lack of natural bodies of water. They had been willing to leave the comforting heat of Florida. Now, Migel, his younger sister, and his parents return every other year to Colombia to stay with the Alvarez elders who still live and always will in San Basilio de Palenque. They all speak Palenquero when they are there.

When people who speak different languages live together, they naturally develop a way to communicate out of both necessity and desire. Linguists call this form of communication a pidgin language. It is a mixture of the languages of the people who need to communicate yet do not have a common language. The grammar is simple and created as needed. However, when pidgin becomes the native language of the next generation, it is then called a creole language. creoles are more complex. Intentional migration, displacement from war, and slavery have all led to the development of creole languages all over the world. Generally, they are roughly based on an oppressor's native tongue. For example, many slaves in Cartagena in the sixteenth century spoke Kikongo (still spoken today by people in the Congo, Angola, and Gabon). The slave traders who transported the Kikongo speakers spoke Portuguese, and their slave ships docked in Spanish-speaking Cartagena. As a result, the Palenquero creole language is primarily a mixture of Kikongo and Spanish and Portuguese—though it remains unintelligible to native Spanish or Portuguese speakers. This language, first documented in the 16th century, is still spoken by Migel's inner family, forming a deep connection to their heritage.

Today, the journey from San Basilio de Palenque to Cartagena is no longer a long trek on a mountainous jungle path to a trade port. Instead, it is a 90-minute car ride on a paved road to a sleek, ocean-side, modern city. San Basilio de Palenque is far from undiscovered— it has been a UNESCO World Heritage site since 2005. Despite its status, it remains a small village of a few thousand, nestled beneath the emerging Montes de María with West African oral and cultural traditions cached among Spanish and still in use today. Palenquero remains the only surviving Spanish-based creole in Latin America.

In addition to Palenquero, Migel is fluent in both Spanish and English like any native speaker there. He majored in cognitive science in college, an incredible field that merges computer science, linguistics, psychology, and neuroscience. After college, when many of Migel's classmates were headed to the biomedical sector, Migel had ideas about doing research, and he needed a Ph.D. degree for that. Migel took a year off after graduation to work, spend extra time in Colombia, and apply to graduate schools. He was at the end of this period, contemplating his undergraduate debt, when Margo reached out to him. By the time he had to commit to her, he'd know where he was going the following year, and if he could be guaranteed that he would be finished with Margo's project by the second week in August, then there was no reason not to say yes to an interview—so he did.

Chapter 3: Binh Tran

"Please, it's no problem," Binh said, motioning for Alec to move past her so that he could get to his plane seat beside her. She tucked her knees to the side, letting Alec slid awkwardly along the folded tray table and sleeping Emma before taking his seat by the window. With the normal commotion, Alec settled in, tucking his feet beside his backpack and buckled his seatbelt.

"Thank you," he said. "I wanted to get up before dinner was served."

"No worries," Binh replied ensured again. She had been willing to move, of course, when Alec got up, but as the woman on her right was asleep, it was just easier for Alec to get out past both of them while she stayed seated. The group had all their seats together on the right-hand side of the 9:50 pm Swiss flight out of Boston. Alec, Binh, and Emma shared a row of three. Theo and Adem sat directly in front of them, while Jiho and Migel were behind, with Margo's seat left empty. Poor Margo had barely her food at the group dinner in Boston, confiding to Binh in the bathroom that she had terrible and unusual abdominal cramps. Two days later, just before the airport meet-up, the group received the text: Margo was in The Tufts Medical Center. Her appendix had ruptured, causing peritonitis. One of her friends had rushed her to the hospital in the middle of the night with a high fever and delirium. The infection had spread throughout her abdomen, and despite emergency surgery early that morning, Margo could not get on the plane. She informed them about the medical emergency over text and told them that she would join them all at the next stop. They'd all googled an appendix rupture; it was horrible sounding. Untreated peritonitis could lead to long-term problems or even death. For now the team was down to seven.

Everyone had something to say about the surprise event – either they had never thought of their own appendix (or anyone else's), or they knew a horror story like Margo's – nothing in between. Binh remembered a girl, Nguyet, from high school, who had trouble getting diagnosed with what turned out to be appendicitis. She had been complaining of stomach pains for many weeks before the diagnosis. The doctors thought it was just acid reflux, then menstrual cramps, and finally, dismissed it as anxiety. Then one day Nguyet had to be rushed to the hospital, and everyone said that she had almost died. She could not attend school for weeks. For Binh's mother, the story was another reason for her encouraging Binh to go to college. "Get educated. Get a good job. Make sure that people care about you and believe you when you talk." Her grumbling had seemed to work as Binh did very well academically. She had loved her psychology classes at UMASS Amherst, and although she didn't have any immediate prospects for a high-paying job, she had been accepted into her first-choice doctoral program. She planned to work as a counselor as soon as she could. With an increasing demand of mental health professionals post COVID-19, and she was looking forward to a stable career.

A flight attendant came down the aisle with a cart, handing out drinks and saying that the dinner cart was just behind him. Binh ordered a seltzer, and Alec asked for water. As the flight attendant turned to talk to the passengers sitting in the opposite row, Binh spoke up gesturing to Emma, "Can she also have water or seltzer, too, please, in a closed container? I think she'll want it when she wakes up." The attendant put a closed can of seltzer on a napkin and handed it to Binh, who took it and tucked it into the seat pocket in front of Emma. Emma had been asleep since they boarded. She had told Binh in the security line that she had been up for over twenty-four hours preparing for the trip and saying goodbye to friends. She planned to skip both dinner and the breakfast and sleep straight through to Zurich. It looked likely at this point. They should have put her in the window seat.

Once the cart of drinks moved further down the aisle, Binh leaned toward Alec, "I've been wondering ever since you said that you were Hopi at dinner on Monday night, does the Hopi language have tones? Vietnamese is a tonal language. We have six tones. It's tough for Westerners even though the vocabulary and grammar are pretty easy. I started thinking about language more on Monday. I have always known Vietnamese speakers, and then in college, most people that I knew had studied French, Spanish, or Latin, and we had a lot of Chinese-American kids, but Hopi is uncommon out east.

I should rephrase that. I've never, ever heard of someone knowing Hopi."

"Hopi is basically non-existent outside of northeastern Arizona," explained Alec, smiling. "It has some variations, dialects really- four, depending on where the people live who speak it, but no one speaks with tones. It's a tough language for non-native speakers any way."

"Like how," asked Binh.

"For example," Alec answered, glad she had cared enough to ask, "In most languages, the concepts that matter to the culture that produced the language are the ones that are embedded in the language itself and have the most vocabulary words. The culture, habits, and ways of thinking, as well as the language itself, evolve simultaneously... I've heard that some languages emphasize where the information comes from, like whether the speaker heard it firsthand or secondhand that there are animals nearby. In English, that's not done, right? You can just say, 'There are deer in this area,' but in some languages, there are markers on the words to indicate if you personally saw the deer, if you heard the information from someone who did, or if it is just hearsay without evidence. Other languages use directional words (the equivalents of north, south, east, and west) but never words like "in front of," "behind," or "next to" Everything is explained as being in the place where the sun rises or sets or whatever. Hopi is very different from English, especially, with time. We think of time as an ongoing cycle, whereas English looks at it in pieces (seconds, minutes, hours, days…). I think that pronunciation, of course, is also what is hard for non-native speakers. Languages vary and the more one can speak or learn then the easier it is to imagine other perspectives and ways of being. I don't think that any language restricts thought. It's just that in some languages, it is faster to convey certain ideas than in others. What's Vietnamese like?"

"Hmm… as you said - some ideas are expressed differently, and so non-Vietnamese speakers often say, 'Oh, I never thought it that way,' but I don't think anyone is incapable of grasping certain concepts. It's just that maybe they were never confronted with an idea in a book or through an experience, and so they don't consider the idea necessarily until it enters their realm. If you had never heard of the country 'Timor-Leste' and then one day you met someone who was from there, and learn that there is a Southeast Asian nation on the island of Timor that just became independent in 2002, you would be able to imagine a slightly larger world. So I agree learning about something just moves it into one's realm of awareness.

"I like that 'realm of awareness.' That explains what I was trying to say. I just wasn't aware of the phrase, but I'm aware of Hopi culture and it definitely influences how I interact with the world- I'm sure that is true for everyone. You know that saying, 'We are all the sum of our experiences?' Tell me something about the Vietnamese language before those dinner trays arrive." Alec smiled. He had a good smile, Binh thought, and he was inherently considerate, it was obvious.

"Well, "she began, "In Vietnamese language, there is no gender for nouns like there is in many languages, and there are no articles. So like Russian or Chinese, you never have to decide between using 'a' and 'the. ' Also, there are no plurals either, so the grammar is much easier than English or French. Those are the other two languages that I know well.

"No plural for nouns? So you'd say 'I want one beer' or 'ten beers' - it's the same?" he laughed.

"No! You say 'one' or 'ten,' but it's always just beer. There is no word "beers." That silly 's' at the end of nouns in English? THAT you don't need. The 's' at the end of beer is just to annoy you and to make nice Vietnamese girls have a hard time in elementary school English class!" she smiled back. The dinner tray cart stopped one row past them, and then a cheerful attendant in blue asked, "Chicken or pasta?"

"Chicken," said Alec

"Chicken, thank you," Binh replied.

"Enjoy your meals," echoed the flight attendant as she turned to the opposite aisle, "Chicken or pasta?"

"That's funny," said Alec, pulling the aluminum covers off his meal, "I guess you are right, though. And then there are all those nouns that don't even follow that rule... like 'person' becomes 'people,' 'mouse' becomes 'mice' and 'child' becomes 'children.' English is weird, I guess."

"Well, I mostly speak it when I'm not at home," replied Binh, forking her filet of chicken until it broke into bite-sized pieces.

"Me too."

"Did you grow up in a large Vietnamese community?"

"Yeah, Massachusetts. About fifty thousand Vietnamese people probably live there. I grew up in Dorchester, which is a part of Boston. The neighborhood that I am from is actually called 'Little Saigon.' so I was definitely 'with the community.'"

"Got it. Me too. I grew up in Northeastern Arizona, on Hopi lands. We have a dozen villages over three mesas. Hopis talking to Hopis speak about which mesa they are from and which clan their family belongs to. I'm from the second mesa—Bear clan. But to most other people, 'Northeastern Arizona' covers it, and no one asks for more." Alec found that he wanted to explain to Binh what he often did not to other people.

"What exactly is a mesa?" she asked.

"You have hills around Boston... They are rounded mounds. Further north, there are mountains that are pointier, or at least with a craggy, not-so-big top—I've seen pictures of lots of mountains like that. Well, a mesa is like an elevated section of land, like a coffee table, that is the size of the base of a mountain, but it never goes up into a mountain. It just flattens off. The legs of the coffee table are steep cliffs on the sides."

"Like the mountain got chopped off?" asked Binh.

"The reverse," said Alec, "At one time, it was a flat plain, but water eroded all the way around one section of it, leaving a high, flat, table-like structure standing around much lower land. A mesa often has hundreds of square miles of flat land on top and in every direction, it drops down steeply. Historically, mesas were a safe, protected place for people to live. They were mini-environments with animals and water and some protection, so villages formed on top of them. The Hopi people have been living in the US for two thousand years, having come up from further south. Did you know that the oldest continuously occupied village in North America is the Hopi village of 'old Oraibi' in Arizona? People have been living in it since the 11th century. It's like a walled castle town or an old-fashioned apartment complex made in mud."

Binh made a mental note to read up on the American Southwest. Listening to Alec, she realized how little she knew not just about mesas but of the people who lived there and the land. All she could really picture was the Grand Canyon, and only because of the images she had seen in books and movies, not from experience. "I've seen pictures of Arizona, but I didn't know about the village. I can picture those high, flat lands with reddish-orange rocks and sand... I just didn't realize that people live up there. It's funny; so many cultures have built walled castle towns, and a mesa sounds like a natural version of the same thing, with more fresh air. I studied French through college and spent a semester in the south of France during my junior year. There are so many walled cities there, and villages up on cliffs, built into the rock. The stones and dirt are a yellowish-tan, though. I remember being surprised that the dirt was not dark brown like at home. Have you ever been to Europe?"

"Dirt comes in many colors—like people," he smiled again. "And this will be my first time in Europe."

"It's a long way from Arizona, I guess."

"It is. When I dreamed of 'getting out' and seeing the world as a teenager, I thought of California, the ocean, and Mexico, even Hawaii and Asia. I never really imagined going East. I do realize that if I went far enough west, I would end up in areas to my east, but I just never thought of traveling into the rising sun. Like the European explorers that changed our land irrevocably, I imagined going west too."

"That's funny. I always think of going east, especially to Asia, even though many flights fly west from Boston to get there." Binh paused and looked towards the window before remembering that the shade was pulled down over it per flight attendant instructions. "What do you think of it out here? On the East Coast, I mean, where we just left. Was this week your first time in Boston?"

"Second. I went out with a classmate once—for a few days, two years ago. It's nice. It's so green and compact. I like the ocean views a lot. I'm used to being able to see a lot further than it is generally possible to on the east coast. There are a lot of people in a small area, though, and everything seems like a city. But it really is very green and brick and built up."

Binh laughed. "You should see Vietnam! Asian cities can be incredibly crowded. Ho Chi Minh City has a bigger population than New York City, for example, and it's very busy all the time. I've only been there once, but I'd love to go back. Speaking of cities, what do you know about Zurich? I was reading about it in Margo's packet before we boarded."

"We'll be there tomorrow morning, but we won't stay long. I'm not sure how much of it we'll see. But as soon as I heard we were starting there, I began reading. It sounds cool and efficient."

"Right, on to Chur. I was going to re-read that section later before I went to sleep." After Monday night's group dinner, Margo handed everyone plastic folders. It held flight details, lodging logistics, and a timeline of the next few months—neatly outlined down to a credit card for meals and transport. It also had a page of links, including a website that she had made to stash uploaded 'location files' as needed. Forty-eight hours later, all of them (minus Margo) were on an overnight flight to Zürich, Switzerland. Their apartments had been prepaid for the next few months with the received salary advances, emails had been returned, friends had been notified, and refrigerators emptied. They'd be back in early August. The timeline started off very detailed in Margo's file, and then it tapered off, and the names of a few countries were followed by question marks. The team would go, be sent, where they needed to be. It would be an evolving project.

"I read Margo's file twice," said Alec. "I downloaded it. I'm planning to get some sleep after dinner so that I can stay awake for the van ride." His tray of bento boxes was nearly empty as he spoke. Their flight would come into terminal two. Flights come into one of two terminals in Zürich called 'Arrival 1' and 'Arrival 2'. It is possible to park a car for a short time in the curbside lane to pick up passengers directly from the arrival hall, and that is where Dr Basig's driver would be. He would have an eight-passenger van with a large sign on the dashboard reading, "Marguerite Duc." Margo had arranged a van for them, sparing the team from navigating Zurich's scenic but intricate train system after a long flight. Honestly, no one who has just gotten off an overnight flight that was really only seven hours and thirteen minutes long wants to change to a second train just after they'd been rocked to sleep by the first train. The train system was laughably simple, but for sleepy foreigners with just a few hours of sleep between announcements and meals, it was just easier to fetch them with a van.

Twenty minutes later, Alec and Binh sat in their seats with their finished meals on the trays extended before them for longer than one might think necessary. *Are there people who dine leisurely in the back of airplanes? Or are the staff all just preoccupied with the needs of the passengers that they can't clear for an hour?* Binh wondered. She decided it was likely the latter. She and Alec had stopped chatting, and they were both hoping to be cleared and reclined soon so that they could sleep for a few hours. Binh closed her eyes and wondered what Dr. Basig and his driver and Switzerland would be like. She fell asleep before she registered any answers.

Binh woke to the gentle clinking of trays as flight attendants resumed their rounds. The scent of warm bread filled the cabin. It was breakfast time in Switzerland. There was bread, cheese, fruit, a yogurt cup, boxed juice and a square of chocolate neatly packed into a little box. Binh was staring at her fingers as they unfolded the flap on the box. She was deciding whether tea or coffee would be better on an airplane when suddenly someone was next to her with a basket of warmed damp towels. A flight attendant with tongs was handing one to each passenger. Binh accepted one, wiped her face and hands, and sat back. Tiny shoots of natural light peered abound headrests from improperly closed window shades, but mostly, the plane was still only dimly lit with night lights. Binh allowed her eyelids to close again. She felt lucky. This would be a great trip; she hoped she'd be helpful. That had been her biggest concern following the job offer. She wanted to be sure that it was clear that she was not an expert in Vietnamese or psychology, for that matter. She wanted to be a researcher, yes, but she had not yet published anything on her own yet. "You are just what we need," Margo had assured her. "We know you are not an expert. We want your opinion, your observations, and your impressions, nothing more. We specifically did not want researchers with agendas and careers. We looked for recent students who would be thoughtful and have novel ideas." So Binh had signed on. Who wouldn't? Lots of people, as it turned out, like most people that she, had time to tell her that she was leaving. Her grandmother feared the worst, her brother doubted it would pay her loans, and even her old roommate had been suspicious of the project. Her boss at the restaurant warned her that when she returned in a week or two and needed money, and her shifts had been given to someone else, then there was nothing that he could or would do about it. She hoped they were all wrong. Her older brother and uncle had read and verified the contract that Margo had given her. Her father had met Margo. In the end, she had, with great satisfaction, been able to go.

Binh was excited to see new places and meet new people. Binh's curiosity about human behavior led her to psychology, where she studied personality, stress, and cognitive biases. She learned about the evidence-based framework for major personality traits. How cognitive biases lead to faulty reasoning that informs people's belief systems. She had learned how to manage stress and think of it as a normal bodily reaction, and she had learned about working memory and learning. Initially, the classes were large, and she didn't have to talk much in class, and the readings were fascinating. By the time she did have to talk in class, they were smaller, seminar-style classes. Binh was with students who were gentle, small in number, and linked to kind-hearted teaching assistants. Binh learned to express herself, defend her opinions, and then advocate for her ideas. By senior year, she was a strong candidate for graduate school. She had applied, had options, and was registered to begin the Master's to Ph.D. program in psychology at Boston University in the fall (which really meant late August). She planned to start work as soon as she had a Master's. Though she had not ruled out being a professor who researches, she was leaning more towards just being a counselor who researches. She had a lot of ideas about the Asian American consciousness of identity and she wanted to write and publish.

Binh's original plan for the summer was purely practical—waitressing to make ends meet. Following 'the take-out years of Covid,' restaurants were busier than ever and thirty percent more expensive. Tips were calculated on the final bill total in general, making waitressing a lucrative summer job for students—better pay than most resume-building internships. She had planned to live at home, save money and pay down loans all summer. Then, she was contacted by Margo. The choice was sore legs, hands that smelled like bleach, and a sprinkle of rude customers each and every long day, or flights, fun, reading, and research work that would connect to psychology. Margo's offer sounded like the fancy summer camps Binh had never attended. So, honestly, Binh saw this trip as a very interesting kind of vacation, and she didn't care how much she would have to work. Alec was particularly nice (and handsome), and everyone else seemed worth getting to know. It was going to be great.

Chapter 4: Margo Duc

Margo opened her eyes to a world of white—cream-colored trim, tan furniture, silver metal bars on the hospital bed—but the whiteness dominated. She was in the Tufts Medical Center, a large hospital at the edge of Chinatown in Boston. Everyone was very nice, but Margo felt utterly miserable. Her misery was partly because she felt a tightness in her abdomen, partly the immobilizing pain, and mostly because her impeccably planned expedition had gone awry. Well, not entirely awry, but Margo had not been able to go, and this was very, very disappointing. Margo glanced at the clock—Flight SWR53 was about halfway to Zurich. While the team slept, she lay in bed feeling aggrieved: all her preparations were thwarted. She'd be offered the chance to plan the whole project from the start and to go on it as the lead. The Institute for Education Sciences within the US Department of Education had contacted her. Actually, a former professor that she stayed in very loose touch with had contacted her, but nonetheless. It was a dream project—rigorous research, a year's worth of fieldwork, and enough data to launch new programs. Margo had planned everything perfectly, right up until 18 hours before the flight. And now here she was. She could still join the team later, but she had wanted to observe the full group together—to see how they interacted, who complemented whom. She had created this team. She had planned on going with them. She was angry and disappointed.

Binh would go along with anyone, masking her feelings effortlessly if needed. The Vietnamese culture was ingrained in Binh enough that she exuded modesty and self-restraint, and yet she was fully fluent in American culture. Her paper on Asian American identities attested to her understanding of the concept of 'face.' Binh's deep understanding of human nature along with her easygoing personality made her so compatible with Alec and Emma—exactly why Margo had seated them together on the plane for that reason. However, they were also the three most outgoing and open members of the team, and maybe they should have been split up. In contrast, Jiho was reserved but wouldn't hold back his opinion if given the space. He could certainly take charge of a group if they ended up in Korea. Adem, the most assertive, followed closely by Theo, could be a powerful combination—or a volatile one, and Margo was so looking forward to finding that out in Zurich. She had been counting on sitting with Migel and Jiho. She had wanted to put Migel and Alec together originally, but after the group dinner two nights ago, she knew that Binh, Alec, and Emma were a good mini-team. She could swap in Migel for Emma maybe later, but Theo and Migel had a lot in common, and they'd have insightful observations. Margo also wondered if Theo and Migel should be together or representatives in each of the two halves if the group split.

Margo grew up in Manchester, NH, a surprisingly diverse city with a population of 120,000 people, just an hour north of Boston.

Following high school there, Margo attended the School of Engineering at Rensselaer Polytechnic Institute. Alice had been her roommate for the last three years of college, but after graduation, Alice moved to Boston, while Margo returned to Manchester. Now Margo was working for the International Institute of New England in New Hampshire, a support and assistance center for refugees and immigrants in the United States. She was basically their entire IT department and software developer. She also worked as a contract coder on the side. After graduation, Alice had taken a well-paying job in Boston, but between mediocre colleagues and expensive rent, she quickly grew dissatisfied. So, eventually, she decided to switch to working remotely for an engineering company in Manchester that produced embedded firmware for medical, robotic, commercial, and industrial applications. She was working remotely until the lease on her very expensive apartment was up on August 15th, at which point, she'd move up to New Hampshire too and share Margo's two-bedroom apartment. That was the plan. A few days before the group flew to Switzerland, Margo had said goodbye to her family and was staying at Alice's small, overpriced rental apartment. When her mild abdominal pains suddenly intensified to the point of screaming, Alice rushed to call an Uber to take them to the nearest hospital. There were ambulances, of course, all over the place, actually, but through her pain, Margo had yelled, "My insurance will charge a fortune unless it's 'medically necessary.' Just call an Uber!" So Alice did. Alice had saved her, and not for the first time. That's what Margo was contemplating when a nurse came in.

"How are you feeling?" the nurse asked.

"Like a truck hit me in the middle of my body, and somehow I didn't die," Margo said dryly.

The nurse smiled. "Creative answers are a good sign! Here are your pills—antibiotics in this cup, painkillers in this one."

"I can take those with this water. Thank you," and she reached for the white paper cup on the right, grasped it, and held it to her lips, and swallowed the pills with water, and then reached for the second cup. She drank some more water, and then, as the nurse was refilling her cup, she asked, "If you had to guess, I know you are not supposed to, but how long do people stay here when something like this happens?" Margo winced as she adjusted herself in bed.

"Another sign of improvement! When people really need help, they don't care how long they stay or what we need to do to them. It's good when people ask about going home. The short answer is that you can go home when you don't need us—when you can take care of yourself, or have reliable help and there's no sign of infection. Someone will go over your prognosis in the morning, but your appendectomy was major surgery. Once the appendix ruptures, we can't use laparoscopy. We had to open your body cavity, which takes time to heal. We need to be sure that the infection in your abdomen has cleared up before we send you home, but your fever is gone, so maybe another day or two? It will be a few weeks likely before you can go back to normal activities still, and it does take a while for your energy levels to return. A doctor will check on it later.

Margo was so annoyed that she planned to spite-heal herself. She'd get back to normal quickly. She said, "Thank you. This just wasn't a good time for this."

"It never is. Everyone says that. Appendicitis most often occurs in people between ages ten and thirty, and it kind of comes out of the blue like this: how old are you again?"

"Twenty-six."

"Right, well, you're young and healthy, and healing won't take too long, but don't push too hard, and be gentle on those stitches. Your body needs to heal. Anything else that I can do for you right now?"

"No. Thank you, though. My parents? Are they still here?"

"They left, but they'll be back tomorrow morning. Get some sleep and ring me if you need anything. Just pull that white cord. I'm here until 7 am."

Margo closed her eyes. She was tired again. Being stuck in bed was infuriating. It really made her feel sorry for people with terminal illnesses and chronic issues. *How did they manage?* Margo wondered. *Well, if she were permanently bedridden or in a wheelchair, she'd make do. She'd make a little office for herself. She'd have her computer and phone. She'd adapt. It's the change that is so annoying. To-have and then to-not-have is misery. She was going to fixate on that for a while. She had a plan, and now she did not have one. She had mobility and communication, and now she had neither...* That was as far as Margo got down the road of self-pity before falling back asleep.

Chapter 5: Dr. Martin Basig

Switzerland, a small but stunningly beautiful country in central Europe, is bordered by France, Austria, Germany, Liechtenstein, and Italy. It is roughly the size of Vermont and New Hampshire combined, or a third of the size of Mississippi or a quarter the size of Florida. It's small. It is also shockingly beautiful, in a profoundly natural way, with ragged snow-capped mountains, even in summer, and villages of sturdily built stone houses scattered across the angled mountain fields. Despite its natural beauty—rugged mountains, lakes, and plateaus—nearly 75% of Switzerland's nine million people live in urban areas, which is unexpectedly high. Switzerland is divided into 26 cantons, which are similar to the states in the United States in many ways. Each canton manages its own education, healthcare, law enforcement, and taxes. These cantons vary in size tremendously, as California and Rhode Island do, with Graubünden being the largest.

While officially, the country of Switzerland has four national languages (German, French, Italian, and Romansch), percentage-wise, less than 1% speak Romansch and those who do mostly live in Graubünden. Dr. Martin Basig is one of them. Dr. Basig lives in Thusis and commutes along the A13 each morning to work in the canton capital of Chur. He works at *Fachhochschule Graubünden,* the Chur University of Applied Sciences, where he runs the university's lab for eye-tracking studies, and this is his particular expertise that Margo's team wants to speak with him about. Margo wrote the emails and arranged the meeting. Early summer was ideal for a visit, he had responded, as classes are out and researchers are available because Swiss Universities run their second semester from February to May, much like US universities. In contrast, French universities, often continue into June, and for that reason, the team was visiting Dr. Basig in Chur instead of Dr. LeFèvre in Marseille.

On Thursday, May 30th, Martin Basig headed into Chur later than he would have on a school day and then continued past the city on his way to Zurich airport. Though he had considered sending a graduate student to pick up Margo's group, her thoughtful rental of an eight-passenger van convinced him to go himself. He was curious, and it was just 90 minutes to the airport if he switched to A15 at the bottom of the lake. Though he often traveled by train or bus, Martin enjoyed car rides, having noticed years ago that they sparked the best conversations. When driving a vehicle, the driver has full control of when to talk and when to seemingly pay more attention to the road. The driver has reasons for not looking other members of the conversation in the eye. There are always options, and it is even possible to stop or prolong the journey. Train rides should be quiet, and it is always harder to make assessments through train car conversations. Everyone sits closely on a train and has few places to look, and the intentionally hushed voices make them harder to gauge. Car rides were instigators of conversation. As he is gathering strangers from the airport, Dr. Basig thinks it would seem too formal if he were to send a driver. Margo had been somewhat vague about her exact hopes for the meeting, and Martin, too polite to press, was still unclear about how his research could help or why so many people were flying to Switzerland just to borrow equipment. He kept up with publishing, and his lab had a website with explanations and links to the lab's published work. What else did they want to know about?

Flight LX53 strode down the tarmac and secured itself to the proper gate tunnel at 11:05 am, as expected. By 11:45, Martin had parked the white van in the pickup lane at Terminal Two. He grabbed the large, handmade cardboard sign from the passenger seat and turned the words "Marguerite Duc" towards the windshield. After a few minutes, he decided to step out of the van, place the sign on the outside of the glass and stand next to the van. Peter, Marguerite's father, had emailed him about Margo's unexpected hospital visit the night before, but he had decided to keep the sign as planned. It wasn't long before a woman and a man came over to him. "Dr. Basig?" the woman said.

Within twelve minutes, brief introductions had been made, luggage was stowed in the back, and all the seats were filled. Emma, the woman that Martin first met, was seated in the front. Behind Martin was a tall man named Jiho, a shorter, darker man with glasses named Adem, and a very European-looking man named Theo. Their pronunciation of various names and places made it clear that none of them spoke German. A woman and two men took seats in the third row, but it would be too hard to talk with them during the drive, so Martin planned to get to know them later.

Martin started the van's engine, exited the airport, and turned onto the highway heading south toward Zurich. It had already been established that none of the travelers had been to Switzerland before, but all had read some sort of the travel packet that Margo had sent them digitally. Thankfully, then, he didn't have to explain Switzerland. Sometimes, international visitors and conference colleagues could not get beyond discussing the mountains and the cows with bells and the chocolate. Some knew a little about banking laws and having multiple national languages, but rarely did visitors know the culture, the history and the contradictions. Many villages and city sections had been using electric vehicles exclusively for many decades, and yet, in 1990, the last canton gave women the right to vote. Like most places, Switzerland was a land of contradictions.

There was small talk in the van, gratitude on the part of the Americans, and general discussions, but soon the van was heading towards Kilchberg. "Are you all from the Boston area?" Dr. Basig asked. "I have been to Boston before."

"No, no," Emma answered. "We are from different places, just working together on a project. We came together from all over. Adem, Binh, Migel, and Theo were living in the Boston area, but I am from Ohio, Alec is from Arizona, and Jiho is from near New York City."

"New York City! I was there once. It's huge and so busy. I went to a conference there five years ago, and I added on some days to see the city. It went on and on and on. It was a machine!"

"Well, I'm not really from the city," Jiho said, "I'm actually from New Jersey, but it's just a short drive into the city. I have lived there for most of my life, so I'm very comfortable going in and out and getting around."

"America is so interesting to me," Dr. Basig said, "so many people from all over the world, so many different little villages. And so much interest in building and improving, there is so much change all the time. Everyone works so hard, though."

The conversation continued in this way for twenty minutes before it fizzled out, and the tired travelers either closed their eyes in the warm, swaying van or turned to look out the window. Either way, the result was the same. A passenger on a night flight to Europe from the East Coast could expect between three and five hours of sleep. Emma alone, seated in the front passenger seat, seemed awake and interested in talking. The others all gave in to the warm sunlight and the moving van.

"If we had gone east instead of south, we would have come to an interesting archaeological site where the artifacts found belong to an interesting and rather advanced culture that lived here six thousand years ago."

"I have read a little about that," said Emma. "I studied anthropology in college. I basically have a four-year degree in studying people and how their culture develops in response to time and place. When I looked up Chur before this trip, I read about the Neolithic people who lived in the Pfyn area. It is fascinating what has been found there."

"Yes, and mostly recently, but during World War II, when it was of great interest to increase farmable land, a group of soldiers were tasked with draining a bog so as to make more land to grow food. This is how the archaeological site began. When the bog was drained, remnants of an ancient civilization were revealed. Seventeen houses were excavated. There were quite large ones and smaller ones, but they were all built the same way and lined up right next to each other. The structures were complex in their height and roofing system, and the area was full of copper axes, ceramics, and man-made wooden artifacts. A true excavation had to be left until 2002, when it could be given proper attention. In 2004, much more excavation work was done, and dendrochronology—the dating from the tree rings—showed that the trees from which the wood products were made belonged to trees that were cut down between 3706 and 3704 B.C.E. There was a singular building period when all of the trees were cut and used for lodging and tools. Many other artifacts were found in the surrounding area as well, that the people farmed pigs and wheat and barley. People have been living in Switzerland for a very long time. "

"It's fascinating. I studied European Neolithic civilizations as a general group, so I have read that they all built homesites that seemed relatively permanent, and they farmed the lands around them and produced tools, weapons, and pottery, but I didn't imagine connected and complex structures that produced a village It's amazing that you live in the same area that humans did thousands of years ago. Well, I guess many people do, including me, but its hard to tell in most places.

"This area is rich in history and natural resources, we certainly try very hard to preserve it."

"Well, we are very lucky to visit it, even for a little while. Thank you again for meeting us," Emma said. She remembered reading that the Swiss placed tremendous value on politeness, and she wanted to be sure that Dr. Basig was thanked profusely for his kindness, so she quickly added, "And we are very pleased that you will speak with us, help us to learn more about what you do at your lab. We've read some of your papers, of course, and we hope to learn more about eye-tracking."

"I was happy to hear that you wanted to visit my lab," Dr. Basig began. I hope I can help you better understand what you have come to learn."

"I'm sure. It was very kind of you to respond to Margo that we could all come and talk to you and learn."

"Oh, I have known Marguerite since she was a little girl; I just don't see her often. Her grandfather and my father were good friends. They grew up in Chur together, but her father left to do work in the United States. He met her mother and decided to stay there.

Her family used to visit more regularly, but now it is sporadic. I am always happy to help her and her family if I can.

"We don't know Marguerite so well—we call her Margo—but she got us all together for this project. It seems to have involved a tremendous amount of planning. We had a long dinner meeting with Margo on Monday, and then we got on the flight Wednesday night Margo was supposed to have come with us." Emma knew that Margo would write software using the data, or at least according to the data that the group acquires. She knew that part of the project required looking into the connection between eye movement and brain activity, which is well known, of course, but their interest was in understanding eye movements when the brain is wandering as opposed to being focused on an activity. "There are recent studies that show that eyes have specific and patterned eye movements when the brain is in different attentional states, and various people in education are interested in understanding more."

"Umm, that is what Marguerite, uh, Margo said to me in an email when she asked if I would speak with you about my research. But why? It's expensive to send so many people to see me. What is the actual application."

"Online learning in the United States is a large and growing business. It's not only schools that offer online classes, —businesses and the military do as well. There are certification programs, webinars, and online meetings of all kinds." Emma was careful to articulate her speech slowly, a skill she had honed teaching English

Language Learning classes, but Dr. Basig's English was impeccable, and clearly, he could understand English at any speed. "There is a lot of interest in understanding whether people are paying attention online, as attention to tasks generally improves performance. We are going to look at some brain scans as well and collect data from them both."

"So you are interested in spying on students to see how much work they are doing?"

"Well, that is one use, of course, but our objective is specifically to learn about eye tracking when people are learning conceptual material versus talking, versus thinking versus participating in a hand-on activity like building something or writing. Eye-tracking allows for more direct, quantitative measurements of student behavior that are more objective and effective than surveys and observations."

"Yes, it is very effective for all of that."

"Effective and profitable. Enough so that it is worth sending us all out to do some leg-work—hmmm, some research."

Adem was sitting in the middle of the second-row bench seat. He had woken up and was largely listening to the conversation in front of him with his eyes closed. He had been wondering about certain things but kept his questions to himself. Specifically, he was wondering right now how it was cost-effective for such a large group to go on such a mission. The cost of the trip, the compensation, how was this efficacious? Adem was a data guy. He thought in numbers.

He calculated by nature; he always had. In his personal life, he worked out the chances of getting into schools, dating women with certain qualities, using one communication versus another, and paying off loans before he incurred them. While sitting in traffic, he gauged the chances of the occurrence of accidents. At work, because Adem now had a Master's Degree in Analytics from Northeastern University, Adem was the Logistics Analyst for a large retail company of building materials and homewares. His job was to make production, distribution, and delivery as effective as possible, literally by analyzing the numbers that were given to him. He used data to identify the potential profit and or loss in a supply chain and to develop cost-saving solutions. He had been at the job for exactly one year, and he had been seeking change when he was contacted by Margo and offered an interview. Adem lived and worked out of a second-floor apartment in Waltham, Massachusetts, just outside Boston. He was saving money paying down his loans, and getting valuable career experience, but he wasn't satisfied. Each week was just like the one before. Consequently, in April, he began exploring his career options. He wanted to travel, and he wanted to meet more people. He had begun looking online at language affiliation groups. He had signed up for a dating app. Adem spoke Turkish, but aside from a restaurant in Somerville that he liked, there were not many opportunities to use it. He had explored group travel, language groups, the Turkish Culture Center, and the National Museum of Languages. In the latter, he had connected with some members online. He had been weighing his networking options and applying for jobs when the offer came along to join this trip. Paying off his student loans fully would really help him and allow him to find the kind of scientific data analysis job that really interested him, whereas, in the year since graduation, he had just worked for the company that was willing to pay him the most. Adem had some job leads, and he planned to pursue them on this expedition and, ideally, start a new gig on September 1st.

Now Adem opened his eyes and more intentionally received the visuals before him. The van was still on the same road, but a small city could be seen up ahead. Adem wondered again to himself how eye-tracking could be of such interest that international travel was justified. There must be plenty of labs that study this in the US. He intended to look that up later.

More people began to appear increasingly conscious of their environment as the van rambled closer to Chur. Dr. Basig had been explaining it to Emma, but now he spoke louder and to the whole group. "I told Marguerite, Margo, to book a specific hotel in Chur that I will take you to now. It is in the *Altstadt*, the old town of Chur. You have four rooms in a hotel with a very unique history. It was a guild house—you know, an association of craftsmen. We have the historical documents that show that the guild in Chur was created in the year 1464 in the house that is now your hotel. Chur is a small city, but the history is very interesting. I think you will like it. It is early to check in to a hotel, but I made arrangements, and they are expecting you all. The rooms are ready for you so you can sleep."

The van had been driving south along the western bank of the Rhine River. They passed farmed lands with neat, ninety-degree angled borders, villages, and signs to Chur with an increasingly smaller number following the word to mark the number of kilometers left until the destination was reached. Huge flanks of mountains rose up all around the roadway, and teeny clusters of houses peeked out between rocks. These houses were always clustered together, not spread out like American houses tended to be. Then suddenly, there was Chur. A city burst out on the left as the van rounded a corner. Buildings and houses were nestled between the Rhine River and steeply rising mountainsides. The van ambled through the winding streets and stopped at the edge of the *Altstadt*. The travelers disembarked and followed Dr. Basig past narrow buildings that shared interior walls to a circular fountain centered in a plaza paved with small grey stones. After the group was checked in to the hotel, plans were established for the following day. Dr. Basig would meet them at the hotel at nine in the morning and walk with them to his lab at the university. The group went up to their rooms, and Martin Basig left the hotel and slowly returned to his van. He'd take it home tonight. He thought as he walked to it. The group was young—he'd expected that. Marguerite was not with them—he'd expected that too. The group was very diverse in their interests, though, and that surprised him. Emma was an anthropologist, Adem a logistics analyst, and two others were brain researchers—one studying psychology, the other psycholinguistics. It was an atypical group to visit his usability lab.

Chapter 6: Jiho Bak

Jiho had earned his undergraduate degree in Neuroscience and Behavior from New York University. As he walked to the Chur University of Applied Sciences with his six colleagues and Dr. Basig on Friday morning, and some of what he had studied was what he contemplated as he walked. He had learned about the four types of eye movements: saccadic, smooth pursuit, vergence, and vestibulo-ocular. Rapid movements that abruptly change fixation points are called saccades. Examples of saccade include the small movements made by the eyes as they search for information on a written page and the broader sweeps that they make when they look at someone's newly decorated living room. These movements are reflexive actions but can be made voluntarily as well. Smooth pursuit movements are the tracking movements that are made by eyes following a moving target. It takes a highly trained person to make smooth pursuit movements when the eyes are not following a moving target. Vestibulo-ocular movements maintain consistent vision as one's head position varies. A runner bouncing along a dirt trail in the woods can maintain a consistent view of the world as a result of the reflexes in the vestibular system. Lastly, Vergence movements are disjunctive—mutually exclusive—where each eye targets an object, such as a finger coming towards and moving away from one's face. Jiho was particularly interested in the neural circuitry responsible for three of these types of movements. He wondered what eye-tracking information would be learned on this and from which movements.

Eye-tracking requires the use of cameras, a light source, and computers. The various eye movement types, pupil position, gaze vector for each eye, and gaze duration are all recorded. When the camera feed is translated with algorithms, data points are generated that are very useful in numerous fields. If one ascribes to the 'eye movements reveal the thoughts of the human they are attached to,' theory then what the eye sees and fixates on shapes human thought. It follows for many then that eye movements if directed intentionally, can influence thought. This is of much interest to market researchers, scientific research, gaming, EdTech, shopper research, automotive research, user experience, training, and assessment; the list goes on and on. Jiho's former professor seemed suspicious of what recorded eye movements could disclose, but many in the industry were not. The reason, he knew, lay in the immense profit that may be gained; data generated could be very valuable. He also knew that product marketing would often run with an idea that science had only suggested was possible. There are numerous studies that connect eye movements to various cognitive processes such as decision-making, attention, and memory. However, it seems somewhat nefarious to control eye movement as a way to encourage certain lines of thought. In many cultures, there is an ancient expression that translates roughly to, 'the eyes are a window to the soul,' and there are now scientific studies that back that up, sort of. Jiho learned about all of this in his cognitive science studies, but he was surprised that anyone beyond academic researchers or anyone not affiliated with the military or private industry would be involved in such work.

The Department of Education in the United States already has more objectives than time or money to address them. In some cases, there is a lack of the knowledge required to address them, but in many cases, academic literature explains what should be done, and the real questions are why no one is fixing the problem or where the money will come from to fix the problem. There are funding issues, equity issues, safety issues, and concerns about the common core and standardized testing. There is controversy surrounding the topics of charter schools and school vouchers and deeper issues rooted in teacher preparation, teacher pay, the high rate of poverty, and disciplinary policies. Certainly, there is value in using eye-tracking for the purpose of understanding concentration, focus, and better assessment, as well as for the training of students, but is it such a high priority considering all of the other problems needing attention that a team should be sent overseas to learn, gather data, and report? Fortunately, it wasn't Jiho's job to prioritize tax dollars, but if it were, eye-tracking wouldn't be very high on the list. Nonetheless, Jiho wanted the research experience that this project offered, and the job was well paid when one considered the twenty-two thousand dollars that he owed in school loans that would be taken care of. He could certainly give up his social plans and freedom seven days a week for eight weeks. So here he was.

The walking party arrived at 9:25 am at a large, rectangular building with many dark silver windows that were evenly spaced in rows across each level. The exterior was what English speakers called 'a nondescript industrial-looking, modern building.' The interior was a surprise. The space was open, bright, and filled with white everywhere. Like their hotel, the interior seemed to have been carved out, painted white, and furnished with high-quality essentials, creating an airy, spacious feel. The furnishings were sparse but very comfortable, and everything needed seemed to be in place. The ceilings were incredibly high, and in the center of the building, the ceiling was three floors up so that open corridors bent around a central, open space, like a courtyard. It was modern, sleek, clean, and intentional. Jiho liked it at once. Jiho was an American kid, but culturally and genetically, he was Korean, and *hanok*, traditional Korean architecture, followed a centuries-old tradition of blending with the environment and using local resources, whether that be stone wood or brick. Modern Korean architecture roots itself in these principles but adds comfort, heating, cooling, and lighting considerations. The inside of this university could have been in Seoul; it was 'modern hanok.'

"At our university, "Dr. Basig was saying, "we focus on the study and practice—applied science. It is 'hands-on' learning, as you say. Let's go up to my office." The group ascended via a sleek, stainless steel, and glass elevator and exited on the top floor into a sunlight-white room. High railing prevented people from falling into the open, center space.

"I love the use of white and natural light," said Emma. "The building itself is beautiful and soothing. Our hotel is like this— everything is either white or light-colored wood, and there are large windows everywhere. It's inviting, clean, and serious all at once. It's not what I expected in a cold climate."

"Thank you. We appreciate our space as well. It is very practical, and it stays bright during the winters." Dr. Basig continued to speak as he pulled out a chair from the enormous glass, oval table and sat down. "Let's take a seat and figure out how I can help you. What specifically are your needs?"

It was Jiho who spoke first. "I studied neuroscience, as you know, but we are quite a mixed group in terms of preparation. Migel here studied cognitive science, Emma studied anthropology and is a teacher now, Binh will continue in clinical psychology working towards a doctorate, Alec is our natural scientist, Theo studies psycholinguistics, and Adem here is our analytics man." Everyone nodded as they were introduced. They had told him this in the car, but it seemed polite to reiterate and put a face to each description. Then he continued, "We are on this international trip to gather information, fuse the knowledge from all the places that we visit, and from each perspective that we have from our respective fields of study. Our end goal is a research report, as we understand it. With it, Margo will write some kind of software program for our central Department of Education. We became a group—we met each other—when Margo hired us all. Because of her medical emergency, you know, she was unable to join us. So, we are seven instead of the originally planned eight. Margo is still guiding the project; she will send us questions to research and answer when she is able to and as we send her information." Jiho paused, hoping someone else would chime in.

"Our first objective," Migel began, "is to better understand about eye-tracking hardware and to get your opinion on which methods will best suit our needs. Additionally, we would like to rent the equipment from your department if we may please."

"Ease of use in the field is a primary consideration," Emma added. "So, weight, overall size, and power requirements are determining factors."

"We have a budget of sorts as well," Adem said, "I investigated pricing a little already. Also, we were discussing this at breakfast and decided that we only need two devices as long as they both remain functional throughout the project. Oh, and ideally, we would like to send the devices back to you once we return to the United States. We expect to be using them in the Philippines, and we'd like to get a direct flight from Manila to New York when our work is completed."

"You will go from here to the Philippines?" Dr. Basig asked.

Binh, Alec, and Theo had remained quiet as the others had said what needed to be said, but now Binh spoke up. "No," she said, "We need to get some information from a university in Kenya first. There is a likely third stop as well, possibly in South Korea. With our practice sessions included here, we will have four physical places for data points and many more cultural variations."

"You have quite an interesting trip in front of you then," stated Dr. Basig without emotion. "Let's get started. I'll begin by giving you a brief overview and then explain the specific types of equipment that we have for researchers to borrow, and you can ask questions as we go. I will start the video presentation for you to watch. It will tell you about what we do here, what I research specifically, and what my graduate students are working on. I will go and assess our inventory of field use devices and cases while you watch and then train you in the equipment of your choice."

Many hours later, the group took a break for lunch and then returned to the facility. By early afternoon, they were thanking Dr. Basig, promising to tell Margo to visit soon, and exiting the University for the final time with data sets from two native Romansch speakers, one native French speaker, and three Americans. They also had two Tobii Pro X2-60 eye trackers, complete with stands. These were portable devices, compactly designed for travel and field research.

The group took a streetcar back to the hotel and regrouped in the early evening at *Bierhalle Chur,* the original version of the microbrewery/ restaurant. They ordered *capuns* (traditional sausage wrapped in Swiss chard leaves and boiled in gravy), *potato rösti* (a better version of the American hash brown), large fresh salads, and the locally brewed *Calanda Bräu*. Everyone was content, but the long table with four seats on each side made conversation strained over the din, and everyone was getting quite tired by the time the food was finished. It wasn't long before a group of three and a group of four started having two very different conversations. Binh, Theo, Emma, and Jiho sat at the end of the table closest to the door.

"I have serious jet lag," said Emma, "And tomorrow, we will lose another hour."

"The fancy problems of international travelers," said Jiho.

"Despite feeling tired for the past few days, I am really excited about this work and the trip. "We just got here yesterday," said Binh. "I can't believe how much has happened."

"I know," said Emma, "but since that meeting on Monday night with Margo, I have been so tired, and the plane ride barely helped. I'm sleeping in tomorrow. I plan to wake up just before check out."

"We have to check out tomorrow by 11 am, which works out well because we are getting a ride back to Zurich tomorrow at 11:15. It's nice that Dr. Basig will drive us once again, although Alec and I told him that we weren't too tired to navigate the train like everyone else here does," added Jiho. "We have an evening flight, so we just need to be at the airport by 3 pm. Has anyone ever been to Kenya? Or even Africa?"

"The Maghreb region," said Theo, "Morocco, Tunisia—nothing sub-Saharan."

"Is that what Maghreb means?" asked Jiho, "not below the Sahara? Just guessing from the location of the countries you listed."

"No, it means 'sunset' in Arabic. When the Arabs conquered North Africa in the middle of the 7th century, it was the western part of their empire where the sun set. The Berbers had been living on the land since Neolithic times and still were when the Arabs arrived, so the people and the cultures today of Morocco, Mauritania, Algeria, Tunisia, and Libya are a mix of Berber and Arab. The top third of Africa is very different from the rest. It has people with different heritages, living in different climates, eating different foods, with different flora and fauna, and speaking different languages. A place like Kenya is entirely…".

"Different," Jiho finished, giving a serious dad look. "Got it. So no one has ever been to Kenya or a part of Africa like it?" No one had.

"Right," said Theo, "The file from Margo about Switzerland was interesting and useful, but I have not gone over the one for Kenya yet, though."

"I finished reading the background info section," said Binh, "It is very helpful. But that is only about 15% of what's in the file. I don't know anyone who has visited Africa. I didn't know anyone from college who was a student from anywhere in Africa, and honestly, Boston public schools didn't really cover African geography, politics, or history in any class that I remember. I had to start reading because I knew almost nothing about it. Were you taught African history in Ohio, Emma?"

"No. I only learned about it from the old National Geographic magazines that we used to have at my grandparents' house. Most of them seem to have sections on Africa, at least as I remember it. The pictures were great, colorful, and exotic. But they mostly focused on traditional cultures, not on modern cities and universities. It's weird that the whole continent is hardly discussed in school—just the people who leave the place or were taken from it. We discussed slavery in many classes, but I don't think any teachers mentioned Africa again. Certainly not the literature or academic institutions. Then, in college, I focused on the archeology of the regions there, so I only heard about conflicts and political coups when they affected the transport of artifacts."

"There is so much to teach in school, and now basic manners and 'how to be a human and handle a hectic life' are being added into the mix, so a huge amount of history and literature gets overlooked. I guess the idea is to instill a love of learning and hope that students continue to teach themselves so that they find out about things, about life, about African cinema, and about what African countries have been doing since the last slave was taken, but it seems to me that a better job could be done at representing the good that comes from the area as opposed to just focusing on the many disasters. Asia is treated the same way. How much have I taught in public schools about the culture and history of Korea, Malaysia or Thailand? If there wasn't a war that involved the West, I didn't cover it at my school," said Jiho.

"But do people teach themselves about the history of Thailand and about African cinema and literature?" asked Emma, finishing her beer. "How many people sit around reading about history and culture? Probably only those who are already aware of such things. Humans naturally fear the unknown, so as long as we don't make time for a basic history of Africa, Asia, and South America in schools, the more we create fertile ground for racism. When schools don't cover topics, they are saying to the students, 'This isn't important.' Migel told me that his family came from Colombia. Well, in school, we study the ancient Incan and Mayan civilizations, and then we never talk about South America again! I've met people who vacationed in Mexico, and I've gathered from Hollywood movies that Colombia grows coca plants to produce cocaine, but I never ever learned anything about the history or how people live or what our political relationship has been like with this neighbor. I also know very little about Mexico, with whom we share a border."

"That's true," said Binh. "In Boston, there is a good-sized population from El Salvador, and one day in high school, some girls at my lunch table were talking about 'the revolution.' I was like, 'What revolution?' and they said that their families came to Boston because thousands of people were getting murdered by the military who was running the government; their friends and neighbors and relatives had died in a massacre, she said. All the girls knew about it, and they had come to the US for the same reason. I was stunned. That happened in a nearby country recently, and no one thought to discuss it in school. Especially in a state that so many of the emigrants came to, why not address it?"

"Like where you said your family lived. Remember, Theo, when you, Migel, and Alec were talking about South America? I had never heard of that country before you mentioned it," said Jiho. "I thought that all of South America spoke Spanish and native languages, but not French. I was really surprised. Sorry, I forgot the name."

"*Guyane française*," said Theo, "French Guiana in English. It is still part of France, and so part of the European Union, but it is in South America. The currency in French Guiana is the Euro. I've been twice with my family because the family of my grandmother still lives there. We stay with my great aunt; that's why my whole family speaks French," said Theo.

"What's it like?" asked Emma.

"It's hot, humid, and the dense rain forest constantly tries to reclaim anything not already covered, so there isn't as much open land."

"Maybe you'll be the most prepared for the Philippines then," said Jiho. "Is it all rural? And how did it come to be part of France?"

"Europe's big spaceport is there, the Guiana Space Center," said Theo. "And the country was a penal colony for France for a century.

The water is warm but full of sharks. There are beautiful beaches, though surprisingly there's no beach tourism. I don't remember seeing any hotels or restaurants on the beaches. They do have prison tours, though. The whole country is basically 'off the beaten path' for French people and 'off the radar' for everyone else."

"A prison in South America for French criminals. How was that ever cost-effective?" asked Binh.

"Well, it's not like they were flown first class." started Theo, smiling. "They were shipped in sailboats that were already headed there. The conditions in French prisons in France were abysmal and harsh. Since the 1400s, many prisoners were housed on 'galleys'—large rowing vessels that were not dependent on sails to move. The prisoners were forced to row. Napoleon apparently asked these rowers for volunteers to go to Guiana, and the conditions were so bad on the galleys that thousands did. The French had been trying to populate the colony since the 1600s and had trouble keeping the transportees alive there, with the heat, the tropical diseases, and the difficulty of producing enough food. Despite this, from the 1850s to the 1950s, French criminals were sent there. They almost never came back. Emma, at some point in school, you probably studied 'the Dreyfus Affair.' Alfred Dreyfus was a captain in the French Army at the end of the 1800s. He was Jewish and convicted of treason (which he was later proven to have never committed). Remember him?"

"Oh yeah," said Emma. "We studied World War II, of course, and there was a whole section before it about how hard it had been for Jews in Europe even before Hitler. I remember learning about Dreyfus."

"Well, Dreyfus was accused of treason, sentenced to life in prison and sent to French Guiana. The French call this event and the many years that followed as 'the Dreyfus Affair,' referring to the years of debate they spent creating, realizing, and trying to solve the problem. It took years. There are a few very small islands just off the coast of French Guiana. One of them, Île du Diable, Devil's Island, was generally used for political prisoners, and Dreyfus was sent there to live in a cage in the heat. When it was made public that the information that proved Dreyfus' innocence had existed but previously been suppressed, there was some public outcry about anti-Jewish sentiments, and the national conversation that followed, an 'affair,' the French called it, had strong opinions and politically important people on both sides. Five years after Dreyfus was sent to the island, he was returned to France, re-tried, and then pardoned. By then, it was 1906. The five debilitating years that he had spent in a small prison cell with bars for a roof, under the relentless sun, subjected to filth and tropical bugs and diseases were not enough to prevent him from hating his country, who knows why. Despite everything, he later served in World War I."

"Oh wow," said Emma, "I won't have done that. Screw any country that does that to me!"

"If you lived to have an opinion! He was being the better man. Anyway, that's a bit about French Guiana. He was our most famous prisoner and one of the few who survived," said Theo.

"Right, thanks!" Emma paused and then added, "Humans—people from every country—have done horrible things so many times throughout history. It's embarrassing," Emma paused again. "So, is French Guiana like Australia, then? Where have past criminals populated the country? I read that many of the criminals sent to Australia were often people who were imprisoned for stealing bread when they were starving because there was no work available that paid."

"Many French prisoners were like that, but not enough prisoners lived and remained really, so the population of French Guiana is still quite small today, like a few hundred thousand people, I think. A lot of the land is uninhabitable. But it is a perfect place for a space station, being so close to the equator. And the people there are French citizens, with all the rights and privileges that come with it. It's an interesting place, but not a big tourist destination. My parents and I, and my siblings were all born in the United States. There are a number of languages spoken there, but nothing like the sixty-two languages spoken in Kenya. That is a huge number. I'm really looking forward to seeing Kenya."

"I started researching Kenya as soon as I heard that we might be going. I had to get a vaccination for Yellow Fever and a visa for entry," Emma said. "I've been really interested in learning about the people and in seeing the land and animals for years—what kid hasn't? But I knew very little—just images, really. You know, if I were ever given a say in how the school curriculum was created, I'd organize it by theme, not by country or time period. This would show children, even through high school, the patterns and the commonalities among humans. Dreyfus could be one example of many, many people wrongfully imprisoned for politics or to satisfy the masses. I think that all cultures think and have thought about the nature of the world, how it got created, what it means, how people should live, and how people should be treated. They've all made terrible mistakes, too. The history of Kenya reads like another tale of humans not thinking about what other humans want or need. It's all about domination. "

Margo has given the group two location files so far. They were digital and jam-packed with information, addresses, and pictures. The location file on Switzerland was mostly about the culture and the Romanche language and how to be respectful while conducting eye-tracking studies (and receiving the equipment being borrowed). There was a section on how the eye-tracking data should be compiled. The plan had always been for the group to be in and out of Graubünden within a few days. The location file for Kenya was substantially larger. It included all kinds of historical and cultural information. It also detailed information on many people and their research ideas. The trip objective, however, was a little more vague than the previous 'Learn which portable eye-tracking devices best suit your needs and borrow it from Martin Basig's lab.' The objective for Kenya said: 'have multiple meetings with Dr. Kimaru Mwangi. Build a relationship. Learn about and document as much evidence as you can for what he told William Beatley at the Fall Conference in London concerning the brain images of patients who talk to spirits. Do as many eye-tracking studies as seems feasible.'

The sun still wasn't ready to set in Chur, but everyone was tired, and 9 pm was late enough. They paid their bill and ambled back to their hotel. Theo and Alec shared the last room at the end of the hallway, and as they entered, Theo asked Alec what he, Adem, and Migel had talked about at dinner.

"Kenya and colonization, mainly. Whether or not domination is an innate desire of humans that was favored through evolution, or it is a learned behavior or a genetic variation of a few who then train and subjugate others. You guys?"

"School, the choices made about what is taught or not, the fact that I have relatives in a country that no one knew existed."

"You're like a Hopi," Alec said, smiling.

"Thanks," said Theo, realizing that it was meant as a compliment, an understanding of shared experience.

"Outside of a small area in the Southwest, few Americans seem to know that we exist. I always get the 'I didn't know there were people alive who are 100% Native American—no offense.' I'm like a ghost. I appear and realize that people never expected to see me because they already thought that I was dead." The men got their door open with an electronic key, swung it inwards, and entered.

Chapter 7: Margo Duc

Margo was feeling much better by Saturday. She was home and capable of firing off emails and making slow, deliberate movements. She was doing just that when Samir popped up in her chat box.

"Hope you are doing better. Let me know when the kids have plans with Mwangi. Make sure they understand the cultural stuff."

"I will. They flew Zurich to Paris and will soon be on the Paris-to-Nairobi leg. It leaves CDG at 9:30 p.m. Arrive at NBO at 6:30 a.m. on Sunday. Monday will be the earliest that I will know more."

"Sounds good. Keep me posted."

Margo had thoroughly covered "the cultural stuff" in her location file. She was sure that the team would read it there. They weren't 'kids' anyway; they were young adults. They all seemed responsible, invested, and interested. They were young professionals. She'd provided a brief history of Kenya, the fact that both Swahili and English are the national languages and linked a series of news articles in English that refer to contemporary views. Other important information followed bios of the people to be met, templates for gathered information, and, of course, the very helpful-to-know bits about Kenya that did not fit neatly into other categories:

- *There are laws against talking on your phone while crossing the street.*
- *There is a law against having single-use plastic in protected areas.*

- *The most common greeting is a handshake. When introduced for the first time, the handshake is short, while among people with a personal relationship, it tends to be longer.*
- *One's physical appearance is noticed by everyone in Kenya. Women are especially watched. Binh and Emma, always keep a 'male escort' with you. Women's hair that is not pinned back, tied or braided is considered highly provocative, especially if it is blonde. Also, always cover shoulders, neckline, midriff, and knees so as to not seem 'suggestive.' Dress conservatively.*
- *Do not wear tight clothing. 'TMI' is still a thing in Kenya. See above.*
- *Do not point with a finger. Doing so is like making an obscene gesture.*
- *Do not rent a car. The street congestion in Nairobi is notorious, and the traffic lights are a mere suggestion. Use taxis or buses for commuting (use caution and common sense here).*
- *Do not begin eating until the eldest male has been served and has begun to eat.*
- *If you are offered food, it is very rude not to accept it.*
- *Do not have a one-night stand in Kenya. HIV infection rates are extremely high.*
- *To formally begin a meeting, each person will stand up and introduce themselves to the others present. Prepare a short intro for yourselves to use at every meeting.*
- *Kenyans often use metaphors, analogies, and stories to make a point. Not being direct is considered to be the most polite method of conversation. If you are unsure of what you were supposed to conclude or if it could be interpreted multiple ways, politely ask if you can repeat what was said. Worst case scenario, write down what was said to you and email it to me.*
- *In June, Kenya is just entering a dry season that will last through September. June also marks the start of the Great Wildebeest Migration. As a consequence of both, an influx of tourists start descending on Kenya.*

Chapter 8: Theo Auclair

Theo and Alec were the first to arrive in the breakfast room of the Garden Hotel on Sunday morning. They were offered tea and asked for coffee. When Jiho, Adem, and Migel appeared shortly after, Theo was already engrossed in explaining Kenya's incredible biological diversity. The group had landed at 6:30 a.m. that morning, but customs had taken longer than expected as several other flights had also landed around the same time. So, by the time the group had maneuvered into two taxis to the hotel, where they were lucky enough to have been given their rooms for a small additional fee, it felt late, but breakfast was still being served. Because Jomo Kenyatta International Airport in Nairobi is Southeast of the capital's center, the group would be spending parts of numerous days at Kenyatta University, at the city campus. Margo had found a hotel for them. The group would be in Kenya for just over a week, which sounded relaxing to everyone, but the reading needed to be finished by Sunday evening, and the meetings would start the following morning. Still, there was time to absorb. Kenya must be absorbed.

After Binh and Emma joined them, they spent breakfast debating how to use the rest of their day. They all wanted to see as much of Kenya as they could, both for their own interests and so that they could show up at the meeting tomorrow able to talk about what they had seen and done. Small talk was always made easier with firsthand stories. Jiho and Adem wanted to see animals more than anything else, and Nairobi has a Giraffe Park just outside the city limits. They would go there. Binh, Emma, Alec, Migel, and Theo decided to squish into a taxi and see Nairobi. From the plane and that first taxi ride, the city looked so unexpectedly big, sleek and modern that they decided to experience it on foot. A plan was made to meet back at 8 p.m. in the airy restaurant lounge at the hotel. Ideally, everyone's readings should be mostly completed by then. Theo hesitated for only a second about going to Giraffe Park; there wasn't enough time to learn a lot, and besides, he was very curious about the people and life here. He wanted to see the city.

Hours later, as they walked crowded streets, slowly peering into open doorways and sliding past large groups of people and people carrying large things, Theo decided that Nairobi had much more infrastructure than he had expected. He could count the number of big cities that he had visited, but he felt that this one was special anyway. The architecture was good and strong. The materials were thoughtful. Modernization was everywhere. The roads had some potholes and other issues, but Boston roads are often as bad, if not worse. There were at least road crews out here- people were working all over the place. Most apparent, though, was the contrast of seeing sleek office buildings and smelling… smelling what? Everything. Nairobi smelled alive. The cab (which had a distinct food-I've been eating smell) had dropped the group off at the National Museum of Kenya (which also smelled). The group backtracked to the University of Nairobi just to see another university really, before heading down Westland Road seemingly unintentionally. There were people, shops, restaurants, apartments, and vehicles of all kinds, and they all had odors of various kinds and one had never completely been small before another came along. Apparently, Alec had been registering the smells as well.

"This city feels so real," said Alec. "I think it is because of the extra dimension—everything has a smell. "It smells like people actually live here and have a life. I guess American cities smell like nothing most of the time, so if you smell car exhaust or human urine in an alleyway, it seems gross and out of place, and people move away from it. Do you guys think of home as having a smell outside I mean?"

"My part of Boston is mostly Vietnamese," said Binh, "and our parents are not afraid to cook with the windows and doors open. But you never smell fish in other parts of town. You're right. The nicer the neighborhood, the more cleansed it seems. College only smelled in the cafeteria or in a room that had a party the previous day and had not yet been cleaned."

"Back at home you don't notice smells in stores or cafes, but here? Dozens of different scents hit me when we passed that clothing rack," said Alec, "but here you do. There must have been dozens of different odors when we looked at the rack of clothes back there. A hound dog would go bananas—any dog would. It made me think of home. One of the things that I love about home is how it smells. The mesas of Arizona smell. Hopi homes and shops have a smell, but the

US schools, shops, and houses never do; They are all sterile." Everyone had noticed it. There was a constant barrage of stimulation to the nasal passages so far in this country: wafts of cooked food, sniffs of rotting food, smatterings of car exhaust, and waves and waves of body smells of passing people and perfumes and dirt and animals and sewage and hot pavement. The pavement had a smell. "The smells here feel so honest that I suddenly wonder why we go through such effort at home to cover them up. I wonder if we seem 'dishonest' to many visitors, you know, like 'we're going to take away one of your senses and see if you can still figure out where you are and what to do."

"I was just wondering what Kenyans must think when they visit the US," said Theo.

"Like we live in a hospital room," said Migel. "I have a lot of smell memories in Colombia but not many in Massachusetts, and I've spent much more time in the latter. I just realized that. If I try hard, I can think of occasions where something smelled strongly, but not many, and they are mostly in the kitchen."

"We sterilize everything," said Emma, "and there's a cultural value, I guess a Western and White value, that is placed on not giving information about the intimate, like how one's body smells. I remember once being about nine years old, and I covered myself in my older sister's perfume. My sister was mad when she found me and yelled until my mother got involved. My mother assured us both that perfume was only correctly applied when it could barely be detected by someone hugging us. One's smell is 'personal and private,' she told us, 'You never want to smell a person.' My sister was angry that I wasted her perfume, but my mother only cared that I learned about the appropriate amount to use. She'd be aghast here. I just smelled many perfumes on people of all sexes and ages and about 15 different hot and sweaty bodies."

"The whole city feels personal," Migel chimed in. "It's sexy. In hot countries, we expect it. Warm skin, perspiration—it's natural to smell people and food. Animals know it's normal, and people in other countries do, but Americans have been brainwashed by advertisers selling washing machine deodorizers, armpit chemicals, air fresheners, sink drain deodorizers, and scented dryer sheets. We've been taught that chemical smells are good and natural smells are bad. But in Colombia, it is good to smell a woman before you see her. It is great to smell *arepas* being cooked and your granny's wool blankets, but it is also good to smell men working outside and the cattle in their fields. On a crowded bus, you should smell people, not laundry soap. The United States is very un-sexy in this way. It seems uptight and embarrassed. It is as if one of the weird religious sects that came here declared that it was too stimulating to smell, and everything should be scrubbed clean, so people didn't walk around thinking about sex all day." Everyone laughed. "I'm serious!"

Binh reflected on these ideas… were smells sexy?

"He's right," said Emma. "Smell has been talked about in a similar way in my anthropology classes. Many cultures value smell as a knowledge source, an indicator, or an ability. In the Andaman and Nicobar Islands, for example, off the east coast of India, 'place smell' is at the center of their knowledge system. The original calendar of the people was created by separating the times of the year into what could be smelled during that time in a given place, like which flowers bloomed, or grasses grew, or fruit ripened. And there are many other examples of cultures all over the world that value smell and believe that it has deep meaning. Many Arab cultures have scent rituals, like scrubbing their bodies clean and then applying different scents to different body parts. People in harsh, dry climates value the smell of rain. I could go on.... It's only the Western world that feels that with advancement should come the denial of this rustic, uncontrolled sense. You can guide your eyes to 'not see' the inappropriate, you know, to 'avert your eyes,' but it's hard to control smell and avert your nose. Smelling is a wild, untamed way of perceiving. It makes most Westerners nervous, but not in other places around the globe—there are even cultures that believe that smell is part of the essence of a person. They believe that tribesmen and relatives all share a common smell. For them, I carry the smell of my great-grandfather. People who knew him would recognize me."

"I can't believe I never took an anthropology course," said Binh, "your classes always sound like they relate so well to psychology. I want to learn more about the psychology of smell when we get back. Aromatherapy is now popular, of course, but with neutral or nice seeming essential oils, and the concept that smells bring back memories is well known, but I wonder now about using smells as a treatment for trauma or other disorders. You guys just gave me a great research idea."

"We're all in fields that relate to psychology," added Alec. "The problem ispeople tend to forget that all the time. Schools focus too much on facts, but facts change, and many are subjectively presented or interpreted. Schools should focus on the process. How we acquire knowledge, how knowledge is stored and used, and how it connects the world like a spider web. Often, what is considered a great invention or a brilliant discovery is simply a person juxtaposing pieces of knowledge that most had never mentally connected, and it's interesting to know that other cultures made similar discoveries via a different path in another part of the world."

"Says the scientist," laughed Emma.

"I know, right? But even in my lifetime, we see in science that what we thought we knew changes when we get more information, better tools, and more knowledge. Science is amazing, but it is fluid, not static. What we think we know can always change. I want to teach. I want to teach about making connections. It pays so poorly, though, but to do it well, it's time-consuming enough that it's hard to research much on the side." Alec stopped. "Where are we going, you guys?"

"I wanted to get closer to that building that looks like a silver bullet," said Emma.

"It's on the other side of the highway," said Migel.

"I see that now. But look at it." They all did. "I watched a video about Nairobi's best skyscrapers, and this one's on the list. High-tech windows, facial recognition, marble interior—I had to check it out. I had expected Nairobi to be more 'developing,' and when I started watching videos of skyscrapers and shopping and museums, I had to see them. This is amazing. That building is gorgeous. Architecturally impressive for Chicago!

"What also looks amazing right now is that sign right there that says 'the Nairobi Street Kitchen.' said Theo. "It looks clean and interesting inside, and I'm really hungry again." They turned and headed for the entrance. Theo thought more about the smell. In the fall, Theo would start his doctorate in psycholinguistics at the University of Connecticut. Though it involved language acquisition, what really intrigued him was the connection between the psychological processes in the brain and language production and use. He remembered that Margo had been particularly interested in his ideas and coursework as if she had her own side interest in this kind of stuff. He thought about how Americans, if not Western European, seemed obsessed with suppressing smells and wondered how this had influenced the olfactory vocabulary. He'd never had reason to think of this before. Medical professionals—some anyway—were interested in olfactory processes, and of course, the prominence of the Covid virus brought to light that some viruses cause olfactory dysfunction, but now he really wondered about the smell as a concept and how it earned such a low place in American culture. The French love a fragrant meal, and avid outdoorsmen love the smells of nature. Hunters knew smells and depended on them. People who worked with wood and paper and food did—he started to think of more and more instances where smell mattered, but so rarely was it at the center of discussion outside of these specialties. The smell of life, of humans, and their environment really had to be completely neutral in the US. It was the culture now. He made a mental note to investigate when that changed as the group sat down at a table near the window. Realizing he'd forget in a month or two, Theo pulled out his phone and typed a note: 'To Research Later.'" He started typing.

Chapter 9: Dr. Kimaru Mwangi

Over breakfast on Monday morning, during breakfast, the re-grouped team discussed their upcoming meeting with Dr. Kimaru Mwangi and reviewed the location file. They had plenty of time as the meeting was set for 11 a.m. The file revealed that the word 'Swahili' originated from the Arabic word for 'coast' and is a mélange of Bantu and Arabic. It had long been the *lingua franca* for the traders. The file had a substantial 'background history' section that was largely new to the American group. They learned that human remains found in Kenya date back seven million years, and although many skeletons are in parts, a complete skeleton of a boy was found that is 1.6 million years old. A twenty-five-million-year-old skeleton of an ape has also been found. In short, Kenya is a central hub for archeologists and paleoanthropologists alike, making the National Museum of Kenya a must-visit.

The group had read that in 2000 B.C.E., Cushitic-speaking tribes from further north had moved down into Kenya from Ethiopia, and groups from other directions arrived over the next thousand years later. Evidence suggests there was much conflict in the region. By the first century C.E., Arab traders began visiting the coast, establishing trading posts, and settling in Kenya., Over the next eight centuries, they intermarried with locals and introduced Islam to the region. In 1498, the Portuguese explorer Vasco da Gama landed on the Kenyan coast and for the next two hundred years, there were Portuguese communities in Kenya in addition. In 1729, the Arabs expelled the Portuguese. However, European explorers continued to arrive, and by the late 1800s, Great Britain had a strong presence in Kenya. Much of Europe, in fact, had discovered the riches of Africa and sought to exploit the continent's resources.

At the Berlin Conference ending in 1885, African trade and colonization were divided into fifty regions of influence and ownership. These divisions respected neither cultures nor indigenous land usage. While France was assigned much of West Africa, and the Belgians took the Congo, Italy was given Somalia and part of Ethiopia, Portugal was handed Mozambique and Angola, Germany took Namibia and Tanzania, Spain got a sliver in Guinea, and Great Britain received a huge portion of the continent from almost top to bottom, including Egypt, Kenya, Rhodesia, Botswana, Nigeria, and Ghana. Not a single African leader was invited to the Berlin Conference. The comments and concerns of the Africans were not considered. British missionaries continued to flock to Africa, and Great Britain officially claimed Kenya as a colony from 1920 to 1963.

Other articles in the file were about specific people so that the group had some base knowledge. Jomo Kenyatta (although not his birth name) was one of them. Jomo Kenyatta was named Kamau at birth and was born to farmers of the Kikuyu tribe sometime in the 1890s (no birth record exists). He was raised by his grandfather after both of his parents died, and he attended a Scottish missionary school, where he converted to Christianity and was baptized "Johnstone." He then worked for the government and as a newspaper editor and in 1929, he was sent to England for two years to speak at the Colonial Office. After returning home for a year, Johnstone returned to England and stayed for the next fifteen years, first as an international student and then as a person who traveled Europe writing and giving lectures. When he published his first book, his name was "Jomo" and not "Johnstone. He learned about the Irish War of Independence and the Russian Revolution. He went to both countries to learn how each transpired. He thought about his countrymen, their needs, and why people should govern themselves and reap the benefits of their own work rather than export them.

Kenyatta returned to Kenya in 1946 and became president of the Kenya African Union and was arrested five years later along with 97 other Black leaders. Kenyatta was tried and found guilty of managing the Mau Mau rebellion and sentenced to seven years in jail. What is referred to in history books as the Mau-Mau rebellion of 1952-1960 was described in the location file as a war: The Kenya Land and Freedom Army (KLFA) versus Great Britain in a ruthless fight for independence. Great Britain "won".

After his release from jail in 1961, he joined the Kenyan African National Union, eventually becoming its president. When Kenya finally became an independent country again in 1964, Kenyatta was made the first president of Kenya, serving until his death in 1978. He is revered across the nation, much is named after him and in

October every year, there is a national holiday in honor of him. In 1965, when the British gave their Templer Barracks in Nairobi to the Kenya government, Kenya turned them into a college to develop teachers for the country and named it Kenyatta College. Today, it is the great Kenyatta University has twelve campuses and houses one of the largest research libraries in Africa.

The next morning, Theo, Migel, and Alec found themselves back at the same table. They had been asked again if they wanted *chai,* or tea, but all had replied that they would prefer coffee. '"It's funny," Theo said, stirring his cup, 'Kenya is known for its amazing coffee, yet most locals still drink tea for breakfast. Didn't you guys think that is weird? I looked it up because Kenyan coffee is sold all over the US, and it is considered to be some of the finest coffee in the world."

"Along with Colombian," inserted Migel.

Theo gave him a knowing smile. "Usually Migel, people think of Sumatran, Tanzanian, Ethiopian, Kenyan, AND of course, Colombian," answered Theo.

He raised his cup. "But yes, Colombian always makes the list."

"How did the people of Kenya get used to drinking tea instead?" Theo continued as everyone else came in and sat at the table. I wondered if it was just the British influence." The restaurant in the hotel had left the eight-top that the group had made on Sunday by pushing two smaller tables together. Now, it was 'their' table. "So I looked it up, but it turns out that when the British ruled Kenya, they had laws that only the farms of White people could grow coffee. 100% of the harvest had to be exported. The Kenyans were sold British tea to drink! Which, of course, was not grown in Britain. The Kenyans also had to have *kipande*, identity cards, that included information about where they worked, so job hopping wasn't very easy. Kenyans were forced to drink British tea at the coffee farms that they were kind of bound to. Kenyans didn't start drinking coffee until they kicked the British out, and international television shows and movies are credited for pushing the cafe's culture. There is a rapidly growing coffee culture here and coffee shops all over, but the older people like our kind waitress are the less likely to drink it."

"No one drank coffee in Kenya before the British showed up to farm it?" asked Emma.

"Well, people in the coastal towns drank some coffee because of the Arab influence and their strong coffee culture. But for most Kenyans, coffee farming was just business—they're only now developing a coffee-drinking culture. Things are still changing."

The waitress served Binh her tea and then put down seven cups, two pots of coffee, and one pitcher of warm milk.

"I wish I knew Swahili; it feels weird speaking the language that these people were colonized with. I feel like an oppressor by affiliation," said Emma. "I didn't realize how many languages are spoken here. I'd only heard of the *Maasai, Kikuyu,* and *Kalenjin,* of course, but I figured there were five to ten more. But there are truly forty different languages spoken in this country!"

Alec raised an eyebrow. "You've heard of the *Kalenjin?"* Asked Alec

Emma nodded enthusiastically. "Yes! that tribe that has been producing the world's best runners for decades. Every year, when the Cincinnati Flying Pig Marathon occurs in May, there is serious TV coverage on the Kenyan runners who are super-human fast," said Emma.

"It's true in New York and New Jersey, too," added Jiho. "But no pigs fly there. I run a little—I mostly follow marathons on the sports channels—and people from that tribe blow most other runners right out of the competition."

"I've heard of the great runners from Kenya, but I didn't realize that so many came from the same tribe," said Alec. "Anyway… The location file was really helpful. Dr. Kimaru Mwangi is Kikuyu like Kenyatta, and he publishes a lot about brain scans. We're supposed to talk with him about that."

"Did any of you find a connection to eye-tracking?" asked Emma.

"No, but presumably, the goal is to follow what the brain is doing during various eye movements. Or changes?" said Binh.

"We'll see," said Adem. But six hours later, they still did not.

Kenyatta University is impressive, large, very modern, and well-equipped by the standards of any country. Dr. Kimaru Mwangi researches and teaches for the Imaging Department in the School of

Medicine. The team's visit with him was long and polite, but it was also inconclusive. It involved several other people. There was a coffee break in the middle, and the meeting started and ended with a lot of small talk and 'What have you seen of my country?' 'How are you liking Kenya?' and then there was more general discussion about sports and food, and there was never a convenient time or a seemingly appropriate opportunity to be blunt. Eventually, the meeting was clearly being ended, and Emma got up the nerve to say, "Dr. Mwangi, if you might possibly have more time, we would love to hear about your discoveries with—"

"Ah, I see. We'll meet again. You'll have more time to explore Kenya, and then we'll talk in more detail. Now, please visit Moobi in the front. Moobi will tell you about my availability. I am happy to see you again. Thank you so much for coming." They all thanked Dr. Mwangi. What else could they do? They pushed in their chairs, and they went to the desk 'in the front.'

A woman with tiny braids, some hair falling over her forehead, sat at the desk. She had a bright yellow shirt, and the name plaque on her desk said "Moobi Kariuki." She had a lovely smile and eyes so dark and sparklingly that they seemed light from behind. She was stunning. Evidently, Moobi had already received all the necessary information because as Emma went up to the desk to speak, Moobi smiled and said, "Dr. Mwangi can see you all again on Wednesday at 11 a.m. Is that good for you?" It was good. Pleasantries were exchanged once again, and the group departed.

"That felt like a sincerity check," said Alec after they had left Moobi, descended the elevator, walked the long hallways, and exited as they left the large cement building that housed Dr. Mwangi's office. "If we seemed to sincerely be interested in Kenya, and if we seemed capable enough and smart enough, then Mwangi would schedule another meeting with us to discuss his work. If not, he probably planned to be 'busy' until we left the country. He was just checking us out."

"Most cultures function that way," said Emma. "It's the Americans who are rushed and direct all the time, followed by the Europeans, but in other parts of the world, life is about relationships, pleasure even, and considering options. We are all from a very direct, goal and profit-oriented part of the world. He was extending a courtesy to us, and he was respecting us by not seeming to be time-pressed. So yes, I guess he was 'checking us out,' but really, he was treating us as he would another African. It was a compliment."

"So, we passed?" asked Binh.

"We passed," said Alec. "The Hopi are similar. As Emma pointed out, much of the world believes that relationships are important and they take time to build. Maybe we'll get what we need on Wednesday, but maybe we'll have another visit. I wish we didn't have plane tickets on Monday morning, though, because it might be tight if Mwangi wants more time. He might want to know us better. We're a big group. It's intimidating. He wants to feel that we are honest, I imagine, and not to sound like I'm fixated on profit like an

American, but maybe he is also thinking that he needs to be sure that we are not going to sell his ideas or otherwise cause trouble for him."

"What would we sell? What trouble could we cause?" asked Binh.

"Everything has a price somewhere," said Adem. "Mwangi has likely noticed something interesting that others have not. He doesn't want people to profit from his ideas that are still unformed, and he doesn't want to cause a big sensation, but I think he will share. He just needs a little more of a relationship with us first. We can certainly fill the time. There is a good restaurant area a fifteen-minute walk away, and I'd love to see the Karen Blixen house and a little more of Nairobi. We could maybe fit in a one-day animal excursion if you guys want. We should make an effort to talk to people and get to know the cultures as much as we can."

"While seeing cool stuff," added Jiho.

"Yes, while seeing cool stuff," said Adem.

"Who was Karen Blixen?" asked Binh.

"Oh!" said Emma, "She was a Danish woman who moved to Kenya in the early 1900s to start a coffee farm with her husband. Kenya was part of Great Britain at the time. Her husband turned out to be a bad farmer and a worse husband, and he left her. She continued to run the farm and lived in Kenya for seventeen years. Blixen wrote letters to her brother while she was in Africa, and when she returned home, she used them for reference and wrote a book and then a few more. *Out of Africa* is one of the books, and it is interesting. Sadly, though, it was made into a pretty big Hollywood movie that is just mediocre because it glosses over a lot of the issues of colonialism. But the movie also gave faces to the African people, explored a small number of issues, and filmed the beautiful land. Blixen documented the colonial period. From her books, it sounds like she was overall a kind person, and she honestly loved Africa, but the fact remains that she sustained the colonial lifestyle, a deeply disturbing form of subjugation where one group of people profit economically from another, the lower class of people who do all of the hard work and reap few of the benefits. Sure, the colonized gain infrastructure, but they lose their identity and their right to rule themselves. Through laws and actions, the native people are made to feel as if they don't belong in their own homeland, and eventually, there is a revolution and the colonizers fight hard to keep what they have, and the colonized fight just as hard as they have little to lose and what they deserve. The history of the world is one group of people profiting from another until the other revolts."

Alec smiled and said, "That about sums it up. Once it got harder to profit off people, they turned to exploiting land and resources." He glanced at the restaurant across the street. "Hey—can we stop here and get lunch? I'm starving." They all agreed, stopped, went in, were ushered to a round table, ordered, and continued talking.

"Look, people naturally get hungry and horny, but they can't go around stealing food and sex from the other humans around them, right?" pointed out Emma. "I think there are human obligations to be fair and respectful, but the definitions of 'fair' and 'respectful' are rooted in a culture, and cultures vary tremendously. The interpretations are cultural. Trying to get humans to never try to profit from each other and to all exist peacefully just isn't realistic. There will always be competing and conflicting interests. We need to teach people to focus on what we have in common, work together, and create rules we can all agree on. That's more valuable than hoping that suddenly, everyone will see each other as equals, get along amicably, share resources, and agree on land ownership."

"It is more hopeless than you think to have world peace." Said Theo. "We can talk about fairness all day, but unless there's a global standard for behavior, people are going to keep doing horrible things. Human groups have so many competing desires over the rights to resources and how people live and behave it's impossible to ever have an agreement. That's what a belief in a 'higher being' is supposed to do: hold humans accountable to goodness. Failing agreement on that, some kind of world contract needs to be put in place."

"A contract will never happen unless the world unites under one government, like in the *Star Wars* movies, and agrees on a higher power, "interjected Alec, "and what (s)he/they says REALLY doesn't work, just look at how the good Christians coming to America treated the native people living there already. In the name of God, there was widespread murder. Cultures and languages were completely wiped out. Whole tribes were destroyed, and the few surviving ones were forced to relocate from desired land and face religious conversion. So much for the concept of 'goodness.' In the name of religion, many of the greatest atrocities of humankind have been committed. The problem with involving religion is it gives people an excuse to do terrible things. They justify murder and destruction by claiming it's 'God's will.'. You couldn't convince me or pay me to be a part of that."

"I know," said Emma solemnly. "It is horrible. I still have faith, but I can see how the history of organized religion has turned many away."

"I can respect your beliefs, Emma, but I think that people should have left Christianity many times throughout history, and I find it amazing how many believers still exist. The inquisitions? The Taiping Rebellion? The—" started Adem.

"What was the Taiping Rebellion?" asked Binh.

"The most important event in 19th-century China," explained Adem. "Hong Xiuquan had visions that told him that he was a son of God, you know, the little brother of Jesus Christ." Giggles broke out. "It's not funny—twenty million people died!"

"Jesus! I mean Hong! How? Seriously?" asked Emma.

"Seriously. Hong Xiuquan organized a God Worshiping Society, gathered followers—mostly poor, oppressed people—and claimed that an angry Old-Testament-style God wanted them to share property, have strict discipline, be obedient, and enact social change. It was essentially a political revolt against the Qing Dynasty: a precursor to communism injected with religious fervor and talk of the will of one true God. You've heard the story before in other forms." explained Adem.

"But how did twenty million people die?" asked Binh.

"Well, the followers became true disciples, and as their numbers grew, Hong called himself the 'Taiping King.' He encouraged the fight for Heaven and so started arming his followers. The Qing dynasty attacked the Taiping group, and amazingly, the religious-crazed peasants led by Hong beat the official Qing army. This fueled the cause. The rebel Christian Communists tried to take over Beijing and failed, but they did successfully take over Nanjing and ruled it for a good decade! It took foreign intervention to free the city of Nanjing and end the revolt." finished Adem.

"Twenty million people died, and I never studied that in school," said Binh. "I learned that the 1800s were about the industrial revolution, social reform, mass immigration, bizarrely tight undergarments for women, emotional poetry, and a lot of great minds and philosophers."

"That's basically true in the USA. The long and complex histories of Asian countries are rarely taught in the US before college, and even then, they appeal to a self-selected group. To take another example, the genocide in Rwanda is still barely covered in school, and it could certainly fit in with multiple units," said Jiho.

"I don't know much about that either," said Binh, "but I thought that I heard it was a tribal conflict."

"It was between two tribes, the Hutu and the Tutsi, but it was a conflict ignited and heated by colonizers. 800,000 people died in 100 days. The Tutsi and moderate Hutus were slaughtered. People were encouraged to kill their neighbors, and even some priests and nuns were complicit in the violence, while others participated directly. Some killings even occurred in churches." Said Jiho, "Whether one sees the conflict as having an ethnic division or not from the start (because the two groups immigrated originally from different areas and so looked differently, and there was tension), there was animosity as the result of social and caste division based on occupation. The tensions were exacerbated by the German colonizers who governed by having African rulers in positions of authority under them, and they favored the Tutsi over the Hutu when handing out high-level jobs. The Catholic church also fueled the division between the Hutus and the Tutsis by favoring the Hutus and stoking racial tensions between them and the Tutsis.

On the plus side, in 2017, Pope Francis officially asked God and the people for forgiveness for the church's sins and failings during the 1994 Rwandan genocide. It was the first time they took institutional responsibility, instead of just blaming individuals. This was positive, and there are a lot of interesting conversations that should be centered around this. They rarely come up because the US schools don't teach much about the history of African countries, and they don't explain how the present relates to the past here. Post-colonialism as a concept is really reserved for college work if one studies literature, history or political science. It didn't find its way into NeuroSci classes.

"Or my psych classes," said Binh, "Which is odd."

"Humans are always trying to one-up each other. Land, resources, power—it's the same story," said Alec. "And I don't know how that can be altered other than through self-realization and education, and that will never happen if the topics aren't covered in schools. People aren't going to change what they don't even know exists."

"I am still going to hope that things will change and world peace is possible," added Theo. "I think it's important to believe that we'll eventually learn more about other people and treat each other respectfully. Otherwise, what's the point?"

"I feel the same way," said Migel. "It's too depressing to have any other view."

"I don't mean to be depressing," said Alec, "but after studying history and biology, you start to notice the patterns. We've always had a tendency to dominate others—like animals fighting for territory. There are repeated struggles of dominance, where often the more technologically advanced group gains power. You can be angry about it, or you can realize that there is probably an evolutionary reason for it and study biology. Plants and animals compete too, you know. The plant and animal kingdoms are brutal and competitive places."

"Everyone ready to move on? We are paid up and free to go," said Adem, who had handled the bill and filed the paperwork in his wallet.

As they all stood up, Emma said, "I grew up with chickens, well, just hens actually, and they literally hop on top of each other. The hen on top will peck the head of the bottom chicken to show dominance. She'll also insist on eating first and picking the best sleeping spot. The other hens generally acknowledge the dominant one and they all assume their places under her. The dominant chickens don't get really mean unless the hens further down in the pecking order try to rank up. I've been thinking it's a lot like colonialism."

"What allows chickens to be higher ranked in the pecking order?" asked Binh.

"Bravery, size, aggressiveness." said Emma, "When you raise baby chicks together, they develop an order peacefully as they grow. Breed, temperament, size, and age are all components, but even when our flock was all the same breed and all the hens were born on the same day, a pecking order was still clearly established a few months after birth. You just need to give them lots of room. Hens with too little space and too little activity get nasty. Hens with room work it out, but equality is not a word I'd use. It's not a democracy in the chicken coop. It's more like a military dictatorship."

"I think humans copied animal behavior. Maybe it wasn't intentional, or maybe it was. Maybe now it is an evolved instinct, but we are going to have to rationalize past it with an intentional desire to change if we are going to have Migel and Theo's love and peace," said Alec.

"We can do it," said Theo.

"I'll be the first to be excited if things change," said Alec, "until then, I'm going to keep studying plants and animals and watch humans act like advanced chickens with opposable thumbs."

Chapter 10: Margo Duc

It was Tuesday, a week since Margo had gone to the hospital and five days since she had been released to her own home with her parents as 'caretakers/watchers for infection.' She had a follow-up appointment in Boston in a few days, and she was doing ok. She'd sent some emails about her halted software projects. Not much was expected of her since she had planned to be traveling for all of June and July, although she had intended to check in periodically. Margo had been tracking the traveling team, both indirectly and directly. Indirectly, she'd looked up who had opened files, when they had been opened, and how long each person had spent looking at them. She read through their posted expense reports. Directly, she shot them a group email and asked them to reply individually. So far, all had responded except for Adem and Emma.

Adem was methodical and calculated. He chose what he said carefully. He most likely had not responded yet because he was deciding on what to say or how to say it. Emma, known for her detailed and idea-packed emails, had likely just not found the time to respond yet. The most recent email had been from Binh. She was thorough. She gave dates, times, and summaries of visits in an objective manner and then offered her interpretation but highlighted it as exactly that.

Margo missed being part of the adventure and getting to know the group better, but she stayed informed about their progress. It wasn't the same, but for now, she was content.

Margo sat at the computer long after she had read Binh's email. She was thinking about Dr. Mwangi. He seemed to like the group, and they seemed to like him; they should be able to learn something valuable. She toyed with the idea of assigning a "Group Communication Lead." She thought of other positions that she had been planning on doing herself and now would be unable to. Adem should be the Finance Manager. He had already started gathering the receipts and spreadsheets of their expenses. Margo decided to group-email them one last time with individual 'leadership roles' based on their individual skill sets.

Chapter 11: Dr. Kimaru Mwangi

On Wednesday, the group reassembled in Dr. Mwangi's conference room. He welcomed them, transferred them from Moobi's domain to his own, and asked about what they had seen and experienced. He asked for their opinions about travel and about Kenya. Had they tried *ugali,* he wanted to know. Yes. "It was served with many meals." It was cornmeal, water, and salt, and it looked and tasted like cream of wheat cereal. Emma described it better when she spoke. Had they tried *Githeri*? Yes. The group recalled that Adem had called it "the love child of a Midwest pot roast, an Indian curry, and a Southwest chili," but Binh just called it a delicious stew. Dr. Mwangi explained his love for these dishes and how countries traditionally eat what they can grow, catch, and kill in their area, and these dishes spoke of his home. They all agreed. Dr. Mwangi continued. He explained that Kenya grew sturdy greens, beans, squash, and maize, and they served a lot of grilled meat, often goat, but beef, chicken, and fish as well. The Americans expressed their appreciation for the food, which seemed to please Dr. Mwangi.

He insisted that the group call him 'Kimaru' and invited them to sit in a half-moon shape facing a large screen. Then, he began his talk on brain scans.

Standing in front of the screen, Kimaru adopted a professorial stance, explaining exactly what the group had come to learn. He was well-spoken and very articulate, which was in stark contrast to some professors they had all encountered. Especially those who, despite their intelligence, struggled to balance the delivery of information in a way that was both engaging and useful.

"There are many teams within this Imaging Department," Kimaru began. "We study brain images, as there are many ways to scan the brain today, each serving different purposes. These scans help diagnose diseases like Alzheimer's, brain cancer, and stroke and assess damage from head injuries. The types of scans we use include positron emission tomography (PET), electroencephalography (EEG), magnetoencephalography (MEG), computerized tomography (CT), functional near-infrared spectroscopy (fNIRS), magnetic resonance imaging (MRI), and Functional Magnetic Resonance Imaging (fMRI), to name a few. Think of MRI as a map-maker, while fMRI shows and measures the activity on that map. When a person engages in different activities, the neuron activity in their brain also changes, and fMRI captures these changes in real-time Screenshots, of course, can be taken at any time. Areas in the brain that are more active require more oxygen, and so blood flow increases to those areas and what we are really looking at is where the blood goes."

Kimaru walked around the back of the group, adjusting his laptop as he began projecting slides onto the screen. "We have questions about brain activity in patients with Down syndrome, Parkinson's disease, those who've suffered brain injuries. We are also interested in exploring brains that have had strokes and brains that have received pharmaceutical intervention." A few eyebrows raised at the mention of pharmaceuticals.

"Oh, certainly," Kimaru continued, "medications have a tremendous impact on the brain, and it is important to understand when that impact is more helpful than harmful and vice versa. Then there's meningitis—an inflammation of the protective lining of the brain and spinal cord caused by infection. The infection can be bacterial, viral, or fungal or result from parasites or amoebas. It is a condition that exists worldwide, of course, but it's particularly prevalent in Africa, forming what's known as the 'meningitis belt,' stretching from Senegal to Ethiopia. We train our students to recognize any irregularities that warrant extra attention and to consider what is likely here versus in other places. I teach and train, and I research, of course, but not perhaps how you may imagine that all occurring in the United States. We have good equipment and ample space, but little of it is proprietary, and we are always seeking more funding. I'm particularly interested in cognitive impairment and have conducted thousands of brain scans throughout my career."

He paused for a few minutes, standing tall in front of the group. "Lately, I've noticed something peculiar in certain scans, something atypical, but it occurs in healthy patients when they engage in certain kinds of conversations.

A few months ago, I had a patient with many concerns. She knew one of my aunts well, and when she was sure she needed a brain scan, my aunt promised her that I would give her one. I did. She was very healthy and didn't need to worry about her brain. However, once that was established, we started talking, and I asked her about her work and family. She was in the MRI tube, wearing noise-canceling headphones, with a talk link to my monitoring room in the back. I should mention that she is well-known as an excellent communicator with God. She talks to her ancestors, even those who passed away a decade ago, and she is regionally famous for offering advice received from these ancestors. As a result, many people come to her for guidance.

Traditionally, in Kenya, we talk to God through our ancestors, even among those of us who consider ourselves Christians, which is the majority. God exists for us, but He is so revered that we do not speak to Him directly. Instead, we communicate with God through our ancestors, as we always have. Some people do not hear the voices of their ancestors as clearly as my aunt's friend does, and so they sometimes contact her or hire her as an advisor. She offers advice on the type of ritual that should be performed to access the ancestors they wish to communicate with, and she assists in the communication process. For Kenyans, spirituality is deeply connected to healing. When we heal traditionally, it is not just with herbs but also with spiritual healing. So, while we have medicine and Christianity, as you do in America, it plays a different role in our worldview. Does this make sense to you all? I know it's not the same in the United States. We have a different worldview. We have an extension of our Christian beliefs—another part that connects us to God differently, but connects us nonetheless. We are Kenyan Christians, and that's not quite the same as being an American Christian, I think.

The group had read about the ideas Kimaru was expressing, and none of them found it unusual. They agreed that if a group of Americans were surveyed about their belief in God, many would say the very existence of God is unverifiable. Among those who believed, their relationship with God would vary tremendously. Muslims would say a person should worship and talk to Allah directly, and members of the Jewish faith would likely say the same—that God should be prayed to directly. However, Christians would give a variety of answers. Some pray to God directly, but many do not. Some pray to Jesus, while others say Jesus and God are one and the same. Some Christians talk to God through Mary, and others pray to saints, who, in turn, speak to God on their behalf. Given the many ways people communicate with God, it did not seem strange at all that many tribes in Kenya communicated with their single creator through their ancestors, even when they considered themselves to be Christians. Jiho explained much of this to Kimaru, who was very happy to hear it.

Kimaru had expected to explain the role of ancestors in greater detail, but when he saw that Jiho and the others viewed the practice as similar to praying through other intermediaries, he continued his explanation. "So, my aunt's friend was lying supine in the MRI tube, wearing high-resolution goggles and earphones while we spoke. Then, suddenly, she said she was receiving a message from me. I was still monitoring her brain and saw a sudden and significant activation in the moments that followed. Surprisingly, the activation occurred in the right parahippocampal gyrus. This is part of the limbic system—an area pivotal to memory formation and retrieval. For example, when looking at the brain scan of a patient with schizophrenia, asymmetry can be seen in this region. However, in mentally healthy people, this region is symmetrical and almost sausage-shaped.

Typically, this region activates on an fMRI when the patient looks at images of places—landscapes, pictures of cities, images inside a building where there is a lot going on. It's also activated when someone thinks of something within a landscape. For example, if someone says, 'You know the orchard at my grandmother's house?' or 'You know that old wooden shed in the center? Inside that shed, on the long red bench,' or 'When you're in New York City, with your back to the southern side of Central Park, walk down Seventh Avenue and in a few blocks you'll see Carnegie Hall.' This region activates when someone has to create a mental image of a complex scene and essentially 'looks' into that scene. It is an area crucial to visuospatial memory.

When a stroke patient has damage to this area, we notice that although they recognize individual items against a background—like a simplified item on a piece of paper or a slide—they cannot 'read' a scene with multiple items and activities. Imagine a living room with a table, chairs, another table with a vase, some people standing by a shelf of books talking, and children playing with toys on the floor. Presenting this scene on paper or a slide to a stroke patient with damage to their parahippocampal gyrus would result in their inability to comprehend what they are seeing, even though they can recognize individual items when isolated. This region is also well-connected to the amygdala and is often used in negative emotional responses, but not positive ones. I know most of you aren't very familiar with brain scans. I want to show you some. Are you following me so far?"

They all nodded. Binh looked as though she wanted to speak. Alec sat up straighter and looked at her, drawing attention her way. When Binh saw this, she said, almost to him, "I'm not familiar with all the regions of the brain and what they do. I apologize. Where in the brain exactly is this area located?"

Kimaru didn't look startled at all. He instead went to his laptop, searched for an image file, quickly found one, and displayed it on the screen. He dimmed the lights a bit more. "Brain mapping is a field unto itself," he began, "but this picture offers a simplified overview. The colors are to differentiate the areas and don't really exist, of course." The group focused on an image of the human brain, composed of various rounded jigsaw pieces fitting together. Each piece had a name pointing to it, and the name was written in both English and what appeared to be Swahili. The brain was shown from above, from the side, and sliced perfectly in half without disturbing the interior. Theo, Migel, and Jiho had seen such images many times before. Others studied them intently.

"Many of these areas are critical to language production and usage," said Kimaru, pointing to the screen. "You see the region called 'Broca's area'? It's paramount to language production and use. Here is 'Wernicke's area,' which is more involved in comprehension. Nearby is the 'angular gyrus,' which is used when we receive visual or auditory stimulation related to language. In the front here, we have the supplementary motor area (SMA), actually two areas together. The SMA seems to be important for performing sequential movements as well as memory. The hippocampus here is particularly important in forming memories. This is just the briefest overview. The human brain is incredibly complex, and there are a number of factors that I'm skipping over, along with other functions of each region. For example, the brain works one way when a process is new to it, but as the process is repeated and 'learned,' if you will, then how the brain looks when performing these tasks changes. More energy is exerted when performing a novel task than a familiar one. Much has been discovered in your country, particularly in Boston. You have some very famous psychologists, linguists, and neuroscientists."

Kimaru looked at the faces before him. They remained intent.

"Worldwide, there are many people interested in aphasia, the loss of language. Consequently, there has been a lot of research since the 1800s concerning where language resides in the brain. In the last few decades, this research has often focused on diseases and problems that occur as the result of drug use, injury, or age that cause people to lose some or all of their ability to comprehend and produce language.

Human language is highly complex. There are words with meaning, a social context, tenses, and stem words with multiple possible endings. In some languages, such as the Cushitic language 'Dahalo' in Kenya, there are clicks made with the tongue that are actually consonants. These clicks are formed by obstructing airflow from the front of the mouth to the back, which is very different from similar sounds made by English speakers. These clicks operate in the brain as language, not just as sounds."

Theo was particularly attentive, nodding. He had covered this in his linguistics courses in college.

"The human brain is very complex—I can't emphasize that enough. We must be careful about what we conclude. However, some information is so interesting that it is hard to ignore. Let me tell you more about my aunt's friend and what meetings with her have led to. You've probably heard about studies, or seen discussions in the media, about what's been called the 'God spot' in the brain."

Kimaru noticed that only some faces seemed to recognize the term, so he explained further.

"This 'spot' was identified by imaging the brains of hundreds of religious people while they had an interaction with a higher being, such as praying or meditating. Essentially, it was concluded that the brains of religious people all over the world, from many different religions, respond in a similar way in terms of what their brain does during these experiences. I don't want to get into the debate about what this means. It's enough to simply observe the regions of the brain that light up on an fMRI for these nuns, monks, and priests during these studies. Commonly used regions of the brain during religious experiences include the frontal lobe (heavily activated when paying close attention or making a judgment), the ventromedial prefrontal cortical loci (where risk and fear are processed), and the nucleus accumbens (our motivation-action center)."

Adem leaned back in his seat. He imagined that Kimaru was going to say that he had first-hand information that this was true. He had just concluded that thought when Kimaru continued.

"So, I noticed that when my aunt's friend talks with her ancestors while in the MRI tube, something different happens."

Adem sat up straight again, and everyone leaned in, focusing on Kimaru.

"For her, it was the right parahippocampal gyrus that illuminated. Initially, I thought that this was because this region processes emotional stimuli. Then, I read more about the studies involving nuns and monks and realized that my aunt's friend wasn't having a religious experience in the sense that others were when their brain activity was documented. I ran a database search of medical journals, using keywords related to the parahippocampal gyrus, and systematically read through all of the results. I discovered a few interesting findings. For example, exercise is considered to have a noticeable effect on parahippocampal function, but I didn't find any other related studies until I came across a few recent ones on telepathy."

Kimaru paused and looked at each member of the group individually.

"It seems that during the COVID-19 pandemic, while the world was focused on infectious diseases, various researchers quietly began running studies that concerned the brain activity of people known as 'mentalists' —you know, people who believe they can communicate directly from their brain to someone else's. Have you read any of these studies?"

Kimaru noted the surprise on a few faces, but no one spoke.

"Well, I'll tell you the findings. The right parahippocampal gyrus of mentalists shows strong activity on an fMRI when they communicate through telepathy, while control subjects show activity in the left frontal gyrus. One reason that I was happy to speak with you all was to get your multifaceted views on what you think of this occurrence. I've duplicated my earlier findings with a number of people now, and I don't think that Kenyans are having a religious experience when they talk to their ancestors; I think they are engaging in some form of telepathy, even if it's one-way communication."

Binh spoke first. "I've studied memory from a psychological perspective," she said slowly. "There's a lot of recent research that's pivotal."

Binh recalled that some team members had different academic backgrounds, so she elaborated on what Kimaru clearly already knew, but Emma and Adem might not.

"Short-term memories are ones that last just a few minutes, while long-term memories are not just longer but more complex. Long-term memories require physical changes in the brain that short-term memories do not. New proteins must be created by the brain in order to expand the brain's 'hardware' so that these memories can be stored. It was once thought that when a memory was made, it essentially became a permanent recording, which would be nice, but it turns out that's not true. Retrieving a memory is not like retrieving a document but more like picking up a canvas with a wet oil painting on it that is still wet and a palette full of colors and brushes. Anything can be added. Anything can be painted over. In fact, when moving around a wet painting, it is difficult not to alter it, even if accidentally, and the same is true of memory retrieval. Experiments on various living creatures, ranging from honeybees to rats to humans show that memories are not permanent at all but are reconstructed each time they are retrieved. This information alone is shocking, although very useful for psychologists. We also know

now that both electric shock and certain drugs can weaken memories by interfering with how they are reconstructed after retrieval. These premises have been used in trauma therapy for years. Is it possible," Binh hesitated, trying not to sound disrespectful, "that your aunt's friend and the others were retrieving memories when they communicated with their ancestors? Could these communications be rehearsed interactions, rewritten to fit the current situation? I don't mean to sound disrespectful at all, but just to…"

"No, no. It's wise to consider all possibilities. I thought of that initially as well, but I've quietly replicated my findings. Memories are not stored in just one part of the brain, and many areas are activated in the brain during memory retrieval. This is not that. I think these people are truly communicating. I was raised to believe this, of course, but somewhere along the way, as I grew older, I came to view religion in general—and talking to God or ancestors specifically—as a faith-based cultural practice. It became a community tradition, part of our collective heritage that was important but not entirely real. I started seeing it as more cultural and artistic than scientific. But now I am starting to reconsider that."

"How many people do you have data from?" Jiho asked, pointing to the screen. "Data that looks like this?"

"I have brain scans from 17 people taken while they were talking to ancestors. All of their scans look like this: they show activity in the same regions. Whatever is going on, it is happening in multiple brains in the same way. I think this is evidence of a kind of communication, even if it's only one-way."

"Are you familiar with recent studies on telepathy, where people from one country send images or words to others in a different country, and those people recreate them?" Jiho asked.

"I am," Kimaru replied.

"What kind of studies?" Emma asked.

"Studies that involve prestigious American institutions, medical schools, and articles in the National Library of Medicine," Jiho said. "Studies that explore telepathy and, to some extent, provide proof of concept, though they're rarely discussed."

"You're kidding!" Emma said.

"It's true," Kimaru confirmed. "That's why I wanted to tell some Americans about my findings. My university doesn't have the extra funds to expand these studies or do more, but someone should. Dr. Beatley, although I don't know him well, seems to have a lot of connections. He got you all here, and I'm hoping that funding in some way will be the next step. There are some interesting things to look into here, things that warrant a formal study. I need time and resources to do more, and I have neither."

The group looked at each other. It had not occurred to most of them. They hadn't realized Kimaru had been hoping to gain something from them as well. They were speechless, knowing they probably couldn't help. Adem, however, had been contemplating many aspects of the project from the beginning, so he wasn't as surprised by the question. He was the first to respond.

"You're right that your project should be pursued. It's also true that there are a lot of American universities that conduct all kinds of research and have deep pockets for funding, from both government and private sources. There's a special class of universities, called R1 Institutions, that spend over five million dollars on research and extend research scholarships in doctoral programs. Over the years, these institutions have played a major role in enormous projects, from the first nuclear weapons to artificial intelligence."

"Are any of you affiliated with any of these universities?" Kimaru asked.

"No, not with any R1 universities," Adem said, "but we can probably connect you with someone who is. We all come from research universities and know professors involved in various projects, Jiho and Migel most directly with neuroscience. Smaller, less famous universities also do important work, and it's often easier to get started there. There are many levels of research, many ways to acquire funding, and many private sources for funding. In short, you don't need to be affiliated with Harvard to do impactful work and secure funding. We'll help you make some connections."

Kimaru felt satisfied. He wanted to pursue his ideas, but he hadn't been able to convince anyone at his university to direct the already limited research funds toward this. He had tried talking to humanitarian groups in Kenya, but there were too many basic medical needs to be met. He had decided to find a way to affiliate himself with a foreign university.

During the third quarter of the nineteenth century, there were important research universities all over the world, and none of them were in the United States. However, shortly thereafter, and well before World War II, Nobel Prizes were increasingly being awarded to individuals affiliated with American universities. It was an incredible change. Having the ability to do the kind of ground-breaking research that could lead to a Nobel Prize, Kimaru reasoned, was proof enough that freedom, time, and funding were available to intellectuals in the United States in ways that were unavailable in other countries. Although Kimaru hadn't returned to the United States since his one extended trip there many years ago, he knew that it was with Americans—and their openness, enthusiasm, and financial resources—that he wanted to work. He had liked this group from the start, and now he believed they could help him.

Chapter 12: Margo Duc

Margo lay in bed, scrolling through an email from Migel. Though she was dressed in loungewear, lying back was still the most comfortable position for her. In the email, Migel described the group had acted exceptionally grateful to Dr. Kimaru Mwangi for his explanations and for sharing his valuable findings. Migel explained the discoveries and their significance briefly and why, in his experience, they were worth pursuing. He even attached a diagram of the brain regions discussed. Jiho had added a note, further convincing Margo of the project's potential.

She decided to call Samir.

"Hi Samir."

"Hey Margo, what's up?"

"I wanted to update you on how things are progressing in Kenya. Is this a good time?"

"Sure, what's happening?"

"Mwangi confirmed everything he had told Beatley before. He explained his ideas, showed them the scans, and discussed his future goals. He has brain scans from 17 different people while they were engaged in telepathy!"

"That's more than I expected," Samir replied flatly.

"It's definitely more than a random occurrence," Margo continued. "The group has been invited to return with eye-tracking equipment to gather more non-invasive data from any willing party. He's really giving a lot of precious time to us. One additional point of interest is that Kimaru mentioned his desire for affiliation with an American university, and Migel has offered to take the lead in helping him, although all of them are willing to help.Mwangi had started looking for funding and was not able to secure it at home, and so had approached Beatley at the conference in London, hoping that his ideas would get back to someone."

Samir sighed. "We knew this might happen."

"We did."

"So let's connect him with someone in Boston. We need the group to focus on their project. We can get Kimaru connected with maybe the neuroscience department or psych faculty. I'll talk to Beatley."

"Great, I'll pass along that we will work the back channels and help Mwangi out. I'll tell them that Beatley will be the touch point from now on and will connect with him soon. OK?"

"Sounds good. Thanks for the update. Migel can also circle back to him when he returns to the States, but I'd like to keep him involved in this project for now. Did anything surprising turn up?"

"Nothing," said Margo.

"Great. Let me know when they leave Kenya," said Samir.

"I will," said Margo.

After they hung up, Margo felt relieved. Everything seemed to be falling into place.

Chapter 13: Alec Nehoitewa

Everyone had returned to the hotel after leaving Mwangi at the medical school at Kenyatta University, north of the city. The hotel was a respite from the hustle, the noise, the smells, and the constant movement of the city. It was a place to think—a retreat from the newness. Some people had later gone out on foot to explore more, but Alec had settled into a corner table made of unfamiliar wood. The breakfast room of the hotel was empty; he had come to use the strong internet connection and enjoy the quiet. It was late afternoon before he saw anyone else. Jiho and Migel appeared as Alec lifted his arms over his head to stretch.

"Hey, Alec, what are you up to?" Migel called out as they approached.

Alec turned his head sideways. "Hey! I'm reading, connecting with people back home, and trying to better understand what Kimaru is working on. I had a few thoughts. What's up with you guys?"

"We were doing the same upstairs. This is more spacious, though—good idea," said Jiho.

"I sent the summary to Margo, as we agreed," said Migel. "It's just after 9 a.m. on the U.S. East Coast, so she'll probably respond by this evening." The two men pulled out chairs and sat at Alec's table. "What did you learn?"

"Well, the catchiest phrase I read was, 'Neurons that fire together wire together.'"

Jiho smiled. "That's a phrase used frequently in every undergrad neuro class. It just means that the more often a pathway between neurons is used, the stronger the connections become. A known pathway is often more readily used in the future—like paths in the woods that animals or people take repeatedly become clearer and easier to follow, so more animals and humans will likely use them. That's one reason why it's hard for humans to change behavioral patterns. What specifically were you wondering about?"

"Well… just more of what people said at lunch. I wanted more information. Like… if a person could try to do something, convince themselves they were doing it, build repetitive neuron pathways, then… I wondered what that would look like on a brain scan. I don't mean to sound disrespectful at all; I'm just curious. If a person fully believes that they're communicating with deities, the dead, or aliens and they build pathways, would they appear the same on a scan as someone who actually had the experience? You know what I mean. I'm curious about perceived reality versus concrete, experienceable reality. Then I wondered how that could be studied and verified anyway. I've been in and out of rabbit holes."

"Dude…" said Migel.

"I see where you're going with this," Jiho replied. "I wish you were upstairs with us for the last two hours. I should have looked for you—sorry."

"Not a problem at all. I enjoyed the time," said Alec, "but I'm partially coming at this from a biological perspective. I can often reduce anything biological to physics and chemistry, but this is complicated. What do we think 'reality' really is? What does the brain exist for? I've thought about this before. At the most basic level, it must aid in survival, or what's the point, right? But how? Does it help by making sense of the world? You know, as in: can I eat those berries, or will they kill me like they did someone else? A brain's function is to allow the organism a better chance at survival by responding to needs like water, food, and shelter but eventually reasoning about the best course of action. There must be brain hardware with software that can learn and adapt. Then I wondered, if a group spends generation after generation trying to talk to dead ancestors because it is so important to their survival in terms of passing on information and stories and dealing with disasters, then… is it possible that they could adapt their hardware to at least have the perception that they've succeeded? Or do they evolve new software? That brought me back to wondering how different the perception of doing something and the actual doing of something would look in an fMRI session. With full respect for these people and their beliefs, I'm dying to know, from a scientific standpoint, what's the difference between perceived reality and actual reality? I'd like to talk to Binh and Emma again, but I was looking things up when you arrived. I'm also mentally comparing Hopi beliefs of kachinas and…"

"Hang on," Jiho interrupted. "I think if the actual 'doing' of an activity involves some other brain region than simply thinking about it, then it would be obvious on a scan. Thinking about mountain climbing and doing it access very different mental regions. To your point, though, I know there have been fMRI studies on meditating monks and praying nuns, with a control group that just sat still and thought. It was a complex, well-set-up study. The Buddhist monks meditated during their fMRI scans, showing more frontal lobe activation than the baseline state of the control group. When Franciscan nuns prayed, their frontal lobe activity also increased over the baseline group but was less than the monks'. The praying nuns also showed activation in the inferior parietal lobe, a verbal, conceptual area that helps in understanding language. In contrast, when Pentecostals spoke in tongues during fMRI scans, the frontal lobe activation went way down, and I think that no other regions lit up at all. The explanation for this was that the nuns and monks were deeply focused and intentional, while those speaking in tongues said that they just 'let it happen,' meaning they were strictly receiving. I can find the study for you online, but that about sums it up, so just as a guess, if the ancestor-communicators are just concentrating and 'sending', then their scans should look more like the monks meditating. If they're sending words, then the scans should look more like the nuns'. When nothing is being 'sent' but only 'receiving' is happening, either believed or actual, then the scans should mimic the Pentecostals'."

"Wow, huh. That's interesting. I'd like to see those scans. What exactly are Pentecostals? I've heard the term, but I don't know much about them," Alec asked.

No one answered for a minute. Then Migel said, "I googled it an hour ago when Jiho told me about the study. I didn't know either. Pentecostals emerged in the twentieth century. They seem to me like very enthusiastic Protestants. They took their name from Pentecost, for reasons I don't fully understand, and want all Christians to have an experience like baptism, where they get filled with the Holy Spirit. They know this happens because the Holy Spirit gives them the gift of speaking in tongues, healing, prophecy, exorcising demons, or other abilities. They believe they're returning to Christianity's original roots because the Bible says that when men speak in tongues, they're speaking to God, not to other men (by which they mean women, too, of course). So Pentecostals try to acquire the language that allows humans to communicate with God."

"I told Migel, and I'm recommending it to you too: read *Snow Crash*. It's a great book, and the Pentecostals play a central role," said Jiho. "Imagine that group going rogue, being exploited, and led by a nefarious figure—it's an awesome story. You guys need to read more science fiction; it's great stuff. In short, though, Pentecostals are a good example of an fMRI of 'just receiving,' whereas nuns 'send' with words, and monks prohibit both 'sending' and 'receiving' through intense focus. By the way, there are a lot more brain scan studies on meditating monks than you'd expect. Many Westerners are increasingly interested in proving or disproving the idea that meditation has physical benefits."

"What's the short answer?" asked Migel.

"Well, it does. Meditation influences physical well-being because it eventually reorganizes some neural activity related to heart function—at least, that's what I read. It's good for you on many levels, but most Westerners don't take that kind of time off from their busy lives, including me. I like the idea of doing it, though. For a busy Westerner to make time for something outside of their culture, there's usually an expectation of tangible benefits; hence, all the studies," replied Jiho, smiling at Alec. The two had recently discussed how, although both American, they had many relatives who related more with other cultures. As a result, Alec and Jiho often found themselves able to objectively look at and even laugh at or be critical of some silly American or Western. They had already had a discussion on the rushed lives of most Americans and the overt and obsessive interest in tangible and personal gain that was the point of origin for so many perspectives.

"So, where does all this lead us?" Alec asked, but before anyone could respond, Emma, Adem, and Binh walked in.

"We went shopping," beamed Emma. "I love the fabric here. And while we looked, we also discussed Kimaru's observations and came up with a theory. Behold, gentlemen! Now I have yards of beautiful fabric and some great ideas. Look at this," she said, holding up a vibrant blue and red design printed on fabric with bold, black outlines. The printed shapes were palm-sized and vivid. "The cotton was grown, spun, woven, and printed right here in Kenya. How often do we see that back home? This is a traditional print called a *kanga,* sold in pieces one meter by one and a half meters. Check out Binh's fabric, too. So, what have you guys been up to?"

Binh held up her own fabric—equally bright but in varying shades of blue. The swirling, dotted, sunburst patterns almost looked like an Indian block print, repetitive yet intricate.

"Nice fabric, but I'm more interested in your discussions. We've been working on what you guys were talking about. We were trying to work out what all of this meant, too, but without the colorful woven joy to focus us. I have thought of a few questions since lunch for you guys specifically. Did you get a *kanga,* too, Adem?" Alec asked.

"I just bought wood," Adem replied, holding up a small carved piece, although not in a way that revealed what it was. "I was focusing on the big picture here. I'm not sure I'm as intent on understanding Kimaru's findings as you all, but I have a few thoughts worth sharing."

"Perfect," said Emma. "Let's meet for dinner and discuss. How about in an hour? I need a shower; I feel dusty. Where's Theo?"

"He's still reading articles upstairs, I think," said Jiho. "But he'll definitely come for dinner; he never skips a meal."

"Great! Let's grab a drink here and chat, then go find something to eat, maybe with a side of *ugali*," Emma suggested, turning to Binh and Adem, who nodded in agreement.

"I smell like everywhere we went today," said Binh.

"I just smell," added Adem.

"Charming, guys," Migel teased.

They agreed to meet back at 6 p.m. Everyone drifted upstairs except Alec, who only needed to store his computer and get a bit more cash before dinner.

Alec found himself enjoying Kenya. It reminded him of Arizona, though it was less arid. The weather was cool, and it hadn't rained during the entire trip, despite Kenya's two rainy seasons— one in spring and one in fall. July, just a few weeks away, was Kenya's coldest month. But it wasn't only the climate, though. Alec liked the Kenyan people, the adventure, and the travel. The team worked well together, each member bringing unique strengths to the group. Alec focused on biological science, while Jiho, Theo, and Migel were the "brain guys." Emma and Binh knew the most about culture, psychology, and expression, and they were the best at starting and maintaining relationships for the team. Adem was a big-picture, analytic person who didn't chime into the conversations as much as others, but when he did, he asked questions that no one else had thought of. They were all more or less the same age and in the same stage of life. It was a well-constructed assemblage, and he knew that wasn't an accident. He also figured that eventually, someone would completely irritate someone else, and he wondered briefly who it would be but began closing tabs on and saving certain articles on his computer instead.

Growing up in northeastern Arizona, Alec had experienced both isolation and extensive perspective building at the same time. Alec had two mostly functioning parents and three involved grandparents. His *kwa'a* (grandfather) preferred speaking Hopi to English and rewarded Alec with time and advice when he came to talk with him in Hopi. *Kwa'a* had little to say in English. More than anything else, Alec's comparatively stable family and his relationship with his *kwa'a* had ensured him a better childhood and brighter future than many kids on the reservation, where poverty rates are the highest among any ethnic group in the U.S. By age twenty, Alec had witnessed both sides of life: the reservation, where friends and relatives dealt with issues like housing, health, money, alcohol, violence, diabetes, and methamphetamine abuse; and life on the outside where there were more kinds of people and a greater variety of problems, but each person seemed to have fewer.

Alec wanted very much to be a part of reducing the number of problems that the Hopis had, and he was planning on coming at it from a biological stance. He was studying mycoremediation and wanted to bring it back to the reservation to help regenerate reservation land and develop new work opportunities. A few years ago, Alec had read an article confirming that fungi, the spore-producing category of organisms that includes yeasts, molds, toadstools, and mushrooms, are able to break down all kinds of agents that are unfriendly to the environment: chemicals, oils, heavy metals, radiation, pesticides, etc. The process of using fungi to remediate soil contaminants is called Mycoremediation. It's been used successfully to clean up high levels of ground toxins created when wildfires burn all kinds of household substances that were never intended to be burned. Using fungi as bioremediation has been effective in cleaning up pollutants in the Amazon and in Denmark.New Zealand, the Philippines, India, and South Korea have the most advanced knowledge of mycoremediation though, so the chance to visit the Philippines on this trip was especially exciting to Alec.

In the United States, mycoremediation is not yet widespread, though research and experiments are underway, such as at the site of the 2017 wildfires near San Francisco. It's a slow process, and despite its successes, it hasn't really caught on as a standard practice in the U.S. However, Alec hopes to be part of using it to restore native lands. When Alec shared this ambition with his *kwa'a*, his grandfather's health visibly improved in a single day. *Kwa'a* declared that the era of people exploiting and destroying nature— evidenced by contaminated food sources and the seemingly endless forms of cancers plaguing humanity— was coming to an end. He believed that the next era would bring a return to valuing nature, with insights from studying Earth's abundance showing how the planet can heal and offer solutions. Alec felt that people are often resistant to change, slow to admit error, and much more likely to focus on short-term over long-term gain, but he is planning on trying anyway. He wants to improve the lives of the Hopi people first, make all reservations better, and offer an industry besides gambling that can bring in money. Alec took pride in his heritage and frequently thought about the limited opportunities available to his family and friends in northeastern Arizona compared to other places.

Alec's childhood had not been without troubles and setbacks, but in addition to his family support, he had a number of teachers at the Cedar Unified School District who really cared about him. Thanks to their encouragement, Alec not only finished high school but studied directly afterward at Northland Pioneer College. When he proved adept at math and science there, his same emotional and intellectual benefactors helped him to get to Northern Arizona University in Flagstaff, where he earned both an undergraduate and a master's degree in biology. He started working at the Southwest Biological Science Center right after graduation and was considering his future options and ambitions when Margo connected with him. He knew he wanted to travel and that he wanted to not be in debt. He was inherently interested in language and the power wielded by language and knowledge.Margo's expedition was particularly appealing, especially with the planned trip to the Philippines. It seemed serendipitous. Alec Hónhoya Nehoitewa was beyond happy when he was offered the job. He had only been in an airplane once before in his life, and aside from the single trip to the

East Coast that the aircraft had afforded him, Alec had not been of the American Southwest.

Looking out the window now, Alec found himself drawing parallels between what he saw and an Indian reservation. Their lunch discussion had included Kibera, the name for the gigantic slum just a few miles from central Nairobi. It was so big, the largest in Africa in fact, that it consisted of several named villages or neighborhoods, like any other city. Unemployment was a problem in Kibera, but it was a lesser problem when one considers the lack of running water, the diseases that come from poor hygiene which results from water scarcity,malnutrition, the high rates of crime, rapeand assault, and the fact that the children growing up there had poor schooling if any at all. Emma had brought up the topic of Kibera as she had been reading about it. Emma had been an adjunct professor at a college in Ohio for the past year and had a lot of students with unfortunate background stories. She was particularly attuned to how living conditions shape attitudes and perspectives. She noted that in the same way that European explorers had colonized the United States and put the native peoples on reserves, so too had the British government in Kenya. In the first forty years of the twentieth century, the British passed laws that required Africans to live in 'Native Reserves. One such reserve, Emma explained, was initially populated by African soldiers who had served in the British colonial army, eventually growing into the enormous slum of Kibera.

Alec couldn't see Kibera from his window, but he thought of it again now. Humans were so commonly overtaken by the desire to exploit, subjugate, and take advantage of one another. Alec understood that while the Hopi were generally passive and had been taken advantage of, other indigenous groups like the Apache, Comanche, and Lakota had fiercely resisted with advanced warfare tactics. Weakness attracts aggression. When one group identifies a vulnerability in another, it's only a matter of time.

Chapter 14: Samir Namboothiri

In 1957, the former Soviet Union launched the first man-made object into space to orbit Earth. This satellite, named Sputnik, meaning "fellow traveler" in Russian, marked a milestone that catalyzed various scientific, technological, political, and military investments by the U.S. government. One such initiative was the creation of the Defense Advanced Research Projects Agency (DARPA). The purpose of DARPA was—and still is—to foster the development of technologies that enhance national security, so it really supports the development of any product that has a viable application for communication, defense, protection, travel, or surveillance. To achieve this, DARPA collaborates with government, academic, and corporate partners.

In 1969, the first computers communicated with each other—one at UCLA and the other at Stanford—thanks to the work of the Advanced Research Projects Agency (ARPA). The "D" in DARPA was added in 1972. The eventual goal was secure computer-to-computer communication and the ability to share information among research facilities across different locations. This capability drew significant government interest. The concept that had been realized was the creation of a link from one computer to another was called the ARPANET, as in 'a net cast by ARPA'. It used packet-switch technology as a way to send and receive data, complete with error correction codes. When the project was brought to Washington

DC in 1973 and demonstrated to important government officials, some of the developers soon found themselves doing contract work from there on out for DARPA shortly after. DARPA was then and is now interested in all technology that has the potential to give the US an edge.

By 1980, the foundational structure of what would become the internet was in place, largely under the ownership of the U.S. government. Within a few years, email was being sent over phone lines using modems, and by 1990, private companies began to create and sell civilian email accounts, leading to companies like AOL, CompuServe, and Telenet. However, due to the Department of Defense's need for secure communication of this nature when cell phone towers were not available, DARPA continued to fund research in these areas.

Now, many years later, Samir Namboothiri was under contract with DARPA, working on a similar objective: providing secure communication across widely dispersed locations. Samir's specific line of research, however, eschews the use of not only cell phone towers but also satellites, computers, and even electricity.

Chapter 15: Theo Auclair

At the hotel in Nairobi, by half-past six, seven people were seated around two tables they'd pushed together, each with something to drink, and the conversation had turned to the nature of consciousness. Binh was answering Alec's question: "Consciousness is a mental state involving multi-faceted awareness. It includes external stimuli, like someone stepping on my foot," she said, "and internal stimuli, like the taste of this cocktail on my tongue. Both can be realized concurrently with me also being aware of my presence in this room with all of you." Binh studied Alec's face; he didn't look confused—he looked intrigued. She continued, "Humans, of course, are conscious beings, and anyone who has spent time around mammals is aware that they are too. The part of the central nervous system responsible for certain cognitive processes and psychological states isn't unique to humans. A cerebral cortex can be found in mammals and certain reptiles like turtles and lizards. The cerebral cortex is often referred to as the 'seat of consciousness,' but there are multiple theories and likely, consciousness is created from many regions working together. One other thing to note is that some argue that consciousness is subjective, while others say it is objective, and a third group argues that brains have the ability to perceive in an entirely objective fashion and are triggered by motivations, but those perceptions are quickly dressed in subjective layers that take the form of emotions and feelings. Regardless, the real question is: how does the brain create consciousness?"

No one spoke for a moment, though Alec looked like he was chasing a thought.

"I understand the connection between consciousness and eye-tracking," said Emma, "but as far as Kimaru's project goes, I don't see why it matters if the subject is consciously communicating or just believes that communication is occurring."

"Cognition is the process of acquiring and contemplating knowledge. I think cognition rather than consciousness is what we're examining," said Theo.

"Alright, cognition," Emma corrected herself. "Does cognition matter for our purposes?"

"I'm wondering about it," Theo replied, "because if someone is cognizant of the fact that they are communicating from their mind into the mind of another, then isn't that telepathy?" As most people took a minute to absorb that idea, Adem chimed in, asking if one of the transmitters or receivers, in this case, was either a dead person or a deity. He also asked if it could be considered successful if one entity was "unavailable for comment."

"It is a matter of religious stance whether one believes that cognition continues after the physical body dies. That's a tough subject to get into," said Emma as she looked around." It's a very personal belief, and it doesn't impact..."

"No, I understand," Theo cut in.

"I've been thinking about telepathy," Adem said.

"Me too," Emma added. "It's central to what Binh and I discussed. We think Kimaru may be mapping telepathy, at least in a one-way transmission."

"Now we're all on the same page," Adem agreed.

"There's some evidence," Jiho interjected, "and a few serious studies that support the existence of telepathy, but I haven't seen any solid proof that telepathy can be harnessed, controlled and used on demand with humans alone. If someone had discovered this honestly, it would have caused a major stir."

"So, where does that leave us?" asked Theo.

"Ready for dinner," Emma said, "and likely with documented cases of mental telepathy on fMRI scans. Migel, how much information exactly did you send to Margo?"

"Enough for her to come to the same conclusion we did. I just started reading a message from her on my phone—here, listen." Migel held up his phone and read slowly and clearly:

Migel, thank you for your updates. I'm very pleased the team is working well together, and the data charts that have been getting filled in by Alec and Theo are quite helpful. Jiho's summary of the scan information was read and appreciated by a neurologist on our end, and confirmed what we suspected. Could he get more details? Adem's spreadsheet and formulas for the eye-tracking data are working out well, and we are deeply grateful for Emma's and Binh's work in relationship management and logistics. Please convey my appreciation and gratitude to everyone.

As I write this, William Beatley is reaching out to Mwangi about opportunities with non-profit think tanks and university affiliations in Boston. Beatley is well-connected, so Mwangi will likely be well-funded soon. For now, there's no need for you to stay in Kenya, and I've booked flights for everyone from Nairobi to Athens with a transfer to Paris. We'd like you to investigate something similar in Greece. Tickets should be arriving in each of your emails shortly from KLM. Please let me know if they haven't arrived by tonight.

Thanks again to all for the hard work and diligence. You'll all have new location files in the morning for the island of Crete. The flight leaves the day after tomorrow, just before midnight. Please see Mwangi in the morning and wind things up with him. I'm going to spend the day figuring out your transportation to Crete and your lodging there, so more on that later.

Best,

Margo

"I've never been to Greece!" Emma exclaimed. "This is amazing!"

"What's KLM?" Alec asked.

"It stands for something difficult to pronounce in Dutch, but it translates to Royal Dutch Airlines," Emma explained, glancing around the group. "Now we have a lot to discuss. Let's eat here and plan for tomorrow. I could do with some semi-Western food, anyway."

Chapter 16: Binh Tran

Everyone sat around a rectangular table in the *Baluba* restaurant in their Nairobi hotel. Under the high wooden ceiling were many kinds of seating options, but from day one, the group had migrated to the rectangular tables by the window. These tables had three seats on one side and a bench on the other. The first time they sat there, they squeezed four people onto the bench side, but a waiter appeared immediately and gave them an extra chair at the end. Since then, whenever the group walked in, a table was arranged for them, and they could sit and talk as long as they wanted.

It was always a long, rectangular table in the corner of the room, by the section of window overlooking the hotel pool. The hotel staff had been vivacious and welcoming from the start, but after the team had outstayed the typical tourist sojourn, the staff literally increased their accommodating treatment. This evening, the group had ordered dinner and was discussing their ideas about the meaning of Kimaru's investigations. Each person tried to generate a deductive argument with premises that they understood through the lens of their individual domains of expertise.

"I move my legs in a parallel fashion when I walk, and I move my legs in a parallel fashion when I swim, but swimming isn't walking," Theo explained. "Both activities use similar muscles in similar regions of the body in order to perform a given activity. Soooo..." he looked around the table, "once I thought of that, it seemed much less conclusive that telepathy was occurring in Kimaru's studies. I don't know why the same brain regions are highlighted, but it seems that this alone doesn't equate one activity with another."

"It could be like that," started Jiho slowly. Despite his confidence and ability to be outspoken, he also had patience and was able to explain his ideas gently in a non-overbearing manner. Binh watched him now and decided that he could be the kind of scientist the public embraced as a spokesperson—the type that gets interviewed by the news or for podcasts. She could imagine him on a panel or a TED Talk because, despite his intelligence, he didn't come across as unable or unwilling to explain complicated material in a way that non-scientific people could engage with, and he was hard to fluster.

"I'm not an expert on this," Jiho began again, "and I am forming the analogy as I speak, but I'm thinking… if you move the lower limbs of an upright body back and forth to propel a free-standing, upright body, it's walking. If different body parts are used, or the body isn't upright, or it's not being propelled forward, then it's not walking—it's something else. The brain isn't like the heart, where the organ is all mapped out. The brain is an organ, but many functions that occur in it, such as thought and the creation of consciousness, are not processes that we know how to represent visually. There is an international organization for human brain mapping—people all over the world are working on this—but a lot is still unclear. People like Kimaru are great contributors to our understanding. He looks at so many brain scans a year, and with so much information about the person behind each one, he can hypothesize so much. I think he is really onto something."

Jiho paused. Everyone was listening. He started again, "I think that the questions are: what level of reality are we talking about? Does it matter? and how can we know?"

"Those are the kinds of questions I was considering when I was exploring textiles," said Emma. Everyone turned towards her. "All humans eventually die; we share that, but there is tremendous cultural variation in the conception of death. Christians mostly believe that when the body dies, the spirit of the person leaves the body and is either rewarded by going to heaven for a delightful afterlife or punished and sent to hell for more pain and suffering. They believe that this happens only once. In contrast, Hindus view life as a circle. After the physical death of the body, that body's spirit is reborn for another life in a new body. The form of the new body depends on one's behavior; poor conduct in life leads to being reborn as an animal or some other lower form of existence, for example. Buddhism also believes in reincarnation. As for those of the Jewish faith," Emma's eyes scanned over heads until they rested on Adem, "correct me if I over-generalize, but as I understand it, the existence of an afterlife is possible but vague, right?"

Adem smiled, "That is my understanding as well. Nothing is guaranteed for the Jews. But honestly, it's not that important.

Judaism is centered on a person's purpose and actions on earth. The most important Jewish text, the Torah, doesn't mention life after death at all as far as I know—but there are a lot of differing Jewish views, just as a lot of people who consider themselves to be Christian have differing views."

"You could be a diplomat. Or a politician," said Theo.

Adem rolled his eyes, "I can't think of much worse; I'm an honest man." He looked at Theo and patted his chest.

"So, my point is," said Emma, reclaiming the stage, "that there are many variations concerning what humans believe happens after bodily death, right? And, as to whether or not cultures other than the Kikuyus believe that the dead can be conversed with, there are many, including those outside of Africa. The ancient Egyptians and many Native American cultures all believe in these opportunities to learn from the dead. I can't help but notice that the cultures that, for the most part, do not believe that it is possible to communicate with the dead are not only the most powerful cultures on Earth today but the most destructive. The cultures that believe that their ancestors see and hear them seem a bit more thoughtful about their actions. The Kikuyus believe that all living things have a life force that connects them to God and that communication…"

"I think we are overemphasizing the importance of who gets spoken to," said Adem. Everyone turned to look at him. "Sorry, Emma, it's awesome that you know all of that, but as far as understanding what is going on here, I think it's the communication that is important here, not who or what is at the other end of that communication. I can talk to a dog and still be speaking. Whether the dog understands me or not is a separate subject of study, and it is really about the dog. I don't think it matters for the time being what Kimaru's patients are receiving—only that they believe they are sending and, for all practical purposes, appear to be doing just that. Is there a related ontological question? I don't know."

"What is an ontological question?" asked Alec.

"An ontological question is one about existence, something like, 'What happens when we die?' or 'Does a god or gods exist?' or 'What is reality?' It's a question that explores, in general, what exists. It's part of metaphysics and not really the kind of question one associates with biology," said Theo. "Everyone has a theoretical framework—a manner of explaining to themselves what they see and what they experience. It's how people understand what they see and do and how they connect new knowledge to their existing knowledge. Frameworks stem from paradigms—ways of seeing the world—and how one sees the world is at the very root of even being able to discuss human behavior and think about what constitutes knowledge. It matters whether one thinks of knowledge as something that can be attained or something that is fluid. It matters whether one believes that knowledge can exist unconnected to culture or if it is produced by cultural assumptions alone. It matters whether one understands the concept of truth as absolute or as something that people construct. All of these beliefs matter when looking at a problem because they influence how the person sees the problem and how they imagine that problem can be addressed."

"Can you give an example of how a concrete answer changes?" asked Alec.

Theo nodded and spoke, "If a person believes in a singular existence of something called 'reality,' then one will come to understand the world by studying it because there is an 'it' that exists."

"That sounds very logical," said Alec.

"Yes, because you are a scientist," said Binh. Others looked at her. This was really her field, but philosophical Theo had done a good job. She continued, "Other people believe that reality is a social construct—something created by humans because it is inextricably linked to the social constructions and cultural practices of the people who live in it. If a policy is created that was intended to help people, but it doesn't. If it is interpreted as aggressive and biased by everyone who encounters it, then what is the policy really, and who gets to decide? Is reality the intention or the perception? And when the intention cannot be known, how would anyone know what is 'supposed to be perceived'? People can be very wrong, even when they believe they are right." Binh paused, more for absorption than drama. "Can anything even exist without a perception of it? Basically, reality for me is the sum of what I perceive, and reality for you is the sum of what you perceive. And since those two realities are never exactly the same, can we ever say that anything called reality exists? Because if we did, wouldn't we just be preferencing a certain perception?" Alec's eyebrows furrowed, but Binh continued.

"Humans can only function and respond to what they believe is reality, and yet everyone creates their own reality. Accordingly, we can say that what people believe is true is all that really matters. You know, when we all arrived in Kenya, none of us had been there before, and we each perceived the reality that we were capable of abstracting. We each zeroed in on what interested or surprised us, and our brains recorded accordingly. None of us really have the same perception of Kenya, even though we experienced it only once and together. There's an old term—a reality tunnel—from an American psychologist many decades ago. It's a proposed hypothesis for why we each experience the world a little differently, offering a metaphor of people each walking through life in their own tunnels. The tunnel walls are created by what people experience and what they believe their experiences mean."

"That makes sense," said Alec slowly. "I didn't see where you were headed at first. I thought you meant the multiple parallel universe thing."

"Well, that's an idea too. The idea is that splits occur when there are numerous ways an event could have turned out. Most people grossly oversimplify, though, because really, everything could have many, many implications, so it's massively exponential. Funny to imagine, but it's just plain silly as a possibility to most people," said Binh.

"How did we even get onto this topic?" asked Emma.

"I asked what level of reality we were talking about," said Jiho. "Sorry, guys. I was thinking about telepathy and wondering if we should consider moving forward on the premise that some people can send mental messages, and Kimaru has captured this on fMRI. Scanning the PubMed database quickly, it appears to me that his work and findings match those of articles published in the past few years by others. That's all."

"I agree," said Theo. Before he could say more, three men slid in dishes from the right-hand side of each person. In minutes, everyone had a warm plate of food in front of them and a full water glass.

"I love this place," began Adem as he looked around, "but listen, we should consider the reality that this business with Kimaru, rather than the eye-tracking data, is the real nature of our project. What do you guys think?" he asked, picking up his fork and trying his fish.

Emma looked at Binh, then put her fork down. She said, "We've sent a lot of eye-tracking data. It's enough to support that there is cultural variation in face-to-face contact, but only an insignificant amount when there is face-to-text contact. This is neither surprising nor rationalizes our journey. Binh and I talked about this, and we agree. We also hope the Department of Education is not hoping to develop a curriculum that is taught through mental telepathy. So, what are we doing here?" She raised her eyebrows and took another bite of her rice.

"I think you're right," said Migel, moving his ugali around with his fork. "I email Margo daily, you know, and convey a summary of our discoveries. I'm careful to sound objective and to omit unproven fodder from our conversations. I try to make each report sound like a lab report with an abstract, methods, materials, results, and conclusions. I keep my communications very academic and about what is known. In the end, I always tell her that we get along well and are not having problems. If we have any issues, like with the original reservation for an extra hotel room, I state that as well. It doesn't feel like I'm sending this information to a professor who is asking me to tighten the writing, hone my ideas, and consider the implications. The information I send just gets... I don't know... absorbed. There isn't feedback or even pushback on anything that I say. I haven't worked much outside of academics; maybe this is just what it's like, but it feels like I produce and send to something that gets consumed only."

"There's not much pushback on the finances either," added Adem.

"This is just what it's like not to be an equal," Jiho offered. "My parents raised me like that. They didn't run decisions by me or ask me about what I wanted or felt. They saw themselves as older and wiser and better positioned to make decisions than I was. Things were ok until they weren't, and when they said 'no,' it was a definite no, not a negotiating stance. I think that the people above us surely talk, analyze, and create plans for action. It's just that we're peons, and we aren't privy to anything that happens after the information gets discussed. We are observers and senders only. Doesn't mean we can't make suppositions, though."

"Agreed. It's a need-to-know basis with this operation. We get the facts that we're thought to need when someone believes we need them," added Alec.

"Works well enough for me," said Emma. "It beats teaching summer school."

"Or waitressing," said Binh.

The team continued to talk through dinner and long after. The hotel staff was always attentive and thoughtful, and the team was always given privacy and space, as if the restaurant workers knew that this was a business trip and not a tourist vacation. Binh felt inordinately comfortable. This might be a job, she thought, but it was a very pleasant one with good conversation, interesting activities, and a chance to travel. Her teammates were good people—hardworking, willing, and smart. Then she wondered what kinds of jobs in psychology came with benefits and similar perks.

Chapter 17: Adem Haimowitz

When the airplane tickets arrived digitally on Wednesday, the team saw that their flight did, in fact, leave Nairobi a minute before midnight on Friday, but the transfer would be at Amsterdam's Schiphol Airport rather than in Paris. Following a short layover in Schiphol, they would continue on to Athens, arriving just after noon on Saturday, and a few hours later, they had a connecting flight to Heraklion, Crete.

At the moment, though, the plane was still over five hours from the Netherlands. It was quiet and easy to think. The majority of the passengers were asleep. Adem was not. He had tucked himself behind his open gray hoodie against the hard, gray airplane wall. Lighting his face was the dim light of his laptop. Every 34th seat or so, someone was crouched in a similar position with a similar device, but the rest of the plane was trying to sleep in the ambient blue glow of the night lights. The overhead lights were off, and only the small, blue LED aisle marking lights, ceiling lights, and exit lights were on. It was enough to see. It was just after 2 a.m., but scenarios and implications of the past few days were igniting thought. He was considering as many perspectives as he could and trying to envision their logical conclusions.

Kimaru had proven to be a very savvy card player. Like a movie camera zooming out on a focused image, Adem imagined a possible, greater picture. When Kimaru attended the Fall Conference in

London to learn about current research and potential uses of direct imaging of neuronal activity (DIANA), he brought his ideas. He knew that they would be interesting and could be funded—just not in Kenya. Kimaru was comfortable with Americans and understood the culture and possibilities well enough. He sought out a Harvard man to entice but withheld enough information so that when the inevitable stream of communication arrived at the right people, Kimaru would be contacted. It had not taken long, and within months, it was arranged that some academics would come in the spring—Adem and his group.

Kimaru had probably anticipated an older, more experienced group, but after spending some time with Adem and his team, they all liked and trusted each other. Kimaru was very generous with his knowledge, time, and facility and created access for the team to work. He shared his research simultaneously with his pitch. Kimaru needed money to track his side interests. As Adem understood it, Margo's friends knew the Harvard man who had attended the conference in London, and he was someone capable of infiltrating various academic departments in the Boston area and securing both funding and clout for Kimaru, all while he continued to reside and research in Kenya. It was impressive and speedy.

Adem recognized their Kenyan trip for what it was: a verification. He and the others had been sent to Kimaru to learn about his work, verify the hypothesis was valid and plausible, and report back to Margo. But why didn't the Harvard man do that himself from London, and why didn't any school send their own people? These were questions that Adem mulled over now.

Adem opened a document where he had written down a few names and places. He was wondering about who would benefit and how. Later today, they would be in Greece, and he wondered what Margo knew. He wondered what Margo suspected. He wondered why he felt suspicious. Adem imagined a dolly zoom.

As a man who liked to watch movies and found himself needing a fine arts credit in college, Adem had registered for and enjoyed a class called "The Art of Film." The course description merely said that the class would explore film through the lenses of artistic and technical merit. Honestly, he imagined watching several films, discussing them, and whipping off a few papers. He did do that, but the discussions were much more intense than he had anticipated, and papers more complex. They were also infused with a set of jargon, much of which he had not known before.

Consequently, Adem thought now of the dolly zoom. He imagined a camera on a track that was dollying toward Kimaru while zooming in on Margo in the opposite direction. He felt uneasy and as if the space between Nairobi and Boston had shrunk down to a couple of yards. He tried to remember who Margo said she worked for exactly at her coding job. Had she even said?

Chapter 18: Emma Miller

The Airbus touched down at Eleftherios Venizelos International Airport and rolled down the tarmac. Emma texted her parents to say that she had landed and to look up who Venizelos had been. She got her answer as the passengers around her got up to open the overhead compartments. Venizelos is considered "the maker of modern Greece." He was a man from the 1800s who, having been born on the island of Crete when it was under Ottoman rule, returned home after finishing law school in Athens to engage in the leadership of fighters for the autonomy of the island of Crete. It was a success.

Crete had been ruled by Rome, the Byzantine Empire, the al-Andalus Arabs, then the Venetians, and finally, the Ottoman Empire before Venizelos helped to earn her independence in 1898. In the next century, Venizelos was an integral part of joining Crete to the country of Greece in 1913, and when he became Prime Minister of the country, he initiated reforms that would help modernize Greece, including a reorganization of the Greek army and navy. Emma learned that Venizelos was keen to unite all of the territories where the inhabitants spoke Greek. It was the language, he felt, that bonded these people of various origins as one.

When airports were named after important local people, she liked to know who they were. It had started on her trip to New Orleans in high school. She'd heard the name Louis Armstrong but could not quite place it beyond the realm of music. When she arrived at the airport bearing his name, she asked who he was and was told to "look it up." She had been doing so since. It was her tarmac activity now.

Before sliding her phone back into her bag, the slow forward shuffle began. Emma quickly stepped into the aisle behind Binh and started pulling down items from the overhead compartment. Jiho helped. Many hours and another flight later, the group would land on the island of Crete, where the people speak Greek.

Chapter 19: Binh Tran

Crete was stunning, even though tired eyes. Smooth yellow-ochre-colored bricks had been organized to form walls, buildings, fortresses, and streets. Twisting paths, which turned out to be roads, wound up from the ports, the city, and the airport into the mountainsides of crumbly-looking yellow-tan soil with stuffy goatees of green. The higher the cab climbed, the broader the view, so she sat twisting back and forth, searching for more glimpses of the beautiful Aegean Sea. Binh was next to her but twisted around less. They always seemed to travel together when two cars were taken: Migel and Theo, Alec, Jiho, and Adem were in the cab in front of them. Both cars had passed the towns of Kallithea and Knossos and now had twice the distance to cover to the town of Archanes, which was barely a twenty-minute car ride from the airport, named after a Greek author who had been nominated for the Nobel Prize in literature nine times. It was a stunning, albeit swaying expedition; driving here was clearly best done by those native-born.

Like many good relationships, the American group had taken on little patterns of assumed duties. Adem was quick with numbers and handled all hotel bills, dining expenses, and cab fares. He made it his responsibility to carry plastic, which was widely preferred in recent years, as well as the local currency, in this case, euros. Jiho frequently worked out logistics—routes, options, ideas, and more recently, neuroscience research. Theo was a linguistic philosopher, and Alec was the researcher and go-to science guy, equally knowledgeable about biology, evolution, and chemistry. To date, it had been Migel who was the main communicator with the U.S., while Margo and Emma handled all local communication, including hotel check-ins, chitchat, and the pivotal role of building relationships. Binh often accompanied Emma, even if Emma was speaking, because her unassuming nature allowed her to easily ask for and be granted small favors when needed.

When the two cabs stopped, one behind the other, Emma and Binh got out and went to the main entrance of the hotel while the others handled the luggage and settled up with the cab drivers. Emma turned and waved to her driver, "efcharistó!" she said and waved. "*Parakalo,*" said the driver as he dipped his head slightly in her direction.

"You are so good with languages," said Binh as they pulled on the outside door.

"I'm not really," said Emma. "I just want to talk to people badly enough that I look up small words like 'thank you' and 'please' and then work to remember them. Did you see the smile on that guy's face? He didn't care that he just heard a quarter of all the Greek that I know. He was just happy that I said thank you."

"Well, your Swahili…" Binh started.

"The four words of Swahili I know," Emma corrected her.

"*Kaló apógevma* — good evening," said a woman walking towards them. "How can we help you?"

"*Kaló apógevma*," said Emma, smiling. "We would like to check in, please. A group of seven? Under the name 'Duc,' please."

There was a moment of paper shuffling and finger-tapping, making it unclear if the reservation system was digital or on paper.

"Very good," said the woman finally, looking up at the growing collection of people behind Emma. "Yes, we have you in four rooms for a week, paid, but the note says that maybe you will need to extend your stay. Is that correct?"

"We are not sure yet," said Binh. "Can we possibly let you know in a few days?"

"You can. We are normally quite busy in the summer, but a group canceled at the last minute, so we have some availability. We will fill in, though, so let me know as soon as you are able," said the woman. She then went about getting keys and handing them cards with WIFI passcodes, breakfast times, and verbal directions to their rooms, welcoming them again. The team gathered their baggage and began walking out a side door to the curved pathway that crossed the garden.

The hotel was either a very large house broken up into many separate spaces, perhaps for parts of a large, extended family, or an intentionally constructed bed-and-breakfast made to look like a local, traditional estate. Either way, it was charming. Tucked behind the main building was a small complex of buildings connected by outdoor spaces. There was a grape arbor with cafe tables under it, a small flower garden, and a little outdoor pool area with a waterfall. Despite parts of walls and hedges between the buildings, glimpses of the rolling hills, the city of Heraklion far below, and the brilliant sea beyond were visible. Benches were set near flowering bushes and a small stone fountain overlooking the expansive vista.

The four reserved rooms were more like small, individual cabins with doorways to the outside rather than an inner corridor. The buildings were together but faced different directions, creating a small courtyard. Binh and Emma went to the one with the longest front porch covered with an arbor of thick wooden beams, and Emma announced, "We'll take this one. And that one opposite us," she said, pointing, "is the one with only one bed." The men shuffled keys, and Jiho headed towards it. Alec and Migel went to the porch next to the women, and Theo and Adem went into the most angular-looking room.

Sixty minutes later, the group was seated at a rectangular table formed by pushing three small square ones together. They were under a cream-colored canvas cafe umbrella on a stone terrace, looking at drink menus.

"We should get ouzo," said Theo. "It's the classic Greek aperitif. It awakens the taste buds and prepares them for the meal to come."

"See, that's what I mean, Theo," said Adem. "Americans don't say things like that! What does it taste like?"

Theo smiled. "Like Pastis in France, a black licorice kind of drink—it's refreshing."

"You're such a gourmand, but I'll try it," said Adem.

"Ugh," said Binh. "I'd rather have wine."

"Me too; let's try Vilana," said Emma "I read about it. It's a white wine grown on the sides of the mountains here in Crete." A waiter came, took their orders, and left. The group discussed the beauty of the village, the fact that sitting in planes all day was bizarrely exhausting, and their pleasure at having been sent to such a gorgeous spot with so much history and delicious food. Then, they turned their attention to the mission.

"The Palace of Knossos and the Heraklion Archaeological Museum are open on Sundays. I checked. We should read up on those first and then try to arrange to meet Dr. Papadakis afterward, Monday if possible."

"I still don't understand how we are going to approach him without sounding like complete weirdos," said Alec.

"I mentioned that to Margo," said Migel. "She said we should mention that our boss is friendly with Dr. Martin Kolsch in the Boston University Archaeology Department. He and Papadakis have apparently met many times over the past few decades. Margo thinks that Papadakis will email Kolsch, verify things, and then be welcoming. Ideally, Margo or someone she knows is talking to Kolsch already."

"Ok, that will definitely make things less weird unless Papadakis wants to know how we like our boss, and we find ourselves not being able to come up with his name."

"We'll use Margo Duc's name if need be, and if he looks blank or suspicious, we'll explain that she is like our direct report within a team of many, presumably including whoever knows Kolsch."

"Is that true?" asked Binh.

"I have no idea. It could be. This must be a bigger operation than it appears, and Margo can't just be a simple engineer," said Adem.

Plates of food were placed in front of the group while Adem was talking. Many had ordered a lamb dish served with broiled tomatoes and *stamnagathi*, a nutrient-packed green that grows wild on the mountainsides and has been used for centuries both as a medicine and salad. Others had *hirina apakia*, a Cretan pork dish that takes days to prepare and involves roasting the meat above a fire fed with herbs so that the meat smells of sage and rosemary. There was a sauce on it, and it smelled of fresh lemon. Binh had ordered a huge plate of fava beans and roasted artichoke halves that came on an oval ceramic plate drizzled in local olive oil, oregano, and bits of colorful vegetables.

Adem resumed speaking when the food was all placed, and the waiter had left. "I get the feeling that someone… Someone that Margo knows wants to explore certain ideas and somehow convinced the Department of Education to fund a research project— or front it anyway. Maybe we are funded privately. We were sent to explore leads. We are an unassuming group, like a group of friendly backpackers. We are all young and approachable. We are not famous, we don't seem like business investors with slick motives and conniving ways, and the fact that we are all just out of school or still in academics lends a certain air of genuine curiosity and naïveté. The fact is, though, that we don't really know what the information we are sending back is being used for or by whom. I'm not concerned, but it's interesting."

"I don't disagree with you, Adem," said Emma, "but I don't think we are going to get any clear answers on this anytime soon. We should be discussing our plans for finding Papadakis and getting him to talk with us. This is an incredible opportunity to be in Greece too, to be honest—Crete anyway. We should be clarifying what we want to do and how we plan to do it. There was a lot of information in that location file, a lot of history. I think that much of that can be talking points with Papadakis. He is not just going to openly discuss something that makes him sound looney; he lives on an island— where would he escape to?"

"I'm just thinking out loud. I'm trying to put this all together," Adem said, glancing at Theo. "Let's go over the location file. What do you think are the important parts to be knowledgeable about, Emma? This is mostly your wheelhouse. What does an older man, who has dedicated his life to the history of his people, hope that we know or care about?"

Emma lit up. She loved to learn about how people live, what they believe, and how they view the world. She had quickly discovered the anthropology department in college, and in a straight six-year stretch, she had earned both a BA and MA in Anthropology from Ohio State University. It is one of those fields of study that made people with clearly defined jobs raise an eyebrow. Anyone whose job is self-explanatory from its title (electrician, engineer, fireman, plumber, data analyst, etc.) was likely to have the follow-up question, "And what are you hoping to do with that degree?" as if the only point of higher education was to acquire a career with a single-word title that makes money. Well, it would help with the loans, but that was just a symptom of a screwed-up system. Emma had mastered her response, though. She looked them right in the eyes and said that studying anthropology developed research skills, cultural awareness, and critical thinking skills, which seem to be particularly valuable at many jobs these days. Only people who knew her family well or were particularly annoying would press it further.

Emma had essentially been studying the human condition: how humans evolved, lived, and diversified linguistically, culturally, and biologically. She had been studying how they had survived natural disasters. What kind of people wouldn't want to study anthropology should really be the question.

"Most American kids learn about ancient Greece in school, but rarely do people focus specifically on Crete. Additionally, the most popular focus is on the Mycenaean Period, about 1450 B.C.E. - 1100 B.C.E. Dr. Lefteris Papadakis dedicated his life to the Neolithic peoples of Crete and the Minoans who developed from them around 3000 B.C.E.," Emma began. "Crete has been an island for five million years, so people who arrived there, until planes were invented, came by boat. It was long assumed that the story of Odysseus is a recount of one of the first attempts to traverse the Greek islands by boat, but in 2010, it was confirmed that Neolithic hand tools, hundreds of them, that were found here, dating from at least 130,000 years ago. So, Odysseus is a great 'sailing the islands' story, but not the first. The earliest human remains on Crete date back to 6,000 B.C.E., and they represent two different body types and skull shapes and apparently lived in two different styles of houses."

"Seriously?" asked Migel.

"Yes. Where we're going tomorrow, Knossos, is where elongated skulls were found among human remains. These remains were found in remnants of huts made from interlaced twigs and branches plastered with mud. These homes had stone foundations and, within them, many advanced artifacts. The second group had a skull shape that was much broader, and these people left artifacts that were simpler, but their homes were very sophisticated, with wooden frames, interior rooms with mud-plastered walls, and reed roofs plastered with mud. We're talking about cultures that domesticated animals and farmed. The olives they ate were likely wild, but they farmed lentils, barley, and wheat, as well as pistachios and acorns. A thousand years later, there is evidence that the people were farming pigs, sheep, and goats in addition, as well as using the animal horn as a manufacturing material. The stone and wood creations from this period are also particularly advanced. The caves of Crete have preserved thousands of years of information. By 4000 B.C.E., the Cretans were weaving, and numerous loom pieces have been found. We are going to look at all these artifacts at the Heraklion Archaeological Museum tomorrow. This is where Dr. Papadakis spent much of his career, and because of his publications and the museum's quality he is a pretty well-known man."

"How old is the museum?" asked Theo.

"It started in the 1880s, but the building you see today isn't the pre-World War II structure. It is from the great renovation of this century that ended in 2013. Papadakis guided the museum through this process, and although he officially retired shortly afterward, he holds so much knowledge that he is still regularly consulted by anthropologists, including Dr. Kolsch.

"Dr. Papadakis is in his mid-80s now, still living here with his wife, and remains an active, revered figure. I was thinking we could visit the museums first, then contact him and see if he has time and is willing to meet us this week."

"The location file said he had no plans to leave the island all month," said Emma, "so I was hoping to meet him by way of introduction rather than email him. You know, let him see that we're young, kind, curious, approachable…" she trailed off. "Do you guys want to walk around or get more wine?"

"I'd like to try the wine," said Migel. "Anyone want a glass if I get another bottle of that Vilana?" Some did, and others wanted to walk around the town. Migel signaled the passing waiter. "Let's go with Emma's plan. This is a social country, like Italy and France. Fewer people hide in their homes, enjoying their private acquisitions; people get out in the community more here. Anyone as well-known as Papadakis is known all over town. This place isn't that big—we'll find him, and I agree, meeting him in person and letting him size us all up is better than sending a random email, even if Kolsch did say something about us."

"Agreed," said Alec, and the rest nodded.

"Meet at breakfast at 7:30 a.m.?" asked Jiho. They all agreed, and Jiho, Adem, and Binh excused themselves to walk around the village. Migel, Theo, Emma, and Alec awaited the anticipated bottle of wine and said that they'd pay and leave in thirty or forty minutes.

"I like the hills and views here," said Alec. "I like the openness, the warm colors, the yellows and browns. I don't mind lush vegetation, but I'm not really a brown-dirt kind of guy, I guess."

"That's funny, I never thought of that. Ohio dirt is always brown. But now that you mention it, pictures of Arizona always seem so… red."

"It's very red where I'm from. Red, yellow, and yellow ochre, like this soil and these houses, I guess. It's dry, like around Nairobi, but with a lot of clay and often salt, like Casa Grande soil. Plants don't like salt, and clay is very alkaline, which prevents plants from absorbing many nutrients like iron. Much of it is characterized as 'caliche,' which basically means that it's very hard to dig in without a jackhammer, and plant roots can't penetrate it either. In order to grow crops, the soil has to have a lot of organic matter added to it."

Alec looked like he was going to stop, but Emma found this information intriguing, so she asked more questions.

"Was the red soil we saw near Nairobi the same, a clay soil?" she asked.

"No… that's laterite, I think," answered Alec. "Laterite is both a soil and rock type. It's very rich in iron and aluminum and rusty-red colored, but it's formed by periods of heavy, beating rain alternating with long, intensely hot periods. It's common around the equator, like in Africa, Southern Asia, and most of South America."

"It's cool that you're into dirt, Alec. I can't say that I know much about it," said Theo. "I can see that there are differences, of course. New England's dirt is brown, the south of France is very light yellow, and I've seen pictures of Arizona's red. That's about all I know. I'm trying to picture the dirt in French Guiana. It's hot and dry on the equator, but also has dense jungle that discharges tons of organic matter onto the ground."

"I'd love to see it sometime," said Alec. "Biology is such a vast field. I always wonder why more people aren't drawn to it."

"I think it's because of how the school curriculum is written, K-12," proposed Emma. They turned to look at her. "Before high school, kids are only exposed to ideas, like gravity or propulsion, or the solar system to water pools, like ponds, marshes, rivers, tide pools, or whatever, depending on location. There's little memorization or connection to industry. In high school, biology classes become faster-paced, full of intricacies, somewhat technical, that require organizational skills and memorization. The teachers are often poor, and many have too many students for written testing, so multiple choice or 'select the best-answer' tests prevail. This continues in college, but by then, 80% of students have decided not to continue."

"Huh," said Alec. "I can't say that I thought of it that way, but it sounds right."

"In many anthropology departments, you can earn a BS or BA based on the amount of hard sciences studied in college. A lot of smart people are not prepared to do heavy college science work, but it's not always from lack of interest," said Emma. "Since I've been teaching, I've thought a lot more about the goals of education and the general quality of it since I've been teaching. Many of my college students are just not prepared to do college-level work—period."

"I didn't realize you were teaching," said Migel. "I just thought of you as an anthropologist for a foundation or something. Where do you teach?"

"I adjunct teach at a community college, a feeder school for the huge Ohio State system. I started after my master's thesis, liked it, continued another year, then got this job. The timing worked out well. I like teaching, but I can see I need a doctorate to be competitive in the job market. It's not as if there are millions of jobs a year in anthropology, at least not in the U.S., so I teach college writing too. But maybe I won't stay in the U.S. now… How do you guys think these buildings came to be painted in all these colors? It's very artsy looking."

"It reminds me of old tempera paints that used egg yolk as an emulsifier, like in Italian frescoes during the Renaissance," said Theo.

"That technique was used in Egypt, Babylonia, Mycenaean Greece, and China too," said Emma. "Another example of people discovering similar methods in unconnected parts of the world. "We should walk around too after we finish this wine and check things out. This is a great village."

So, they did just that. They talked, finished the Vilana, and paid the bill. The group had, from the beginning, eaten most meals together and put the bill on one card. Adem kept track of expenses, and there was never any pushback. The hotels included breakfast, so they ate lunch and dinner out, expensing them on the cards Margo had supplied. They ate local food at inexpensive places, which was healthy and good and frankly of much higher quality than what they had sustained themselves on during their college years and in their post-academic apartments—those who had them.

The group started walking out of the plaza and down a narrow street lined with colorful yellow and orange houses, vines climbing up their walls. Flowers seemed to grow everywhere.

Chapter 20: Dr. Lefteris Papadakis

The Heraklion Archaeological Museum appeared very clean and quiet on the morning of Sunday, June 10, as museums typically are, minutes after opening. The group went directly to Room One: Minoan Prepalatial. The location file for Crete included a lot of information on the Minoan civilization. Everyone had read through it, although most were initially wondering why there was so much coverage on a Bronze Age culture. In the file there was a strong recommendation to start the area and stay at this very museum. Emma was the one who made the connection that since this was Dr. Papadakis's area of expertise, being knowledgeable and interested in it was a good way to initiate a conversation with him.

Migel looked around him in wonder. What he saw was from the Stone Age, 7000-3000 BCE. There was a small white marble figurine of a man's body. The head and left leg were missing. There were mini pottery bowls decorated with lines incised in the clay, taller ceramic shapes like vases, and carved and smoothed stone axe heads. "These people were very industrious and creative," he said. "None of this stuff is easy to make with hand tools alone."

"They had food and fresh water within a short distance. That is the defining factor in what a culture can and will do," said Emma. "There are many cultures in Africa living a full day's walk from water and even further from hunting grounds. When most of the week is spent looking for a water source and trying to catch or harvest the next meal, there is a lot less time to make pots and philosophize and less impetus to build permanent housing. Crete has fresh springs that don't dry up in summer and lush greenery that ensures hunting, trapping, and wild crops. It seemed reasonable that the people, with the luxury of staying put, relatively protected, eventually began cultivating crops where they wanted them and in quantities that would sustain them."

"That makes sense," answered Migel, his face up against the glass case of wide-mouthed pottery jars with handles that had been found in a cave. They were 6,000 years old. He thought about that and continued to walk, look, and periodically talk to Theo and the others. It was late morning before the group had toured all the rooms. They finished, left hungry, and walked in the direction of a plaza with a church, a fountain, and many restaurants with more seating outdoors than in. They sat at an outdoor table facing the church. It was just a short walk from the museum, and they were still talking about what they had seen despite holding menus. While in the museum, Emma and Migel had spoken with one of the room guards. They had learned that one of the women at the ticket booth in the museum reception area was a friend of Dr. Papadakis. Finishing the museum tour brought them down a set of stairs right near the ticket booth, and so Emma walked over and introduced herself in her friendly way as a student of anthropology from the United States, hoping to meet the famous Lefteris Papadakis. She then learned that Dr. Papadakis came to Heraklion every Tuesday and Thursday to eat, drink, and meet people in the same plaza cafe that he had been patronizing for many decades. He was known to arrive at about 9 a.m. and often came to the museum afterward. Additionally, Emma learned that on Saturdays, he and his wife arrived in town early to sell their orange marmalade and talk to neighbors at the open-air market in the section of Heraklion directly south of the port, known as Pateles. Emma thanked the woman profusely, gushed about the chance to meet such an important archaeologist, then walked to the plaza, found the cafe that Papadakis frequented, and guided her group to one nearby.

"What should we prioritize until Tuesday?" asked Binh.

"The Palace of Knossos, for certain," offered Jiho. "More research on Dr. Kolsch, too, I think, and time spent on our eye-tracking records. We shouldn't ask him immediately, of course, but depending on how things go with Dr. Papadakis, maybe we can ask if he knows anyone who might be interested in participating in our study."

*****

The opportunity to speak with Dr. Papadakis came on Tuesday morning. He had arrived at 8:55 a.m. and selected a table facing the plaza, away from the other occupied ones. He was seated with a woman who seemed too young to be his wife. Emma spotted them as the group entered the plaza at 9:05, and she walked forward to introduce herself and her friends. Binh was standing next to her, with the five men loosely behind them. Although priding herself on her beliefs in gender equality, Emma also realized that women are often trusted more easily, believed to be less threatening, and, in short, better, in many countries, to be the ones approaching a stranger to represent a group. This was not true in the cultures that expected women to stand back and not have an opinion, of course, but Greece was not like that in most ways.

Dr. Papadakis was neither surprised nor annoyed by the introduction. "Please sit," he said after the briefest of introductions were made. They did, using the neighboring empty tables and chairs, and soon, nine people were seated. The Americans introduced themselves, and shortly after, the woman, who identified herself as Cora, made an excuse to leave. She turned out to be the middle-aged daughter of Dr. Papadakis. She had appraised the group, finished her coffee, and left.

The conversation that followed began as many do among people in complementary fields of academics when one party is hoping to impress and gain information from the other. Papadakis had nothing to prove, and he was in no hurry. The group of twenty-somethings explained the agreed-upon version of what they were doing in Crete. They mentioned Dr. Kolsch and were grateful when details of his whereabouts and work were not required. They explained their recent visits to the Heraklion Archaeological Museum and the Palace of Knossos. Emma commended the doctor's work and mentioned purchasing a book in the gift shop that he had written. Dr. Papadakis was in his early eighties and could remember excavation dates, historical facts, and events. He had good posture, spoke clearly in impressively pronounced English, and his eyes shone like brown jasper. Perhaps his body was aging, but his mind did not seem to be. It was an hour before the conversation slowed enough for Papadakis to ask the group the much-anticipated, "Is there something in particular that I can help you with, show you, or tell you about?" He waited. Legs crossed, coffee finished, hands moving into a folded position in his lap, he waited and then seemed to know from body movements that Migel would speak next. Papadakis looked directly at him.

"Well, sir," Migel began, "although we have all, I think," Migel said, looking around at the others, "been fascinated by what we have learned of the Neolithic cultures on Crete and the Minoans in particular after that, we are also trying to understand how these people might have evolved mentally and from a linguistic point of view." Dr. Papadakis looked at Migel, nodded, and responded that he would really like to have them to his home to meet his wife and see his plantation of orange trees. There are citrus groves all over the island, he explained, particularly on the western side, but there were smaller groves everywhere. "Did you know," he asked, "that according to Greek mythology, when Zeus and Hera got married, Gaia, Goddess of the Earth, provided citrus fruits as a wedding gift?" He smiled and waited.

Binh understood immediately. She smiled back and said, "We enjoy learning about Crete very much; it would be our pleasure to see your groves. We can help, as well, if you have any heavy lifting to do or items to move. We'd be very grateful to learn more about the oranges that grow here and how they are used."

"My wife, Eleni, makes the best marmalade from our trees," he responded. "Can you come tomorrow? At about ten in the morning? I will give you an address to put into those phones," and he did.

After Dr. Papadakis left the cafe, he went to visit Viktoria at the museum. She had called him, of course, two days ago, and she had sent a message to his wife, her childhood friend. Dr. Papadakis had talked with his wife and his daughter, and he had emailed Martin Kolsch. He had planned what he would say to start and what he might say later. Eleni had planned on them for lunch on Wednesday, and she and their daughter Cora had most of it prepared. There were things that Dr. Papadakis had been wanting to understand, and a cognitive scientist, a neuroscientist, a linguist, a biologist, a psychologist, and an anthropologist had just arrived at his doorstep. They were young, kind, easy to talk to, naturally curious, and aware of recent studies in their fields. Everyone would learn something tomorrow.

Chapter 21: Theo Auclair

On Wednesday, the group walked to the home of Lefteris and Eleni Papadakis. North, in the direction of Heraklion, east of the main road, the houses were spread out, each with its own gardens, citrus groves, and long driveways. When they arrived at the one that belonged to the Papadakis family, there was an initial walking tour of the orange grove. While they walked, Dr. Papadakis explained that from January through March, the trees he tended bore the most delicious fresh citrus. He spoke of the cycles of the trees, the watering, and the feeding. The group listened and asked questions.

Dr. Papadakis turned deeper into the grove and started speaking of his museum work until his retirement and his research in Cretan hieroglyphs. He had been decoding them for many years now. The hieroglyphics that were etched into tablets and pottery pieces found on Crete were still undeciphered. Some patterns had been worked out, and educated guesses had been made about which were syllabograms and which were logograms.

At this point, Adem and Theo, who had been closest to their host, with the others in pairs behind them and Emma tailing them in the rear, stopped. "Wow! I didn't know that hieroglyphics existed outside of Egypt," he said. He was being sincere. He had never heard of hieroglyphics that weren't Egyptian. The others came closer. "I did see the markings on the tablet and pottery, but I didn't realize that the symbols weren't ancient Greek. I can't even read modern

Greek." Adem started scanning his memory of the museum; there had not been attention drawn to the many pieces with unknown markings.

"Yes," said Dr. Papadakis, "but our hieroglyphics are much less famous than the Egyptian ones, as they are undeciphered. They look like scratches, markings, and shapes to many. They date from the early Bronze Age in Crete. Most interestingly, they are found on pieces that date 100 years earlier than those using Linear A, but the latter does not appear to have replaced the former. Rather, the two writing systems coexisted from about 1800 BCE to 1450 BCE. Linear A has never been fully translated, either. It is a language like hieroglyphics but different, and it appears not to have evolved from the writing systems of Mesopotamia or Egypt. Cretan Hieroglyphics are true hieroglyphics, but we don't know yet what stories they tell."

"I am astonished," said Adem, and then, "Linear A seems like an odd name for a language."

"It was an effort to be descriptive. When archaeologists found clay tablets with this written language in the last century, the symbols were noticeably different from the hieroglyphics that had been discovered, which seemed more like pictures. The newly found symbols were mostly made up of linear lines," answered their host.

"I see," said Adem.

"I can show you pictures and good photocopies of Cretan hieroglyphics in the house. I have a nice copy of a piece from Phaistos." Dr. Papadakis registered the look lacking recognition and explained. "One of the most important centers in Minoan civilization was the city of Phaistos, located just over an hour south and west of here."

"So, is it generally thought that the Minoans developed two writing systems? Cretan hieroglyphics and then, about a century later, Linear A?" asked Theo.

"That is correct. It is thought that the Minoan people created a Neolithic culture around 3000 BCE and then became much more sophisticated around 2000 BCE, remaining that way, with their two writing systems, until about 1450 BCE. At that point, they merged somehow with mainland Greek people. These mainland Greeks probably sailed to Crete, and many stayed, explaining the cultural influence of mainland Greeks spread across Crete starting around 1450 BCE. Perhaps it was a political conquest as well—we don't know—but it was certainly a cultural expansion for Crete. Around this time, another language appeared in written form that we call 'Linear B,' which has, in my lifetime, been shown to be the earliest form of what we call the Greek language today. It shares a few logograms with Linear A but is a separate written language. It has been translated. Linear A and the hieroglyphics have not."

"That is so interesting," said Adem, and he meant it. It's so strange what people talk about and what they do not.

Jiho and Migel came up from behind and, after reminding the doctor of their names and areas of study, told him an abbreviated version of why they had been in Kenya last week and what they had come across. They pointed out that shortly after they reported their findings to their boss, they were booked on flights to Crete.

They all walked along in silence for a bit. Theo had just thought to speak again when Dr. Papadakis said, mostly to Jiho and Migel, "That is fascinating. I suspect that Dr. Kolsch wanted you to meet with me then, not because of my interest in hieroglyphics but because of my interest in telepathy. I study that as well, in a way, but I lack some knowledge and data, so perhaps we can help each other to understand more." It was a statement, really, but when Dr. Papadakis raised his voice slightly at the end of the sentence, looked at Adem and Theo next to him, and raised his tidy gray eyebrows, it was clear that he was looking for some confirmation.

The two younger men stood still for a moment, and when Dr. Papadakis stepped forward to examine a branch, he was temporarily alone until Binh was near him, quietly saying, "We've had some experiences of our own recently." But then, quickly as she saw the expression on the man in front of her, she added, "not among us, but we were witnesses to such interesting occurrences. We are working to make sense of them. Jiho and Migel studied neuroscience and have explained some background information to us. Jiho made us aware of some recent studies, and we are all more interested and aware than we were a month ago. It was a surprise to me, but apparently, such activity has been a quietly discussed topic at several universities and written about in many studies. It's not a topic that you hear about, but when I searched the databases, the studies were there, just as Jiho said."

"Do any of these studies mention Crete?" Dr. Papadakis asked. The group that had quietly assembled around him glanced either toward him or each other. The doctor knew then that all he said was novel to them. No matter, he had anticipated that. So, he turned west and said, "We can walk back to the house now and talk there."

They picked their way up the narrow trail between the trees. Theo couldn't stop thinking. It was like suddenly finding out that lots of people had a third hand, and he just didn't know, had never noticed. Telepathy was a thing. It was something that academics studied. It was something that some people talked about. Do any of these studies mention Crete? What did this mean? He had not said a study on Crete, a researcher from Crete, or a family from Crete. He simply said "Crete," which implied the whole island and … And then Theo realized that despite his easy-to-understand English, Dr. Papadakis was not a native speaker. How could Theo have forgotten? Countable and uncountable nouns were problematic. Even American grocery stores couldn't get their signs right. "12 items or less" was just offensive. The word 'less' was for uncountable nouns, like 'information,' 'money,' and 'food.' However, the error was pervasive among native speakers. Why did he expect Dr. Papadakis to be error-free? He had always thought that if every college student had to take one linguistics class and one English for

Language Learners class (at an accelerated pace, of course), then the country would be in a different place.

The octet exited the grove and walked the short distance between the trees and the house. The sun was heating them uncomfortably as they approached a large patio. The patio was covered with a wooden structure of beams crossing at perpendicular angles above most of it. This created a suitable amount of shade, as woven among the wood in one direction were sky-colored canvas strips going over and under the crossbeams. Theo focused on a long table under the shade wrapped in a woven cloth and covered with ceramic plates and glasses. Theo was dying for a glass of water.

A younger woman, who Theo recognized as the daughter, Cora, was pouring water from a pitcher, and an older-looking woman in a full-body apron was facing them. As they came closer, she shouted, *"eláte sti veránta!"* Come to the terrace. Dr. Papadakis raised his right hand to signal that he had heard the directions, and the group moved towards the shade and the cold drinks.

Chapter 22: Alec Nehoitewa

They were ten now: Dr. Papadakis, his wife Eleni, their daughter Cora, and the seven Americans. Introductions for Dr. Papadakis' wife took many minutes. When they were all seated around the long table with drinks, large platters of dakos started to be passed around. Dakos is a traditional dish of Crete, a bit like Italian bruschetta. The bottom layer is crunchy and does not get soggy easily. To the Americans, it seemed like toast, but Cora explained that it was barley bread baked two times, so 'a rusk,' and it was called *paximadi*. Cora demonstrated with her hands that it should be rubbed with a clove of garlic, sprinkled with salt, and then have *myzithra*, a cheese, crumbled across it. *Myzithra* is a local cheese that has the texture of feta and the taste of salted fresh ricotta. The cheese then must be topped with a few tablespoons of high-quality olive oil, chopped fresh tomatoes, whole olives, capers, and finally, fresh oregano. The result was outstanding.

When all mouths and hands were busy with the dakos, Dr. Papadakis began speaking.

"Because Crete is an island, there were many centuries for the people on it to evolve in response to their surroundings, relatively isolated from other people. Those of us from Crete for as many generations as we can trace have relatively similar genetics, as neighbors married their neighbors and friends for thousands of years in some cases." He paused and looked at his dining companions. "It appears that some people in Crete evolved a language that is entirely mental, and that among the people whose families have lived on Crete, there is a certain percentage that has this ability now. Perhaps it is a gene. I cannot, but some people can correspond with one another directly from one mind to the other." Dr. Papadakis leaned back, took up his water glass, and allowed the Americans to consider what they had heard.

The Americans were careful not to gasp. "I am so interested in hearing this," said Emma. "I'm sure we all are. Within anthropology, there is great interest in understanding humans today as a response to our evolutionary past, as people whose attributes are the answers to the needs of previous generations." Wow, she was quick with that thought, thought Alec, who realized that he was still surprised. Emma continued after a brief pause, "Just as voice boxes evolved and languages evolved, there is no reason to suppose that telepathy couldn't have evolved. I just, well, until last week, I never considered it. It never came up in any class. I never read about it as a possibility... But logically, it makes complete sense. Have you seen it, ah... in situ, like occurring naturally among people from your island as opposed to in studies?"

Dr. Papadakis said something in Greek to his family. At once, they put down their glasses and forks, and then Cora said, "I can do it. And my mother, too."

Alec didn't miss a beat this time. This was a biological discovery of immense proportions. He said, "We'd love to hear about it if you don't mind." He spoke clearly and slowly. When he finished his sentence, even though he had not planned to say more, he could tell that it would put the family at ease if he did, so he continued and tried not to sound too eager. "There must have been a need, maybe geographical, many years ago that favored the evolution of an internal language in addition to an external one. Maybe it was a possible attribute of people who live in certain areas where it would be advantageous. Perhaps it exists in many areas but needs to be tapped into and honed and utilized in order to get passed on through natural selection." Alec hoped that he was making it sound like an advantage and an interesting biological development because it was. He didn't want to seem overly nosy, disbelieving, or like he didn't take this seriously. He wanted to hear more.

Cora spoke English well. She could not speak as well as her father, but she was much better than her mother, so Cora did the explaining; none of the Americans spoke Greek. Alec wished he could record this moment, but there was no way to ask without affronting the family. Nobody really wanted to be recorded except the people who made reality shows, and normal people felt that none of those actors really considered what they were sacrificing or revealing in trade for money and notoriety. Of course, now Alec would sacrifice his whole day, and many more, as well as his chance to talk whenever he wanted, just to hear, to learn about what Cora had to say.

"When I was little, I remember sometimes just knowing what my mother wanted me to do. I knew she would call me to dinner or to come help her out some seconds before she said it out loud. I didn't think this was strange. I mean, children are supposed to know what their parents expect of them, right? Isn't parenting just teaching children to recognize what their parents, religion, and community will expect from them as they grow? So, I was a teenager before I ever had a conversation with my mother about it. There is a specific day that I remember that is significant. I attended high school in Heraklion. I took the bus to and from Archanes. I walked from the bus stop in the city to school and from the bus stop in Archanes to this house. One day, I was still in town, walking to the Heraklion bus stop, when I thought to detour onto a little street that has a very good dairy product store. I knew that my mother wanted me to come home with a specific cheese and some milk, but as I was selecting it, I realized that I did not remember her telling me directly that I should do it. I just knew that I should, and so I decided that I would purchase what I thought she wanted and bring them home." Cora paused; she knew what was coming.

"How did you know? Um, exactly?" asked Alec apologetically. He didn't want to sound challenging or combative, but he really wanted to understand.

Cora appreciated Alec's tone. "Well, the same way that you know anything, I guess. How do you know you are interested in my story right now? It's because you are thinking about what I say and thinking of questions that you want to ask me, and you are processing what I say, right? But you don't really know what happens in your head. On that day, I knew, like I knew that my shirt was white, that my mother wanted the cheese and the milk. My father was in Athens for a few days for museum business, so it was just *mitéra,* my mother, and I at home, along with my younger brother. It was a long time ago, but I remember knowing that my mother wanted me to detour to the shop that she liked and to purchase the items. I realized that I didn't remember a conversation with her that morning about these items, but I thought that maybe she had mentioned it the night before when I was studying or sometime before my father left. Like, maybe she said that if I brought these things home while he was gone, then she wouldn't have to go to the city to shop while he was away. Anyway, I stopped wondering when I had learned the information and just did what I thought I was supposed to do. It wasn't until I was walking home from the bus stop in Archanes, walking down the road to our house, that I saw my mother outside watching for me, and then I knew too that she was very happy and proud of me, even though the distance was too great to see her facial expression.

"I was seventeen, and my mother didn't normally stand at the door waiting for me to come home like she did when I was young. My mother saw me with my folding shopping bag on my arm and my backpack over one shoulder, and finally, I was close enough to see her smile as she came to meet me. I walked toward her. She said something like, 'I was trying to send you a message to pick something up for me.' 'Milk and cheese?' I asked. 'Because I knew that you wanted them somehow, and so I stopped on the way home to buy them.' We went inside, and my mother explained things to me. She explained my family history with this ability and the fact that, although it was not only women who could do this, neither my father nor my brother could. It was more common with women, she thought, but not limited to them, as her father could do it. She explained that she had not wanted to discuss it with me when I was young for fear that I would say something at school and other kids would tease me. But she said that she had been getting me to respond since I was little, and she could never get my brother to respond."

That made many people laugh quietly. It was a challenge to get young boys to respond to directions in any language Cora had translated from her mother. They are very busy and interested in everything, and it is the rare boy or the sick one who takes pleasure in being still and quiet and learning directly from the lecture. Why should mental communication be any different? But of course, they had already learned that it was not this at all. It was that the son, Dimitrios, could not communicate as Cora and her mother could.

"So that occurred over thirty years ago, and it has been the same since." Cora finished speaking and resumed eating her dakos.

"Can you also send messages to your mother?" asked Binh gently, meeting Cora's gaze.

"Oh yes, of course, and to other people—some people we know," replied Cora.

"Do you think of a person and then send words to them?"

"No, the opposite," said Cora. "I think of an idea and then shape it into a summary. It's like when you indicate on a test what the 'main idea' of a reading is. I do that—I reduce something to a main idea. Then I direct the main idea to someone else, to someone who can receive it."

Jiho had been patient, but now he was leaning forward against the table, and he had to speak. He had so many questions; they all must. It was important to be careful not to bombard the woman. "How do you identify a person who can receive the information?"

"Trial and error. I mean, I didn't know when I was younger—I had no idea, but after that time in high school, my mother explained our family history to me. Her father and her grandmother could do this, so my mother was not very surprised when she realized that I could, too. She realized it was a family trait sometimes, like a fiery temper or almond-shaped eyes."

"Do you know who you can send to and receive from? I mean, if you don't know the person, can you tell who they are?" prodded Jiho carefully.

"Kind of. Um… you know how when you are in a public place, and you turn on WIFI, and you get a long list of hotspots and WIFI networks near you? It's a bit like that without the list format and the password-locked access, I think. But it's not always accurate. It's like hearing the radio or a person talk. You can choose not to listen, but if you are within range of the sound, you hear."

"Can you prevent someone from sending it to you?" said Jiho.

"No, but you don't have to listen closely. It's like, you know, if you go to a crowded train station, or restaurant, or bar, many people are talking, and it doesn't bother you. It's normal. You can focus on a particular conversation and listen to just that one. You can't control what you hear, but you can control what you listen to."

"So, people don't know everything that you are thinking?" asked Alec.

"No, no, not at all," said Cora, laughing a little at the idea. "It's not like the alien movies with mind control that my brother used to like. Some people just know how to understand the language when they essentially 'hear it.' You know, because it is nearby or directed to them. Like if you go to a busy place and all the people are speaking in Russian, and you don't know Russian. You sort of tune it out, but then if you hear one person start speaking in a language that you know, say English, you tune in. Your brain recognizes it. I don't know how it works, but it seems like people either hear it or they don't. I just did it while you were speaking, and none of you heard me. Neither did my father, but my mother did. So it seems like a special ability to hear, but ears are not involved."

"That makes sense," said Binh. "I am a native English speaker, but I speak Vietnamese with my family and friends from home.

When I am somewhere where everyone is speaking English, I register it immediately if someone near me starts talking in Vietnamese, especially if I am not near home. I often turn to see who I heard speaking."

"Exactly!" said Cora.

Alec had been dying to ask other questions, but he didn't want to bombard Cora or give the family any reason to stop sharing, so he'd been patient and waited. Now, there was an opening, as Cora was sitting back down at the table. "So, the belief is that some people on Crete evolved to have this skill? And it is congenital, I mean genetic, because it seems to run in families? It's the people who can do this?"

Alec looked at Dr. Papadakis quickly, who nodded, and to Cora, who said, "Yes."

Dr. Papadakis had been quietly enjoying his food, watching the faces around him, and listening to the conversation. He had the same questions many, many years ago. He helped himself to a bowl of room-temperature, olive-oil-coated beans. Something was said in Greek at this time by Eleni, and Cora stood up and began clearing small plates. Emma stood up instinctively and picked up the platters despite protests, and there was a change of dishes. The used, empty ones went to the kitchen, and clean ones and platters full of food emerged and were brought to the table.

Something occurred to Jiho. He said, "Do you have a name for this process? This way of communicating?"

"*Glóssa Schimatízontas*," said Dr. Papadakis. "It means the forming of language—sort of."

Everyone thought for a minute and moved platters of food around, and then Emma asked, "Do you suppose that there are people off of Crete who can do this?"

Cora finished chewing and began her story. "Yes. And this is why we share today. The process of Glóssa Schimatízontas is bigger than just us. We recently learned this. My mother was in Heraklion and went to see her friend Viktoria at the ticket office at the museum. You met her. They have been friends since elementary school. Viktoria can use Glóssa Schimatízontas also." The Americans all silently noted this. "On the day that my mother was there, a family from South Korea had arrived at the museum, purchased tickets, and was orienting themselves when my mother heard the Korean mother. My mother does not speak Korean. However, somehow, she knew that the mother was talking, doing Glóssa Schimatízontas to one of her two little boys. The little boy looked at his mother and nodded. The family went on to tour the museum, and my mother and Viktoria started a conversation that ended in the evening with my father's input. Now, we are wondering if it is possible for all humans to think in the same language and if this language is what *Glóssa Schimatízontas* is in. This would explain why my mother understood the Korean woman, who spoke neither Greek nor much English. My mother heard it in her head the same way she heard me and Viktoria. There was no language barrier and no accent. It was the same.

The father in the Korean family had purchased the tickets from Viktoria; his English was good. He said "thank you" in Greek, but like a tourist who only knows a few words. Viktoria appreciated it and asked in English where the family was from and how long they were visiting the island. Viktoria doesn't remember what city or region the man said, only that they were from South Korea.

When relaying the story later that evening to my father, he proposed that perhaps this solved some archaeological mysteries of Crete. Maybe the reason that Cretan hieroglyphics coexisted with the language called Linear A from 1800 BCE to 1450 BCE is because the hieroglyphic language is a representation of the thinking language, and Linear A is a representation of the spoken language. Cretan hieroglyphics have never been translated; you know." Cora finished and looked around at the young academics.

No word in Hopi or English easily describes what Alec felt. All he could think of was the slang term for surprise; he felt "blown away."

Chapter 23: Migel Ngubá

The group sat on the outside porch of Binh and Emma's room in the semi-shade of the wooden beams. It was comfortable; however, the wooden shade structure was not as complex or nice as the one at the Papadakis' house. Still, it worked well enough. Despite its latitude, Crete in June was not as hot as one might expect. The porch had two chairs, but some people brought their own from their own porches, while others opted to sit directly on the twelve-inch elevated wooden decking. They were discussing the events of the day. They had left the Papadakis home in the early afternoon, walked for a while, and found themselves going back to their own lodging to sit and discuss.

First, there were explosive exclamations of surprise and interest, the reactions that everyone had suppressed while they were guests at someone's house. Next, Adem pointed out that he was now certain that eye-tracking was not their primary objective. All had agreed. He had then mentioned that it seemed too coincidental that there was a known Korean speaker at large who could speak mentally and that they happened to have a team member who could read and speak Korean. All had agreed again. They had briefly returned to expressing awe and implications. Now, they were in the third phase: clarification and analysis. For Migel, Jiho, Alec, and Theo, the experience of the day was a real-time lab experiment without enough pre-lab work. They wanted to process what was happening, but they yearned for quantitative data. Binh and Emma were more interested in the qualitative aspects: what all of this meant, what the experience was like, and what the ramifications of the information would be.

Adem was constantly running patterns through his mind, predicting potential outcomes and projecting analytical results. Alec pointed out that in physics, a "three-force member" is a body that remains in equilibrium while three non-parallel forces act upon that body. He felt like the people who could communicate, the people like Dr. Papadakis who knew about it, and the people who knew nothing of it, had maintained the existence of *Glóssa Schimatízontas* in an equilibrium that would now be disrupted, as they, a fourth force, had gained knowledge. It had been an underappreciated analogy. No one was fully ready to consider the consequences. Someone had poured more water. Binh had gone into the room behind them to use the bathroom, and then the conversation had continued.

Theo mentioned that he was contemplating whether mind-to-mind communication was signaling or actual language. "Signaling is not the same as language," he explained. Many animal species signal. Many birds make warning calls to their flock when a predator is seen or heard. Animals can posture; they use their eyes, wave their arms like chimps, or stamp their feet like elephants. Animals have mating calls. In addition to these visual, tactile, and auditory signals, there is also a way for some to signal chemically; for example, some animals change their color as a result of pheromones. Rhinoceroses can read messages in poop piles; they gather information from the chemicals that are smelled about the age, gender, and reproductive readiness of other rhinos who pooed in the same pile. "Signaling is defined as behavior intended to alter the behavior of another being because of the information it conveys. But this is not language," he explained. His linguistics courses had covered this thoroughly early on: human language had distinct features. "Cora and Eleni might just be sending signals."

"Well, that's more than I can do," said Migel wishfully. "And maybe it is signaling. As I understood the explanation, what gets sent is almost like a simplified thought message; it's only a concept, right? Mostly nouns, it sounds like. Cora explained that the sender thinks of a person intently and then thinks, 'I want X,' or 'I need X,' or 'Go to X, and I will be at X,' where the X is an object or place, something depictable. Cora made it sound like the more concrete the need is, such as 'eggs,' the more easily the image comes through to the receiver. Trying to send a message like 'I want to change our evening plans' would not be conveyed well. This makes me think that the 'language' is not complex, and it sounds like if there is an attempt to involve verb tense or switch around syntax, then it doesn't even work. It is really, I guess, behavior intended to alter the behavior of another, as Theo said, but it's still cool."

"It's amazing. And it does lend itself to hieroglyphics," said Emma. "I am dying to try to figure them out now. I can imagine a symbol for 'I want/I need' and then symbols for what was commonly needed over 2,000 years ago. Someone at the bottom of the cliff could bring a needed item to the caves without requiring a communicator to run up and down the path in the heat. There's an idea: maybe this evolved to conserve energy and water in hot climates. Kenya gets hot. It gets hot here. Isn't South Korea hot, Jiho?"

"It can be; there are many mountains, but the latitude of much of the country is similar to here. Nairobi, Kenya, is just south of the equator. We are north of it now. Hang on, I'm looking it up…. We are right now at the same latitude as the southern region of South Korea. Huh."

"And what is the latitude of the Philippines?" asked Emma. "Oh," she said before Jiho could talk, "I know that it runs through Indonesia, which is south of the Philippines, so the Philippines are just north of the equator."

"As is French Guiana," said Theo. Everyone looked at him.

"Have you ever heard of…," started Migel.

"No," said Theo, "but I also never asked. I didn't know that any humans could talk without words." They were all quiet for a minute. Then Alec spoke.

"Has anyone pulled up that list of the hieroglyphics online yet? It could have been a fluke that people were naturally selected for this ability because it made daily life easier. As it was not a necessity for survival, plenty of people without the gene survived as well and eventually outnumbered the people who did have the gene. Maybe the people capable of *Glóssa Schimatízontas* made the hieroglyphics when those who knew it were the dominant group. Then, when there were enough people living on Crete who could not do this *Glóssa Schimatízontas*, about one hundred years later, they created a written language based on what they spoke. That could explain why there is a set of hieroglyphics in one language, and ten decades later, a completely different written language appears, and the two coexist for a century."

"That seems plausible," said Migel regretfully. "I was so surprised and unprepared for the discussion that I didn't ask the right questions. I keep thinking now of how I could have elaborated on what I said. I am missing a lot of information to form too many ideas. Alec's idea assumes it's a genetic capability, which it might be. It could be an inherited trait."

"What do you wish we knew?" asked Binh.

"Things an fMRI would show," said Migel. "I'd kill to do more research here. I'm not sure how we could ever ask for an fMRI or where we would go to get one that is not in a hospital, but I wish we could see what is happening in the brain when this communication occurs. I wish we had Kimaru and his labs."

"I wish I had asked if new sentences and analogies can be created or if there is a limitation as to what is available and representational through imagery," said Theo. "I was wondering if an idea can be communicated as the will of a third person, like, can there be an image of father and then 'I want' and then an image of daughter and then house so that Eleni could convey to Cora that her father wants her home now? Can the images be built upon like blocks, and if so, how many symbols or images are in a grouping? It's like a computer program of sorts—I want to see what it can do. I want to play with the program. Is it a matter of how the input gets fed in? Do you think these guys have already spoken to other researchers or not?"

"Easy, Theo," interrupted Jiho. "I know this whole situation is linguistic porn for you." He smiled. "I'm not giving you a hard time, dude. If parts of the brain suddenly got mapped out, I'd be all over it. I get it. But we don't need to have it all worked out on the first day. We're not leaving yet. We're not even reporting yet. What exactly would we say anyway?"

"Guys," said Emma, ignoring Jiho's question, "is it possible that we all think in the same language and that this thinking language is somehow only understood or accessible by a small number of people? That's what, in theory, happened, right? Eleni understood the Korean woman's thinking language?"

"That's the premise," said Jiho. "There are some studies to back that idea up." Silence ensued, then, "What do you think, Alec, of the evolutionary possibility of this?"

"Well… Theo pointed out earlier that the unique-language-for-thinking hypothesis is not a super popular idea. Even if such a language does exist, it's not necessarily universal to all humans. So, there's that... but I think that human language evolved in many places in many ways. Presumably, thinking evolved in a number of ways, too. The idea of forced mind control from other parts of the world seems like an impossible activity to evolve, but those kinds of evolutionary developments are theoretically possible, just improbable... just as unlikely as the exact same language developing in two unconnected parts of the world.

Other ideas, though, like this—the concept that some people wrote down the language of thought—it has never been known to have occurred, but it's possible. As Emma pointed out, there are scenarios that could have encouraged evolution but not prioritized it to the extent that only that one approach was naturally selected. If you don't know something exists, that's way different from being sure it definitely doesn't exist, you know?" Alec had spoken clearly and slowly, and everyone had followed his intent. He had become the lead of these kinds of conversations, having dedicated over six years to considering evolutionary traits and adaptations of flora and fauna.

However, Jiho and Migel were the brain experts, and Theo had the greatest specialty in the language-brain connection. No one knew theories of psychology as well as Binh, culture and geography as well as Emma, or identified patterns and statistics as well as Adem. They were, in fact, kind of an ideal mix of people to be exploring this topic. Migel assumed that this was not an accident.

He had been sitting quietly, processing what everyone said, but he was getting ready to talk.

"What is known about how people think? And what language or format is it supposed to occur in?" asked Emma.

"The assumption previously was always that everyone's brain worked the same way," began Migel. "I mean, of course, throughout history, there were always people who believed that their brain functioned better than other people's did, but those people aside… scientists, right into this century, believed until the past few decades that what we all experience in our heads is the same. It's not, it turns out… We all make cells and grow hair and move blood about the body in the same way, but our inner monologues and how we think are not universal. Some people have a strong inner dialogue, a controllable voice that chats nonstop. Others do not. All thoughts are in a language that a thinker understands. My inner voice speaks in English, but I can make it talk to me in Spanish or Palenquero, too. I always assumed that everyone has and uses an inner voice as I do, but in the past few decades, it has been shown that some people have less chitchat up there than others, and some people hear no words at all; they just experience images, emotions, and sensations. Fortunately, this does not line up with skin color or religion or geography, or we'd all be screwed. But some people, all over the world, think better and more deeply internally and talk to themselves in ways that others, again, all over the world, cannot or do not. Some of the people in this latter group describe the experience of talking as the result of translating their thoughts into words. When questioned in studies, these respondents make the translation process sound cumbersome and tiring, so these people claim that they often prefer written to oral communication.

I thought of this when Dr. Papadakis spoke of translating the language of thought as if the hieroglyphics assigned a symbol to each thought and the later language translated the spoken language of the island. However, maybe he intended to express that some people have to actively translate their thoughts. Maybe we are all translating thoughts into words, but some of us do it fast and naturally and are unaware of the process. Maybe others, those who think in images, without the chatty voice, might have less motivation or need to translate, or maybe it's entirely genetic, like having different hair color, and people adapt to what they get. Anyway, because those people describe it as having to translate their thoughts into words, the whole idea of a universal language of thought seems a little more possible to many of us now than it did twenty years ago."

"Are these real studies, Migel?" asked Emma. "Or are we talking about college kids asking people in the dorm if they have a voice in their head?"

"These are real studies!" said Migel. "Go to PubMed. Seriously, this is new stuff."

"It's true," said Binh. "In the last decade, several studies have furthered what has been known about how people communicate in their own heads, with their conscious self. Several of them involved having study participants wear beepers, and when the beepers went off, the participants wrote down what was going on in their heads."

"The responses that you mentioned are interesting, but I don't see how it is ever possible to know for certain what a person means when they self-report on their own mental processes," said Adem. "People experience things so differently. I have a niece who has perfect pitch; she literally hears sounds in a way that I don't. Some people are color-blind—a lot apparently, particularly when it comes to distinguishing various hues—so they see in a way that I don't. Some people can picture the faces of others who are not in front of them, and others can accurately draw a map of a complicated route through a city. These different abilities and perceptions have to influence how we perceive experiences, and assuming that they do, then how can anyone really ever know what another person is experiencing when they describe it?" Everyone was quiet for a minute.

"Welcome to psychology," said Binh finally. "Therein lies the interesting part."

"It feels unattainable to me, too," said Theo. "Part of it, I mean. I'm sure it is possible to get someone else to realize some of their own problems and make many people feel better, but can anyone ever understand the experience another person has? Or how that experience impacts them? I don't think so. What really matters is the person's understanding and interpretation of their experiences, and that can never be known. I think it is only possible to understand how it affected them and deal with that. How reliable is any interpreter of their experiences, and where do these women fit in? And can't a person only ever understand something by attaching the knowledge that they already have to what they learn? Because if acquiring new knowledge is based on earlier knowledge, then no one ever really can know what another thinks, right? So, any attempt to explain one's own experiences to another is practically useless."

"I think that is a very philosophical way to look at it, Theo," said Emma pragmatically. "But maybe we should stop trying to understand and authenticate and take it instead at face value and move on. Maybe we should just collect the artifacts and knowledge that we can and save the interpretation for later. It's hard to know what a puzzle will look like when one only has a few pieces. An event occurred that gave us new knowledge. We certainly need to document what we know. Beyond that, all we can say is that there is a possibility that there is a written historical record of this activity and that, possibly, this activity is related to something that appears to occur in Kenya. We also have a trail that leads to South Korea, though we don't know where, but fortunately, we have someone with us who speaks the language and knows the culture. Should we advocate for heading to South Korea next to gather more puzzle pieces?"

"I think so," said Adem. "And I think we need to sit together until we work out what we understand and believe, even if that means that we don't all agree. We will still likely not have more than a few hypotheses. Then, we need to decide how much of what we believe should be relied on by Margo, who is, without a doubt, expecting news today. Next, we need to determine how to proceed, and a consensus would be good to have on that. We should help Migel plan out his communication so the burden doesn't all fall on him, and after all that, we can call the workday done."

"You're a good project manager, Adem, thanks," interjected Emma. "I'm interested in getting some fresh fish with Binh in an hour or two with whomever else is interested."

"I'm not a fan of eating things out of the ocean unless I have to," said Alec, "but I am already getting hungry, and I agree that dropping an update to Margo should not all fall to Migel. We'll do it together before dinner."

"Let's skip right to the part about writing to Margo," said Jiho. "How much are we willing to say? How much are we holding back?"

"We should definitely hold back a little; it's unclear who we are working for." Binh looked around and then started again, "And who knows what is being done with the information we deliver? Chasing leads around the world about mental communication isn't likely a project of the Department of Education. Personally, I feel a bit uncertain about outing people capable of mind-to-mind communication in general, but especially when I don't know who wants the information or what they will do with it. Won't some military come and abduct these people and try to force them to spy on foreign governments or something? Or a big tech company? Or some billionaire who wants a new toy? I think that transferring too much information can put Eleni and Cora's lives in danger, or at least disrupt their quiet existence, and we don't have the right to take that away from them. We should be very vague this evening. I think we can say what we know and what Dr. Papadakis suspects, but not who can do it."

Chapter 24: Margo Duc

It had been two weeks since Margo's surgery. She could move around well, although she didn't feel like she had one hundred percent of her energy back, but that bothered her less than missing the big trip. Maybe she had never been necessary? Worse, really, was that the group seemed to be fine without her. That was an annoying thought. No one wanted to feel superfluous. She pushed that thought away.

Samir had been very happy to hear that the Papadakis family had embraced the group and was sharing information and resources, and Margo felt that she should be credited with this; she had selected the team. It's not that no one had thanked or complimented her, but it wasn't a recurring event. The project just kept chugging along, and as it did, her team, with their specific skills, areas of expertise, and personalities, tackled each obstacle like pros. They succeeded beautifully and carefully documented their achievements and conclusions along the way. Each time it happened, Margo thought, "I did that. I picked these people. I made this happen." She hoped, expected maybe, that others would recognize this as well and call her up and congratulate her all over again. No one had. Didn't people wonder at the way that the group connected and easily moved through situations that many other groups would not have been able to? Gratitude, for many, is a temporal obligation, and this was what Margo was considering when the phone rang.

"Hello?" said Margo, in the atavistic way that people still do these days, even though caller identification comes on every phone, and it's rare not to know who to expect at the other end of the line.

"Hi. It's Samir. How are you feeling?"

"Really well. I'm fine, thanks," replied Margo.

"Great. I wanted to check in about South Korea, and it seemed easier to do that by phone. Do you have any more information? The country has been on our radar for years, but we didn't have a specific area to investigate."

"No additional information. We don't have much at all. We only know that a single family from a country with over fifty million people may be part of this. The group was vague. We learned that the Cretan woman understood a Korean woman a few months back in the absence of verbal language. The Korean woman was traveling with her family, and we don't know where they live in Korea."

"I know." (pause) "I have some people trying to get a look at the museum cameras. If we can just hear that family speak amongst themselves, we might be able to place them regionally by their pronunciation. Then, put your team on it. With even a vague idea, I'd like to send at least some of them to South Korea, but we need to be able to dial in the location. Just the fact that a South Korean woman is in the story makes it worth checking out. It means that the other pieces of news gathered over the years were likely true."

"What other pieces of news?"

"Just chatter. Rumors. Nothing concrete."

"What can I do to help?" asked Margo.

"It was helpful already that you got someone on the team who spoke Korean. I wasn't sure how likely it was that we would need that, but I sure am glad now. I want to investigate; I just need to get a precise location. If we split the kids up, the Korean speaker and a few others could go to South Korea. It would be easier for them to get around in a small group, and they'd be less conspicuous. Get the kids to ask around about the Korean family. Even if we knew the hotel that the Koreans used on Crete, it would help. I'll work on trying to figure out where they come from through other channels."

"A good plan."

"Any more clarification or detail on the specifics of the day with the Papadakis family?"

"No. Not more than what I already sent. I think things are going well, though. The team is busy and tired, and they probably don't have the complete picture. They'll learn more tomorrow, I imagine." As Margo said this, she realized that it sounded defensive. Why did she need to defend what had happened? It was a funny reaction. She wondered if Samir had noticed.

"OK then. Carry on. Keep me posted."

"I will. Thanks."

"Talk soon," said Samir, and the line disconnected.

Margo thought about the very brief conversation for a while after it ended. Samir had called the team "kids" again. They were literally just a year or two younger than she was: each between one and four years younger, to be exact. What did it mean to not be a kid? Or was it just the connotation that bothered her? She thought about the work next… she would need a location file on South Korea in general, and then she could add to it as she knew more. She could begin the general language and culture part now. Margo crossed the room to fill the electric teapot with water. She flipped the switch down to close the circuit and turn it on. She thought briefly of her mother, who insisted that the "o" seemed like it stood for "on." Margo had explained that a better analogy was for the line to represent a bridge that power could cross and the zero to represent a hole – no crossing could happen. Lines and circles made her think of the Korean language. As a non-speaker of Korean, looking at words in the language had a greater visual impact on her than an auditory one.

Margo had never been to South Korea, either. Man, was she missing out? Shortly after she was released from the hospital, Margo had held onto the hope that she'd be sent to join the team as soon as she had healed enough. Eventually, though, it became clear that she was never going to be sent. She would remain the East Coast Liaison.

The group had gelled without Margo. They were reliable and functioning, and she wasn't needed. It would change the dynamic if she popped in now. Beyond that, neither her doctor nor her parents wanted her to hop around the world for several weeks. Margo was going to miss the whole trip. She sighed. The water boiled, the kettle dinged, and her thoughts were interrupted. She poured the hot water into the mug that she had dropped a tea bag into and plodded back to her workstation. That's when she remembered that she had felt defensive on the phone.

She flashed back to when she had interviewed Binh. They liked each other very quickly and talked easily. Margo had found herself more than a little curious about what Binh had learned in her six years of study. Who doesn't want to know how people tick? Their conversation had been finishing up when there was a reference to a very public event in professional football. Margo loved watching football and couldn't help mentioning that the coach involved seemed awfully defensive when he spoke on camera about the much-covered event. That one word, "defensive," had prolonged the conversation another fifteen minutes as the two women discussed the psychology behind a human's verbal defense mechanism.

Margo had learned a few things that, at the time, she related to football players past and present and the attention-seeking coach. Since then, she had applied the knowledge to other scenarios. People defended themselves verbally in response to a perceived threat, like criticism. When no criticism is forthcoming, the person feeling defensive may be reacting to shame or guilt. A defensive person might also be hiding the truth or fearing failure. Warm mug in hand, Margo sat down and realized that she probably felt defensive of the team in Crete because Samir was putting into words what she had already thought, and it made her feel guilty.

Margo had thought that the email was oddly vague. She had dismissed the notion of intent as it was the end of a long workday in Greece, but when she had read Migel's email, it had not seemed as full of detail as she had expected. It was a very concise and vague email, unlike his other emails. There was a certain lack of specifics, and the eye-tracking questions could be read as sarcastic. She was careful not to assume tone, but Margo had hoped that clarification would come the following day. Then Samir had called, and it made her feel like she didn't really know what was going on. She moved those thoughts to the back burner and started a location file on South Korea.

Chapter 25: Adem Haimowitz

Everybody has some innate sense of allegiance. Adem knew that. People felt allegiance to their family, culture, or country, and often to some kind of community, if not a higher power. Humans are animals that live in groups, and their groups—even their sports teams—earned a place in their hearts. Much has been discussed (and studied and published, although Adem had not read it) about a feeling of allegiance to an employer—a sense of duty, an obligation to do what was expected. When Adem had broached this topic with Binh, however, she had pointed out that traditional employment allegiance wasn't simply a matter of recognizing the trade-off of time and skills for financial compensation and benefits; there is also an emotional investment that employees make. Binh had said that people often reacted more strongly to a breach in that emotional investment than to infractions of more clearly defined areas. She cited that in recent decades, employees were, in general, reducing their sense of allegiance to their employers and increasing their understanding of allegiance to themselves, their ideals, or whatever else. Even some military employees had outed work that they did not personally agree with. Adem thought this was inappropriate and should be considered treason, but nonetheless, he was drinking the coffee he'd made in his room and thinking about it. He wondered how much allegiance he felt toward Margo, the project, the team, or even humanity. The last one seemed a bit pompous, but really, who wouldn't think about humanity when they learned of a secret that, if known by all, would change the trajectory of history? Adem wondered what "the right thing to do" really was. He had already encouraged Migel to write up a report that was the truth, but not the whole truth. Margo and whoever she worked with obviously had leads but no answers.

There was a knock on the door, and Adem knew it was Binh and Emma. Adem wanted to continue the conversation about allegiance. He had more questions now. He went to the door to sit on the porch with the women. Together with Theo—if he ever got out of the shower—they'd walk to the fish restaurant across town to the west. Jiho, Alec, and Migel had gone north of town, toward Heraklion, to a traditional restaurant with grilled meat.

"I pulled up a list of the Cretan hieroglyphics online," said Emma as Adem walked onto the porch. "There's a great website of ancient writing systems. I'm imagining all kinds of meanings for the symbols."

"I've been thinking about why Dr. Papadakis talked to us. What motivated him, and why now?" said Binh.

"Aside from wondering why Theo's showers are so long, I was thinking about what we owe Margo and whoever she hired us to help."

"We need a table and pens and a notebook. I can't think without holding a writing utensil," said Emma. The door opened, and Theo appeared. "You guys ready?" he asked.

They grabbed a notebook and pens and walked across the village. Adem led the conversation through his ponderings, as any part that was overheard would be benign. He used himself as an example and covered who and what he felt allegiances toward. He felt surprisingly sentimental as he listed certain promises to people, relatives, Jewish traditions, and schools. As he ran down the priority list, probably boring people, he made his point that while everyone has many allegiances, it was those of family, country, and culture that appeared at the top, followed closely by ones where he had made a personal promise and felt an obligation to some inner sense of self. As they neared the restaurant, Adem said that he had worked out that his sense of obligation to Margo and her group was strictly financial. He felt obligated to do what he said he would in exchange for monetary payment, and beyond that, he had no inner sense of obligation to a business he didn't even know the name of. "However," Adem continued, "I got to thinking that allegiance was an emotional attachment. I realized I feel an emotional attachment of sorts to you all and an obligation to work with our group and do what we agree upon. Six months ago, I didn't know any of you, so I guess it's the time we've spent together that's making me feel this way. That's it, really—Margo seemed nice enough when we met her, but I haven't spent enough time with her to feel that I owe her interests over ours."

"That's so analytical," said Binh.

"That's how I roll," said Adem.

"Well, an intro to psych textbook would tell you a similar thing," said Binh, "but I'm much more impressed that you worked it out by yourself, and … I agree, by the way."

"I hadn't thought about it," admitted Theo as he held open the door to the restaurant, "but it makes sense now that you mention it."

"Thank you, kind sir," said Emma, sliding past Theo's arm and into the restaurant.

Within minutes, they were seated at a table with only empty tables around them. "It's 8:45 p.m.," said Emma, "it's already later than I like to eat, but it will give us the restaurant alone for the next fifteen to twenty minutes until the Greeks think it's worth coming in for a pre-dinner drink. Are we all in agreement with Adem's soliloquy?" Emma bowed her head slightly to him. "And as to Binh's topic, let's just use pronouns and not names here, ok? And…"

A waitress came by asking about drinks. They ordered water and wine, and the woman disappeared again. "What motivates someone to disclose such a secret to… well, essentially strangers?" asked Emma.

They all looked at Binh. "That's what I've been thinking about— why us?" Binh said. "There's age, of course. People like closure at certain points in their lives. It's also a chance to solve a riddle with the…" She gestured and made signs in the air, and everyone understood. "There's the desire to unburden oneself, which is an innate and natural process. There have been a lot of recent studies on humans talking about themselves. Did you know that thirty to forty percent of daily conversation involves a person relaying their own private experiences to others? Also, eighty percent of all social media posts consist of people telling other people what they have just done, seen, or heard. We humans are just dying to divulge. So, I've sort of worked out why he talked, but why us, as the audience, is harder to answer. Firstly, I'm wondering if he was under any pressure to talk or if we just seemed distant, young, and non-threatening. Who are these contacts at so many universities that 'Pap' and 'Kim' seem to know, and how did they gain access to a vague idea that they sent to Margo's group but also need us to extract all of the details? I'm also wondering if, since we are young and non-native speakers, there is an intent to claim that we misunderstood if all goes sour." Binh looked around the restaurant. Only other tourists were seated and hoping to eat. It was safe to continue.

No one responded immediately. Then Emma said, "We are a unique group—young, but knowledgeable and interesting… and we are affiliated with many universities and specialties. We seem like delegates, I think. Our arrivals get pre-announced, and doors seem to open."

"It's still a burden," said Theo. They all glanced at him. "We become the keepers of information, and it becomes our decision if the world knows secrets. We didn't quite consider Kimaru's position enough, I think, but he was already getting his ideas out. We didn't start anything for him, and he wanted and was already actively looking for a university affiliation in the West. It's a good fit for him and his work. Kimaru is charismatic, and if not for us, someone else would have heard him and gotten involved, and that person could have been up to no good. We at least associated him with a good place, but Dr... I mean 'Pap,' he has more to lose from unwanted attention. What is clearly an actual occurrence of a highly desirable skill is not common. I think he would sincerely like to establish what the sign images might mean, but we have to continue very cautiously."

"I agree, Theo, but couldn't he have looked into translating them quietly himself?" said Emma.

"Maybe, maybe not. He would have had zero evidence for where his suppositions came from. With no studies, no evidence, and no reasoning, no one would publish his ideas or take them seriously. He also wanted to know more about how things happened in order to guide his translation work. Or maybe it's just that he had a big job, and people love unsolved mysteries... or maybe the thought just occurred to him recently?" added Adem. "He's in a tough position."

Wine and water arrived. They ordered food, and the evening moved along. The conversation came easily but regularly shifted to the subject of human rights and the responsibility to safeguard the mind communicators of Crete.

"The basic problem with the concept of 'human rights' is that it is impossible for everyone to have them. Who gets to decide? Who has the right to deem one culture or practice more important than another? We should all understand this now since the disaster of colonialism. Human rights can sometimes only be granted to one group of people at the expense of another group. I'm not trying to solve world problems here. All I'm saying is that when we say that some people have the right to knowledge and other people have the right to peace and privacy, it's often impossible for both groups to get what they theoretically deserve. Add in violence, torture, fair practices, and justice, and there is no way to argue a point without being hegemonic. There is no way to attempt to protect everyone without exercising ideological, social, and cultural influence. It can't be done. History has shown this over and over."

"I can't say that I've ever thought of it from that perspective," began Theo. "I have generally been a fan of human rights for all."

"I don't mean to sound like a jerk," started Adem, but he knew that he kind of would. Most people hum along in life, thinking that world peace, human rights for all, and a prejudice-free existence are plausible. He knew better. He was realistic. Statistically, if people could have all learned to play nice, they would have by now. Theo was a good kid and a philosophical thinker, but he didn't have enough real-life experiences, hardships, and ugly encounters behind him to be realistic. Adem liked him, however, and wanted to be gentle, so he said, "I think that all good people are pro-rights until they realize that it's not possible. But who gets to grant the rights and decide on the deserving party when there is opposition, like when two or more groups claim their right to land?" Adem interrupted himself. "It's complex because as soon as you decide in favor of one side, you are against the other."

"I get it," said Theo. "What you're saying makes sense. I need to think about it more, but what is true? There will be no way to address the translation without exposing the glossa–" he stopped. "The L shapers. If that is done, there is no chance that their rights or privacy will be protected."

"Exactly," said Adem as he leaned back.

"What should we do about SK, then?" Emma asked, trying to lighten the conversation. "You know what I mean? The country? I wonder where that family is from?"

They ate and discussed it, then talked about home as they started walking back to their hotel, discussing human rights again. Emma's question was answered the following day.

Chapter 26: Emma Miller

When Emma woke up on Thursday, she had to remind herself that she had not yet been on Crete for a full week. A lot had happened, and she was already accustomed to the time zone and culture. Long before she met the group at the agreed-upon 8 a.m. breakfast time, she had made a mental list of questions to ask the "brain boys" (Migel and Jiho). She had read academic articles about the correlations between Cretan hieroglyphs and their likely ancestor, Egyptian hieroglyphics, and she had contemplated possible matches for various symbols and ideas. It had been a productive morning. Binh, on the other hand, slept until 7:30 a.m., then showered quickly and was ready to walk to the dining area at the same time as Emma.

"I was wondering," began Binh as they closed the door behind them and stepped out onto the porch. "What do you think Migel, Alec, and Jiho discussed last night? Do you think they came to similar conclusions?"

"We will see shortly," said Emma, "but I won't blame them if they just drank wine, relaxed, and discussed life. Yesterday was a long, provoking day."

Ten minutes later, the group of seven were seated at a table and being poured coffee. "What did you gentlemen do with yourselves yesterday evening?" asked Emma as she reached for the milk.

"We had dinner and figured out where that Korean family was from," said Alec.

"WHAT?" said Binh. "How on earth did you work that out?"

Jiho, Alec, and Migel enjoyed the surprise. They picked up bread to eat instead of answering. Migel began the story. "We started off by walking to that little restaurant we said we were going to. Then, we got talking about that family at the museum." Migel looked around to make sure that no other guests could hear him. "We basically decided quickly to catch a bus into Heraklion, eat there, and ask around. Do a little detective work."

"It's better than that," said Alec. "We initially decided to pretend that one of us saw the woman without her kids and husband and thought she was beautiful, so we pretended we were trying to track her down. We ended up—"

"Wait!" interrupted Emma, "What! How on earth would you even do that? Didn't this family visit a while ago? How would anyone remember her so many months later?"

The men all laughed, and Migel said, "OK, ok. We're sorry. We are just fooling around. What really happened was that we ate in town, and when we got back to our rooms, I had an email from Margo. Her people worked something out. They did it. They placed the accent to a region." He looked sheepish and bit into his bread. "There are video surveillance cameras all over the place. Margo must have connections because some got pulled and listened to. Most don't have sound at home, but they do here."

Everyone had to smile, as it was pretty funny. "So, what did the email say?" Emma asked.

"Well," said Jiho, "it said that 'her people' had acquired a videotape from the security camera at the museum, and they verified the family has an accent from the southwest of South Korea, the Jeolla dialect to be specific. There are a number of dialects in South Korea that sort of align with the province boundaries, but not exactly. I read up on it. The Southwestern region, the city of Gwangju, and the area below it, for historical reasons, speak in a specific way. In particular, they pronounce the vowel 'a' differently, but it's more than that. There are also grammatical differences in some verb structures and variations in vocabulary."

"There are a lot of regional differences in pronunciation in American English, too," added Theo. "It's possible to guess the approximate childhood location from the speech of most people who grew up in the United States. Regional variation includes vowel pronunciation and vocabulary choices."

"Margo also said," began Migel, "that there have been rumors for a few years now of people who lived near a national park in South Korea who could communicate with thought. There are so many national parks in South Korea that it wasn't worth investigating. However, the only national park in South Korea where the Jeolla dialect is spoken is the country's smallest national park: Wolchulsan National Park. So, we are going to get a location file on small towns in that area."

"Oh!" said Binh, who registered shock. "We have a lot to do here yet. Are we supposed to leave here soon?"

"Loosely," said Migel. "We did cover that last night. We thought that… some of us should go with Jiho to South Korea and explore that lead, and others of us should stay here on Crete. Margo is allowing us to figure out the details ourselves, such as who goes and when. We know a person here who would like some translation help, and there needs to be an official explanation of things. Without telling anyone what they should do, we actually thought that Theo would like the linguistic work there is to do here, Emma would like the archaeology hunt, and Binh would be very helpful with the psychological work to be done. We are all open to suggestions. Of course, that was just an idea."

"I'd like to stay, and I'd like to have Adem stay too for the analytic help and pattern work," said Emma, looking at Adem. "But otherwise, it's a good suggestion."

"I would like to stay as well," said Binh.

"I definitely want to be here a while longer," said Theo. "Are you guys willing to go with Jiho?" he asked, looking at Migel and Alec, who were seated near each other.

"Yeah, but we thought of taking Adem, too. That was the ideal we thought of last night, but we were going to run it by you guys this morning."

"I feel so popular," said Adem. "Thanks, guys, but I'd like to stay here, and not just because we get to eat cheese at breakfast every day, which I love." He smiled. "I'm interested in how this situation here gets managed. I've been thinking a lot about our obligations in this, um, predicament. Do you need a visa for Korea?"

"Not with a U.S. passport," answered Migel, "and proof of a ticket out of the country within ninety days."

"Well, if you guys can hang here with us for a few more days, that would help us a lot. We have some brain functioning to understand. Maybe you can take off sometime after the weekend?" suggested Binh.

"That sounds smart," said Migel. "I don't know how much our financiers care, but a plane ticket bought too close to the departure date is normally pretty pricey. As far as the trip goes, our idea was to kind of bill ourselves as college friends. Alec and I would be getting shown around by our Korean friend—a visiting-the-homeland kind of trip. It's summer. We'll seem like any other group of young tourists, and three is very believable and manageable. One hotel room required."

"All the more reason to be three people instead of four," said Adem.

"To be clear to the rest of you," said Jiho, "I've never been to Asia before, and I think I read Korean at, like, a sixth-grade level. I'm basically used to talking to my family and the people in our neighborhood."

"That is a lot more than we can do, Ji. You can understand and talk, and that's invaluable," said Adem. "And didn't you say that you come from an area called Korea Town?"

"I do," said Jiho, smiling. It's always nice to have others remember. "I am from Palisades Park, New Jersey. It's one of the biggest, if not the biggest, Korean American communities in the U.S."

"Well, that is so much more Korean experience than I have. I eat bibimbap and beef bulgogi a few times a year, and I order from the menu in English," said Adem. "You're going to be amazingly helpful, Jiho. I think that leg of this project would be impossible without you."

Jiho seemed pleased, thought Emma. He was handsome when he smiled. Often, it was hard to read his face, but now he looked happy. He actually looked content and proud.

"Great," said Migel. "If we are set then on the travel, the next order of business concerns what we should say to Margo. Maybe I just feel guilty, but I feel like she knows that I know more than I am saying."

"Actually, can we continue this conversation on the lady porch in fifteen?" asked Alec.

"Gladly," said Emma. "See you on 'the lady porch,' but please pass that pitcher of coffee before you go." Alec moved the pitcher and stood up to go. Emma poured herself more coffee from the insulated carafe that came her way. Adem had a second cup as well. The rapid breakfast eaters stood up and left. The conversation resumed among Adem, Binh, and Emma. "This will be good, right?" said Emma.

"I think so," said Binh. "I'm sorry to miss the next adventure, but we can't all just walk out of here. They were right to think about splitting the group up. We did, too. It makes sense to divide and conquer. As well, I'm glad you are staying with us, Adem. You had some good ideas last night."

"Wow, just last night?" asked Adem.

"No!" said Binh. "You know what I mean. Also, we should try to meet up with the Ps again as a smaller group. Us and Theo, of course. We need to figure out what we should do next."

"I was working on that this morning," offered Emma. "Matching symbols, coming up with a story, and figuring out how to protect the island."

They talked a little longer, and then Adem and the women stood up to go. They walked down the stone steps to the garden path, and Emma said, "Let's bring up the eye-tracking device again. If we don't need any more data—if we even ever did—maybe we can send the devices back now. It would be a smaller charge to send them from within the E.U."

"Yeah, let's bring that up," said Binh.

Emma thought about how well the group got along. She felt lucky. It would have been a less fun trip if one of them had been super annoying, or if two people had started sleeping together, or if someone had been one of those very fussy eaters. Emma kept the daydream going for a few seconds more and then realized that all of these things were unlikely on this trip, even though they were common in real life, because this group had been hand-picked. They had been carefully vetted. She made a mental note to run this by Binh later, as the lady's porch was just ahead. Within one minute, all seven were assembling themselves on the wooden porch of Binh and Emma's room. The morning sun shone between the slats above them, creating long shadowed strips of cooler and warmer places to sit.

Chapter 27: Jiho Bak

Jiho had been talking with Alec as they walked, but they had stopped, and now he was just thinking to himself. The group was on their way to their second meeting with the Papadakis clan. Jiho, Alec, and Migel had received their digital airplane tickets for a flight leaving in exactly one week. They would fly from Heraklion, Crete, to Munich, Germany, and then directly to Seoul, South Korea. Jiho had been elated when he found out he would visit South Korea, but his family dampened his enthusiasm slightly. When he had told them of the next leg of his journey, they had been more suspicious than happy and more inquisitive than helpful.

After the first meeting with the Papadakis family, the group of seven had all agreed not to tell anyone they maintained contact with about their exact activities. Locations could be discussed and eye-tracking, but nothing mind-related. This made all conversations that weren't with casual friends seem dodgy and vague. It made eye-tracking seem overly valuable. The group turned down the driveway. They could see the front door.

Eleni Papadakis was at the door as soon as they arrived. "*Geiá sou*," she said as they entered, "hello." Dr. Lefteris Papadakis appeared at her side. "Nice to see you again, please come in." The group entered, expressed their happiness, and were seated out on the veranda for a second time. Drinks were served, and the group began with a talk about where and what they had eaten. Jiho's mind drifted to the fact that a Ph.D. in archaeology and a revered museum worker wanted his opinion and input on neuroscientific discoveries and current trends. Before he wandered too far in this direction, the conversation shifted to discussing the topic at hand. Dr. Papadakis prompted Jiho and Migel to explain thought formation in the brain as they had promised that they would when they were leaving the last time.

"We have a way to explain it, sir, that supports your ideas as well," began Migel. Binh and Emma leaned in, as this was new to them as well. Migel selected his words carefully and spoke more slowly than he normally did. "There has recently been more evidence that thought and language are separate. In fact, many of our cognitive functions appear to be separate from our use of language. We believe that what your wife and daughter are able to do is send and receive thought in the form of visual images. The historical record of language may explain how your hieroglyphics connect to this. Jiho and I can help with information about how brains work."

"Do humans need language to speak?" asked Dr. Papadakis directly.

"No. Thought is not dependent on language," began Migel again. "We know that now, although the two are often connected. Brain imaging over the past thirty years has explained a lot. fMRI technology has been particularly helpful since it was invented in 1990. For example, it has been demonstrated repeatedly that when people who suffer from brain damage from accidents or strokes lose the ability to produce language, they can still think. Additionally, while people use language regions of their brain when they read, they do not when they listen to music or compute in math. We talked about an inner voice when we saw you last. A person's inner voice is connected to their sense of self. A person's sense of themselves starts to develop in early childhood, and the progression is fast in the early years, as is vocabulary acquisition. It continues at a different, slower pace throughout a person's lifetime. When we think about ourselves, it is our medial prefrontal cortex (mPFC) that is activated. Our inner voice is our internal conversation partner. This is, well... talking to oneself in a human language that we understand. Thought is different. Thought can be in images or in words. It can exist as a mental representation."

"But what is thought considered to be?" asked Emma. "What is thought made of?"

"Human brains have many, many neurons," said Jiho, "about 100 billion of them. They emit chemicals called neurotransmitters that essentially contact neurons nearby. Thoughts are essentially a wave of these neurotransmitters. Recently, some researchers used fMRI to capture a person's brain activity to look at a physical representation of a brain wave that represents a thought. It is quite amazing. The non-invasive technique of fMRI was used to record the brain waves of people that were then decoded and translated into speech. It is cumbersome, but it works. A set of neurotransmissions can be translated into verbal speech that captures the idea, though not the exact syntax. To ensure that the fMRI records brain waves of thought alone and not speech, some of the tests involved participants watching movies without sound. The viewers are asked to think about what they see, and their brain waves get recorded and then decoded and translated into speech. Guess what? The speech transcript at the end is basically a verbal summary of what the viewer watched."

"That's unbelievable!" said Dr. Papadakis.

"It is. It is also time-consuming, but one day, helpful medical devices for impaired people can exist, and we might be able to understand the level of a person's coma. Imagine that thinking is a representation of what brains feel emotionally or perceive with the senses or design as a plan in order to achieve through a certain action." He let that sink in a moment. "Thinking is also just an electrochemical process. Some thoughts simply appear and disappear, but others can be stored as a memory, which is also a physical change. Neuron connections get generated as the structural molecules change."

"Some studies have also looked into visual versus verbal thinking," added Migel. "It appears that visual thinking is more deeply rooted and less controllable. There are ideas out there from writers, thinkers, and scholars that describe thinking as existing in the primitive part of the brain. Think of a brain as three separate parts. The innermost part controls our most basic needs for survival:

breathing, eating, sleeping, and the desires for self-protection and reproduction. This section is called our Primitive Brain. On top of it is a layer that is responsible for our most basic emotions, such as fear and aggression. This is called the Limbic Layer. On top of that layer is the outermost layer, a prefrontal cortex that is sometimes called the Executive Brain, and it is here that our ability to reason, experience, and explain complex emotions resides. It is thought by many that dreaming comes from the primitive brain and occurs for many reasons, such as the need to process emotions and memories. While the specifics and underlying reasons that we dream remain unclear, researchers are actively investigating brain images of individuals during sleep. There is data that we have observed already or are confident about based on earlier studies. For example, it has been observed that significant chemical alterations take place during the REM cycle of sleep. We also know that there is a lot of activity during dreams in the part of the brain that processes emotions. We know that all images that are dreamed about come from the brain, as human senses do not receive input while sleeping. We know that humans need sleep to live, and we know that all humans dream, even if they don't remember their dreams. Anyone who has ever owned a dog has watched it dream in its sleep, which demonstrates again that dreams (so thought) can occur without language. Accordingly, many posit that dreams come from this inner, primitive part of the brain, and they occur in images (although words can be attached to them quickly upon waking if the images are remembered). Current research then all supports your idea that the hieroglyphics could be tangible representations of visual thinking, and specifically of thought." Migel finished.

"Humans have been around longer than they have had language, right? Is there evidence of that?" asked Binh.

"Well… Homo erectus, humans as we know them today, have been around for the past 300,000 years," said Theo. Many scientists believe that it was not until this time that humans used oral language because of the lacking, physical anatomical parts in the brain and vocal cords necessary to make sounds and connect images and ideas with words. Others think that this could have happened much, much earlier. We just don't know yet. I suspect that first, there was likely thought, then hand movements that allowed communication within seeing range, and then language, which allowed for communication outside of seeing range. It is certainly possible that some people maintained clear, visual thought images well after verbal thinking became more common, and these people both standardized the symbol for certain images and relayed information through thoughts by writing in these symbols. We are still working on a hypothesis explaining how one mind communicates visual images to another, but we'd like more data."

"If we could write down a list of words that can be sent versus not sent, that would help," said Migel.

"They are ideas, not words," interrupted Dr. Papadakis. "Ideas that get conveyed without complex grammar, as I understand it—no verb tenses, no pronouns, just concepts. I had questioned Eleni a lot about it when I first realized what she could do. Then it became just another talent, like doing math quickly in one's head, playing a flute, or throwing a ball well. There are many talents that I do not possess." He chuckled. "Only recently, after the experience with the Korean woman, did I realize that I had misunderstood what was sent as communication, that it was an idea that may just be a thought. Migel was explaining that ideas are represented as images, not words, in dreams, and possibly sent from our primitive brains.

"I should tell you that I reached out to a psychic in Athens once when I was there—this is not the kind of thing that I would do on my home island. I even said that I came from someplace else. I did not want a trace of this, but I did want to know if people who believed they were psychic thought they acquired information through images or through language. That was as far as I got, and later, when I was home, I started wondering about our hieroglyphics as symbols and ideas, as opposed to sounds and phonemes. I want to understand more, and I would love to help decipher the hieroglyphics, but I do not want a lot of attention here. Eleni and Cora do not want a lot of attention, and so previously, I have not discussed this with other people. I have known Hartwin Kolsch for over forty years, and I trust him, but still, he only knows small parts. I explained some of my ideas to him, but not enough for him to understand exactly, and I did not mention my family." He paused, perhaps wondering what the young scientists were thinking. After taking a sip of water, Jiho spoke.

""I know that there are sometimes occurrences that cannot be explained with scientific knowledge. We refer to them as 'paranormal' in English. The prefix *para* comes from Greek, I believe," Jiho saw Dr. Papadakis nod, and he continued, "We attach it to English words to add the meaning of 'outside' or 'beyond' the word that it is attached to. Events that occur outside or beyond our known scientific understanding are those that we cannot explain other than from folk tales, oral stories, or other non-scientific bodies of knowledge, such as the tales that all old cultures have. Paranormal events are those that there are no laws of nature or science that we know of that can be applied to explain them."

Jiho's comments seemed to encourage Dr. Papadakis to go on. He said, "From the psychic, I learned that for my purposes, there are three different types of activity that are distinct. Clairaudience is the ability to hear paranormally, clairvoyance is the ability to see paranormally, and clairsentience is the ability to feel paranormally. So, I came away thinking that Eleni and Cora have clairsentience. They can feel or know what another transmits. I think that this occurs because of their ability to receive thoughts as images, and these images translate to feelings but not words. I think they come from the innermost part of the brain that you mentioned, the one that is under the part that creates and uses language, but I cannot prove it. I am wondering if our hieroglyphics are the images themselves, as I have mentioned. It would make sense if the hieroglyphic symbols explained quantities of stored, traded, or sold items. Manpower and archaeological products could be accounted for. Many scholars before me have come to this conclusion about the hieroglyphics as well."

Dr. Papadakis settled back into his chair.

"What specifically can we help you with, Dr. Papadakis?" asked Binh.

"It was a great help already to have heard from Jiho and Migel. I don't want to involve the people that I know here who can explain such things. We have a very good university here, but I don't want to start asking too many questions. There is a published, comprehensive set of hieroglyphics that have been found on artifacts in Crete. I'd like to look at them with you and see what you think," said Dr. Papadakis. "I will show you what is suggested by others, such as the symbols that seem to represent a quantity, one that seems to mean 'amount paid' or 'sum.' I can summarize for you the work that has been done, starting with Arthur Evans, the tireless British archaeologist. He was born in 1851 and did not come to Crete until 1894, but he later returned after his initial visit to stay for a quarter century, when he dug up the Palace of Knossos and made tremendous discoveries. We have all built upon his work."

"I would be immensely grateful to have the opportunity to learn from you," gushed Emma. "And I do maintain contact with some people from the anthropology department at Ohio State University if that helps in any way."

"Us as well," said Adem, gesturing to the people on his right and left sides. The group explained the plan. Dr. Papadakis marveled at the speed at which more information about the Korean family at the museum had been obtained. He was nervous until Jiho promised they would reveal nothing about their time in Crete. Adem, Theo, Binh, and Emma made plans to meet with him in a few days, on Monday. He recommended readings for them until then, and the group left his patio and began ascending the road to Archanes once again.

Chapter 28: Samir Namboothiri

The headquarters for the United States Department of Defense, generally referred to simply as *The Pentagon*, has an All-domain Anomaly Resolution Office (AARO) that, according to their website, has a process in place as of the fall of 2023 for employees past and present to report securely and digitally on their first-hand knowledge of anything relating to Unidentified Anomalous Phenomena (UAP). Samir finds this to be seriously entertaining. He would be respectful, of course, but he deeply believes that some UAP are deflating balloons carrying spy cams and that some have too vague of a description to ever be identified. He feels confident that none are aliens in spacecraft. He knows of many countries and groups that the U.S. government has annoyed over the years and that some enjoy playing games with Americans, while others go to great lengths to spy on American military bases and support structures. Samir is adamant that until there is evidence of higher-order life on other planets (he does expect to find protozoa and the like at some point), he is just not intrigued. More than that, he is frustrated and embarrassed by it. Samir likes proof and likes people who look for proof, and he assumes that there is an explanation that can be found. Therefore, although it would surprise many people if they knew, Samir is a believer in paranormal communication. The explanation is simple: he has proof.

On July 15th, Samir was sitting at his office desk, looking out his window and watching the sky. He didn't always come to work on Saturdays, but he did with more regularity than other people. It was very quiet at the right time. Saturday mornings were great for running errands as many people slept in. Grocery stores and highways were uncrowded, and as the sun crossed the sky and they filled up, people who had dropped by their office in the mornings had left, and the office buildings were particularly quiet. Samir watched the sky and thought. Then he checked his email and Slack again and wondered if he could call Margo on a Saturday afternoon or if that seemed too presumptive. He decided rather quickly that he could not. He did want to go over some questions and ideas that the two groups should consider, look out for, and explore. He sighed and decided that an email might be more appropriate. Samir understands communication very well; it's the touchy parts with on and off hours, women versus men, and colleagues versus subordinates that make it all tricky territory.

Samir's job relates to secure communication transfer among entities in diverse geographical locations. All militaries and all governments that have the bandwidth to consider this option are very interested in it. At DARPA, Samir works with all kinds of communications. He is a radio wave expert. He is excellent with a HAM radio, of course, although they are not officially used by the military. He works with the Military Auxiliary Radio System (MARS), which is still active and dates back to 1925, the Airborne

Radio System (SINCGARS), which hops frequencies, and the short-range tactical AN/PRC-126. He is an expert at using, fixing, and addressing issues with these communication devices, but his main research focuses on Mesh Networks. American off-gridders often use a version that has limited functionality and a small battery to communicate without a cell phone tower or satellite. Samir has a serious system. His construction of it and work with it are classified. In addition, he does sort-of-sanctioned research into the abilities of living people who work to verify claims of telepathic abilities. He was a background figure in some of the studies that were conducted, two of which Jiho and Migel know about. As with any quality research institution, he has relatively free reign to explore ideas, and he has sufficient funding. Samir repays this privilege with hard work and results.

Qualitative research methods and assurances have been described in academic literature for decades, with many seminal voices in agreement. At the most basic level, qualitative research is about asking a question, gathering data, and then using the gathered data to answer the question. It produces knowledge from the very start, whereas quantitative research identifies and utilizes pre-existing knowledge. There is very little verifiable pre-existing knowledge on clairsentience. In contrast, there is a lot of research on clairaudience, the ability to hear paranormally, as many religious people claim to hear voices, as do schizophrenics and other mentally ill patients, certain self-proclaimed psychics, and a few political leaders in history. Some indigenous people hear knowledge from plants, and others talk to dolphins, and there are thousands of other claims. Samir, however, is a "doubting Thomas" until he has proof, and so to date, he is only interested in clairsentience and only in those abilities that can be proven. There are sometimes abilities attributed to clairsentience that are not interesting to Samir. He does not compile information, for example, on people who sense energy. He doesn't believe that people have energy or an aura around them; and if they do, he has never seen it or felt it and has no way of determining its validity. He also feels ambivalent about people who claim to experience physical sensations that others do not (such as a tight feeling in the chest as a ghost enters a room); again, it is a problem of proof. In addition, Samir is not even a little impressed with the claimed abilities of emotional awareness, such as those who "sense" another's emotional state or "sense" an unseeable being nearby. And yet, all these abilities are associated with clairsentience; people with these abilities are typically considered to be clairsentient. Samir, however, is uniquely intrigued by those people who have intuitive knowledge, that is, people who acquire knowledge when there is no logical explanation for how they came to have it. Samir keeps a database of everyone he knows of who falls into this category.

Samir knows of an elderly Hopi woman in New Mexico, two Haitians in Boston, a couple from Nigeria living in Texas, and a fisherman in Nova Scotia who is originally from Ecuador. They all have the same abilities. He has had leads to follow up on in Kerala, India, Nairobi, Kenya, the northern islands of the Philippines, an island in Greece, and South Korea. He has verified all of the others personally and would like to visit Kerala personally, but he hired Margo to build a team and work for him in order to investigate the other areas. These other areas had complications associated with them that would require time and some skills that Samir doesn't have. The time required was the hurdle that led to him hiring Margo because the search for people with intuitive knowledge and people capable of mind-knowing was not specifically a DARPA-funded expedition. It is a benefactor-funded one. A very clever Malaysian-American businessman, investor, and philanthropist named Syed Bin Abdullah makes it possible. It is that simple. Because Samir works at DARPA and has a high-clearance position, he has access to interesting databases, information, and people, and because he has a supporter of his interest, he is able to explore it. Nothing that he is doing is explicitly illegal, and he never uses his professional credentials, time, or money in order to pursue his personal interests. They are entirely separate except for the fact that he only has one brain, so what he knows, if not classified, is a usable resource.

Chapter 29: Theo Auclair

Studying linguistics was a common choice for an African-American college student in the US when Theo began his trajectory; the statistics expressed that clearly. However, Theo loved what he read, learned, and discussed in class, and he had a few ideas about how to make money in the field. His first choice after finishing his Ph.D. was to secure an appointment as a professor at one of the universities in California. He had already been accepted to a doctoral program in the fall in Connecticut. It was the college that had offered the best financial package last spring, and thanks to this opportunity, he wouldn't be dragging his undergraduate loans with him when classes began. New England froze and sleeted its way through the winter, and the warmth didn't return until late spring. This didn't quite align with Theo's blood, which was 100% equatorial, but he would manage. He had survived Massachusetts, after all, and Connecticut was further south.

Theo had devoured his time in Kenya, surprised to feel much more American than African but nonetheless comfortable. Crete had seemed ideal. It had the comforts and security he was accustomed to and the temperature of both air and people that he preferred. Theo lay back in his porch chair with a hat tipped over his face, and he thought about language. The last few days had yielded some very interesting thoughts. He and Emma, Binh, and Adem had toured the Heraklion Archeological Museum again. They had spoken with

Alec more about the evolution of language from a biological standpoint and other major transitions in human history that had spurred radical change. Alec started rather far back but cited a number of examples, such as the addition of DNA to RNA and the emergence of eukaryotes alongside prokaryotes. Theo had considered language as a biological aptitude before, of course, but never in such a serious context. How exactly language might have evolved has been a question among linguists (and others) for centuries.

Animals can clearly communicate, but none can quite do what humans can. Human words, though limited in every language, can be combined in an unlimited number of ways. In addition to the concrete and routine "I want to eat now" communication of a household pet, humans can say, "How about having dinner later this evening, say about 8 pm?" Humans can express abstract ideas, like the hypothetical production and use of a new tool, and consider another's viewpoint and how it may impact future actions. The human language capacity is unique. The age-old question is, why? What made humans develop language as they did, and why is their linguistic ability so unique? This seemed very important to think about now because it might give insight into why language shaping existed.

After years of school assignments and thinking, Theo had invested both lecture time and hours of reading in trying to grasp what he thought was likely the reason humans have language. He concluded that it's a combination of the larynx and the brain.

In the late 1960s, it was suspected that the human larynx was unique among other mammals, the larynx being essentially a straw in one's throat that enables sound. Some refer to it as a 'voice box.' It carries air from the throat to the trachea and then the lungs. Human babies and other mammals are born with a larynx high up in their throat, which allows for simultaneous breathing and swallowing, a convenience not enjoyed by humans over age two. Humans acquire a lower larynx proportionally as they grow and so at about age two, when most humans begin to speak, the larynx has dropped into the neck. Despite the great idea that this was unique to humans, it was discovered in the 1990s that other mammals also have a lowered larynx, particularly in the males of certain species. Another group of mammals was found to have a larynx that can be lowered at certain times for the express purpose of making specific kinds of vocalizations, such as the ones made when one is trying to act large and scary in order to ward off a predator. This ruled out the idea that a lowered larynx was the sole reason why only humans have the ability to produce complex sounds and language, but it doesn't mean it's not beneficial. Apes and monkeys can lower their larynx temporarily to sound older, larger, and more frightening but still lack the vocal membranes attached to the larynx and a brain that enables complex language production and rapid acquisition. The two together seem to be the magic combination. Humans produce language with these, and those who cannot make sounds can speak with their hands. These are universal traits among humans, just as any human language is for any human baby. Bring an infant from any human population to any other human population, and that baby will become a native speaker of the language of the people it grows up around. That never ceases to amaze people; it's fascinating.

So burrowing through Theo's thoughts now was the impetus for the development of human language. Specifically, he was considering if it seemed reasonable that variations of communication existed. Every known human population had language in more or less the same manner, coupling either hands or a larynx with the brain, but what prompted the need? It could have been simply communication, Theo thought, or perhaps the driving force was reproduction, clan forming for warfare, or the development of the internal voice. Theo considered academic studies. There was concrete evidence that when brain damage impairs an individual's language from a processing and production level, multiple forms of complex thought can still occur. These studies have led to the belief that thought has to be separate from language, so why couldn't thought have its own concrete and representational form? It could, Theo reasoned. It seems redundant if language exists, but Theo started to contemplate how thought could be an image language only and how those pictograms could be transferred to another person. Hadn't he heard that dreams were a series of pictograms that the brain gave meaning to? These would be the same ones. A pictogram, also called a pictograph, is an image that represents words or phrases. Theo knew that the most famous of such images were the Egyptian hieroglyphics, which originated around 3200 B.C.E. and remained in use until the 5th century. Theo adjusted his position in his chair in the sun and realized that everyone assumed that the Egyptians spoke and that their pictograms were their "writing system."

"Do you have sunscreen on, Theo?" came Emma's voice as she approached. "You'll fry sitting there all afternoon."

Theo opened his eyes and held up a hand across his brow, watching her come to his porch.

"Hey, Emma, I was just thinking," began Theo, "is it possible that the Ancient Egyptians used pictograms to express thoughts as well? I read that the first thousand years of hieroglyphics look like representations of recognizable animals, people, and objects—could they be just that?"

"That's a cool idea, Theo, but no," said Emma. "There are really four periods of Egyptian hieroglyphics. 'Old Egyptian' does not have much grammar, so I know it seems like *Glóssa Schimatízontas*, but the Old Egyptian pictograms are mostly found on items in or related to pyramid burials. The next thousand years of hieroglyphics are markedly different in that they seem to have been stylized so they could be written much more quickly with a brush and ink on papyrus. These are mostly found on documents for legal or literary purposes, autobiographies, and temple inscriptions. Many people are interested in the third and fourth periods of hieroglyphics, but I like the older ones. Egyptian hieroglyphics were always symbols for phonetic sounds as opposed to concepts, and experts claim that the use of letters much later was not an evolution from the pictures."

"But how do we know for sure? Couldn't—"

"Because," Emma interrupted, "in 1799, the Rosetta Stone was found."

"I've heard of it, but I don't remember exactly what it is," said Theo.

"Literally one of the coolest archaeological finds ever. It was found by accident by soldiers in Napoleon's army at the end of the 1700s when they were in Egypt, looking to take over the land in that area. The Rosetta Stone is a huge piece of polished stone a few feet high, and it's part of a much larger tablet. The tablet is like a marketing campaign for King Ptolemy V of Egypt. It explains some of his past great deeds and some planned future great deeds, such as tax reduction, and there is support for elevating the king to an even higher status. The same message was carved in three different ways: in hieroglyphics, in the script version of that, and in the Greek alphabet. By doing this, literate priests, people, and government officials could all read it. The translators working on the stone knew Ancient Greek and were able to not only decipher the message but to be the first to announce that Egyptian hieroglyphics were alphabet letters and syllables, not images representing complete concepts or ideas, as people had previously imagined. The Rosetta Stone translators put together a list of hieroglyphs and their Greek counterparts, and this allowed for future translations. Without the Rosetta Stone, it's likely that no one would have figured out how to translate Egyptian hieroglyphics because people had certainly tried."

"I see," said Theo, a little disappointed. "Sounds like we need a Rosetta Stone."

"We do," said Emma. "But I'm still in awe of the communication that Eleni, Cora, and Viktoria have, even if it's not related to the hieroglyphics."

"Me too, but it is slow," said Theo. "I guess I thought that if mind-to-mind communication were ever possible, it would be better than speech. It would be faster, more secure, and more efficient. This seems more like having a flashlight and knowing Morse code."

"Ha!" Emma laughed. "You imagined something that evolved after oral language. I think this Language Shaping that they do, this *Glóssa Schimatízontas*, is either a remnant of a simultaneous stage that got out-competed, or it's a fluke gene that just sometimes pops up, you know, like when people have eyes that are two different colors, one green and one brown, for example. It's not common, but it happens. If there are people around who can do it, and we know of three, there are likely more. There is the Korean woman who was somehow on the same radio station as Eleni was, and—"

"That could be it!" interrupted Theo.

"What could be it?"

"Language Shaping could work on radio waves," said Theo.

"I thought humans can't detect radio waves?" asked Emma. "But I don't know much about waves."

"We can't. Maybe they can?" said Theo.

"I don't know. That's Migel and Jiho's department. Is it possible?" asked Emma.

"Not as far as I know. But I can't send a thought either," responded Theo. "Maybe some people have a way to transmit on radio waves? Eleni said that she can't send information very far and that the other person needs to be able to recognize the reception. Maybe they transmit and receive?"

The door to Jiho's room opened to the outside, and Migel, Alec, and Jiho came out mid-discussion. When they saw Emma and Theo on a nearby porch, they walked over to talk.

"Hey, you guys," said Alec. "We were just planning for South Korea. The Wi-Fi is very good and fast right now, and we wanted to work some things out. We downloaded a bunch of reading for the flights to add to the location file that Margo sent. What are you two up to?"

"We've been talking about Language Shaping. What do you guys know about radio waves? Is it possible that some people can hear them and use them to communicate?"

"No," said Jiho. "I don't think so. Radio waves are at the lower end of the electromagnetic spectrum. They can be a fraction of an inch long or hundreds of miles long. Human eardrums cannot hear radio waves in general, and it seems unlikely that some people have ears that can. I think there is another explanation."

"Wait, back up. What did you mean by 'in general'?" asked Emma.

"Look up the Frey Effect," said Jiho. "I know that's what it's called. It turns out that some people can hear microwaves. I don't know how far-fetched it is that some who do could also hear some radio waves. It would be a disadvantage, I would think, in evolution and not an advantage."

"So, you don't think that is the explanation for Eleni, Cora, and Viktoria?"

"No," said Jiho, shaking his head.

"I don't either," said Alec, "but I do have an idea." Everyone turned to see him a little better.

"What is it?" asked Theo.

"Humans have minor variations, right? Minor ones. Some people have longer toes, longer eyelashes, larger nostrils, or bigger ears, and some have differences that cannot be seen, right? Some people are just better at hearing tones in music, for example," said Alec. "Well, research is repeatedly supporting the fact that most human genetic variation occurs within a given population, and only a small amount of variation exists between various populations. Also, genetic variation is pretty evenly distributed; human groups are mostly all the same with the same subsets of prodigies and problems. Take two humans from anywhere in the world, take samples of their DNA, and you will find that their genetic variation is 0.1 percent, meaning that only one base pair out of every thousand base pairs of DNA is actually different."

"That's surprising, but keep going," said Emma.

"A person's genetic code, their DNA, tells the body how to grow and function, right? If a mutation—a change that occurs in the DNA during cell division—occurs, it creates a permanent change in the DNA sequence. You with me?" asked Alec. "Mutations are more common than you might think because so many letters have to be transcribed—remember the A-C and T-G pairings? A random gene mutation caused by an error in cell division that either replaces, adds, or removes a letter in the DNA sequence could cause a terrible problem and kill the person, or it could make that person's survival easier. If it does the latter, that person becomes more likely to pass the variation on from one generation to the next. What was once a mutation becomes a normal part of the human genome."

"Hmm," mumbled Jiho.

"So, I've been wondering if being able to send a thought wasn't at one point a mutation that has now become something that is passed on in the genes of some people. Maybe this gene requires linkage, or maybe it requires both alleles. I feel like it must be recessive, but it exists as a possibility. Because of what I said first about the very little difference among all humans genetically, and the fact that maybe someone in Korea and some people in Kenya can do something like the language shaping that we see here, maybe that is evidence of a mutation that is now part of the genetic code. While some mutations cause a cleft palate, webbed fingers, or cancer, others protect people from disease or maybe, in this case, give improved communication capabilities."

"Cancer is a mutation?" asked Emma.

"That's what you took away from that?" asked Theo.

"Not entirely, but the rest of it made sense," responded Emma. "I thought that cancer was self-induced from the sun, or chemical exposure, or there was a gene to get it."

"Some kinds of cancer are caused by genetic mutations. Others are environmental, which is why we are all supposed to eat well, exercise, not smoke, and avoid too much radiation. Obviously, if you think you broke your arm, go get it X-rayed, but never play with an X-ray machine. Look, I simplified a lot, but the basic idea works, and I think that Language Shaping is a likely variation in many more human populations than just the ones that we know about."

"You're saying the original mutation could be something that occurred randomly?" asked Theo.

"It could be. Of the many things that occurred randomly in nature—some worked out, and some did not," said Alec. "We all have the ability to think visually, and sometimes, when we are thinking of a specific person, they call us, right? Maybe that occurs because all humans have a very underground, not very usable way to connect with each other mentally, but only when the DNA sequence reads in an atypical way is this ability actually a viable tool that a human can access. Instead of saying, 'Oh Mum, I was just thinking of you when you called,' Cora can literally send a thought to her mother." Everyone was quiet. "Maybe doing so is the result of a mutation."

"How plausible is this idea?" asked Jiho. "Could it only exist by accident?"

"It's possible, and it's plausible. I don't know how likely it is. I know of some interesting studies about the CCR5 gene. It's a gene for coating human immune cells with a protein. Some viruses infect humans by binding with this protein and a few others. Having a mutation in the CCR5 gene that changes the structure or expression of the gene means that the coating is a little different. Populations that have numerous people with a mutated CCR5 gene have decreased HIV infection because it is one of the viruses that needs to bind to the proteins on the surfaces of immune cells. So, imagine that another kind of mutation could be responsible for how accessible human thought is. Clearly, we all don't have the exact capabilities when it comes to thinking. Maybe the people who speak about translating their thoughts into speech have it a little harder, and maybe some people have it a little easier in that they have greater access than others to their own thoughts. This could be a fluke from an error in mitosis or meiosis, but it could also be a remnant of an older way of doing things, or it could be a mutation from ages ago that eased survival and so became favored, as only people who live long enough to reproduce, and do, are the ones who pass on their genes. The DNA of anyone who can shape language would have to be studied, and honestly, that brings questions and attention, and there are a lot of ethical obligations to consider. Aside from exploitation, what are the possible outcomes?"

"That is the central cultural anthropological question," said Emma. "Is it more ethical to bring the modern world to an uncontacted group of people, or is it more ethical to leave them alone? All the comforts and ease of modern cultures come with the attached cost of problems, illnesses, and the destruction of the social and cultural systems that hold people together, not to mention bacteria and viruses that isolated peoples have no immunity to. The bottom line is that when all of the ramifications are calculated, intervening in a people's way of life has never proven historically to have been a good idea. Should we expose a private group to genetic testing for the curiosity of humanity? I say absolutely not. We focus on the hieroglyphics and get out."

"There are many Hopi who would agree with Emma. They would attest to the fact that the trade-off for modernization was not worth it for us. We lost land and culture, and our language is dying quickly. Many Native people suffer from depression, drinking, and the diseases that come from not eating well. Reservation life is desired by very few. Most native people do not consider themselves improved because of the intervention of foreign people. I'm not trying to make anyone feel bad, but contacting other people and saying, 'Hey, look what we have! Show us what you have!' inevitably leads to one culture telling the other that they can be 'improved' with a freer government, a better standard of living, equal rights for men and women, or by changing their lifestyle and believing in a new higher being. It's always one group imposing their ideas of betterment on another group, and it is usually forced. I say we tread very, very carefully with this."

"But Margo is sending a group to South Korea. She knows something, and whoever is behind her knows too that there is something worth knowing."

"But she will only know for certain what we tell her," answered Theo. "So again, let's respond judiciously." Alec's ideas had made sense to him. Subjugation seemed to be a routine response for humans, and the more he thought about it, the stronger he felt they should work to protect the Language Shapers, who might just be the victims of a cool genetic mutation that others would kill for.

Chapter 30: Binh Tran

Binh was staring at her laptop screen. She had searched her stored articles for psychology, Sigmund Freud, and telepathy; she was sure that she had read something years ago when hunting for fodder for a research paper, and like any good student, she downloaded and saved journal articles that were currently or might in the future be useful. They were all organized on her desktop in folders; she just had to remember what she had been writing when she saw it and find that group of publications. It took a little while, but she found the article that she remembered reading. In the 1930s, Sigmund Freud proposed that telepathy could have predated language in the course of evolution. *This was his idea,* thought Binh. She kept reading the article. Some later psychiatrists posited that all humans continued to be born with the ability, but the development of language and of an independent ego displaced access to it. People who fail to develop an independent ego often become schizophrenic, and many of these people claim telepathic abilities, which are generally considered to be a symptom of their schizophrenia. Binh pondered an idea. *What if Freud had been correct almost a century ago?*

Binh had other papers in the files on her desktop, proposing that all human thoughts are generated through analogy-making. Clearly, some people just understand and can create analogies better than others. The ability to make and use analogies is considered an integral component of critical thinking, and again, some people are better at critical thinking than others. If creating and using analogies helps a person to communicate complex ideas and ignites creative thinking by highlighting new connections and patterns (it does), then maybe somehow it allows access to mental communication as well. Perhaps everyone has the innate ability to do what these Greek women do, and it's accessed through analogy-making. Maybe it is simply an accessibility issue. If a human develops within the range of normalcy, then the ability remains dormant, overshadowed by language. If a human develops differently, maybe they gain access to these hidden yet innate abilities. It made sense to her. It was possible. There was a nagging question, though: how could this have remained undiscovered for so long?

Binh thought next of the many times that she had been studying late at night and woken up the next day with a better and clearer understanding of what she had been studying the night before. Many people have experienced and written about this. In one of her undergrad classes, she learned about oneirology, the scientific study of dreams. She remembered a required reading on a German professor of organic chemistry who, in the mid-1800s, had been the main creator of the theory of chemical structure. Seven years after that, he proposed that the structure of benzene, previously an enigma, had the structure of a ring. This discovery revolutionized organic chemistry as a field. In commemoration of him, a quarter century later, the professor stated in his speech that the idea of the ring structure occurred to him because he had a brief daydream of a snake with its own tail in its mouth, forming a circle. The professor woke up and considered a circular ring structure. The implication was that dreams could connect the subconscious with the conscious. Binh's ideas clicked one after the other, and Binh was just about done fully forming a hypothesis for *Glóssa Schimatízontas*. What did they say that meant, "language shaping?" when Emma entered the room.

"Hey!" Emma said.

"Hey," returned Binh. "That was a long walk."

"Actually, I came back a little while ago. I stopped to talk to Theo when I saw him on his porch. Then Jiho and Alec came by, and we all started talking, and guess what? Alec has a proposition, an explanation of language shaping. It's a good idea—a hypothesis, maybe even," said Emma. "Isn't that great?"

"Great!" replied Binh. "I just put together an idea myself. I wonder if they are the same?"

*****

Later, but still before dinner, Alec explained his hypothesis to everyone, and Binh explained hers. Their ideas were not the same. Alec proposed a genetic mutation that occurred in some humans across the globe that became part of that person's genetic code and thus inheritable. Binh posited a dormant innate ability existed in all humans that some humans were able to utilize. The others were impressed.

Migel wrote to Margo again, explaining that although they had evidence for what they were calling "language shaping," a loose translation of what it was being called on Crete in Greek, they were still working on understanding the details. He elaborated on the ideas of the team going to South Korea and proposed that Emma be the touchpoint for the group in Crete, while he remained the communicator for the South Korea group. In a final paragraph, he had, as the team had decided, asked Margo who she worked for. He also asked what would be done with the information that was imparted to her about people who had telepathic powers.

The team agreed to gather at 8:30 pm and walk to a group dinner. At home, a group of seven people was not easy in a restaurant. It required a reservation or at least a "wait here while I get a table ready." On Crete, it seemed normal. People were often going out with friends, meeting family, walking about, and socializing in large groups. They decided on the small family-run taverna up the road, whose patio was filled with large wooden tables amidst a jungle of plants. Migel pointed out that this taverna had incredible *apaki*, pork meat soaked in olive oil and herbs and then roasted in a wood-fired oven. He and Theo were interested in becoming connoisseurs of the art of *apaki*. It was that good. The group walked and talked up the partially cobbled streets.

Chapter 31: Alec Nehoitewa

"Our penultimate dinner!" said Emma when they had arrived and been seated. "And who doesn't love an opportunity to use that word?" Emma was like a diamond, thought Alec. She's all sparkly and desirable, but not in a "too much" kind of way. She resonated well with most people and many situations.

"It's a great word, Emma, but it's going to take second place for now to that 'o word' that Binh used earlier," said Migel.

"Oneirology?" said Binh.

"Yes. I'm going to work that into conversations periodically from now on," Migel said. "Is that what you want to study, Binh?"

"Oh no," said Binh, and she looked down. But then she began to speak, lifting her head and looking at everyone. "Honestly, I'd like to work as a clinical psychologist. I often tell people that I am interested in research because it is so fast, easy, and vague, and I am interested in it, but on the side. What I really want to do is work with teenagers. I'm sure that dreams will come up in my work, but it won't be my focus. I'm very interested in identity, and I hope to work with middle school children and teens. I have an idea for my dissertation already, and I'd like to develop it into a book one day. My end goal is to open my own clinic, an old-school, private practice that helps people and takes insurance."

"Wow, Binh, that's amazing!" beamed Emma. "You're going to command BU!"

"Command what?" asked Alec.

"Boston University. It's where I am going for my doctorate in the fall," said Binh. A waiter took their orders and left. Alec remembered an early conversation they had had when he didn't really know her. He was impressed from the start. Binh was smart, kind, and pretty.

"What are you interested in writing about?" Migel asked.

"It's no big deal, just something that I have been thinking about," said Binh.

"Come on, tell us," said Migel. "What's your dissertation idea?"

"I want to study and work with Asian American teenagers on how they construct their identities outside of the stereotypical 'good at math and excels at playing the violin or piano' stereotype. I have an idea about how, if expectations are consistent among families, they function as cultural norms. I'm calling my idea the Asian-American Consciousness of Identity Theory. I want Asian-American kids to know about Ang Lee, George Takei, Viet Thanh Nguyen, Jerry Yang, and Tammy Duckworth. I think it matters. Kids need role models. I have a lot of research ideas, and I'd like to be a 'reach for the stars wherever you see them' kind of therapist. I think that a lot of high schoolers don't know what they want to do. Families who might not be willing to allow their children to go to a therapist might be willing to let them read a book."

"That's a great idea!" gushed Emma, "but I don't know who the people are that you mentioned. Seriously. Who are they?"

"Anyone?" said Binh coyly.

"Ang Lee was the first non-white director to win an Oscar award. He is Taiwanese American," said Adem. "Man, I learned a lot in that one film class! And I'm a tech nerd, so I know of Jerry Yang. He was one of the two guys who founded Yahoo. He invests in a lot of tech now. I don't know his cultural background."

"Also, Taiwanese American," answered Binh.

"I know Tammy Duckworth!" offered Emma. "She was a U.S. senator from Illinois, the state next to mine. She was in the House of Representatives before that and famous for being a badass retired army officer, high up too, and a double amputee. She never complains; instead, she encourages people to strive for the life they want. She was born in Thailand. I remember that she is Thai-American and very attractive."

"She was a lieutenant colonel in the Illinois Army National Guard," said Binh.

"George Takei was on Star Trek. He played Hikaru Sulu. I know that," said Theo, who then suddenly looked embarrassed. "What? Star Trek is iconic! Just a great, great show. Who is the last one, though?"

"Viet Thanh Nguyen is a Pulitzer Prize-winning author," said Binh, "and an English professor in California. He's Vietnamese American. Anyway, that is a short list, but my point is that Asian Americans contribute in many ways beyond the STEM fields. Regardless, there is a lot of pressure on Asian children to only focus on math and science, and that is hard on teens who realize that they would rather write, paint, think about finance, or teach," said Binh. "So, I've had this idea for over a year now. It was part of my application essay for doctoral programs."

"It's very thoughtful, Binh," said Migel. "You'll be a great therapist."

"You've been quiet, Jiho. What do you think of Binh's idea?" asked Emma.

"It's a good one. It's important. There is a lot of pressure. She's not kidding. I honestly liked science, though, so it was less of a big deal for me, but my family would not have been thrilled if I had decided to study the humanities, and I think I would have been disowned if I had wanted to be an artist of any kind. Fortunately, though, I can't draw or paint or sing, so I was kind of saved there."

The conversation wandered. They learned that while Jiho could not dance, Theo could. Binh revealed that she was able to draw well but had been told not to 'show off' at school. Migel had always wanted to draw because his sister could, but he could not make a pencil do his bidding. Then dinner was served, the group ate, and some shared updates of what was happening in their lives back in the States. After the table was cleared, they switched to discussing Margo.

"It depends on what she responds with, of course, but I say we continue to project cordial and compliant," chimed in Theo. "We don't want to upset Margo and get ourselves withdrawn and shipped home or accused of a breach of contract. We just really need to consider what..."

"It's Margo!" said Migel, picking up his phone just after he noticed the incoming message notification across the top of his screen. "Hang on," he said as he quickly unlocked his phone and opened the email. He read more slowly than he normally spoke and out loud:

Hi Migel,

It sounds like everything is going well; however, it was unclear from your last email how many people you have encountered who can communicate like Eleni. Please clarify in your next update. As for the chain of command, your concern is noted. We do have additional funding from a source that prefers to remain anonymous, but I can assure you that the aim is not to exploit people. I copied Emma on this email. She should take over your position as head correspondent in Crete, and you should continue your contributions from South Korea, please. Adem's spreadsheet work should continue (column ideas attached). And do keep aiding Lefteris Papadakis with his translations. Thanks for the update. Let me know when you know more.

Best,

Margo

"Pretty short and sweet. And it doesn't say much that we couldn't have figured out by ourselves," said Alec.

"It doesn't," agreed Emma.

"Claiming not to exploit people seems vague to me. A mysterious funder can easily have nefarious intentions, telling Margo one thing and doing another. Who pays her salary? I vote that we be somewhat vague and uncertain," said Alec. "We can always add newfound information to the records that we send, but we can never take it away." Alec had been thinking about the concept of cultural norms since Binh had brought it up. He knew that it meant the shared rules and expectations that shape and often dictate behavior within a social group. He had been thinking about the respect for traditional artisans within Hopi culture; producers of pottery, weaving, carving, basketry, and even painting were all respected. Kwa'a had loved that Alec wanted to study science, but this was not a cultural norm of the Hopi people in general, although, loosely, it did put him in touch with nature, the land, and helping family. These were as Hopi as clans were. Alec thought about Americans in general and the cultural norms of the many subgroups he had encountered.

Binh broke into his thoughts, saying, "Alec, how can we both report as expected and withhold information?"

Alec turned to face her. "We continue to explain Eleni and Cori. We don't mention Viktoria at all. We decide case by case about any other people we learn of on Crete in the future, but the goal is to report on as few people as possible. The normal conclusion will be that it exists but is very rare. We'll see what we find in South Korea. We will report on as few people as possible. I guess I am assuming that we will find some, as we seem to be following up on leads that were already established as likely. Rare and elusive is what we should convey."

Adem offered to help Emma generate honest but not fully accurate texts. Alec was grateful. He thought it would be hard for Binh to feel deceitful, and Theo had never wanted to be the head communicator. Alec spoke again, "I can't believe I have become a part of reporting on a new people. How ironic is this? I know they are not undiscovered people, but their abilities are. Think of how humans have handled things in the past. Humans have a bizarre obsession with identifying differences. The explanation in biology is that our evolution favored pattern recognition, but I feel like that hypothesis is missing something."

"We evolved to recognize patterns and become obsessed when the pattern doesn't work or fit?" asked Theo.

"Something like that," said Alec. "There is also a very strong biological drive for self-preservation and for group or community preservation. I think that is what gets us into the most trouble."

"It is so fortunate that we are the team working on this. We are thinking about things. We are trying to be sensitive to the needs and desires of opposing groups," said Emma. "Not just any group would do that."

"We were not randomly selected, I don't think, but yeah, I think we are doing a pretty good job," said Alec. "I assume some of these efforts are unexpected."

"I'm sure our thoughts in these areas are unexpected," said Emma. "As we discussed the other day—one group is always just imposing their value system on another. You'd think that there would be big brains in the government. I mean, for people who dream of meeting sentient life from another planet, our interactions with new people are not very impressive. I hope that meeting aliens is a long way off. No one seems ready. Do we really want to repeat the errors in the history of 'first encounters'? When I write about cultures that were technologically less advanced than others, I look at ways that they were intellectually more advanced in terms of thinking about their resources, communities, and the people they encountered. That all matters, you know. People get conquered and exploited if they have gold, make good slaves, or don't have refined wayfaring capabilities, but few people consider advancements that are valuable beyond the tangible and the obvious. Managing a community so that it handles outliers is valuable. Considering environmental impact is valuable. Encouraging the preservation of language and culture is valuable, and promoting a culture that values elders is valuable. I'm rambling; I've had a lot of wine, but seriously, it seems like humans are slow to figure out what matters, and because of that, we really need to preemptively protect language shapers. We can't assume that anyone will 'do the right thing' because they understand what matters, okay?"

"We're trying, Emma," said Alec. "This has turned into a big undertaking."

Chapter 32: Margo Duc

"Damn, damn, damn," said Margo out loud after she read Migel's email. Then she re-read it. She was fully aware that Migel was holding back. His emails had gone from reporting every unnecessary detail to being vague and short. She looked sideways and tapped a finger on her desk. "Damn!" she said out loud again. If she had been able to travel with the team, they would have liked her. They would have looked to her for guidance, and she would have been a part of forming the groupthink. She would have had some control. Now, she clearly did not. Maybe she wasn't being fair to assume groupthink just yet, but this smelled of it. The team members were similar thinkers, and they honestly liked each other, but there had been unanimity for a while now on every decision. It gave her the horrible feeling that she was being lied to, or at least not given the full story.

Margo dialed Samir's number. The call went straight to voicemail. She set down the phone and started an email to him. Should she give a little background about people who feel a deep obligation to do what they think is right? Ugh. The group was thinking as a unit, she could feel it. Should she point out to Samir the unquestioned morality of a group's decision? The illusion of invulnerability? Should it be pointed out that next, there would be the mind guards against dissenting information, and she'd have no control? No, she decided. No proselytizing. No "I told you so." It was the right decision medically for her to remain in the U.S., and that made her not part of the team. Now, they were experiencing and reacting without her, and this was her problem to deal with.

Margo had already sent a quick reply to Migel, but there had to be more information forthcoming. Now, she had to change her mind. It was so much easier to help form opinions than it was to change them once they had been created. She sighed, tapped her finger on the desk, and decided to write a list of details to ask Samir about. She pressed the checklist button. She'd email him and ask what she could reveal. The information would help. She needed the group to feel more of an obligation to her, to the goal.

Chapter 33: Migel Ngubá

Migel looked up at the screen in front of him. There were four hours left of the flight. The plane was quiet. Migel was thinking about mental images. It's hard to explain to another person exactly what one pictures in their mind. And even if one does a particularly good job explaining what they are imagining, it's still hard to know if the image that another person conjures up from that description is accurate or flawed in some crucial way. Migel stared out the window and wondered if Eleni, Viktoria, and Cora formed and created mental images in the same way that he did. Migel created a mental image of himself as a child, then of himself on the plane, and finally of himself returning to his family and friends after this trip. He could easily create a mental picture of an event in the past, present, or future. Was there another option? Migel watched the stratus clouds below. It seemed like trying to imagine a color that humans couldn't see. The retina in the human eye is made up of about 120 million rods and six million cones. The rods provide peripheral vision and the perception of light and dark, and the cones allow us to see color. Human eyes have only three types of cones, but mantis shrimp have twelve, so they can also see ultraviolet and polarized light. Migel had read this, and now he wondered if some brains had receptors or transmitters or some other part that allowed for the transmission of thoughts. The Zurich study revealed that brains, much like fingerprints, exhibited unique characteristics, with no two being precisely identical. This topic was a recurring discussion in many of his classes. Both the anatomy of each human brain and its functioning are slightly unique as the result of many factors, some genetic and others not. His professors had been clear that, in the earlier part of their careers, the assumption had been that the human brain had very few individualized aspects. Migel remembered that the study had specifically noted that professional musicians, golfers, and chess players had recognizable physical areas in the regions of their brains where their skills demanded repeated and specific use. He wished again that he could see an fMRI of a few brains in Greece. It was just such a…

"Hey, what's up?" Jiho interrupted.

"Hey. Just thinking," replied Migel. "About human brains. I don't feel like sleeping while sitting up anymore. And I'm excited to see Korea."

"Me too," said Jiho.

"I know, but it will be less of a surprise to you," said Migel. "It will feel familiar, I bet. When I visit Colombia, it feels familiar."

"That's the strong pull of identity. We're hard-wired for it. I've never actually been to Korea. I was reading about Seoul before I fell asleep. We should be able to see a few things before we head south."

"I liked the sound of Bukchon Hanok Village, a preserved 600-year-old village with just under 1,000 houses made of clay and stone. They're still inhabited. I'd like to check that out. It's in the northern part of Seoul but not far from the Gyeongbokgung Palace that Alec mentioned wanting to see," said Migel.

Jiho smiled. "Great, let's plan on that then." It sounded a little "Disneyland-authentic-village" to him, but what the heck. At least the houses were real. "Where is Alec, anyhow?" said Jiho, nodding to the empty seat.

"He's stretching in the back. People walk to the bathrooms and hang out in the space in front of them for a little while and stretch. This is a great flight. It's much more civilized to fly these long hauls."

"Yeah, it's like they're afraid to cramp people too much and have medical problems in the air!" said Jiho. "The last time I flew was to Florida, same class, and I had a third of the space these chairs do."

Alec soon reappeared and sat back down in his seat between Migel and Jiho. He said, "An-*yom-a-say-oh*," and looked at Jiho.

Jiho smiled again. "Close enough. Where'd you learn that?" he asked.

"In the back of the plane. It took over ten minutes, though!" said Alec. "The first guy said it too fast, and I couldn't get it. A flight attendant finally helped me out. She says this is the best greeting to learn because it is polite and general."

"It is," said Jiho. "It is literally a question too, asking, 'Are you at peace?' but use it like saying 'hello' to people in a polite way. It's not 'Hey, what's up?' But because it's really a question, sometimes people reply 'ye,' meaning yes, before they repeat the greeting to you."

"I'll learn as much as I can, but Korean is not an easy language, dude. Not even when the Hangul letters are translated into an alphabet that I can read," said Alec. "There are some tough letter combinations to pronounce for the unfamiliar. And some seriously long words," he said, raising his eyebrows.

"English is no dream for Koreans at first either. Many words that are pronounced the same have very different spellings or arbitrary pronunciations. And many Americans don't articulate when they speak. They mumble."

"Fair enough," said Alec, smiling.

"So, we land, clear customs, get to our hotel and then do some sightseeing?" asked Migel. "We can get to that palace that interests you, Alec, and an area that I want to see near it, and whatever Jiho wants to do."

"Let's figure it out now," suggested Jiho. So, the three men dug into their bags under the seats in front of them, retrieved their papers and laptops, and started discussing their options.

Chapter 34: Emma Miller

The lines were often straight on the hieroglyphics, but not always. There were circles with dots or a cross in them, and there were curved lines that typically formed a somewhat recognizable image, such as an animal head, a hand, or a bird of some kind. Emma and Theo sat hunched over their computers with many tabs open on each laptop. A few sheets of hieroglyphics were printed out and laid across the table. Emma thought that often repeated sounds might have simplified logograms, and maybe the very complex logograms stood for sounds or words that were privileged, perhaps the sounds that were present in the king's names, for example. Some of the hieroglyphs in the printed charts had phonetic notations in the box next to them. The notations were symbols, largely from Latin script, that represented human speech sounds in a standardized form per the International Phonetic Alphabet, created in the 19th century. Next to many symbols was a blank box. They also had a sheet that Eleni and Cora had written out for them of commonly used ideas or words from language shaping. Emma studied the hieroglyphic shapes and then the list of words and concepts from the Papadakis women. She stared at them and then went back to the texts she was reading, repeating the ideas in her own words in her head every few sentences. When something was particularly interesting, she wrote it down and often interrupted Theo's thoughts to tell him. The goal was to see how certain ideas mapped onto the hieroglyphics, which was, so far, not very well.

The hieroglyphic language is thought to be of Sumerian origin. Theo was particularly interested in this. The civilization called Sumer was part of Mesopotamia 6,000 years ago and not very far from Crete by boat. Sumer developed in the very fertile lands between the Tigris and the Euphrates Rivers in what is now the countries of Syria and Iraq. The floodplains allowed for excellent farming, and as the culture ate well, they had sufficient extra time to develop theories in math and astronomy and to create a written language. Civilizations that spend 100% of their time trying to survive understandably don't develop much math and astronomy. Emma and Theo studied a map, read articles, and stared at logograms, pictures, symbols, and words.

Theo read out loud that the total known number of Cretan hieroglyphs attributed to the Minoans is just under one hundred. This is too few for the symbols to be logograms, representations of entire words, and too many for them to represent individual alphabet letters. The general assumption has been that each symbol represents a syllable of speech. It has even been proposed that, since Crete has been documented as being a multilingual society in the second millennium BCE, and since so many of the artifacts with hieroglyphics were found in and around the great Palace of Knossos, there may have been a common set of phonetic symbols — a manner in which to write numerous languages with one script, by representing the sounds the languages made. Writing would have been rare then, and having a central place where it occurred made sense. Emma thought for a moment, conveyed the idea to Theo, and then said, "I know that's the most common view of scholars, but I still want for these symbols to be documented, simplified, representational ideas of what was expressible by some from one mind to another. Many cultures throughout history had various sorcerers and witches for the kings and courts. The Palace of Knossos might just have had telepathic masters and maidens, and these artifacts could detail important transactions. I still think that it makes sense for a language that isn't spoken to be recorded in a different way than a spoken language is, and this accounts for the simultaneous coexistence of two written languages."

"Maybe," started Theo. "Listen to this: the Minoan Palace complex of Knossos covered over two football fields and was surrounded by a town. Palace construction began around 1900 BCE and continued for the next 500 years, either as expansion or renovation of damaged areas. There is evidence that humans have lived in Knossos since 7000 BCE." Theo dragged his finger down the article he was reading for a few minutes and then continued out loud. "The palace complex had water storage and waste systems. Freshwater arrived by aqueduct from a spring in Archanes. The water was transported through the complex via clay pipes. There were rooms with enormous clay pots for holding grains and oils, fish and beans, and the walls had elaborate frescoes." Theo looked up at

Emma. "This was a seriously advanced civilization, even more than I thought when we visited the ruins. At least a portion of the people lived and ate very well. Accounting tablets have been found in the Palace Complex, as well as numerous coins from communities on other islands and the neighboring shores of Syria, Egypt, and Sicily. The Minoans enjoyed extensive exporting as well as importing."

"Well, that explains travel to Sumer," said Emma. "Maybe the telepathic ability originated there? When Binh and Adem return, we should talk to them about meeting with Dr. Papadakis again and, of course, trying to get some more time with his wife. Or maybe we should try to spend time with Viktoria? It's hard to imagine a translation for something that I don't really understand. And if the logograms represent sounds, then we'll never figure it out."

Chapter 35: Jiho Bak

On Saturday, following an email from Margo, the Americans followed the directions, taking a hired ride to a nondescript office building in another neighborhood of Seoul. They were greeted in the lobby by a lovely woman who could be anywhere from twenty to sixty years old. Her English was excellent, and she said that her name was Ha-Yoon. Shortly after she welcomed them, Ha-Yoon began walking them to a collection of elevators. She pressed a button to go up, and minutes later, they were entering a suite on a high floor and being greeted by another welcoming woman. The two women guided the men down a hall and into a room with a round wooden table.

Just that morning, the American men had acknowledged and discussed the importance that Koreans place on age and status at meetings, and they had all come to the conclusion that although Alec was the oldest and Jiho was the youngest, Jiho looked and spoke Korean, and he should be given the role of the group head. Despite parallel roles on the trip while in Africa and Greece, in South Korea, Jiho's skills and the responsibilities he would take while they were in the country should give him the greatest status. It was agreed that he would speak first.

Dr. Bak arrived ten minutes later. He was a tall, very upright man with glasses and thin streaks of gray through his neatly styled hair. The younger men bowed slightly, stopping at about 40 degrees.

It was Jiho who lifted his eyes first and looked at Dr. Bak. To the great relief of the Americans, Dr. Bak spoke English clearly and with excellent pronunciation. When Alec, Migel, and Jiho had been sightseeing earlier that day, their general impression was that most of what they did would have been impossible had Jiho not spoken Korean. It appeared as though no one spoke English, although they had read in the location file that English was a mandatory subject in elementary school.

Dr. Bak was kind and direct, but they had a very short meeting. The takeaway, after he apologized for making them wait and asked if they were enjoying Seoul and what sightseeing they had done so far, was that he knew someone who knew Margo. He had been called upon to meet the men in the afternoon, between patients, and to welcome them and to arrange for them to get to the South Jeolla province on Monday morning. He explained in general how this would work, and he said that Ha-Yoon would help them with the details. He asked if they had any questions, then asked them to send kind words to Margo from Bon-Hwa Gim, and with just a nod, the meeting was over. The entire interaction took just three or four minutes.

Before the group could wonder how they would leave or what would happen next, Ha-Yoon, the smiling woman who had met them in the building lobby, reappeared. She brought them to another room, where she had maps and books on a table, as well as tea and small plates of things to eat.

"I am pleased to sit with you," Ha-Yoon said. "Dr. Bak is a *uisa*, a medical doctor, and a busy doctor, but I am not in a rush. We can have some tea, and we can talk as long as you like. These are *dasik*," she said, pointing to beautiful round cookies with designs punched into the dough. "Let's look at a map and talk about your trip. Additionally, I have arranged for your travel south."

"*Gamsahabnida*, thank you so much," said Jiho. "We are grateful." He nodded his head. It sounded to the others like *Kam-sa-ham-ni-da*, so they repeated it.

"Is it hot for you today?" asked Ha-Yoon as she began to pour from the teapot into the cups. "July is not our tourist season. It is quite warm, and there is much rain."

"It's not a problem," offered Alec. "We have rain at home, too, and we all live in areas with hot summers. We are enjoying our visit. Today, it was cloudy, so the pictures will not be great, but we walked in many interesting areas."

"Yes, Seoul looks like an amazing city," said Migel. "It is an interesting blend of old and new, and there are an incredible number of people everywhere." Migel had read that almost ten million people lived in Seoul.

"It is raining now!" responded Ha-Yoon, gesturing to the tinted windows, where the most polite and disciplined raindrops were rhythmically landing against the glass. It was mesmerizing.

"That was abrupt," said Jiho.

"It often is," said Ha-Yoon. "The whole month of July, so be careful in the south. Especially when you are in the mountains, the rains can be very heavy, and sometimes there are strong winds too."

"We'll be careful. Thank you," said Jiho.

Ha-Yoon passed the teacups around and then told the group that they were booked on a train from Seoul Station Monday at 10 am. They would arrive in Gwangju three hours later.

"A driver will meet you in Gwangju," Ha-Yoon said. "The driver will find you when you get off the train and have a sign that says all three of your names. He will drive you to a town near the Wolchulsan National Park, where a hotel is reserved for you. Buses are more typical for this kind of journey, but it will be easier for you to have a direct car this time."

"That is very kind. Thank you again," said Jiho. "I hope it is not trouble for you to help us. I do know some relatives of friends that I can contact if necessary, and people seem to understand my Korean here," he smiled at her, "But your help makes the transportation very easy. Thank you."

"It is no trouble at all," said Ha-Yoon. "Welcome to Korea."

"Is it typical for doctors to see patients on Saturdays here?" asked Migel.

"On Saturdays, yes, but for a shorter workday than Monday to Friday. Dr. Bak is often very busy," she smiled and then offered more tea. No one except Jiho had drunk it as fast as had apparently been expected. Ha-Yoon poured more.

"So, you are going to Jeollanam-do. Do you want to know some history?" The Americans told Ha-Yoon that they did, of course. "Jeollomon-do is the name of one of our eight provinces. In the year 1413, Korea was divided into eight provinces, and these boundaries remained for the next 500 years until 1895, when a king decided to change the system. He re-divided the country into 23 districts, but this new system was not popular, and it lasted only one year. In 1896, we returned to our system of *Paldo*, eight provinces. Because the boundaries of these eight areas are marked by natural features, such as rivers and mountains, they reflect not only territory lines but also minor cultural and linguistic differences in the people of the eight areas. They made sense to people. Where is your family from, Jiho?" she asked, but Jiho felt like she already knew.

"They are from a small town in the Gangwon-Do province, the southern part that did not become part of North Korea in the 1950s. Both of my parents went to the United States in the 1990s with a group from their region that had little family. They married when they grew up. I am their second son. My brother and I were both born in the United States. This is my first time in Korea."

"Then this trip will be an adventure for you as well, Jiho. I welcome you all again, and I hope you will enjoy your visit and not be too bothered by the rains," Ha-Yoon smiled. She continued to be informative and helpful. She did not ask what the men would be doing in the South. She continued to refill teacups and answer more questions about place names and trains. She suggested areas of Seoul worth visiting the following day, reminding them that their train would leave early on Monday morning. After the men had said thank you repeatedly, Ha-Yoon expressed that they must be tired, and since the rain was lighter, she could order them a car back to their hotel. It was all smooth and quick and pleasant, and in less than an hour, the men were back in their hotel room.

"I am writing to Margo," said Migel. "We're fourteen hours ahead of her, but she keeps weird hours, it seems, and she'll want to know that we have train tickets."

"Thanks. Thank her for making that so easy, too," said Jiho. "I'll work out the trains and bus systems in the next few days, but Ha-Yoon's plans will get us where we need to go correctly and quickly."

"I will. But for the record, when she said that we didn't have to worry and she'd have someone meet us, that wasn't exactly what I expected. Also, I had started trying to figure out the hotel options in Jeollomon-do, and it sounds like we are all set in that department too now," said Alec.

"There's a new message from Margo," said Migel as soon as he logged into the Wi-Fi. "She says she sent more information about the south, the hotel, the park, and what she is hoping for," he said as he scrolled. "She says that she knows someone who works at Celltrion, a Korean biopharmaceutical company whose U.S. office is in New Jersey." Migel looked up. "That explains Dr. Bak and the medical building. I guess someone owed her a favor..."

"Ha-Yoon was super helpful. A very nice person. Really. I wonder how old she is?" asked Alec.

"Korean lady magic," said Jiho. "You can rarely tell, and they never do!"

"That sounds complicated," reasoned Alec. "How do you know if you are going to dinner with a fourteen-year-old or a forty-year-old?"

"Ha!" said Jiho. "Don't invite too fast! A more interesting issue is that until recently, Koreans counted babies as being one year old as soon as they were born. Apparently, some very ancient counting systems did not have a concept of zero or something, so people started counting at one. Then, on New Year's Day of every year, everyone acquired another year of age. It was just recently that a law passed that switched all Koreans over legally and officially to counting age the way the rest of the world does, with one's age only going up on the anniversary of the person's birth. It's confusing, and many people became a year or two younger during the switch, depending on when their birthday falls. It's supposed to be easier for official work in the future, after the complications end, of course."

"I just assumed those things were standardized a long time ago," said Migel.

"Well, they are now," said Jiho, "but Korea held out until 1960 for legal documents and until 2023 for everything else. Look, you guys, I am suddenly exhausted. The jet lag caught up with me. I need a nap before dinner. Can we take a break for an hour or so?" Minutes later, as he lay on one of the three single beds in the room, Jiho thought about how comfortable he felt in Korea, even though he had been there for less than 24 hours. Jiho knew that with every new experience, nerve cell connections realigned themselves to adjust to the new experiences. He thought of how his brain would accommodate his experiences of today. This made him remember discussing a study in school that demonstrated that a specific part of the brain, the ventromedial prefrontal cortex, is likely where one's sense of self is constructed, as people with abnormal growths or injury to this region have difficulty discussing themselves and telling accurate stories about themselves.

Jiho reflected on his sense of self. He decided that he did identify partly as Korean. He identified with many groups and two nationalities: American and Korean American, which were culturally a little different. Here, he was experiencing a related yet third culture that he felt connected to but not a part of. He recognized people as ancestors but did not feel like they were part of the family. Maybe it would be different outside of the city. He reflected again on how very American he was in his cultural expectations for noise, space, availability, waiting in line, communication, food… the list was long. People must leave their own country to realize how much they embody its ideals, culture, and opportunities, he thought.

Then, Jiho found himself considering World War II. He had learned that in the United States, many Japanese citizens had been interned, essentially collected and kept separate from other Americans after the attack on Pearl Harbor in 1941. That had been covered in school. Not covered in school was the fact that in Australia, people of German, Japanese, and Italian ancestry, many of whom were naturalized citizens, had been interned or incarcerated. In Canada, anyone who lived in Canada but was originally from a country that was at war with the British Empire was considered an "Enemy Alien" and subject to internment during both World War I and World War II. Not covered in Jiho's school was any discussion of why these governments had made such decisions or what could have been done instead.

Cultural identity lives deep, thought Jiho, but for him, it did not overshadow citizenship. Governments want to ensure that everyone in their country has allegiance to that country, particularly in a time of war. He understood that. He also could imagine that any immigrant can develop a greater allegiance to their new country than their birth country, but doing so requires the new country to be welcoming, kind, understanding, and supportive. Citizens are created by sharing common feelings, loyalties, and culture; they are not made through a test. He wondered if people who were less supportive of immigration understood that. Allegiance is built.

Ostracization breeds resentment. Resentment can build and cause serious problems. Jiho fell asleep.

294

Chapter 36: Adem Haimowitz

The group sat on the patio at the Papadakis house for the third time. Despite the insistence that it was not necessary, Eleni and Cora had made and were serving a lot of food. The Americans were figuring out how to give back, however. They stopped asking what they could do and just arrived with items that would make the occasion easier for the hosts: carbonated bottled water, fruit, fresh bread, and sausages from the local market in town. From the city, they had brought a large box full of pastries, including *portokalópita*, literally "orange pie," but actually, the traditional moist, orange-flavored cake. The gifts were warmly accepted and brought into the kitchen while the guests were escorted around the side of the house. The large yellowish rocks near the house were heating up in the sun, but the patio was still shaded and cool. In town, the adjoining buildings that flanked narrow streets meant that shadows were cast all day, offering respite from the heat. When farmhouses were built in isolation, as the Papadakis home was, staying cool required angling the structure appropriately, strategically planting trees, and building patios with shade-producing features. The visit would be comfortable despite the heat.

Everyone ate and talked about Greece, the United States, the weather, and the world in general, minus the political turmoil. When the last plates were being cleared, Dr. Papadakis began to discuss the hieroglyphics and the language that had no sound. Eleni and Cora disappeared into the kitchen.

"Has the work been interesting to you?" asked Dr. Papadakis.

"It has," Adem began. "We have been looking at the hieroglyphics. Emma and Theo have been searching for meaning, Binh has been considering what their use was, reading research papers and trying to extract translation from that, and I have been searching for patterns from what they give me. I can't say that we are making great progress, but it is a very interesting project to rearrange the symbols and consider them with the pictures that you gave us. We have a few possibilities we'd like to show you."

"A lot of people have worked for many decades at translating those hieroglyphics. It's not an easy project," admitted Dr. Papadakis, "but you bring fresh eyes and a possible reason for their existence that others likely did not consider."

"Maybe we have an advantage, knowing about Language Shaping, *Glóssa Schimatízontas*. Having an idea of what the symbols might have been used for might uncover the meaning."

"Ísos. Maybe," said Dr. Papadakis. He swirled his drink and looked out past the orange trees. The lines around his eyes undulated as he processed what he might say. "What do you expect to do with the information about *Glóssa Schimatízontas*? Will you write about it?"

"We will not write about it," said Binh. "We are just following some leads. We are looking into stories about people who have information about various kinds of telepathy. It's more of a documentation project of an academic nature to explore genetic variation."

"We don't want attention," said Dr. Papadakis.

Adem understood. This had been mentioned before. The family had revealed that they had not talked to outsiders previously, as they were concerned there would be unwanted attention and their quiet life would be disturbed. Adem wanted to make sure that this did not happen. Binh had been quick and helpful in her response. He would back her up. "As Binh said, we are just documenting the existence of ideas. We are not judging or selling the information. We are just students, really. We have all finished university and are at various stages of finishing the degrees necessary for our careers. We are all interested in language. I'm interested in language and data patterns, too."

"What are you thinking about the hieroglyphics and *Glóssa Schimatízontas*?" asked Dr. Papadakis directly to Adem.

"Well... I work with data science and analytics to visualize data. I make statistical models and images with visual data. I was switching jobs when the opportunity to travel with this group came up. I've been wanting to travel more, and I wanted a break. This seemed like a creative project, really. Even though it has been different from what I anticipated, I am very happy that I came along.

It has been a chance to learn and to visit new places. I have been reading about topics that are new to me and putting together information," Adem paused to see if anyone else in the group wanted to talk. No one did, so he stopped buying time and started to answer the question. "I am very grateful, we all are, for the opportunity to consider your hieroglyphics and to learn about Language Shaping, um, *Glóssa Schimatízontas*. I have been reading a lot about ideas concerning such abilities. It seems that a common thread in both the academic literature and in online blogs is that there is likely a human capacity for communication from one mind to another. Well, this isn't popular belief, but among people who think about and research this sort of thing, much has been written about the ability in animals as well. There are a lot of interesting studies that beat the odds of chance by a significant amount concerning knowing who is at the other end of a telephone call from the first ring. To make a call or send an email, there is an intention that requires selecting an email or phone number and, at the very least, pushing send and waiting. It's uncanny how often, in that time period, the receiving person thinks of the sender partial seconds before they are contacted. So, I found a lot of interesting research work from scholars who are supportive of 'the innate ability hypothesis,' as we are calling it. Being able to access the ability on demand, however, and use it at will is not as common, we don't think, as none of us have ever met anyone before who was able to do it. It's also not present in any high-quality studies that I have found so far. So yes, it would bring a lot of attention to the island if it were ever advertised that Crete is a location where such skills thrive."

"Thank you for recognizing that we don't want such attention," said Dr. Papadakis. "It is the main reason why we didn't speak to anyone sooner."

"We have another hypothesis, too," Binh began. "Cognitive Theory of Mind is one way that psychologists refer to the capacity for a human to understand the emotions, beliefs, and intentions of another person. This is what we do when we judge or analyze the actions of others. Humans have always exercised this ability, sometimes for survival and often for gossip. Gossiping—and I mean repeated heard or suspected information without evidence or permission—has caused an incredible number of problems, but fascinatingly, it seems to exist in every human culture. All humans like to judge the social appropriateness of the actions of others. One characteristic of 'autism spectrum disorder' is the inability to do this. Do you know this English word?" Binh looked directly at Dr. Papadakis and waited.

"Yes, aftismós," he said. "I know of it. There is a center in Heraklion, Zoodochos Pigi, for people with many kinds of mental conditions, including this one."

"Well, there are so many people with *aftismós*—autism—now in the United States that we have a number of centers that only help people with this condition. There are researchers in various fields who investigate it: educators, social scientists, neurologists, biologists, psychologists," said Adem. "The drive for greater research and more answers is strong."

"Interesting," said Dr. Papadakis. "What is the connection? No one in my family has this condition."

"Well, I learned something interesting. When it was discovered in the 1990s that there were neurons in the brains of primates that reacted to what was observed as opposed to just an action enacted, there was a tremendous amount of hype—ugh, discussion and reporting about them."

"I know this word 'hype,'" said Dr. Papadakis.

"Well, these neurons found in primates were named mirror neurons because they mirror behavior. They activate not only when the person who has them acts but also when that primate observes and witnesses the actions of another. Mirror neurons are not a kind of neuron in the brain but a function of an already existing neuron. They are just differentiated by their response pattern. When I pick up fruit and eat it, a similar neuron process in my mind occurs in those who watch me pick up the fruit and eat it."

"I think I have heard about this," said Dr. Papadakis. "This discovery was considered very influential for studies of early humans. It explains how a lot of learning could have occurred pre-language. There were articles about this in my journals."

"This is not my field, but I think I see a connection to *Glóssa Schimatízontas*, and I ran some data. Post-discovery of these mirror neurons, many researchers thought that they might have a quick explanation of and help for people with autism. The hope was that studies would easily demonstrate that people who lacked the ability to learn socially and understand intention would simply have fewer mirror neurons activating than people without autism. As sometimes happens in my country, the news coverage was extensive before there were enough studies and enough facts. The emphasis was misplaced, and the ensuing expectations became unrealistic. When it became evident that mirror neurons could not swiftly and definitively provide insights into autism, interest in them largely diminished. Funding for scientific studies is somewhat linked to the interest of the general population, so perhaps that is related to the declining interest, too. But studying autism is still important, and so is the study of mirror neurons. I found myself reading about mirror neurons. I'm sorry if they can't explain autism, or maybe they will one day, but I'm wondering if they can explain the ability to communicate without sound. I've texted our brain boys in Korea for some help because all of this came up after they left. I haven't heard from them yet, but perhaps Language Shaping is the result of being more attuned to the behavior of others. Maybe some people have an increased number of mirror neurons, or they function differently— or maybe better. The hieroglyphics, if they are related, could be action representations, the command form of verbs and some nouns. This aligns with what Cora explained to us. I understand that it is thought each image represents a syllable, but maybe the command form of certain verbs, such as 'go' or 'sell' or 'buy' or 'move,' are single syllables in this language and so easily represented by a single symbol."

"That's quite an idea," confirmed Dr. Papadakis. "I have to admit, I've spent less time contemplating how *Glóssa Schimatízontas* is possible than you have. I ignored it for many years and only recently became interested in its connection to the artifacts that we have from previous civilizations. Mostly, I haven't wanted to discuss it. I guess I assumed that it's not a newly acquired ability but a remnant from the past, though I'm not sure now why I assumed that. Perhaps because there are other, older people around who have the skill and know that some of their relatives before them did as well."

"We're interested in considering all options, Dr. Papadakis," said Emma, who had until now been quiet. "It could exist only in recent generations, or it could be centuries old. If we could possibly ask your wife a few more questions about how it works, when it's convenient for her, of course, we could learn more."

"Of course. I'll get her. And Cora too," said Dr. Papadakis as he slowly got up from the table and shuffled toward the door on the far side of the patio that led to the kitchen. The Americans waited. Binh took out her phone and looked at the notes she had written there.

When Dr. Papadakis and his wife and daughter returned, they brought a new tray of cold drinks, and the conversation continued. This time, the team was prepared for what they would hear. This time, they had better questions. Theo asked about the form of communication and the process. He asked about grammar, distance, and timing. They learned that the sender thinks of what she wants the receiver to know in the simplest terms. The receiver doesn't instantly know the information but must instead think of the person who sends the information and, at that time, is able to know what was sent. They learned that just like when everyone sometimes thinks of their mother or a friend, and then that person calls, typically, the receiver just thinks of the sender as soon as the message is sent. Adem thought of email: a person may send an email to another, but the other person must either log in to an account or otherwise agree to notifications of the received message in order to access it. They also learned that, in addition to Viktoria, the family knows of other people, some of whom are men, who can do this. They all come from Crete, and they all suspect there are others.

Walking home late in the afternoon, Adem smelled the air and thought. He was shoulder-to-shoulder with Theo. Emma and Binh were walking just in front of them and chatting. He wondered what Alec, Migel, and Jiho were doing. They were seven hours ahead of Greece in time. It was odd thinking of them. His brain treated them like friends he was close to rather than co-workers who were unknown to him four weeks earlier. Travel accelerated relationships, he decided. It was probably because of the cognitive theory of mind that Binh brought up. It wasn't the going places *per se,* but the constant experiencing and trying to understand what another might be thinking or intending. The group had grown accustomed to each other, but more importantly, they had deep connections and respect that he, now that he actually thought about it, had previously developed only with people he had known for many years. Adem noticed that Theo was lost in his own thoughts too, so Adem continued to consider how this new information would impact his dating. Adem looked at the moving feet of the women in front of him. He felt closer to understanding Binh and Emma than he had his last girlfriend. Huh. Maybe the one before that, too. He decided that he should take a trip with the next person he dated. It would accelerate things, and he'd either like her more or less when the trip was over. At least he'd know her better.

Chapter 37: Alec Nehoitewa

The southwestern province of South Korea is Jeollanam-do (the 'do' meaning province); it is the greenest and least developed of the provinces. In a country of rolling hills and mountains, the relatively flat and temperate Jeollanam-do is the breadbasket of the country, with enormous rice fields and the mighty Sobek Mountains to the east, featuring picturesque hiking trails in multiple national parks. In other directions, there are the terraced green tea fields of Boseong County, bamboo forests near Lake Danyang, wooden slat boardwalks winding through reed-covered wetlands at the edge of Suncheon Bay, and thousands of miles of coastline, off of which there are almost 2,000 islands. If this area were in the United States, thought Alec, it would be a busy and expensive year-round tourist destination. It would be more developed and covered with inns, resorts, hotels, and motels. There would be miniature golf and ice cream venues. The small roads would be overwhelmed with traffic at various times of the year, and so junky souvenir shops and unhealthy food stops would sprout from the congested lanes. But here, in South Korea, a country that not many Westerners venture to, he saw nature and carless roads. Salty winds blew through the spaces between trees, and the open views were astonishing. The three Americans rode southeast towards Wolchulsan National Park, peering out the windows of the hired car and discussing what they saw.

Modernization has altered how people in rural Korea work and live in significant ways, but small hamlets of traditional life still exist. Realistically, though, since World War II, probably no area has been completely untouched by foreign influence. There has been an increasing quietness and emptiness in the villages for decades as the younger generations leave for city lives. However, thanks to a recent government initiative, people can apply to a program that provides free housing and training in farming to those willing to relocate to rural areas and work the land. Over one hundred villages participate in the program, and until that number increases, there is competition for a spot. The idea is for South Korea to grow more of its own food, for the cities to be alleviated of their unnecessary populations, and for the traditions of the countryside to be preserved through agrotourism and farming. When Alec read this in the location file, he imagined the impact that such a program would have on population distribution and food production in the United States. He thought it would be very helpful.

From the car window, Wolchulsan National Park's small but bald, rocky peaks rose nearby. The iconic red steel suspension bridge, over 170 feet long, could be seen connecting two ridges. Looking up information on this area always brought up images of this hiker's bridge; it was even more impressive in person. Eventually, the car arrived near the entrance to the park, close to a village that was nestled between a forest and open farm fields. The car slowly made its way through streets with businesses and then along the narrow road until it stopped beside a property tucked behind a stone wall. Two rectangular buildings with dome and bracket-style roofs that sloped up at the ends and extended past the edge of the building structure rested about forty feet from the wall. One of these buildings was, in theory, the inn where Migel, Jiho, and Alec had a reserved room. The driver spoke in Korean, and Jiho responded. Alec heard *gamsahabnida*, thank you, and repeated it while looking at the driver. It was one of the four things that he could express in Korean so far. Migel followed. Everyone got out of the car and walked toward the building, where a man was emerging.

Thirty minutes later, Jiho, Alec, and Migel were walking on a small street that appeared not to have seen foreigners in a while. Surely, this wasn't true, but people stopped, looked up at them, gazed for a second, and then returned to working, walking, eating, or whatever they had been doing. No one just ignored them; it was the opposite experience from the one that they had just had in Seoul. Alec felt uncomfortably happy. No one looked like him, but then again, no one looked like Migel either. They were probably a hard-to-place group. Jiho looked Korean, and his friends didn't fit any stereotypical American image that foreigners often have from Hollywood movies, so the local people probably assumed they were European. Everyone looked interested in them, and no one was too busy to notice them.

"Thoughts on how to spend the rest of the day?" ventured Alec as they walked. "I've had about enough sitting, but I'd rather be in town right now than on a nature trail."

"I'll second that," said Migel.

"Well, we can walk the area that we drove through with the businesses and see if there is anywhere we want to come back to this evening to eat dinner. I'd love a coffee if we can find one. We can go back to our room, clean up, and come back out later with a destination in mind. Maybe there'll be someone to talk to." They walked to the approaching corner, turned right, and were surprised by the commercialism. It seemed busier than it had from the car. Jiho quietly read the storefronts out loud for the others as he saw their large signs, mostly with black characters on large white rectangles. "There is a bank on the left," he said, "then a fried chicken place, a coffee shop, a convenience food shop, a different fried chicken place, and a pharmacy. Oh, and that's another fried chicken place on the right."

Small apartment buildings were interspersed among the shops, and freestanding buildings like their small hotel could be seen in most directions. The three travelers walked the streets, peered casually into windows, and eventually went into a coffee shop. Inside, they were immediately surprised to see that it looked like many American coffee shops, but without the crowds of people using their fifth hour of free Wi-Fi while hogging a table. Jiho ordered three iced coffees, and they found a table to sit at.

"Minus the menu that I couldn't read, this feels like home," said Migel.

"I know it," said Jiho. "This is more than a village. It's more like a small town or a small suburb back home. There is a lot going on in town, although it's quiet, and I really didn't expect a café." They drank their iced coffees and commented more on the area.

Then Alec said, "So now, how do we think we will approach people here? I think it will be weird to ask direct questions about Language Shaping, but I have been trying to think of another way and can't."

"We'll have to make a relationship with some people," said Jiho, "talk to them many times and then somehow allude to the fact that we heard about it … it's a long shot, but it is all we can do, I think."

"Right. Unless Margo magically sends us a lead," said Alec. "Which isn't impossible. Is there Wi-Fi here, Ji?"

There was. Jiho got the password from the barista, and they all logged onto the café Wi-Fi and checked their emails. They responded to friends and family. They looked at pictures and tried again to use Google Maps. It was not good for distances. A message kept coming up that directions were impossible. Jiho went up to the counter where he had purchased coffee and spoke in Korean. When he returned to the table, he said they needed to download 'Naver Map' or 'Kakao Map' because, in the name of national security, the South Korean government required that all mapping data be stored on local servers, and Google Maps didn't fully comply. Accordingly,

Google Maps doesn't work very well in South Korea—or at all in some places.

"Ugh," said Migel. "It's not a bad idea, you know, storing such information only locally."

"It really isn't," said Alec. "It keeps control where you might want it one day. It's funny what the U.S. wants absolute control over and what they don't seem to care about."

The men spent the next hour talking, downloading useful mapping apps, and trying to work out the bus schedule online. The latter proved amazingly easy.

"Hey Alec, can't scientists look at ancient remains and tell if that human had language capabilities? I was just wondering if there is physical evidence of Language Shaping that could be seen without neuroimaging," said Jiho.

"How do fossils have physical evidence of language?" interrupted Migel.

"Oh, they do!" said Alec. "Have you guys ever heard of *Australopithecus afarensis*? The most famous skeleton of one is 'Lucy,' who was found in the 1970s in Ethiopia. Heard of it?"

"Vaguely. I know that a lot of old human fossils have been found in Africa. There is the whole 'we all originated from Africa' theory," said Migel "Lucy and fossils like hers have been found in Ethiopia, Tanzania, and Kenya. Lucy is the most complete skeleton found, and she is a bit over three million years old. She was dated using an argon-argon method. Carbon-14 is the dating method that most people have heard of, but it works best on things from the last 50,000 years. It worked well on the leather shoe that was found in a cave in Armenia, for example. That shoe is 5,500 years old," said Alec, smiling. The others didn't seem as enthralled. "Anyway, dating language requires looking at the fossil evidence for brain size, skull shape, and spinal cord. It's a super cool science. Lucy and her kind had small heads and brains, but her pelvis, spine, and feet show that she walked on two legs. Although hundreds of fossils with identical anatomical features have been found since, people seem to only recall "Lucy." It is generally believed that her species—and I say this because she wasn't quite like us—did not have language or speech. She had an ape-like skull and vocal tract. This is Theo's department, but basically, as I understand it, having a high larynx and short pharynx like modern chimpanzees do seriously limits the range of sounds the body can produce. So, when human remains are found with that type of skull and neck, we believe they were only capable of making the sounds that many modern chimps can. They probably relied much more on hand gestures. Also, these fossils have very narrow spinal cords, meaning they had far fewer nerves than modern humans. The way humans breathe and talk at the same time requires a more complex nerve system to control the breathing muscles responsible for this, and narrow spinal cords aren't sufficient infrastructure. No offense to Miss Lucy, but she also had a very small brain, so she was likely limited to simple sign language.

Again, we'll talk to Theo, but I was taught that modern sign language, such as American Standard Sign Language, is a complex and mature language with many rules and even accents. I'm not talking about that. Lucy's brain wasn't complex enough to handle it, but communication is important to any species, and clearly, she had something going on. However, all evidence points to the fact that it was not at all what we can do vocally."

Migel thought and rubbed two fingers together. When Jiho looked at him with an expressionless face, Migel started to speak. "So… I've been thinking about what language shaping might require for production, and I can't think of any physical requirements that would be visible to the naked eye. I've been thinking of the capability as the result of a mental process, not a physical one. This is a long way of saying that I agree with Jiho, and we're going to have to make connections here and talk to people." Jiho nodded. Migel looked up and started asking more about fossils and why Alec switched to focusing on plants and mushrooms.

When the men returned to the hotel—if one could call it that— the proprietor, Hwan Kim, was waiting for them. They were really staying in a home; a "bed and breakfast" is how it would be marketed in the States. Hwan spoke to Jiho in Korean but looked at everyone as he spoke. He had planned to serve them dinner. He could do it every day if they wanted, and he would serve breakfast, too. He seemed very interested in talking to the Americans. He said he knew some English and watched some movies in English with Korean subtitles. Jiho arranged a time to return to the front room for dinner, and then the Americans went to their room to get their story straight. Hwan was very kind and curious; he was friendly and interested in them. It occurred to all of them that they could probably forge a relationship with him.

Chapter 38: Theo Auclair

On June 27th, across the world, Theo was once again lounging on the front deck off his room. His chair was pulled out past the semi-shade of the wooden arbor. He was like a lizard absorbing heat and loving it, but unlike a reptile, he was considering the origin of human language. While in school, he had decided that he was most drawn to the gestural theory—the idea that human language evolved from gestures. To him, it made the most sense logically, and there is interesting evidence supporting it. For example, when certain brain lesions are found in the left hemisphere, people who use sign language experience the same issues as vocal language users because gestures and verbal language have similar neural structures. Modern brain imaging has also offered the opportunity to see how the brain works when a deaf person watches someone sign. The fact that very similar regions of the brain work when non-deaf people watch someone speak verbally suggests that gestured and spoken languages are processed in the same areas, although it is yet unclear if they are processed in the exact same way. The discovery of mirror neurons is also a huge boost for this idea, as they explain how ideas could have been rapidly transferred among people as language was emerging.

Theo had spent part of the morning reading about mirror neurons, and he was now in contemplation mode. Lying around with his eyes closed was how he did some of his best work, and the sun was a bonus. Adem, on the other hand, was out walking to think. Adem moved when he thought, then he stared at a computer screen for a while, and then he moved around again. It was like he had to stir up something internal to create a reaction; his thoughts needed agitation. Not Theo. He just needed to vegetate with his eyes closed, preferably in a comfortable position.

Theo briefly wondered why people have always been so fixated on physical differences and beliefs, such as religious ones, when these mental differences were so much more interesting, and then he went back to considering how mirror neurons could produce what Eleni and Cora had explained. He couldn't work it out. Theo thought about Adem again and what he had said about knowing how often people can sense who will call before the phone rings. Theo had also read about people who woke up knowing information that they did not know before they went to sleep. He thought he'd experienced it himself when studying in college, but it was always unclear what he had retained the evening before and what was newly acquired by morning.

Perhaps, he thought, our minds are in our bodies but not limited to the physical space there. Perhaps they reach out somehow for an undefined space. Many cultures had a loose version of this, he thought, although he couldn't recall many details. He considered a young boy who asked for something outrageous and then was not surprised when he didn't receive it. Did the child predict the behavior of the parent, or did he "read" the information somehow in a way that all kids can but then they outgrow the skill as they develop? Theo had not contemplated the topic much, but a logical hypothesis would be that kids learn what their parents consider reasonable boundaries and then adapt. But is that what really happens, he pondered, or do kids read their parents' minds externally? Perhaps everyone is born knowing how to do this, but the ability atrophies when it goes unused as most people grow. Kids probably don't remember even doing it. Perhaps this is a neglected ability that we all share, but in families such as the Papadakis family, where some people expect the ability to show up, it is looked for, then practiced. When it appears, it is met with encouragement and becomes more developed. Does this account for the numbers?

Theo was jolted out of his thoughts by a bug. Something flying had landed on his upper arm where his tee-shirt rode up. He swatted it. It was too late; there was blood now, and itching would follow later. He stared at the small lump of bulging skin, then stood up and stretched. He walked over toward Binh and Emma's door. He called out as he arrived, not in an annoying way but to announce his presence. It worked. The door opened, and the women came out onto their larger, more shaded porch.

Binh began talking to Theo almost as soon as he sat down. "In a nutshell, Eleni can think of a simple thought to transmit, then think of Cora, and Cora knows her thoughts. Cora doesn't suddenly know it; she must think of her mother first, and when she does, she knows what her mother wants her to know. This works both ways between both people, right? But aside from people that they happen to know can do this, they don't advertise. No one wants to stand out at best or be run out of town at worst."

"Agreed," said Theo.

"We've been reading," began Binh again. "We found an article published in *The Journal of Nervous and Mental Disease* in the 1970s—"

"That's a title?" asked Theo.

"I know, right? We found it in the Psychology database at Emma's university," said Binh. "The bottom line is that at the time of publication, it wasn't uncommon for people admitted to inpatient psychiatric units to claim that they had telepathic abilities. It's not uncommon now, either, incidentally. But in the 1970s, the inpatients in these facilities were noted for being disproportionately women, and none of them, if able to complete a test given for telepathic abilities, were able to score any better than chance. Therefore, the study concluded that mind communication was nonexistent and basically closed the door on the possibility of mind-to-mind communication."

"Now, on the other hand," said Emma, "not many years later, in Cora's childhood, if the distance was reasonable—between towns or within town—she and her mother were communicating and were 100% accurate. Very few people seem to be aware of this. The interest in disproving any type of paranormal activity was so strong in the United States that even when the participants were already diagnosed with a mental illness, a study went out of its way to show that it didn't exist and wasn't possible. This had Binh and me thinking, once again, that it would be awful if any of this information about what sometimes happens on Crete gets to unfriendly people. It's a real concern, Theo. Are you worried about this?"

Emma and Binh continued explaining to Theo what they had been doing and thinking and how, at the very end of the discussion with Eleni and Cora, Emma, in her most compassionate and slow voice, had asked the Papadakis family how many people they knew total who could shape language.

"I asked as if we had never discussed it, you know? Because they didn't give a number the last time," said Emma. "But I acted like maybe a number was given, and I just couldn't remember, even though, of course, we had asked. It was initially implied that it was just them, then Viktoria and the Korean family, and then that grew."

"People are much more inclined to be open and truthful when it seems like the listener is amenable and an ally," added Binh. "The Papadakis family didn't know us weeks ago, but now they trust us and like us, and they know that we are being and will be careful with their secret."

"Eleni said that she had lost count since she was young of exactly how many people she had known. That alone tells you that it wasn't a single-digit number, right? A person remembers when just one or two other people are like them, right? When Eleni discovered in her childhood what she and a sibling who is now dead could do, a family member or two guided her and disclosed that they could as well. She remembers that there was also the odd person here and there on the playground, one in a nearby house, two in school, and a parent of a friend of her son in elementary school. She mentioned her friend Viktoria, whom she befriended as a teenager. It adds up, Theo. There were quite a few people!"

"And Cora!" exclaimed Emma. "Cora currently knows ten people her age! She just hadn't mentioned this before. We played it very cool, but Theo, Language Shaping may not be all that common, but it is not exactly rare here either."

"I've been wondering how many people there really are here who can do this, and how we would ever know. Good job, you guys," said Theo, raising his chin toward them. "Huh. That's more to think about."

"But you had come over to us. What were you going to ask about?" said Binh, then, suddenly remembering that she had seen him sleeping on a deck chair, she added, "Or, you know, did you guys talk about anything worth passing on?"

"Well," Theo began, "I was lounging. But I think well that way. I had been reading a lot of articles earlier today about mirror neurons and talking about it with Adem, and when I felt cross-eyed and tired from it all, I said that I wanted a break. Adem said that he was thinking of one too, and he'd go for a walk to circulate his blood and his thoughts. He does that. He moves when he does heavy thinking. He'll even pace in a room to jolt his thought process. Not me. I need all processes to direct their energy to thinking, so I declined the walk. I stretched out on a deck chair, closed my eyes, and started processing what I had been reading."

"And?" asked Binh."And Adem is still out walking. But I went off on mental tangents. I'll spare you the tendrils, but I got to thinking that maybe all humans can shape language mentally." He saw Emma raise her eyebrows higher than they seemed like they should go. Binh directed her gaze right at him and opened her eyes wider. He knew what they were thinking. "Just listen, you guys… think of what Adem said about the phone call and email studies, OK? You also know how you can take a baby from any culture in the world, bring it to another country, and it will grow up to be a native speaker of the language of that new country? That's because all babies can babble all kinds of sounds, but these babbles eventually reflect only the sounds that the baby hears. A baby may babble in sounds that belong to the Chinese language when they are very little, but if the baby grows up on a farm in Nebraska, far from a Chinese community, then eventually that baby will speak English. And if no one speaks to that child in Chinese ever, then the ability to make the sounds in that language will be forgotten. Also, have you ever heard a music teacher say that anyone can sing? They claim that some people need more training and practice to sound good, and other people sound great right from the start, but they all roll their eyes when people like me say, 'I can't sing.'

"Last point," Theo took a deep breath. "I have thought a bit about the origin of human language. It's come up in some of my classes. Basically, there are several theories that are prevalent and not mutually exclusive. There is the (1) a God exists who created people and gave them language, and (2) people had to develop language on their own, which is harder than it even sounds because no other known species of animal can make the variety of sounds that humans can. So, how did humans just evolve a language that allows for layering? Also, there must be a way to explain grammar, so there are several theories and ideas about how that might have happened. (3) There is a theory that language rapidly evolved via mirror neurons from gestures. It's a tricky topic, but I always favored that third option. The earliest humans only gestured, but eventually, as they grew taller and stood straighter, they had better vocal capabilities and a larger and more complex brain that could support more vocal sounds and a complex language or, if needed, a more complex signing system. Vocal language, at that point, would have been favored, when possible, over gestured language because it would allow people in various positions, at distances, and in poor light to communicate. For many reasons, I've felt in my gut—don't laugh, you guys—that humans developed language by gesturing first. It seems the most natural, and it makes sense." Theo offered the evidence that he knew could support the idea, and then he told them what he had read about mirror neurons. Then he said, "So imagine that a kid grew up around people who can send thoughts to others. Maybe the kid was conscious of what the others did, or maybe not, but essentially, the mirror neurons copy the action enough that if the kid tries it, then, having both the physical equipment needed and a few neuron pathways, it's easier to learn, easier to repeat, and finally, easier to retrieve. Like the baby that was going to be a native Chinese speaker but then wasn't because it stopped hearing the sounds it would need to mimic. It's possible.

"I don't know how much Chinese you guys have listened to, but it is a very complex language for an adult with no prior experience to learn. For example, there is no alphabet in Chinese. People learn Chinese by learning the pictograms or characters as they are usually called, and there are over 50,000 characters in the language. Good news, though, ladies: it does turn out that one can make a decent conversation with a knowledge set of only about 20,000 characters or so. Anyway, the system has worked for years. There are animal bones in museums that are over three thousand years old and have Chinese characters engraved on them. The hard part is…"

"We haven't gotten to the hard part?" asked Emma.

"No, the hard part for us is that Chinese is a tonal language, so the pitch, such as high or low or neutral, of a word determines the meaning. This might not be as hard for Binh, as she has the concept of tones already, but an anglophone adult who has never been very involved with music would likely have a terrible time even hearing the difference in pitch pronunciations."

"I have a whole new respect for all speakers of Chinese. Wow. I wasn't exactly about to learn it, but it just moved further down the list," said Emma.

"It's hard," said Theo. "But when you were a baby, if a nice Chinese family had adopted you and moved you to Beijing, then today, you would be a tone-differentiating guru and a character-drawing machine."

"And, according to your idea, if she had been raised on Crete by people who could communicate mind to mind, then she would have picked that up as well?" asked Binh.

"Yes," answered Theo. "That's what I came up with."

"It's an interesting idea, but how do you explain why all the children of a given woman who could shape language are not equally skilled?" asked Binh.

"I don't know," said Theo honestly. "I haven't finished thinking it through yet. Maybe the kids who pick it up from their mothers are the kids who spend more time trying to emulate the parent who shapes language, or at least the kids who watched that parent more closely. A lot of these families are traditional; maybe more women can do it, and they pick it up from their mothers. Maybe Cora's brother was off doing other things when Cora saw it, or she paid more attention, or she watched her mother more, or worked side by side with her more in the garden or the kitchen or something. Their father was certainly working long hours, and Eleni cared for the kids alone much of the day. Who knows? I'm just saying that if we think of language shaping more as a gesture that anyone could learn with proper exposure and practice, then we can rethink the numbers that we now know exist and consider all the places on earth where it may be present. Most people that I have met could have been trained to do a split in a gymnastics class, sing a song on key, or learn calculus, but most of them didn't have enough training and practice in at least one of these areas and can't do it very well at all. See what I mean? There are a lot of basic human abilities that people can do but just don't. People with talent can do the same things earlier or maybe with less training and practice, or they can go further in that field, but most humans can do a lot of things that they just never try or practice. Just look at how few Americans speak a second or third language well. It's not because they are not capable. It's exposure and cultural attitude, right?"

Chapter 39: Margo Duc

Margo had been researching, sending, and assuaging for weeks. The two teams were now functioning on their own in different locations, and both had been appropriately convinced that they were not exploiting humanity. Samir had allowed her to explain, in part, his position that he was a communications expert, a radio guy, and a person interested in communication in general. She was aware that the assumption was that Samir held an academic position and conducted research, and Margo did nothing to alter that, but she didn't lie either. He worked for the federal government, as several professors did. Samir just wasn't actually a professor; he was a researcher. He wasn't doing anything harmful with the information. He was just collecting it, cataloging human diversity, exploring communication techniques, and gathering data that might be useful. However, for the first time, Margo found herself asking: useful to what end?

Now that Margo had worked so hard to persuade the team, though, she found herself questioning what she knew. Did she have proof that Samir only gathered information for research? No. Did she know who would view the research? No. Was she certain that a government would never promote, ostracize, manipulate, or otherwise mistreat people who had skills that the average person did not—skills that could change tactical warfare and international relations? Again, no. Margo wondered why she had not been more suspicious and why she had not asked more questions about the use of the research information. She had not even questioned his work until the team kept pushing.

But she knew why. Samir was kind and unassuming. He was almost aloof. He was a thoughtful, thorough, nice guy. He researched to understand; he was altruistic, right? He worked for the government just for the money and the challenge, right?

Margo had passed on to Samir that there were three mind communicators on Crete whom the team had met, and that others existed. She had reported that the group was looking into various explanations for why language shaping existed, as well as the connection between the communicating ability and the undeciphered hieroglyphs found on Crete. Samir had not known that there were undeciphered hieroglyphs in Greece, and this had interested him. As for the men in South Korea, she had reported on their progress and their relationship-building with Hwan, and she wondered what they would learn. Margo also wondered at her own naiveté and how much trust she placed in Samir and then at her jealousy of the team members' experiences.

Before she felt too self-deprecating, though, she circled back to the great group and how much they were able to consider, and she took most of the credit for that. Again. Then she went back to wondering what information was being or would be withheld and how it would affect the outcome.

Chapter 40: Migel Ngubá

Over the course of many days, Migel, Jiho, and Alec had many conversations with Hwan. They were careful to be complimentary about Korea, which wasn't hard, and to be inquisitive about the culture and the area attractions, which was also easy and natural to do. In turn, they learned a lot from Hwan, for example, about dolmens. There are about 40,000 in Korea. Dolmens are formed when two or more enormous stones are stood on their side, and a third stone is placed on top to form a giant-sized, rustic dinner table. Stonehenge in England has many dolmens, but they are also found in much of Scandinavia and the United Kingdom, down through Europe, and in parts of Africa. There are a few thousand in Russia. Surprisingly to Migel, Jiho, and Alec, no country has more dolmens than Korea. The megalithic structures are man-made and very, very old, and no one can imagine either how they were made or why they exist in many places around the world. There are peck marks on the dolmens from tools chipping away at irregularities. There are often human remains under them and fossilized charcoal from the fires that were evidently built inside the structures. Stone tool parts and pottery pieces that largely date from 4000-3000 BCE have been found around many of them, too, but despite studying all of this, no one knows why they were built or how. The word for dolmens in Korean is *goindol*, which means "the propped stone." The American men discussed *goindols* with Hwan.

"Do you know of any nearby?" asked Alec. "We'd love to see one."

"Oh yes," was the answer from Hwan. "The Koch'ang dolmen site and the Hwasun dolmen sites are nearby, and both are UNESCO World Heritage sites. Both sites have over 400 dolmens from the second and first millennia BCE." Hwan had functional English, but through Jiho, the men told him about the Casa Grande ruins in Arizona, and Alec explained the only known prehistoric site cut into bedrock on the East Coast of the United States, The Miami Circle at Brickell Point, in Miami, Florida. Hwan was interested in history, fascinated by nature, and intrigued by what mankind has done and not done. The men had good and casual conversations every time they met.

Another day, the men returned to Hwan's from a morning spent visiting Dogapsa Temple, the first Buddhist temple ever built in Korea. The temple is near Wolchulsan National Park. When they entered the reception room, Hwan was there and offered them tea. As they drank tea, the Americans explained what they had seen and wondered. Hwan was happy, and so he was explaining Korean Buddhism to them. Buddhism, he said, is a religion and a philosophy founded by Siddhartha Gautama in India over 2,500 years ago, but Monk Marananta was the first Indian monk to spread Buddhism to Korea. Around the year 384, he built the Dogapsa Temple. At the time, most people practiced Musok. Jiho knew about this, and he told the group that Musok was often translated as "Korean

Shamanism," but this is a poor translation, he said. He said it was more like an old-fashioned folk religion that believed in many gods, most of which were female. He had heard of this from his parents and their Korean friends.

Buddhism, Hwan had explained in Korean through Jiho, co-existed with Musok, then was suppressed when the Joseon dynasty ruled from 1392-1910. "At this time, Korean Confucianism was more important. The Japanese had been looking to colonize Korea for a long time, and from 1910 to 1945, they officially did. Korean place names were exchanged for Japanese ones, the police of Korea became the Japanese military, Korean cultural artifacts were relocated to Japan, religious Shinto devotion became obligatory, and land ownership became more often Japanese than Korean. Also, under this colonial rule, however, Korea became more industrialized, infrastructure grew tremendously, and a public education system was created, so it was not all bad, but bad for our sense of culture," Hwan explained. "Korean cultural identity suffered. But since World War II ended, so did Japanese rule, and Korea has been rebuilding itself and Korean Buddhism along with it, and it is now followed by about fifteen percent of the population, including me. Most people in South Korea state in polls that they have no religion, but this is only partially true." Hwan said, "There are only about twice as many Christians as Buddhists in South Korea, but Korean Buddhism, like Korean Confucianism, remains part of the cultural and historical fabric of the nation, specifically in the concept of *hanmaeum*." This word had to be explained, Hwan said. *Hanmaeum* is an indigenous Korean word for the concept of "one heart, one mind," used often in the last century by a Buddhist nun named Daehaeng (1927-2012). She was a teacher that Hwan admired.

Jiho asked Hwan to explain *hanmaeum* further because when Jiho added to the translation for Migel and Alec, he added his own words for their benefit about how all minds are individual, but from one, the men all saw where the conversation could go if gently guided. Migel verbalized an opportunity to ask about language shaping and suggested in rapid English that Jiho try. Jiho said that he wasn't sure what he would call it in Korean, but he ended up explaining it when Hwan looked at them curiously.

Hwan replied that Daehaeng taught that humans had three parts: an eternal part, a bodily part, and a consciousness. "The three parts work together to create life," Hwan explained. "All people share *hanmaeum*, and so all human beings are connected to each other. Daehaeng said we are connected in the air, like space."

Migel heard Jiho speak, and then he looked at Alec. What Jiho had said was, "Can people connect to each other by talking in *hanmaeum*? Can their minds be so connected that they talk without using words?" Migel wasn't sure he understood *hanmaeum*, but the question sounded plausibly related to him. Hwan was still for a long time, but he did not seem upset. Finally, in English, he said that there are many non-Western views about how people are connected. The American men nodded and encouraged him to continue.

"The question is 'what is a self'?" Hwan said, "And what is self-identity? They are not the same, I don't think, in Western cultures and for us. It can be hard to see here when your eyes were grown in America."

That makes sense to me, thought Migel. Migel and Alec looked at Hwan and nodded. Hwan continued, switching back into Korean halfway through so that Jiho had to translate every few sentences. Basically, he said that Western bias influenced how Westerners saw the world. He thought that they emphasized individual knowledge and individual actions when thinking about who people were, whereas Koreans emphasized their part in a collective. Thinking of 'Self' was not realizing one's individual uniqueness in Korea, as Westerners believe, but realizing one's place and purpose in a social, hierarchical web. "For us, people are already connected," he said, switching back to English. "All people can talk when they are connected. Some people can connect from one mind to another, and some always need words and hands. Koreans already recognize the connectedness between people. Maybe it is strange for those who don't see the connectedness already. In Korean Confucianism, a root of our culture, the individual is tied to..." Hwan waved his hand upwards. "Harmony for me connects to harmony in the world. Maybe Westerners are not thinking of it in that way, but we are thinking in that way in Korea." Hwan seemed done, but then he added more. "Some cultures want to break a self away and be a complete individual as a goal. The goal is a separate self. Our goal here, my goal, is to make myself disappear and be a part of everything that I see and everything that I do, and that is when I will be a full person. When two people have a deep connection, and self is not in the way, then these people can connect without words."

Migel was stunned. Alec was thoughtful. Jiho was respectfully silent, and then he said, "I think you are correct. My family often speaks about being a part of a whole, but no one explained it to me before in this way. Thank you."

It seemed best to lighten the discussion and not seem driven to discuss telepathy, and so Jiho then talked more about the idea of what makes a good human. Alec chimed in about how different cultures consider individual versus community needs, and then they rolled the conversation toward plan-making for the next day. They discussed dinner, and then the three Americans excused themselves, left the table, and headed to their room. They had been bursting to talk to each other privately for twenty minutes. Once inside, Migel said, "WOW."

"I know," said Jiho quietly. "We need to not seem fixated on it, though. We need to stay cool and let it come up again sometime. We can't rush this, or we won't learn anything. Pointed conversation will seem suspicious to him. We need to seem like we thought of things and then just returned to the topic with questions."

"It was interesting hearing what Hwan said about one's sense of self," said Migel. "The truth is that we all see the world through our own culture, and one must know another culture or cultural idea well before considering what it means to see the world in another way. Everyone can only know what they have seen with their own eyes and, in a lighter way, what they have read and heard."

"You don't seem amazed, Jiho. What do you think?" probed Alec.

"Well," said Jiho… "when people come from isolated areas, over many centuries, they develop a distinct culture, naturally. The people become more similar and more aware of how things should be and are expected to be. In Korean, there is a word for this. People can often complete the thoughts and phrases of another person. This is not mind-to-mind communication. It is recognized reactions, shared expectations, and similar thought patterns from shared cultural beliefs and education. When you say hello, and then I say hello back, and you say, 'How are you?' and I say, 'Fine, thank you,' we are not mind-reading. We are following a cultural script. These are short and few in the US, but they are long and many here. Despite the small size of South Korea, there are many somewhat isolated villages because of the mountains and the rivers. People living there know their culture well and have less change and variance than people who live in Seoul. I don't want to push, but I want to be sure of what we are all talking about before I get too excited. We'll talk to him at dinner. For now, let's figure out how to share this with Margo and the Cretans. They will all want an update, but let's be clear that we are not sure if the comment can be taken at face value yet or not."

Chapter 41: Binh Tran

Seoul, South Korea, to Manila, the capital of the Philippines, is an easy flight. Many airlines schedule direct, inexpensive flights regularly, so Jiho, Migel, and Alec arrived easily at Ninoy Aquino International Airport, just south of Manila, on July 1st. Flying to the Philippines from Greece is a different story; there are no direct flights. Theo, Adem, Binh, and Emma had to fly to Istanbul, Turkey, and then take an eleven-hour nonstop flight to Manila. The time zones traveled were also uneven, so the Grecian group moved six hours ahead in time by flying to the Philippines, but the Korean group moved back just one hour. It was impossible to coordinate landing times, so the teams agreed to meet at the hotel that Margo had sent them.

It was a small two-star hotel in the old walled section of Manila, the Intramuros, literally meaning "within the walls," and it was perfect for their needs. It was clean, equipped with suitable rooms and food, and had a large outdoor seating area with a view into history. The muros, the walls, had been built in 1571 by the Spanish for protection, and they had successfully fended off Dutch, Portuguese, and Chinese attempts to penetrate Manila. When the Philippines was a colony of Spain, from 1565 to 1898, the entire city of Manila had the walls built around it for protection. Now, the vibrant city spilled out over these barriers in every direction possible, and the walls simply designate 'old town.' Manila, as a city, is much, much bigger. The thick, high stone walls simply cuddle the interior cobblestone streets and the buildings with second-floor balconies and interior courtyards of the 'old town.' History, beauty, and death are all bound in the tired and pitted charcoal-colored masonry.

Binh watched the walls of old Manila grow as she approached from their twenty-five-minute taxi ride from the airport. When the taxi stopped just inside them, in front of a hotel, Alec, Jiho, and Migel were sitting at an outdoor table facing their direction of arrival. Migel got up as soon as he saw them and pulled over a nearby table so that they could all sit together. Alec walked toward the parked car.

"Hey, you guys!" called Emma as Theo paid the taxi and began unloading bags. "How have you been?"

"Less tired and busy than you all," said Jiho, who had gotten up to help with the separation of people and bags from the vehicle.

"Since we got here yesterday, we've walked around a bit already. Margo has arranged a meeting for us tomorrow with a woman named Mirikit, but we are free until then. Do you guys want to go up to your rooms? We checked you in already," said Alec. "Take showers?"

"We will. Hang on. Stories first!" said Emma. "We have juicy news."

"As do we," countered Migel with a sly look.

"Give us the details!" said Emma.

Binh recognized that her anxiousness from awaiting their arrival was dissolving into happiness at seeing the men. She'd missed them. The seven of them had become a tight, little interdependent group that trusted each other to do what the group decided. In the end, there is no better description of a well-run team. They'd kept in touch while on separate continents, but it wasn't the same, and the communication had been light on specifics.

"You catch us up first because we know how your story starts," said Jiho, "and we can picture the place and people already."

"We're like a mini version of 'The Canterbury Tales,'" said Adem, "but we already ate!" He laughed a little at his own joke, but no one really seemed to get it.

"What?" said Alec.

"'The Canterbury Tales' by Geoffrey Chaucer?" Adem retorted. "It is a story written over 600 years ago, in thousands of lines of poetry, so it's a super long poem with a good plot, basically. It tells the story of a group of pilgrims walking from London to a shrine in Canterbury, England. They are a diverse group of people of various trades and social status, like a knight, a cook, a miller, and a nun, but they are all walking for the same reason, and they all tell stories as they walk to pass the time. They declare it a competition. The person who tells the best story will eat a free meal at the tavern at the end of the trip. It's written in a very old version of English that is hard to understand, but we read a modern English translation in high school."

"I don't think that was even mentioned in my high school!" said Alec. "But it sounds interesting. I'll look it up. When was it written?"

"At the end of the 1300s," answered Adem, "I don't remember the exact date."

"OK, so, we are like that. And here is our tale…" blurted out Emma. There was nothing like the weird tiredness that comes from sitting in a plane for a long time, doing nothing important, to wind a person's energy up. "In addition to what you already know…" she began dramatically.

"You can't start a tale like that!" said Adem.

"Fine. In addition to Viktoria, Eleni, and Cora," she looked at Alec, "there are about two dozen more people, at least, who can shape language, and they are either currently on Crete or were when Eleni was growing up. This little piece of new information means that there are probably more, and so we don't think we are talking about a weird genetic mutation within a family or two."

"You guys met another two dozen people?" asked Jiho.

"No, no, but we gently asked again if there were more people that they could think of, and it turns out that Eleni knew some people growing up and has, over the years, known more. Cora has known a lot, too, and at least some are still on Crete. Considering how long it took them to mention this to us, I assume it is probably even more than they said," explained Emma.

"In all fairness, they didn't know what we would do with the information," said Binh. "They sort of ended up being forced to tell us what they did when they had only barely known us, so I think they downplayed a lot in the beginning."

"That makes sense," said Alec.

"Yes," said Emma, "but it does change a little bit how we think about this. We have, as a group," she looked at Theo and Adem, "posited that either this is an innate human ability, atrophied or ignored, or… it is something that everyone can do. However, it only gets accessed by some, when an action, or a gesture, perhaps 'ignited' through mirror neurons at a young age and strengthened over time with practice. It would be interesting to know if anyone who can do it had never known someone who could until they were older. We suspect not. These ideas make the hieroglyphic piece seem more likely to be connected in that there easily could have been a population of people who language-shaped living at the palace. After a lot of studying and reading, it does seem as if the pictograms might represent concrete items and amounts of goods stored or transferred. We worked a little bit with Cora, and the content of the pictograms best explains the concept of how information is sent in language shaping. Cora called the sent information 'idea packets' once. Unfortunately, proposing this officially means that there will be unpleasant questioning and unwanted attention. After all these years, one needs a strong backstory as to why the epiphany is on meaning now. We talked mostly about that on our final visits with the Papadakis family. They are good people," concluded Emma.

"After so many years of museum work, it's not that Dr. Papadakis is not regionally well-known," said Binh, "but everyone thinks about what their lifetime of contributions are as they get older, I think, and Dr. Papadakis probably wondered if translating the hieroglyphics should be something that he put his name to. He has been mulling it over for decades, I suspect."

"The family lives in relative isolation, and they seem to have been wondering about how much to share with the larger world. It helped them, I think, to be able to discuss this issue with a nonbiased party," added Theo. "Yeah, I think it helped them to hear from us that it's not paranoia when people really are out to get you," added Adem. Everyone laughed. "Seriously, a media craze would just be the beginning. There is no way to guess how the government of Greece might react, and what if the European Union decides that it is in the best interest of EU security to understand the ability and force testing? Worst-case scenario, the family could be kidnapped by a less discriminating group wanting to run some tests. There are many options for how many ways their peaceful and productive lives could be ruined. I think they were hungry to talk to someone, to be able to have open discussions and to have outside advice, and that is why Dr. Papadakis had, after so many years, leaked a little information to his buddy Martin Kolsch. You know, the source via which we ostensibly ended up here?"

"I remember," said Alec quietly. "It's still surprising that it was us. That it is us, you know, doing this. Learning the secrets. Trying to figure this out."

"Well, we only officially have to document it, not figure it out," said Theo, "but only a total dolt wouldn't wonder. I'm still amazed. Remember that weird non-disclosure thing we signed months ago? This is why! At the time, I thought it meant that we were going to learn about some screwed-up aspect of the US education system and weren't supposed to discuss it with anyone. Ha!"

"There's no one better than us," said Adem quietly. "None of us are affiliated with any companies that might have interests. I had just left a serious, unrelated job, and the rest of you, no offense, were still working through what you would do and how long you would stay in school. Together, we're knowledgeable enough to be thoughtful, not connected enough to cause trouble, and not educated enough or famous enough to be cocky. If I had to guess, Margo was careful about our personalities as well—none of us are likely to go rogue and sell the others out. I'm not sure who would believe us anyway."

"There's some truth to all of that. People do seem unguarded about talking to us," echoed Migel. "Hwan opened up to us pretty quickly and told us more each day."

"What did you learn?" asked Theo. "Well, our story ends in roughly the same place as yours, but the journey was different," said Jiho, and he proceeded to tell the group what he had not in his short emails. He described Hwan and his old building, their relationship, and finally, about their conversations on the last few days. "I was concerned initially, of course, about the cultural tendency for social learning, but it wasn't that at all. As Hwan explained it, there is actual mind-to-mind communication occurring, not that we witnessed any of it, but we heard the explanation."

"And what is that?" asked Binh. She liked hearing Alec explain his natural science concepts. He was a natural teacher.

"Well, Hwan explained the communication between minds as happening in the space around the people," said Migel. "Information gets transferred across space and time but not physically. I clarified that he wasn't talking about auras. He was talking about energy in space, in the space around us. He talked about the Korean concept of connectedness among people. Hwan says this is possible because people's perceptions extend beyond their brains and their bodies. He talked about what could occur in these fields of perceptions."

"What?" said Emma. "I don't get it."

"Have you guys ever heard of tree mycorrhizal networks?" asked Alec.

"No," said Binh. "When a forest is healthy," Alec began, "every tree is connected underground to other trees. They share water and nutrients. Fun fact: studies have shown that trees recognize their own relatives by their root tips and favor them when passing out supplies. Importantly, this is how the large, older trees with very deep roots keep the younger saplings alive in times of less rain. There are cool studies where trees are fed non-toxic dye that comes up in other trees in the forest, showing how the resources are distributed among groups of trees."

"What Hwan was describing is like a web that we can't see," said Migel, "where humans feed each other, or at least offer information for access. But not just humans in his mind. He says that all living things have webs among their own kind."

"Actually," said Alec, "there are biologists who believe that plant life does this because molecular biology alone does not explain how certain organisms, like free-living bacteria cells, organize themselves into complex structures. One hypothesis floating about is that organisms share a collective memory that exists outside of them in a kind of field. The field or area around all organisms influences development because it contains communal information for growth and development, allowing that organism to learn from past knowledge and experiences of the same kinds of organisms. The theory is often called morphic resonance theory; it describes how forms resonate with a field and information is sent between the form and the field in both directions. Every organism, from a pine tree to a developing human embryo, can both access and offer knowledge because a field connects all similar type species. According to this idea, successful patterns are reinforced, and new habits can be created. There is a lot to this idea, and I have been reading more about it for a few days now, but essentially, Hwan was saying that all information is not in one's head, and so while clairsentience seems paranormal to us, that is only because we conceive of our bodies incorrectly and as unconnected to the bodies of others. If we consider that all of a kind are connected, and that knowledge can exist outside of bodies that bodies have access to, then knowledge is not limited to existing within one's mind. A human mind is not limited to being only in one's head. We are partially, maybe even mostly, in our own bodies, but there is also, according to this, a shared knowledge of minds outside of individual organisms. 'Where is human consciousness?' is a philosophical question that has existed for centuries: is the conscious mind physical or mental? Is the conscious mind a creation of the human brain, or is it a non-physical entity? Hwan believes in the latter, a concept generally called 'dualism,' where the mind is considered to be separate from the body and not a physical entity, although clearly, some aspects of perception are brain-dependent. There are a few theories proposed on how this might work. In opposition are the materialists who believe that the mind is the body and it creates consciousness."

"Huh," said Adem. "Not having put much thought into this before now… I guess I assumed that the human mind was a product of the brain and so the brain was the place where consciousness resided," said Adem.

"That makes you a materialist, and that is basically what's taught or alluded to in school," said Jiho. "The seat, as it is often referred to, the seat of human consciousness is in the brain, specifically, in the cerebral cortex, and consciousness is the result of brain activity."

"Maybe it is. Maybe it isn't, but the answer to that changes what mental communication is," said Alec. "A month ago, I had never thought for very long about clairsentience. A few weeks ago, I considered it to be an unusual skill contained within a given human population and accessible by only those humans. Today, I think that mind-to-mind communication exists, and now I'm just wondering how prevalent it is and how it works. Now that I have been listening to Hwan explain that there is shared knowledge in a shared field and that anyone can access it, the idea that people can transfer knowledge within the field is not so weird sounding. One person puts knowledge in a field, and another takes it away. There's more— this idea transcends human abilities. I mentioned trees in a forest earlier. The idea is that all life forms have this ability may alter some understandings in biology. Maybe animals navigate via this kind of field, as opposed to having an embedded kind of compass, as many predict. Maybe birds fly in a synchronized flock, and fish can swim in a coordinated school because of these fields. Perhaps people know what others think sometimes, or when they want to contact us because of these fields as well? The scientific explanation, that not many scientists acquiesce to, by the way," said Alec, "is that these fields are called Morphic Fields, and Morphic Resonance is how these fields have what is essentially memory. The origins are in plant biology, which is how I heard of it, and I've been researching it more since we met Hwan. It sounds like he is describing the same thing."

"You know the idea from biology because of the connected root systems? I thought those were physical connections?" said Binh.

"Oh, they are. Sorry," said Alec, "There was a theory proposed in the 1920s about Morphogenetic Fields. It basically says that chemical signals and gene activation alone aren't enough to explain how specialized cells develop, and so it proposes a field where cells within that field acquire the information needed to specialize. It's been brought back by some scientists in the 1980s searching for an explanation for what appears to be mental telepathy among animals."

"What is the explanation for how the physical human brain interacts and communicates with the non-physical field-type place—or are they all one?" asked Adem.

"There isn't one," said Migel, "No one knows how Magnetic Resonance works for certain, but there are some ideas from scientists who study it. The most popular of these is an idea from a quantum physicist who thinks there could be essentially a world that we can observe that has more to it that we have not observed. Space and time are located in the unobservable world, for example. The phenomenal states of consciousness, the parts of the experience that are perceived, such as feelings and mental imagery, are not clearly tied to a specific brain state either, so no one is sure how they happen. Hwan was basically saying that the brain doesn't contain all consciousness, just some of it, and that the rest resides in a communal field that we can tap into."

"Is it… likely? What do you guys think?" asked Emma, her sense of reality slowly evaporating. Communication without sound or hand movements was strange enough, but she'd at least heard of that before as a concept. Fields of invisible information were a lot more to accept.

"There are studies," offered Alec, "concerning bacteria and other microorganisms, demonstrating that they share information with each other using electromagnetic fields. We're not bacteria. We have nervous systems that are complex, but neurons do respond to magnetic fields. I'm still reading about how this could work between humans. I found a study that was quietly done during COVID, but it was published, and it wasn't that hard to find. It piggybacked on the studies that found iron particles in human brains ($Fe3O4$) and posited that they function as weak magnets to a field, um, like the one that we are talking about now. I read some of those studies, and then I read the study that found cryptochrome in the human retina as well as the human brain and confirmed that the cryptochrome perceives magnetic fields, such as the one that might be connected to us via the trace amounts of $Fe3O4$ in our brains. It's a lot to take in, but I'm trying to be open-minded."

"Knowing how mind-to-mind communication works seems crucial to knowing what questions to ask," said Binh. "Not every detail, of course, but generally understanding how it's possible helps me to think about it. I have a hard time thinking deeply about what I can't understand."

"You and everyone else," said Jiho, and Binh understood that he meant it sincerely and not in a snarky way. "The concept of electromagnetic fields being a place of shared information is tricky. If real, they force questions about what we believe about energy and certain scientific assumptions."

"They do. And it is not popular to question scientific dogma," Alec continued, "One can get seen as a kook at best and a dissenter or dangerous, anti-science agitator at worst. Remember when medical doctors and scientists who spoke out against the official explanations of and the official protocols for COVID-19 were de-platformed and branded as conspirators? We saw that people like the expression 'thinking outside the box' a lot more than they like to hear the ideas that exist outside of the box. If there are people who have something to gain by maintaining the status quo box, then disruptors will be persecuted. So, it's taken me a few days to really explore this idea properly. Most scientists who are curious about this idea are quiet, but a few are not. There are some carefully worded articles and published studies of value. There are books. I think that science is and should be about asking questions, and when questioning makes people angry and uncomfortable, we should ask why and look deeper. Controversy shouldn't be something we silence; it should be explored. I have no vested interest in any explanation of the world. I'm just curious. I have friends and relatives who claim to hear the corn talk. I know that listening to nature and to dead ancestors is common globally, yet we, as Americans, have a tendency to discount cultures that didn't invent a stock market. I don't know. It was an odd experience to hear a Korean man recounting what I had recently heard in Kenya and had also heard many times from poor and marginalized people in Arizona. Then I looked up a bunch of published studies by seriously impressive scientists, and guess what? There's alignment. That's a long answer, I guess. The short answer is that I'm not discrediting anything yet, but I don't know."

"Wow," said Emma after a second. "That is a lot to take in. Animism, you know, the idea that spirits inhabit what Europeans and Americans consider to be non-animate objects, like trees, rivers, and birds, is well known in anthropology. It's an ontological perspective that exists on every continent around the world among the indigenous people. I was raised to think of humans and some animals as having a life of value, and to view ideas to the contrary as pre-scientific, as primitive, and the kinds of ideas that people come up with to explain the world to their community in the lack of scientific explanations. But it is hard not to notice that the dominant cultures that eschew such ideas, the ones dominated by people who don't hear plants talk, are quite literally destroying the earth at a rapid rate. Maybe that's not disconnected from all of this."

"Wouldn't it be ironic if the old Africans were right?" suggested Theo.

"Not just African cultures, but all native cultures that I've ever studied," said Emma, "which is a lot. Ancient Polynesians navigated using 'wayfinding' techniques that essentially meant being so mindful and in tune with nature that the smallest changes in water pattern offered information. The Yanomami in the Amazon Forest have been listening to the plants talk for generations to learn how, despite the tens of thousands of plant species in the Amazon, the people can know which ones combine in which ways to gain certain medicinal effects. These examples of interconnectedness between humans and the natural world conflict with Western views of single truths, compartmentalization, linear timelines, and individualism. But they make a lot more sense if there are electromagnetic fields."

"So where does that leave us?" asked Adem.

"In the odd position of finding what few would suspect in an unexpected place," said Alec. "The little I got to know of Korean culture, it struck me as more reflective of a holistic tribal community than the modern buzzing K-culture movement or country-setting trends. Did you guys know that the V&A Museum in London had an exhibit in 2023 on the current Korean cultural exports: food, fashion, film, and music? That's the Korea that I was expecting to meet. But the Korea that I visited in the south felt more like spending time with long-lost relatives. There was an indirectness punctuated with directness. There was silence. There was a reverence for the natural world. Things felt more circular than linear. There was a connectedness. There were conversations that were familiar. I truly enjoyed Korea."

"I know some nice Korean girls that you can date when we get back home," said Jiho, and he laughed. "You guys can talk circles and connectedness." He smiled.

"I was being serious. I liked eating *Ddukbokkie*, *bibimbap*, and *Kimchi*. But Hwan made sense, too. People feel differently in the United States. It's hard to explain."

"I know what you mean, dude. I'm just giving you a hard time," said Jiho. "I see the difference. Koreans are more spiritual and open in many ways than Americans are not, but less religious and more closed in other ways. They like order. Hwan was also more typical of the countryside than the city. I think there has been a river emerging and widening between city and rural people for a long time in every country. Before the Industrial Revolution, maybe the river was between landowners and people who worked the land, but that became more of a stream when a deepening and widening divide sprang up between city dwellers and rural people. Either people live with nature, or it's a hindrance. Either they value time over almost anything else, or they value almost everything else and are patient with time. People driven by numbers and power are not of the same mentality as people who produce, raise, and grow products. For many rural people, acquired skills rival studied knowledge, so Kwan reminded you of Arizona, but the people in Seoul, if we talked to any for very long, would have reminded you more of the US, I think. Kwan represents Korea, but specifically rural Korea."

"Hey, I'm all for continuing this conversation, but right now, I am dying for a shower and maybe a nap. Can we meet up for dinner and continue then?" asked Theo. All agreed. Binh told Emma to take the first shower, and she'd follow shortly. Migel and Jiho walked off to find somewhere to buy the local halo-halo, a Filipino ice cream and fruit dessert. Alec and Binh remained at the table.

"So, you really liked Korea?" Binh asked.

"I loved it," said Alec unequivocally. "Seoul was gigantic and busy. It's how I imagine New York City. It had everything: old, new, large and small, but the south seemed like the heart of Korea. I wish you could have met Hwan. He was warm, kind, and helpful but private at the same time. We ended up paying him to make us a lot of meals, and we talked a lot then about everything while we ate. And Crete?"

"All that you remember, the food, the rooms with the porches and the walking in the hot sun," replied Binh.

"This isn't cool, but it's not sweltering, and it feels dry. It rained a lot in Korea. Every day, I think, but never all day," said Alec. He fiddled with his glass. "Glad we're all together again," he said and smiled, "I hope Mirikit can help us."

"Me too," Binh said. She was tired, didn't have much else to say, and felt silly now for wanting to talk more to Alec. She said, "I bet it's my turn in the shower," and got up to push her chair in. "Traveling makes me feel grimy. Pick out a good place for dinner, and I'll see you in a few hours."

Chapter 42: Emma Miller

The Location File for the Philippines, sent by Margo, was particularly useful. While 20-something-year-old Americans tended to know a little bit about the Philippines, they tended not to know a lot. The information about the history and culture would prove invaluable. The group already knew that the Philippines is an archipelago in Southeast Asia, but they learned that where Hawai'i is an archipelago of 137 islands, the Philippines consists of 7,641 islands. These islands are all tucked together south of China, north of Indonesia, and east of Vietnam. There is evidence of human habitation as early as 700,000 years ago and also that people moved onto the Philippine islands as the result of a prehistoric seaborne migration sometime before 2000 BCE. These people used boats with sails, and they navigated.

It was also learned that the indigenous belief system of the pre-colonial Philippines included both animism and polytheism. Pre-colonial mythology in the Philippines consisted of gods, creation stories, and mythical creatures. Bathala was the creator of earth and man among the Tagalogs, Laon among the Visayans, and the Ilocano people believed in Kabunian. These gods were great beings, inaccessible to regular people who accordingly often communicated with the secondary deities called anito by the Tagalogs and diwata by the Visayans. The stories with these characters explained national phenomena, a reason for existence, and a direction for the future.

Until the sixteenth century, the people on this group of over 7,000 islands were of many cultures, each with its own beliefs, language, religion, and lifestyle, whose stories were passed through the generations orally. Today, the information and tales have been diluted and influenced by the Hindu, Buddhist, Shinto, Muslim, and Christian peoples who came to live on these bountiful islands, and the past is hard to know for sure.

A discussion of the Philippines' culture and history is incomplete if it does not consider the influence of the Arab traders who arrived in the Philippines and stayed. Sulu, now a province at the southern end of the archipelago, was eventually chosen as the site for the first Muslim ruler, Muhammad Sharif Kabungsuwan, who became the first Sultan of the Sulu region. The Sultanate of Sulu rapidly became known as a center for Islamic study. Kabungsuwan and his successors flourished and continually fought attempts to be overthrown by the Spanish, who started arriving in 1565 when Miguel López de Legazpi announced that a small community in Cebu would be the first Spanish settlement in this new land that the explorer Magellan had named for King Philip II of Spain a few decades earlier. When the Muslims and the Spanish discovered their conflicting aims, they fought until 1726, when a peace treaty was signed between the Sulu Sultanate and the Spanish Colonial government. It said that the Muslims would remain, and so would the Spanish. In this way, Islam in the Philippines survived 300 years of Spanish colonization and the US colonization that followed, although the US government took power away from the Sulu Sultanate in 1915. Islam, nonetheless, remains the longest-lasting foreign influence in a country that has also been shaped by Chinese traders, the Japanese, the Spanish, and the Americans. The Philippines was the one place where Margo had said that the team would go from the beginning. Emma had recently learned that this was because Margo wanted the group to connect with Marikit, who would not be back in Manila until July. Marikit, Emma was surprised to learn, had studied in the United States for a semester of college, courtesy of the US government. Evidently, since 2008, the US Department of State has funded the Global Undergraduate Program, whereby strong students from one of over sixty economically developing nations can apply to come to live and study in the US for a semester, fully funded. The idea is to develop future leaders and influencers. It seemed like a good idea to Emma; she just had no idea that such a program existed. Now, here was Marikit, sitting with them at an outdoor table and explaining her experience in the United States in fantastic and only slightly accented English.

"I will take part in school administration at some part and work in curriculum and access, but I teach now," Marikit was saying. "I met a friend of Margo's when I was in California, and we stayed in touch. Margo has been emailing me about your project and connected me to you. I picked the hotel that you are at," she smiled, "I hope you like it."

"It's perfect," said Adem, "and so is the location. We have been able to walk around a lot, and there are plenty of places in the areas to hang out and get food. Thank you."

"It's great to meet you," said Jiho. "Thank you for making time to talk with us." Marikit smiled, and Jiho continued, "How exactly did Margo explain our project to you? Because, um, it has evolved for us. I just want to be sure we are all on the same page." Marikit smiled and nonchalantly stated that, as she understood it, Margo and her friend were studying language communication and were interested in sending a group of researchers, who she supposed were who sat in front of her now, to meet the people with *nagsasalita sa ulo*, the head talkers. She furthered that her help was no trouble at all, and she had planned on meeting the group today and taking them to the islands in a day or two. It wasn't even an inconvenience, she said, because she had family up there that she wanted to visit. The team was in awe.

Alec recovered first and said, "Yes, that is exactly what we are working on. Do the *nagsasalita sa ulo*, live near here? Is that what you call them, 'the head talkers?'"

"Yes, we call them 'head talkers' because they can communicate language from one head to another. They are not from here. They live up on the Batanes Islands in the far north of the Philippines. This is a group of ten islands just 150 kilometers from Taiwan. Only three of the islands have people living on them: Batan, Itbayat, and Sabtang. I will go with you up to Batan and show you what we have here for information. I told Margo that I could, and I was happy to help. Most people speak English there, but everyone speaks Ivatan too. I speak Ivatan and have family up there. You can meet them." "That's so kind of you," said Binh, trying to act as if this was a normal thing to hear. "Thank you. I knew before this trip that the Philippines had two national languages, Filipino and English, but I have recently read that there are over 120 languages spoken here, somewhat separated by area. Ivatan is the language spoken in the Batan Islands, I assume?"

"Yes, but there are two dialects of Ivatan, and English is commonly spoken there too. People in the Philippines often speak two or three languages: the local one that they speak at home, Filipino, which the schools are taught in, and English, which is also taught in schools. The longer one stays in school, the more English they know."

"The languages are very fascinating here," broke in Theo, "I am studying linguistics. However, I was never taught about head talking in school. Is it common here?"

"I don't know how many people speak *nagsasalita sa ulo*," said Marikit thoughtfully as she scrunched her nose towards her eyes. That's such a universal human gesture, thought Emma, and it was also her opening to talk. "Are you taught about head talking in school?" she asked.

"Oh no!" said Marikit, "It's a... well, we have a lot of superstitions here that many people believe, for example, we don't sweep our floors at night so as not to sweep out our good luck. We don't let brothers and sisters get married in the same year to prevent bad luck, and we eat pancit and noodles at all celebrations to make sure that we have a long and healthy life. There are many beliefs like this, but people are generally very religious as well, and it is ok to be more one way than another. My family is Christian, but they all also believe in the old spirit world and an old Filipino indigenous religion. People who can head talk are said to be spirit communicators, so the people who don't believe in the spirit world just don't believe in head talkers any more than they believe deeply about anito, the spirits of our ancestors."

"We read about anito," said Theo, "before the Spanish arrived, the people here believed in a human world and a spirit world and many gods. The Spanish understood the word to mean just the carvings of these spirits, but really anito are the souls of the people who used to live here. Is that right?"

"Exactly. There are many words for the spirits and the gods due to the different languages spoken here and the many different groups of people pre-colonization. The Tagbanwa people, for example, have their own language in which they explain their complex mythology, and they have an old written form, Tagbanwa script, which many still know today."

"I heard of it just recently," said Theo excitedly. "It is an alpha-syllabary, a language where each character or symbol represents a syllable, like pa, ka, yi, or mu, as opposed to English, where each letter represents a sound, and we have to make the syllables by putting sounds together. We were just working with a language in Greece that functions in a similar way. I had looked up other alpha-syllabary languages." When he said this to everyone who had not already immediately seen the connection to Cretan Hieroglyphics, Theo continued, "Can these people head-talk as well?"

"I don't know," admitted Marikit. "They live in an area south of here that I have never been to, near Indonesia, the Palawan Province. Palawan Island is very long and thin, so it has a very big coastline. The people are farmers, fishermen, weavers, and hunters—I don't know much more about them."

"Can we go?" asked Theo. "How long would it take? Are we expected on a certain day on Batan?"

"It would…," began Marikit, but Theo cut her off.

"The base of the language is related to certain scripts in Indonesia, which themselves are based on old scripts from India," said Theo. "We could go and check out the connection."

"It's Wednesday," began Marikit again. "We'll go to Basco, the capital of Batan, on Friday morning. Maybe in the middle of next week, I can take you to Palawan," said Marikit. "It depends on how long you stay."

Chapter 43: Jiho Bak

Most chicken breeds have feet with three toes pointing forward and one little toe pointing backward, just like theropods, the dinosaurs from the late Triassic and early Jurassic periods. The Philippine islands look a little bit like a chicken foot. There are three island clusters pointing south of the large island of Luzon, where Manila is located, and then a little archipelago, the Batanes Islands, north of Luzon, like the tiny back claw or toe on a chicken foot.

The flight from Manila to Batan Island is direct and takes less than two hours. The airport is in Basco, the capital of the province of Batanes, located at the north end of the island. It is more like a town than a city. The group arrived there, and shortly thereafter, were picked up by the shuttle bus of the inn where they would be staying. The inn was in the center of Basco and exactly a third of a mile from the airport; it was all very walkable without luggage. Marikit had helped the group to the inn, which seemed entirely unnecessary, and then continued to her parent's home after promising to pick the Americans up in two hours for lunch.

July is not quite the rainiest month. August, September, and October are, but July is right behind them. So, no one was surprised by the light rain that was falling when the plane landed. "I told you that the past two days in Manila were unusual," Marikit had said. But the rain didn't prevent the beauty of the island from emanating from every green hill. The island of Batan was lush with pastures. It was the opposite, really, of the island of Crete. Yellow-ochre is the dominant color on Crete, but on Batan, the dominant color is the deep green of chlorophyll-rich plant life. Jiho had more recently been in South Korea, and so was not as jolted by the difference in islands. Everyone else commented on it.

"As the group walked up stairs and down a hallway, Jiho said, "We have four neighboring rooms and time to unpack. I know we bought one-way flights, but I bet we are here for at least a week."

"Oh wow, did you guys connect your phones yet? This is the strongest Wi-Fi we've seen in weeks. Go figure, we're in the middle of an ocean!"

"I read about the internet here," said Jiho. "I was wondering if it would be satellite or underwater cables. I learned that the satellites in operation are slower than the speed at which information travels via the undersea fiber-optic cables. Then I looked at an undersea cable map, and I saw that the Philippines, Malaysia, Hong Kong, and Taiwan are all seriously connected," said Emma.

"Here's the first room; the others are that one," said Jiho, pointing across the hall, "and those two up there."

*****

Marikit showed up just after noon, as expected. The group had unpacked and walked the area a little bit by the time she arrived. Together, they walked west towards the coast to a restaurant run by Marikit's aunt. As they walked, Marikit pointed out buildings and shops. They talked about her plans for getting the group together with some head talkers. She said she'd be happy to answer all their questions at lunch.

It was hard for everyone to walk close enough to hear the conversation, so Emma, Binh, and Adem walked with Marikit, and the others walked behind. It made sense for the people who were skilled at small talk to be at the center of it. So that everyone could hear, Emma waited until they were introduced at the restaurant and seated at a table before asking about the anito.

"We read about them," said Emma, "but how do you explain them? We are trying to understand the connection to the head talkers."

"Ah, ok," said Marikit. "Anito is a group term for all the invisibles. They can be souls of people who are no longer living, or spirits who stay in a certain place, or ones who wander. Many people say the anito of the recently deceased can become visible briefly and appear before them to ask for small solutions to worldly problems to explain the needs of someone who is still living. These anito show themselves in black, generally. Anito who appear wearing dark colors need prayers to release them from the state they are in, often suffering. Anito who appear in white are at peace. My people have believed in anito for a very long time, even before the Spanish came, and so some people today dismiss the discussion of them because they are a part of folk religion."

"And the people who are head talkers speak with the anito?" asked Binh.

"Oh, probably, if they see them, but head talkers can also talk amongst themselves. Many people don't pay attention to Filipinos with old religious beliefs, and the same people who ignore people who talk to anito also ignore any discussion of anitos or to each other in their heads. This is what I said about people knowing but not caring. The head-talkers are not in hiding, but many people just don't believe that they communicate with each other any more than they believe that they communicate with anitos."

"Ah! Now I understand," said Emma. And Jiho did, too. He had brought up with the group that perhaps the head-talkers were community members who interacted with the dead on behalf of the living, as the people that Kimaru studied. The group had a lot of questions, but they had been following Marikit's directions about where to go and generally talked about it. It had seemed too forward and too pushy to have asked for clarity sooner. Jiho was happy to have it now, and it helped him to orient his thoughts because it wasn't easy for him to believe that some people have mental telepathy and others don't, and the two groups live side by side in harmony. That had seemed unlikely. But if one group looks down on another in some way, and doesn't value or believe in their cultural ways, well, then it suddenly seems plausible. Beliefs are everything. They had also learned from Marikit that although the Philippines became independent from the United States on July 4th, 1946, this was not a holiday because, in 1964, the president of the Philippines moved the holiday to June 12th because, on June 12th, 1898, the Philippines won their independence from Spain. The group and Marikit had enjoyed a long discussion on the purpose of national holidays and the power of belief.

They also clarified, on this day, the difference between Bataan and Batan. Adem had apologetically asked about the Bataan Death March of 1942, when the Japanese army forced 76,000 prisoners of war (approximately 66,000 Filipinos and 10,000 Americans) to march to Camp O'Donnell, over five to ten days, depending on when they joined the march. The Filipinos and Americans marching were beaten often, many were beheaded, and all faced a life-threatening lack of food, water, and unsanitary conditions. Only 54,000 people were alive to arrive, and of those, many died from unsanitary conditions and starvation shortly afterward. It was one of the great atrocities of World War II. Marikit had explained that the Bataan Peninsula was just west of Manila. The group was going to travel to Batan Island in the "Batanes," which is far north of the country. That was when the group unanimously decided to spend July 4th visiting the World War Two memorials and taking a historical tour.

It was only twenty-four hours later, and Jiho was listening to Marikit and others chat about some groups not taking different groups of people seriously. He thought of what had been discussed yesterday on the bus ride home: under no circumstances were any of them comfortable sharing data that other countries or various domestic groups might have flagitious ideas. No one wanted to have a part in starting another world war.

After everyone had finished their meals and the table was cleared, two people came out of the kitchen and introduced themselves: Bernila, another aunt of Marikit, and her son Alejandro. They introduced themselves and sat down at the table when Marikit asked them to.

"These are some of the people that I wanted you to meet," Marikit began, still in English. "They are head-talkers." She looked at her relatives and said, "These are the people who are working to help Samir collect more information. They only pass information to Samir and his assistant. Will you show them, please?" Bernila smiled, and Alejandro looked slightly bored, but both put their hands out. Marikit took a notebook from her bag, ripped out two blank sheets, and handed one to each of her relatives. Bernila passed hers to Binh on her right and said, "Think of a word, something that you eat or a place to go or something in a house. Write it down here, and don't show Alejandro."

Binh turned a little to the right and used her left hand to form a cup and shield her right hand as it wrote the word 'lamp.' She folded the paper over twice when she was done and handed it to Bernila. Bernila looked at it quickly, and Alejandro wrote down 'lamp' on his paper. They continued with other words and short phrases: sailboat on the ocean, snow on mountains, a girl singing, pineapples. After six transmissions, it felt to all like a dog was being asked to demonstrate his tricks. Bernila and Alejandro could transmit information back and forth without speaking. No one was in doubt. The group spoke casually for another ten minutes, and then Marikit's relatives excused themselves and went back into the kitchen. The inconceivable, which had turned into a supposition and then a single island anomaly, was now quite clearly a human ability.

As they found their way down the street fifteen minutes later, the Americans were quieter than they usually were when all seven of them were together. They had left Marikit at the restaurant with plans to meet up again on Saturday at 10 a.m. They had refused the many offers to be accompanied back to their hotel in favor of aimlessly walking, but with the verbal excuse of seeing more of Basco. They moved in the direction of the ocean, ending up in the small, lush park just before the town pier.

"I feel like less of a man," Theo articulated.

"You and me both," said Emma. They all laughed for a minute. "I used to feel pretty together, but that was before I learned that my idea of a whole self was, in fact, just a fraction. I feel like just a fraction of a person suddenly, as if everyone else has been using three hands instead of two, and I just found out."

"Don't," said Adem. "People all over the world have skills that I don't have. It's analogous. I can't sing, as you know, or paint, or compose songs on a violin. Head talking is a skill like any of those others that I can't do either. I don't resent people who hear musical notes in patterns in their heads; it's the same thing."

"I'm not sure that everyone will see it that way," began Jiho.

"Right? Now that we are out of shock," started Theo.

"Are we?" asked Alec.

"We knew this was coming," said Migel flatly. "Eventually. There was too much talk and too many opportunities. It was inevitable that we'd see it."

"What are we going to do with this knowledge?" asked Theo. "I've read a new theory about the burden of knowledge since artificial intelligence became mainstream and more accessible, how new knowledge will force the choice of using it to help or hinder progress."

"Old Testament, Ecclesiastes, the Burden of Wisdom," said Adem. "This is not a new idea. It's a seriously old one. Theo's question still stands, though, even if someone reworded it in a snappy way. What is the right thing to do? And can we live with ourselves if we do nothing? One idea is to ask Margo for a video call. What exactly do we want to ask, though?"

"If we are sure we trust her, which we agreed last week, we do, then we tell her what we know," offered Binh. "But I think we need to start off being upfront about wanting more information from her, as we have information to give. Information that comes with a burden."

"Or we clarify once and for all who she works for and why our project exists, and then decide," stated Alec.

"And who is financing it," added Adem.

"To summarize," said Emma, looking around out of instinct despite the lack of anyone within hearing distance, "On three, probably four continents, there are people who can shape language in their head and convey it without sound. The ability appears to run in families, but it is unclear if it is genetic or learned behavior and if everyone has access to the skill developing like swimming, or if a certain talent or gene is required in addition. We have seen fMRI scans of just one of the groups, and they are using their brain in a way that matches only the studies on mental telepathy, that is, brain regions that typically engage for memory recall, speaking, reading, or other related abilities are not activated in the same manner."

"You can make the call," said Migel. "You've got this."

"I was just recapping," said Emma.

"And you did it so well," said Theo. "You got the job!"

Chapter 44: Margo Duc

Adem listened closely as the call began. Migel had proposed a FaceTime, Zoom, WhatsApp, or whatever she wanted to call it. Margo had offered many times that she was available. Here they were. It was 9 p.m. Friday night in the Philippines and 9 a.m. Friday morning in Eastern Standard Time.

"Hello, Emma!" Margo answered.

"Hello!" Emma replied and then swiveled her laptop. "We are all here."

"Fantastic! Great to see you all. You guys have had quite an adventure. I am very happy with your work. Thank you for all of your efforts. How is everything there?"

"You're very welcome. We've had a good time, too, and learned a lot. The Philippines are beautiful, although it's obvious why there is so much green— it rains a lot, but parts of each day are very sunny. Marikit is very helpful and so nice."

"Good to hear. I thought you all would like Marikit. She probably told you that we know her because she was a student here."

"Yes, she told us. And today," Margo decided that it was time to get to the point, "earlier today, she introduced us to some of her relatives. We will meet more tomorrow.

"Would you all consider their abilities to be authentic? Accurately advertised?"

Emma moved her laptop around so that its camera could scan more faces than just hers.

"We would," said Jiho, who was standing in the back.

"I am really, really sorry to have missed that experience," said Margo. "The whole trip, actually. I am still disappointed."

"Oh, how are you?" said Binh loudly and apologetically.

"I'm fine now, practically normal," answered Margo. "Thanks. Listen, tomorrow, write down as much data as you can, including any personal information that you can get. You can even record if it seems possible."

Emma used Margo's brief pause to interject. "Of course. We just want to clarify where the information was going, if we could, please. You were going to talk to someone named Samir?"

"Yes. I did. I officially work for Samir, and you do, too, for this project."

Binh's chest felt uncomfortably full. Her paranoid family was right about this expedition. She clenched her teeth and then said clearly, "As opposed to the Department of Education? This is not work assigned by them as the contract stated?"

"The contract said that your loans would be cleared with the Department of Education, and they will be, but not because the DOE is paying off your federal student loans, because Samir will. He will also pay the rest of what we owe you, of course. Nothing has changed."

Binh could breathe better again and was silent.

"Where is Samir getting the money? Is he just independently wealthy, or does he run a business? Or does he have a philanthropist, benefactor, or foundation behind him?" asked Adem.

"It's one man, a funder. To be honest, I don't know all of the details, what category the funder falls into, or even how he made his money. I do know his name, and that he was born in Malaysia, but he is an American citizen now. I know that he has been good friends with Samir for a long time. Nothing about it seemed weird to me until you guys started asking so many questions. I can see that I should have asked a few myself, but I did not. I had not questioned the funding as much as I should have, I think, but Samir is a good person. I believed that he had a very wealthy friend who supported some of his research. I still do, but I didn't question if the donor had rights to the data discovered, and I didn't question the funder's intent. I will learn about both. Samir is a good guy. I'm sure of that."

"I believe you," said Adem, "but the good guy is not the end of the line. This funder guy is. We are a little concerned about passing on the identities of language shapers and head talkers when we don't know who has access to the data or why someone might want to fund an expensive project such as this one in the first place. Aside from the fact that it's cool, of course. And very interesting. We are all very happy that we came, Margo. We just want to do the right thing. You can just imagine which groups might like to have this information."

"That makes sense," said Margo as she realized that she was not going to get more information until she came up with some herself. She started feeling a little blindsided, politely blackmailed, grateful, and proud of her people-selecting skills all at once. She said, "I will talk to Samir today and get back to you as soon as I can. In the meantime, collect all the data that you can. Details matter. Please. This is a personal project for Samir, and, uh, I know it means a lot to him. I have written some software for him, and his enthusiasm for this project is genuine. He's a good person."

"We will," said Emma, trying to soften the conversation because they were really grateful. They'd talked about it. "We are doing everything that we are supposed to and as much as we can in addition. We are just trying to be, um, ethical, if that's the right word. We need to be able to live with ourselves for the choices that we make."

"Of course," said Margo. "I'll dig deeper. I'm sorry for not doing that earlier, and I'll get back to you."

"Great, bye for now then," said Emma.

"Bye," and the connections across the world were broken. I'll just have to find out more from Samir, thought Margo. I wonder how he'll take the inquisition? No, it won't be that. A short set of direct questions should do it. I just need to make it clear that I will support him no matter what he tells me to be sure that I get truthful answers. Margo wondered briefly if she was angling because she did not trust Samir, but then decided that just because she honestly liked him and believed his intentions, it didn't mean that he was not in a grey area with respect to the money.

374

Chapter 45: Migel Ngubá

Migel, Jiho, and Alec sat together with multiple tabs and studies open on their laptops before them. They were discussing the morphic field hypothesis, which had initially seemed unlikely. It was a bit like reading that aliens currently visit the world in high-tech spaceships, and the people who know this are trying to keep everyone else in the dark. Migel was one of the ones who knew about the aliens. But then the theory became more palatable, and finally, it felt like a plausible explanation or at least part of an explanation. Interestingly, Alec was the most open-minded from the start, even though it sounded unlike anything that a scientist of his kind might avouch. It didn't hurt that one of the most acclaimed scientists who upholds the theory is himself a plant biologist or that Alec had known of the idea for so much longer than the others that he had pre-processed it already. Migel, Jiho, and Alec were not so much attempting to derive a complete explanation of how mind-to-mind communication works but to develop a working theory that could drive the questions that they could ask when Marikit introduced them to more head talkers. There are always only a limited number of questions that one can ask, and it's best if those questions are well-used and designed to elicit specific information.

"This article here is saying that historically, it has been valuable for humans and prey animals to be able to sense when they are being watched," said Alec. "We've all seen that in films of animals, you know, the deer looking up as the camera zooms in. People have it too. They know when they are being stared at. They feel it. So, what explains that? Not much, it turns out, but this hypothesis does."

"Have you read anything about the connection between animals and humans?" asked Migel, because I was just scanning a study.

"The one about dogs knowing when their owners were heading home?"

"Yes!"

"That also fits with this idea—it works the same way."

"Enlighten me," said Jiho.

"There are a number of studies that have been conducted in which dogs left at home when their owners went to work are videotaped. They go to the window and look for their owners periodically, no surprise, but they do it repeatedly when their owners leave work, even if they are thirty minutes away. The studies account for the ability of dogs to gauge time by having the owner leave work on different days at different times and using different modes of transport to get home. The dogs always seem to know when their owners are on their way home. The data is impressive, and though it doesn't surprise most dog owners—how could a dog know when its owner leaves work? But they do. And… the results are not explainable with the science that we are certain of."

"So… people to people and people to pets, at least dogs, and wild animal to wild animal?" clarified Jiho.

"Exactly," said Alec. "With animals, the examples are not only with prey animals and their predators. Homing pigeons, for example, can find their way home from hundreds of miles away, even when that 'home' is a moving ship. The hypothesis—maybe it's a theory—offers a possible explanation for animal navigation as well."

"Is part of this idea that there is one mind, in a sense, that connects all living things?" asked Migel.

"No, no. No. That's a different hypothesis. That's WAY out there and doesn't seem plausible to me at all. I don't understand how the science behind that works would even. This is different," said Alec. "This idea purports that there are mini, mini magnets in the brain that connect to a field. There is evidence that trace amounts of iron acting as magnets are linked with memory. If this is a possible explanation for what we see happening, then the questions that we want to ask should shed light on whether the magnets are inherited, environmentally acquired, or present in every human from birth. Is there variation in the quantity of magnets in the human brain, or do we all have equal amounts?"

"What kind of questions would we ask to generate any data on any of that?" asked Migel.

"I've been thinking about that," replied Alec. "I think we should ask if the connection works better between people who are already emotionally bonded to each other. I was also wondering if anyone who does NOT drink well water can do this. We can also chart where the people live. We'll get Adem to come up with categories. We'll ask about jobs and exposure to certain metals."

"What are you wondering exactly?" asked Migel.

"Air pollution. I'm wondering how the metals get into the brain. Are they always there? Do people inhale them? Basically, are we talking about people in areas who are exposed to some kind of fog that results in the inhalation of certain magnetic particles? I want to try to rule out the fact that magnetic particles arrive after birth from unintentional sources. Here, for example, maybe a huge factory in Taiwan blows smog into these islands."

"Maybe," said Migel while he was still thinking. "But Eleni knew of many previous generations who…"

"I know, but maybe those ancestors might have smelted copper, gold, silver, or iron or been exposed to the pollution of it? It's just an idea. I'm looking to explain the metal," said Alec.

"Yikes," said Migel. "If this is true, then between the microplastics that they keep finding in human organs and arteries and the inhaled metals in our brains, humans are going to kill themselves off from the inside out."

"It's uncanny how many bad ideas people have had that have proven detrimental to their species," said Alec. "Sometimes I think we'd be better off if we moved all major decisions to coin flipping. Statistically, we'd be less destructive."

"Ok," said Jiho, "I'm interested in this. What other questions should we ask? What other commonalities are we looking for? We need to chat with people and ask about their lives. We'll tell them about ours, too, so that it isn't weird." The conversation continued in this vein for another hour, and when the group met Marikit, they had a series of questions concerning the syntax of sent messages, where the head-talkers lived, and what their lifestyles were like.

Chapter 46: Samir Namboothiri

On the west side of India, in the far south, and along the coast, lies the state of Kerala. Samir's ancestors are from this region. They are part of the Malayali Brahmin caste: the feudal elite. Kerala is a stunningly beautiful Malayalam-speaking region with animal sanctuaries, stunning beaches, lush landscapes, and a history of religious tolerance.

Kerala, "land of the coconuts," is first noted in written historical records in the third century BCE in a rock carving that was ordered by Emperor Ashoka. Christian tradition claims that St. Thomas the Apostle, the very person from whom the expression "a doubting Thomas" derived when he did not believe that Christ had resurrected and wanted proof, visited Kerala in the first century. Before Thomas, however, Jewish immigrants had arrived in Kerala, and Greeks and Romans before them. In the sixth century, Arab traders arrived and brought Islam with them. So, although Hinduism is the main religion, the Pardesi Synagogue in Kochi was originally built in 1568 by the Jewish community and had a clock tower dating from 1760, with inscriptions in Hebrew, Malayalam, Roman, and Arabic alphabets. Even today, mornings begin with Hindu Temple music, muezzins from Islamic mosques, and church bells in Christian churches.

Samir's grandparents, though, lived within walking distance of the Pardesi Synagogue, and they left because life was too agricultural. Coffee, tea, rubber trees, and spices are all cultivated in this region, and before the internet boom that caused major software companies to move offices there in the giant tech parks, Samir's grandparents imagined a more cosmopolitan life, so they worked against the more common trend to move to London, and they made their way to the New York City area.

Samir's paternal grandmother came to America with her son and his wife. She was small, colorful, and kind. She said, often as she got older, and mostly only to Samir, that she could hear the simple desires of some people even when they were not being spoken out loud. Only Samir paid much attention to this.

One day, when his grandmother was making Samir's breakfast of appam, the Kerala version of a French crepe, with fermented rice flour and coconut milk substituting for the eggs and milk, she told Samir again that his name was from *Samīra* in Sanskrit and meant 'the wind.' "I know, Muttaśśi," Samir had said. "I won't forget." And he didn't because that was also the morning that she proved to him that she really did know what some people thought—not him, not everyone, but some relatives. She proved this to him more times before she died, and Samir has always carried this information with him.

In college, Samir met Hartwin Kolsch and Andrew Johnson and confided in them one evening over a beer about the abilities of his Muttaśśi. Years later, when Hartwin and Andrew became college professors at different universities in Boston, they would pass along bits of information that they happened to hear about anyone with 'mind knowing' abilities, as they called it, to Samir. Samir carefully recorded the data. Hartwin had accepted a position at Boston University, and Andrew had done the same at Harvard. Samir, when he taught, worked at Northeastern, but he had not stayed in academics long. Despite departing a decade ago, however, he is still in touch with a large number of former colleagues. Many of Samir's academic connections are aware of his interest in any kind of brain-to-brain communication. Most, either entertained by it or curious themselves, continue to report all snippets of information to him, typically third or fourth-hand. Samir collects these stories, rumors, hunches, and folk tales alongside any actual, factual evidence. He keeps all his data coded and securely stored in a very academic manner, which was helpful when he was trying to acquire funding. Samir tried for many years to fund his project. He tried academics, but they never had money. He tried religious groups, but they had an agenda, and so finally, he talked to think tanks and non-profit organizations, but surprisingly, they lacked untethered money and the ability to maintain secrecy. And so, Samir was funding himself, without ties, commitments, or contracts to any group, when he met Syed Bin Abdullah serendipitously in Kuala Lumpur.

The capital city of Malaysia is Kuala Lumpur. The population is slightly under half Malay, with almost as many of Chinese heritage and just over ten percent with Indian heritage. So, while Islam is the dominant religion, ten percent each are Christians or Hindus and double that are Buddhists. In addition to its diversity and interesting culture, Kuala Lumpur is a welcoming, pleasant, and easy-to-get-to city that is, as a result, afforded the opportunity to host many conferences every year, particularly in healthcare, biology, economics, and sustainability. It was at one of the latter that Samir initially heard of Syed Bin Abdullah when he was first out of graduate school. Syed had been about Samir's age, and he had presented a very interesting sustainability talk about the fishing industry in Malaysia and how it has been changing. Samir attended the conference in order to learn more about extreme solar geomagnetic disturbances (because they are a natural way in which an electromagnetic pulse could destroy a grid in the same way that a cyber-attack or thermonuclear detonation can). Samir learned a lot at that conference, but most importantly, he attended some talks that were interesting but unrelated to what he was researching at the time. In doing so, he also made a life-long friend: Syed Bin Abdullah. Samir had always been altruistic, curious, and hardworking. Syed had always been those things as well, and he had money. The women in his family did not work, but the men were all involved in the fishing industry, and they were all good businessmen, though not formally educated. Syed had gotten himself educated, and he had invested much of his family's money and done well. Five years after the conference, Samir left his university position and began working for DARPA. Two years after that, some of his side interests were funded by Syed, who was a newly minted US citizen.

It was late in the morning, and Samir had just ended a phone call with his friend Syed when Margo called him. She always attempted a different form of communication first, yet had not this time, so Samir was intrigued as soon as he saw her name on the caller ID panel. He answered. He listened. It was about the kiddies across the ocean. They wanted to know about Syed.

Chapter 47: Theo Auclair

Margo did not contact the team in the Philippines before they went to sleep on July 6th, but she did, late in her day, send an email, copied to each of them individually so that they would each be able to read it upon waking Saturday morning. What Margo wrote satisfied them. They discussed it briefly over breakfast, and then Adem sent his additional spreadsheets and pages of hypotheses and ideas to Margo. Theo participated in all of this lightly, as he was so excited to meet more head-talkers that he could barely finish his coffee. This was a linguistic experience that would top most.

For the zillions of times that humans had sought to identify how another group of humans could be marginalized, for all of the differences that they had found or invented between humans, it was beyond Theo how so many people had missed what he was experiencing. He thought to himself while he played with his coffee cup: Superficialities like height, skin color, accent, beliefs, and manners all paled into nonexistence when one considers that some people can head-talk and others cannot or do not. So many exceptionally misguided people in history. How would this have changed warfare, education, business, politics, etc., if everyone had known?

Painfully slowly, 10 a.m. on Saturday finally arrived. Marikit brought the Americans to her parents' home east of the airport. The day had begun rainy, but when it cleared up at about 10:30 a.m., the festivities were moved outside. Everyone was moving tables and food outside as the bulk of the party-goers arrived. Bernila and her son Alejandro were there, of course, but so were Datu, Chrisanto, Diwata, Corazon, Angel, and a baby named Aurora. The central attraction was the lechon, the roasting pig, that was already being cooked outside under a corrugated metal-roofed lean-to. Smoke puffed out around all sides of the roof, and the smell was delicious. Emma and Binh had dragged Theo and Adem shopping that morning, so they walked in carrying large woven baskets of fresh fruit and flowers to donate to the event. It was an event! Marikit was home; she had brought Americans to visit, and baby Aurora was just starting to walk. Everyone was happy and talking and eating, and the music went on for many more hours than it ever would have in the continental United States.

Theo likened the event to parties at his relatives' home in French Guiana. He marveled that the more developed a nation became, the shorter their parties were, the less people danced and sang at them when they were held, and the more stress inviting friends over seemed to cause the host and hostess. On a remote island, off the more populated but still remote Philippine islands, developing nation fun was in full swing. People had much less, and they celebrated much more.

After a few hours, those who were head-talkers were identified to the Americans. Guessing games were played with transferred information, and most of Migel, Jiho's, and Alec's questions were asked. The Americans learned that genetics or strong family relationships were crucial to developing head-talking. They learned that not all siblings in a family had the ability or cared to. They heard stories that were similar to what Cora and Eleni had related in Greece, and the explanations for such stories were either existent or something like what Hwan had said in Korea: people are connected somehow. Nothing definitive was established at the party, but an additional five people—Bernila and Alejandro—were politely verified and documented as being proficient in head-talking. Some of these people were in-laws of Marikit's family, so they were not blood-related. Two of them grew up on purified city water in Luzon, as opposed to well water with possibly unpredictable mineral content. No one had any obvious excessive exposure to welding pipes, working at landfills or old U.S. Army bases, or had a hobby of metallurgy. By the time the Americans left, they were sincerely tired, very grateful, and mentally stretched from having to think of unique ways to introduce their questions, such as, "Oh, my uncle was a welder, and you remind me of him. Do you weld, or are you a plumber?"

Chapter 48: Adem Haimowitz

The days spent in the Batanes were among the most relaxing and the most beautiful that the Americans had ever experienced. The Filipino people are happy, and they seem to enjoy life every day. The Americans laughed when discussing this because they realized that this was a statement that could not be made about most people that they knew. It is common for people in other locations to spend large parts of their day expressing their disappointment, angst, and frustrations. It probably affects their health to complain so much, and it certainly affects those around them. Such attitudes and activities seemed distinctly absent in the Philippines, and that alone greatly combated the almost daily bursts of rain, and it made everyone think twice before discussing the weather negatively. It turns out that group thinking can be valuable in certain situations.

Adem spent a few days after the Saturday party working and documenting, asking Marikit questions for her to ask her relatives, and trying to find ways to pay her back. Marikit had no immediate need to return to Manila, so she ended up staying with her family for the full week and spending every day with the Americans. She was accommodating, curious, and fun, and Adem found himself promising to return to her islands.

One puzzle that had been nagging at the group, however, was the Cretan hieroglyphics, and they were on a document that was constantly open on Theo's laptop. One afternoon, while everyone was working to assemble the new information into Adem's files, Theo squealed. "You guys!" he said. "Remember when I mentioned that I wanted to see that island where the Tagbanwa live?"

"Yes. and no," said Jiho. "The people that have a language that you read about?"

"Yes. The Tagbanwa are the dominant ethnic group on the island of Palawan and are one of the oldest peoples in the Philippines. Well, I realized that we just are not going to get there on this trip, right? Margo is wrapping this up, and we will fly home soon. But I pulled up a copy of the script. Good, I love the internet, and guess what?"

"You recognize it?"

"Nooo, duh. But it is alphasyllabary like we think the Cretan hieroglyphs are, and… I see some similarities in the shapes," said Theo.

"Seriously?" asked Binh, looking up from her computer.

"Yeah, look at these." Theo held up a printed page of Cretan hieroglyphics up to his computer screen, where there was an alphabet of drawn, mostly curved lines. "Look at the outlines of the symbols of each. The Cretan hieroglyphs are often painted or carved in stone and so are filled, but imagine them with just a line outlining each shape. The bent arm of the Cretan hieroglyphics looks like what the Tagbanwa are using for a 'ya' sound. The Cretan symbol of two branches coming together at the bottom had a similar shape to the 'yu' sound in Tagbanwa. Both scripts have a complete circle as a symbol. The animals' heads that point to the left from Crete look like the 'ma,' the 'mi,' and the 'mu' in Tagbanwa."

"I agree they are similar, Theo, but maybe those are the easiest kind of scratches to make in stone."

"No stone!" said Theo. "The pre-Spanish people in Palawan wrote on leaves of palm trees and bark, but mostly on bamboo. I'm trying to get a copy of a publication from 1604 by a Jesuit missionary from Spain who went to the Philippines to convert the people, obviously, but he wrote about the high level of literacy that the people had, and he described how they wrote and with what tools. Paper, pen, and ink were all introduced by the Spanish."

"You think the scripts are related?" asked Jiho.

"No, not by travel," said Theo. "But I think it is possible that both are some written form of the language of thought, and that is why they are so similar. I plan to write Dr. Papadakis and attach the alphabet and see what he thinks."

"I still like the idea of the language of thought," said Emma, "but I don't see yet how any kind of hypothesis can be developed. We all saw that the head talkers are essentially eschewing verbal language and sending ideas, but we really need more concrete information. I think we need to talk to Margo and Samir in person. We need to consider if it even matters or is worth pursuing."

"I think it's possible. I think it is very interesting, and I really want to get to Palawan sometime for a few weeks and look into this. In the meantime, my nerdy linguistic websites have a fair amount written about the language of Tagbanwa, and hopefully, I can get ahold of some of the first encounter accounts written in Spanish. I'll get Migel to translate them for me if I can't find a translated copy. All kinds of cool documents are digital now. You'd be amazed at what is available."

"I'm glad that you are going to write Dr. Papadakis. I will, too," said Emma. "I want to let him know what happened and where this all led to."

"Do we have those answers?" asked Alec, and it was obvious from his tone that he was entertained and not being challenging.

"Well, we know more than we did when we arrived in Crete, and I'll tell him that. Margo said that it was alright if we passed on to language shapers that head talkers exist and that we think it is the same thing."

"I'm going to propose to Margo that we explore Korea more. We can find people. It will just take time. It's a more private culture than the one here."

"Can I just say one more time that I don't think that there is a happier culture in the world than the one here?" said Theo. "I wonder if that is preserved when Filipinos migrate to North America or Europe. I don't actually know anyone with Filipino heritage at home, I don't think," said Theo.

"Happiness is a state of mind," said Binh. "It is a way of looking at the world and interpreting experiences. I think that it is a skill to be happy and one that is culturally transmitted, but that also has a genetic component like everything else. Hormones can control a lot, but I think there are other components that get overlooked. I want to return here and study the art of being happy."

"Bottle it, bring it home, and sell it for millions," said Jiho.

"Speaking of home, let's keep making the docs for Samir and Margo. I think we want another category on this file, Adem, for interesting data that we learned, but that doesn't seem to be immediately connected to anything but might be down the road. We can stick your Tagbanwa script info there, Theo. Maybe there is a connection."

Chapter 49: Dr. Syed Bin Abdullah

Small-scale, coastal fishermen traditionally comprise the majority of fishermen in Malaysia. Lately, however, they have been going out to sea in their small boats less often as unpredictable ocean weather makes doing so dangerous; typical winds turn to gales these days. The waters are also more acidic, and changing ocean temperatures are altering marine habitats and affecting the coral reefs where fish breed and live. Crabs are not as abundant as they have been for the past fifty years, and it's not as safe for fishermen to go out further, for longer hours, and for a smaller catch. Older fishermen are retiring, and younger men are not joining the industry. Syed Bin Abdullah attended Universiti Malaya, in Kuala Lumpur, for the express purpose of studying these changes in fishing and learning how to address the problems that they create.

East Malaysia refers to the part of Malaysia near or on the island of Borneo. It is an area with a very diverse population of elasmobranchs (sharks and rays), and it was discovered in 2014 that these fish use electroreceptors to perceive magnetic fields. The magnetic fields aid in fish locomotion and spatial awareness. Changes in these magnetic fields, natural ones or those from human power lines, lead to delays in the development of the embryos of these fish. Syed learned this while looking into impacts that have altered traditional fishing grounds and quantity and became mildly interested in magnetic fields and how they affect fish activity and communication in general.

Syed wondered briefly if humans experience what the fish do, and a quick search led him to find studies that examine the effects of artificial magnetic fields on human embryo development, as well as some studies concerning human magnetic fields. It turns out that all humans have magnetic fields that result from the electrical currents in the body that generate them. Nerve impulses (electricity) are constantly being generated by the human nervous system and the brain. Some human body tissues can conduct electricity (muscles, the brain, the heart in particular) and so using the right tools, one can measure the magnetic field of a human heart. The most impressive field is the one generated by the human brain when it sleeps. Technically, the condition of epilepsy can generate an even larger field, but it is not desirable to do so.

When Syed told Samir that he was studying fish to see if they could geolocate their places of birth by using the earth's magnetic field, he was ahead of his time. This was very fringe thinking. He was wondering, in particular, if climate change could be impacting Malaysian fishing, as large solar storms cause fluctuations in the earth's magnetic field. Samir had wondered out loud to Syed that it would be interesting to know if humans could access magnetic fields in the environment as well, and if so, why didn't they geolocate. Samir quickly made the connection to what Syed had said about the largest human magnetic field emanating from the brain when it sleeps. Every serious student he knew had at some point studied until they fell asleep and woke up knowing more than they did when they stopped putting in the effort. Within the hour, a joint project was born.

It was slow at first. And Samir initially pretended to care about fish. Eventually, though, the fish studies took off on their own under other researchers, and Samir concentrated on people. Then, there were other studies exploring whether humans could access magnetic fields, a few involving very prestigious medical schools. Finally, Samir proposed the big expedition. The one that was currently taking place. Syed had thought that it would be fruitful, although Samir recognized that it meant bringing new scientists into the fold and the risks involved. The decision was to limit information, at least initially. Margo's proposal was to identify younger-than-usual scientists. Now, it all seemed prudent, and Syed, Samir, and Margo felt that it had been a great success. Once given all of the background information, the group of seven was fully on board as well.

Adem's ability to sort, use, and analyze the data was remarkable, and both Syed and Samir came independently to the conclusion that he should be hired for the great fish project. Samir would gladly pay him for any work that he could contribute to the language project as well. Adem was thrilled once informed, as his future employment prospects all seemed much less interesting after his jaunt around the world managing new knowledge.

Syed is still very interested in addressing the changing needs of Malaysian fishermen, of course, and exploring the role that climate change indirectly and various human activities directly play in this process. He came from a long line of men who earned their living from the sea, and even though he had gone to college for a different life, it was important to him that he help the occupation survive because, without intervention, it didn't seem like it was going to. His country depended on fish.

Chapter 50: Alec Nehoitewa

On a Friday in mid-July, during the on-and-off rain, Jiho, Migel, Adem, Theo, Alec, Binh, and Emma boarded a Japan Airlines flight from Manila to Boston with a three-hour layover in Tokyo. It was the nicest flight at a reasonable price. The group was tired of the clothing that they had been wearing for the past many weeks, and their bags were overstuffed with purchases and presents.

The group was flying home earlier than had been anticipated, but all had agreed to spend two nights in a Boston hotel, downloading to Samir and Margo jointly and handing off their work files. Afterward, Binh, Theo, and Adem would return to their apartments by car services, and the others would be flown to their home airports. All seven would then work from their respective homes for the following two weeks to help Samir understand and think about the data. They anticipated a morning and an afternoon video call, all together, Mondays through Fridays, so the long flight home from Tokyo wasn't really 'goodbye.' Each had been paid generously for the project, including full payments for their student loans. It was a more-than-fair arrangement, thought Alec, and it was a great experience on many levels. Despite a certain lack of conclusions, however, there was no point in staying overseas any longer unless Kerala was going to be visited, and Samir had said that he wanted to be a part of that trip. He insisted, though, that it not occur during monsoon season. South Korea, also, as Jiho insisted, would be fruitful to visit again. There was so much more to learn there.

Alec felt that the magnetic field theory persisted in being the most likely explanation for how people communicated from one mind to another, but he still had a lot of questions. What hardware allowed for it to work? Or was it software? Who had access to it? Most importantly, what would the future be like if more people became aware that all humans are actually not equal, but not in any way that they had ever imagined? Alec wondered if any of this connected to his ancestors who listened to the corn. He looked forward to exploring electromagnetic fields when he returned. There was also still the open question of the equator. Kenya, Crete, South Korea, and the Philippines were all nearer to the equator than not, even Kerala, India. There were still no ideas about whether that was by coincidence or if it was a factor in determining what could or could not happen or to whom.

Migel and Jiho wanted to dig deeper into the studies of the ancient reptilian brain. They expected more answers to lie there. Emma had agreed to teach again for the fall semester, but she planned to explore doctoral programs now that she didn't have the weight of school loans on her, and she could better imagine interesting careers that an anthropology degree would help her find. Binh was looking forward to starting her Ph.D. program but was considering shifting her focus to, or at least integrating, her previous ideas with the study of happiness. There was, after all, a great need in the United States for people willing to research and work in mental health. Theo was really looking forward to going to Connecticut and had dreams of getting to Palawan in the Philippines to study Tagbanwa as soon as possible. He was thinking of concrete projects for which he could apply for a research grant. Adem had been offered a full-time job with benefits starting August 15th, working for Syed Bin Abdullah's NGO as an environmental data analyst. It was almost like settling down; his parents would be thrilled.

Later that day, after noodle soup in an izakaya at the Tokyo airport, the group moved to their gate to sit, charge devices, and wait. The area was very quiet and compulsively clean. Alec watched Binh gather herself and lean over towards Jiho, Theo, and Migel and whisper, "Do one of you fine gentlemen have the seat next to me? I'm 28B?" She waited as they all checked their tickets. Finally, Migel looked up at her and flashed his digital boarding pass. Binh smiled at him and quietly asked if he'd be willing to swap seats with Alec, who had the desirable 29C. Alec was embarrassed, but everyone laughed. No one was surprised.

Works Referenced

Acharya, S., & Shukla, S. (2012). Mirror neurons: Enigma of the metaphysical modular brain. *Journal of Natural Science, Biology, and Medicine, 3*(2), 118. https://doi.org/10.4103/0976-9668.101878

Carles, G., Ginhoux, R., Riera, A., Thanh, N. T., Chauvat, H., Berg, M., Juli, A., Pascual-Leone, Á., & Ruffini, G. (2015). Conscious Brain-to-Brain communication in humans using Non-Invasive Technologies. *Frontiers in Human Neuroscience, 9.* https://doi.org/10.3389/conf.fnhum.2015.218.00011

Carpenter, J., Green, M. C., & Vacharkulksemsuk, T. (2016). Beyond perspective-taking: Mind-reading motivation. *Motivation and Emotion, 40*(3), 358–374. https://doi.org/10.1007/s11031-016-9544-z

Chan, M. M., & Han, Y. M. Y. (2020). Differential mirror neuron system (MNS) activation during action observation with and without social-emotional components in autism: a meta-analysis of neuroimaging studies. *Molecular Autism, 11*(1). https://doi.org/10.1186/s13229-020-00374-x

Grau, C., Ginhoux, R., Riera, A., Nguyễn, T. L., Chauvat, H., Berg, M., Amengual, J. L., Pascual-Leone, Á., & Ruffini, G. (2014). Conscious Brain-to-Brain communication in humans using Non-Invasive Technologies. *PLOS ONE, 9*(8), e105225. https://doi.org/10.1371/journal.pone.0105225

Greyson, B. (1977). Telepathy in Mental Illness. *The Journal of Nervous and Mental Disease*, *165*(3), 184–200. https://doi.org/10.1097/00005053-197709000-00007

Hewitt, M. A. (2014). Freud and the Psychoanalysis of Telepathy: Commentary on Claudie Massicotte's "Psychical Transmissions." *Psychoanalytic Dialogues*, *24*(1), 103–108. https://doi.org/10.1080/10481885.2014.870841

Hosseini, E. (2021). Brain-to-brain communication: the possible role of brain electromagnetic fields (As a Potential Hypothesis). *Heliyon*, *7*(3), e06363. https://doi.org/10.1016/j.heliyon.2021.e06363

Kulick, D. (2017). Human–Animal communication. *Annual Review of Anthropology*, *46*(1), 357–378. https://doi.org/10.1146/annurev-anthro-102116-041723

Maiseli, B., Abdalla, A. T., Massawe, L. V., Mbise, M., Mkocha, K., Nassor, N. A., Ismail, M., James, M., & Kimambo, S. (2023). Brain–computer interface: trend, challenges, and threats. *Brain Informatics*, *10*(1). https://doi.org/10.1186/s40708-023-00199-3

Pile, S. (2011). Distant feelings: telepathy and the problem of affect transfer over distance. *Transactions of the Institute of British Geographers*, *37*(1), 44–59. https://doi.org/10.1111/j.1475-5661.2011.00458.x

Pophof, B., Henschenmacher, B., Kattnig, D. R., Kühne, J., Vian, A., & Ziegelberger, G. (2022). Biological Effects of Electric, Magnetic, and Electromagnetic Fields from 0 to 100 MHz on Fauna and Flora: Workshop Report. *Health*

Physics, *124*(1), 39–52.
https://doi.org/10.1097/hp.0000000000001624

Rao, R. P. N., Stocco, A., Bryan, M., Sarma, D. D., Youngquist, T. M., Wu, J., & Prat, C. S. (2014). A direct Brain-to-Brain interface in humans. *PLOS ONE, 9*(11), e111332. https://doi.org/10.1371/journal.pone.0111332

Sheldrake, R. (2006). Morphic fields. *World Futures: The Journal of New Paradigm Research, 62*(1–2), 31–41. https://doi.org/10.1080/0260402050040624

Sheldrake, R., & Smart, P. (2005). Testing for Telepathy in Connection with e-Mails. *Perceptual and Motor Skills, 101*(3), 771–786. https://doi.org/10.2466/pms.101.3.771-786.

Sheldrake, R., Smart, P., & Avraamides, L. (2015). Automated tests for telephone telepathy using mobile phones. *EXPLORE, 11*(4), 310–319. https://doi.org/10.1016/j.explore.2015.04.001

Stafford, O., Gleeson, C., Egan, C., Tunney, C., Rooney, B., O'Keeffe, F., McDermott, G., Baron-Cohen, S., & Burke, T. (2023). A 20-Year Systematic Review of the 'Reading the Mind in the Eyes' Test across Neurodegenerative Conditions. *Brain Sciences, 13*(9), 1268. https://doi.org/10.3390/brainsci13091268

Venkatasubramanian, G., Jayakumar, P. N., Nagendra, H. R., Nagaraja, D., Deeptha, R., & Gangadhar, B. N. (2008). Investigating paranormal phenomena: Functional brain imaging of telepathy. *International Journal of Yoga, 1*(2), 66. https://doi.org/10.4103/0973-6131.43543

www.ingramcontent.com/pod-product-compliance
Lightning Source LLC
Chambersburg PA
CBHW070347170726
48291CB00001B/212